T0316069

PRAISE FOR THE BLIX & RAMM SERIES

'The new novel by the stellar Norwegian crime-writing duo Jorn Lier Horst and Thomas Enger ... tense, brutal and fast-moving' *Sunday Times* Book of the Month

'An international sensation' *Vogue*

'Grim, gory and filled with plenty of dark twists ... There's definitely a Scandinavian chill in the air with this fascinating read' *Sun*

'The most exciting yet' *The Times*

'What happens when you put two of the most distinguished writers of Nordic noir in tandem? *Death Deserved* by Thomas Enger and Jørn Lier Horst suggests it was a propitious publishing move; a ruthless killer is pursued by a tenacious celebrity blogger and a damaged detective' *Financial Times*

'A stunningly excellent collaboration from Thomas Enger and Jørn Lier Horst ... It's a brutal tale of fame, murder and reality TV that gets the pulse racing' Russel D. McLean

'Superb Nordic noir. Dark, intricate and extremely compelling. Contemporary Scandinavian fiction at its best' Will Dean

'Darkly twisty' *Crime Monthly*

'A devilishly complex plot, convincing red herrings, and well-rounded characters help make this a winner. Scandinavian noir fans will eagerly await the sequel' *Publishers Weekly*

'This tale often surprises or shifts in subtle ways that are pleasing and avoid cliché. As the opener for a new series this is a cracker. Long live the marriage of Horst and Enger' *New Books Magazine*

'Hands down, the best book in the series so far and it will satisfy even the most demanding readers. It has a little bit of everything: action, drama, suspense, mystery, and a strong whodunit element' *Tap the Line Magazine*

'A fast-moving, punchy, serial-killer investigative novel with a whammy of an ending. If this is the first in the Blix & Ramm series, then here's to many more!' LoveReading

'Jørn Lier Horst and Thomas Enger's electrifying narrative is irresistible and *Victim* is another exceptional instalment in a series that consistently offers the very best in crime fiction. The piercingly honest exploration of some distressing, tragic topics is heartrending and yet ultimately it is a novel imbued with the promise of hope. Thrilling, emotive and completely unmissable, I cannot recommend it highly enough' Hair Past a Freckle

'A suspenseful mystery that is fast-paced and chilling, it is Nordic Noir at its best. I think *Victim* is my favourite of the series' Catherine Poe Reads

'One of those jaw-dropping "what did you just do" kind of conclusions that will leave fans of the series reeling' Jen Med's Book Reviews

'Blending a gripping storytelling structure with thrilling tension and heartfelt moments that may bring tears to your eyes ... The Blix & Ramm series is one of my favourite Nordic noir "hidden gems", and if you're a fan of writers like Lars Kepler, Stefan Ahnhem, and/or Søren Sveistrup, you won't want to miss this thrilling crime-fiction series' Crime by the Book

'The series offers everything you would expect from Scandinavian suspense literature ... An absolute must for thriller fans' *Krimi Couch*

'Great entertainment! *Stigma* is perfectly poised suspense'
Verdens Gang

'*Stigma* surprises on many levels, ... a completely nerve-wracking story' *Tvedestrandsposten*

'Horst and Enger simply write wonderful detective stories and *Stigma* is living proof of that' Thriller Zone

'The collaboration between the two authors has resulted in some excellent books, and that level is absolutely maintained in this unusually angled crime novel' *KrimiFan*

The Blix and Ramm Series – available from Orenda Books:
Death Deserved
Smoke Screen
Unhinged
Stigma
Victim

ABOUT THE AUTHORS

Jørn Lier Horst and Thomas Enger are both internationally bestselling Norwegian authors. Between them they have been published in more than fifty countries and sold more than eleven million copies across thirty-eight languages. Jørn Lier Horst first rose to literary fame with his no. 1 bestselling William Wisting series. A former senior investigating officer in the Norwegian police, Horst imbues all his works with an unparalleled realism and suspense. Thomas Enger is the journalist-turned-author behind the internationally acclaimed Henning Juul series. Enger's trademark is his dark, gritty voice paired with key social messages and tight plotting. Besides writing fiction for both adults and young adults, Enger also works as a music composer.

Death Deserved, the first book in the bestselling Blix & Ramm series, was Jørn Lier Horst and Thomas Enger's first co-written thriller and was followed by *Smoke Screen, Unhinged* and *Stigma*. The latest instalment, *Victim*, was shortlisted for Norway's prestigious Riverton Prize in 2023.

Follow Jørn Lier and Thomas on Instagram @lierhorst and @author_thomas_enger.

ABOUT THE TRANSLATOR

Megan Turney is a literary and commercial translator and editor, working from Norwegian and Danish into English. She was the recipient of the National Centre for Writing's 2019 Emerging Translator Mentorship, and holds an MA (Hons) in Scandinavian Studies and English Literature from the University of Edinburgh, and an MA in Translation and Interpreting Studies from the University of Manchester. She has previously translated the Blix & Ramm Series by Jørn Lier Horst and Thomas Enger and *Thirty Days of Darkness* by Jenny Lund Madsen for Orenda Books. You can find a list of her other translations and work at www.meganeturney.com.

VICTIM

THOMAS ENGER & JØRN LIER HORST

TRANSLATED BY MEGAN TURNEY

ORENDA
BOOKS

Orenda Books
16 Carson Road
West Dulwich
London SE21 8HU
www.orendabooks.co.uk

First published in the United Kingdom by Orenda Books, 2024
First published in Norwegian as *Offer* by Bonnier Norsk Forlag, 2023
Copyright © Jørn Lier Horst & Thomas Enger, 2023
English translation copyright © Megan Turney, 2024

Jørn Lier Horst & Thomas Enger have asserted their moral right to be identified
as the authors of this work in accordance with the Copyright,
Designs and Patents Act, 1988.

All Rights Reserved. No part of this publication may be reproduced in any form
or by any means without the written permission of the publishers.

*This is a work of fiction. Names, characters, places and incidents are either products of
the author's imagination or are used fictitiously. Any resemblance to actual events,
locales or persons, living or dead, is entirely coincidental.*

A catalogue record for this book is available from the British Library.

ISBN 978-1-916788-34-3
eISBN 978-1-916788-35-0

This book has been translated with financial support from NORLA

NORLA
NORWEGIAN LITERATURE ABROAD

Typeset in Garamond by www.typesetter.org.uk

Printed and bound by Clays Ltd, Elcograf S.p.A

MIX
Paper | Supporting
responsible forestry
FSC® C018072

For sales and distribution, please contact *info@orendabooks.co.uk* or visit
www.orendabooks.co.uk.

'All that I am, or hope to be, I owe to my angel mother.'
—Abraham Lincoln

PROLOGUE

The moon cast a dull light over the car park. A quick glance at the dashboard told him it was 1:34am.

He had returned to the area numerous times since burying her but had never ventured all the way to the exact spot. But despite the fact it was dark, he felt confident that he would find it. He knew the forest well.

It had rained the night before.

The grooves of his hiking boots would make deep, distinct impressions on the forest floor, which was why he had bought a pair he knew you would find in thousands of Norwegian homes. As for his clothes, he'd opted for a green waterproof coat, to blend in with his surroundings.

Planning, he thought.

Alpha and Omega.

He grabbed the bag from the boot. Locked the car and headed off down the trail. The air was cold, biting. Black clouds floated across the sky above him. A whiff of cool decay rose from the ground. His footsteps startled a couple of birds, who scattered violently into the air. After a few minutes, he could feel his scalp beneath his cap wet with sweat. The lenses of his glasses had fogged up.

It had not been without risk, carrying her into the forest as he had. Half of Norway was looking for her at the time. She was also much heavier than he'd expected. But it was night, like now. Besides, as always he had planned ahead.

Three nights beforehand, he had taken a collapsible metal shovel with him and tried to dig out a good spot. At the first potential burial plot, there had been far too many stones, the rock bed far too deep. As for the next, it had been impossible to dig deep enough – he didn't want to risk some animal catching her scent and digging her up. Only on the third attempt had he succeeded in finding a suitable place, which was also hidden behind a clump of trees, bushes and ferns. Before going back, he had carved a symbol into the nearest tree.

The spruce had grown significantly since then. Its branches wider, maybe also a little thicker. He put down his bag and took out the shovel, glad to see the ground was not yet frozen.

The first plunges were the hardest. He had to penetrate a thick layer of heather and moss, roots that stretched out like a grid beneath the forest floor. It took him a while before he finally reached her.

He dropped the shovel and continued with his hands, to avoid tearing the plastic sheet he had wrapped her in. His gloves tunnelled into the damp ground. More and more of the plastic came into view.

He opened his jacket pocket and took out the piece of folded paper, carefully, not wanting to risk ruining it. Just as gently, he pulled back the plastic, layer by layer. And there she was: free and exposed.

There was a time for everything, he thought.

And now, the time was right for this.

During the day, the forest was a popular hiking area. People let their dogs roam off the lead, run freely among the trees. And if it did take too long for her to be found, he would just report the discovery himself.

The last thing he had planned to do took him less than a minute. Once completed, he stood up and looked around, satisfied. Above the treetops, a cloud drifted aside, and the moon peeked out, illuminating the burial site.

It was Tuesday morning. Now 4:15am.

He smiled.

It was going to be a good day.

1

The ground in front of him was a grey-brown, speckled with white spots here and there from the chewing gum that had been trampled into the pavement. Alexander Blix kept his eyes a metre ahead as he did his best to steer clear of the litter and old dog poo.

A sudden gust of wind made him pull his jacket collar tighter around his neck. Above, the clouds had started the gather. It would only be a matter of minutes before the first drops of rain would fall. It had been sunny when Blix left home just a short while ago.

Oslo, he thought.

Summer one second, autumn the next.

Only when the Grønlandsleiret 44 building, with its tall windows, appeared on the left did he lift his gaze and come to a stop. A woman stood smoking by the front door. A little further away, someone was shouting in a foreign language. Red and yellow leaves were strewn across the grass of the park next door. A stubby-legged dog darted back to its owner, holding a stick between its teeth.

They must have finished their morning meetings by now, Blix thought. Nicolai Wibe was probably propped up by the coffee machine, bragging about something he had accomplished in the gym that morning. Tine Abelvik likely snorted and rolled her eyes, while Gard Fosse, overbearing as he was, probably told them to get on with the day's work.

Blix's eyes were drawn to a car emerging from the building's basement car park. As soon as it pulled out onto the road, its sirens blared. The car's blue lights flashed over the façades of the buildings lining the road.

Other motorists pulled aside. The uniformed officer in the car's passenger seat cast a long look at Blix as they passed. He couldn't remember seeing her before.

He wondered what they were responding to – whether it was a burglary, an accident, a murder or something else. The car continued wailing towards the city centre, the sound gradually disappearing as it blended in with the sounds of the city, just another instrument adding to the cacophony of Oslo's orchestra.

Blix turned back to the police station. A raindrop hit him on the cheekbone, and more quickly followed. He pulled back the sleeve of his jacket. A glance at his wristwatch made him realise he was late.

He turned around.

Noticed a person do the same – they immediately picked up speed and crossed the street at an angle without turning to check the traffic approaching. A motorist blared its horn at him. The man disappeared into the throng of people on the other side and continued with hasty steps.

The same guy, Blix thought.

The same dark-green waterproof, the same black backpack. Blix had seen him in the street outside his apartment, sometimes late at night, other times early in the morning. He had seen him at the shop too, and once – *maybe* but he wasn't one-hundred-percent sure – in the courtyard of his apartment block.

Blix tried to speed up himself, but quickly realised he wouldn't be able to catch up with him. The man disappeared down the steps into the subway station at Grønland Torg and vanished.

Blix continued towards the city centre, faster now, no longer concerned about where he put his feet. He turned often, each time with the feeling that everyone was staring at him. But the man in the green raincoat was not one of them.

2

Eleven minutes later, Blix arrived at the entrance to Leirfallsgata 11. An electric bike was propped up against the wall. It was raining lightly.

Hesitantly, Blix raised his index finger to the intercom beside the door, but paused and pulled it back.

You don't *have to*, he told himself. You could just turn around and go home. Regardless, he found Krissander Dokken's name on the wall panel and drilled his index finger into the light-green doorbell. A mere second later, the door's locking mechanism clicked open.

Blix took the stairs up to the second floor, where a door stood ajar in the short corridor. He tentatively pushed it open. Inside, Krissander Dokken met him with an outstretched hand and a measured smile. In his other hand, he clutched the cane he was leaning on.

'Please, come in.'

Blix took off his shoes and hung up his now-wet jacket. Without saying anything, Dokken showed him into a room where two chairs were placed at a good distance from each other with a small, round coffee table in between them. On the table was a water carafe filled to the brim, along with two glasses. A thin, white tissue poked out of a small, square box.

Blix sat down on the chair furthest from the door and crossed one leg over the other. A deep breath provoked a sharp pain in his chest. He tried to tell himself to relax, but it did nothing.

Krissander Dokken took a seat in his regular chair, placed his cane next to it and lay a notepad on his lap. On the wall behind him was a familiar print of a Vincent van Gogh painting. On the floor next to a white bookcase: a terracotta pot with a luscious green Guiana Chestnut plant.

'So,' Dokken began, adjusting the round glasses that barely covered his eyes. 'How are you? How have you been since we last spoke?'

Dokken spoke slowly in a light, dry voice. Blix didn't know how to answer. He could say that it still felt like an invisible force was pushing him down into his bed when he woke up in the morning, keeping him there. That there wasn't a minute of the day when he didn't think about Iselin and the man who had killed her. When he didn't think about all that he, himself, had done afterwards. His time in prison. The time since he had been released.

Instead he said: 'Good.' And swallowed. 'I guess I've been … pretty good.'

'What does that mean?' Dokken looked at him intently.

'Uh,' Blix said, shrugging it off. 'I don't know really.'

'What does it mean to you to be *pretty good*?'

It took a few moments for Blix to answer.

'That's a good question,' he said. 'Maybe I don't really know what that means or includes anymore.'

Dokken nodded slowly. 'What do you think you have to do for things to be or feel better?'

Blix thought about it. Thought for a long time.

'I don't know,' he said. 'I've no idea.'

'Have you tried meditating yet?'

Blix shook his head. 'I've … not quite got round to it.'

A long silence stretched across the table between them.

'What have you been up to for the last few weeks, then?'

'Not much, really. I … read a lot. Newspapers, books. And then I tie … flies.'

'As in … flies for fly fishing?'

'Yes, it's an old hobby I've taken up again.'

'That's good. I'm glad to hear it. Do you fish a lot?'

'Not anymore. Before, I did. In the old days.'

'Maybe you should test out your new flies sometime soon?'

Blix shrugged. 'Maybe.'

Dokken waited a moment, then asked his next question.

'Are you eating?'

'Yes, I'd say so.'

'Are you eating *healthy* food?'

Blix thought about it.

'Not as often as I should do, no.'

'We are what we eat, you know.'

Dokken tried sending him a small smile. Blix didn't return it.

'What's your sleep pattern like?'

'A little disturbed. As it's almost always been though, even back when I was working.'

Dokken moistened his lips. 'Do you still do your usual morning walk?'

'Mostly.'

'The same route?'

'Yes, I've not really made many changes. I guess I'm a creature of habit, like almost everyone else.'

Dokken brought his hands together and steepled his fingers. 'Do you still feel like you're being watched, or like someone's following you?'

Blix had forgotten that he'd told Dokken that.

'No,' he answered, a wave of heat rising to his face. 'But a lot of people know about me, now,' he added. 'After ... everything that happened. Someone always seems to recognise me when I'm out on the street or shopping or whatever.'

'Ah, the price of fame,' Dokken said with a faint smile. 'I'm glad I'm not famous.'

Blix said nothing.

'Are you still receiving the same amount of letters?'

Blix thought about it.

'Maybe a little less now.'

'What kind of letters *are* you receiving then?'

'I don't know, I don't really look at them.'

'Why not?'

Blix considered the question. He didn't really have a solid answer.

'Do you keep in touch with anyone?' Dokken asked.

'Emma,' Blix replied. 'Emma Ramm. Occasionally.'

'No former colleagues? None of them message, invite you out for a beer or anything?'

Blix shook his head.

'So there's no one *you* reach out to either?'

'No. Unless we're counting Merete. My ex-wife. But even that's only every so often.'

Dokken stared ahead for a few moments, as if he were deep in thought.

'What about your parents?'

Blix looked up at him abruptly. 'What about them?'

'Are they still around?'

'Do you mean, are they still alive?'

'M-hm?'

'My father is...' Blix said with a heavy sigh. 'My mother died a long time ago.'

'How old were you then?'

Blix pushed himself up a little in his chair. Quickly scratched his cheek with an unexpectedly sharp fingernail.

'Sixteen.'

'Do you have any contact with your father?'

Blix put a hand on his thigh and squeezed a little on the muscles under the fabric.

'Not so much.'

'Why not?'

'He's ... in a nursing home.'

'Does that prevent you from having contact with him?'

Blix looked down and interlaced his fingers. Didn't answer.

'Why is he in a nursing home?' Dokken continued. 'If you don't mind me asking?'

'He ... can't take care of himself anymore.'

Dokken nodded slowly. 'Where is this home?'

'Just outside Gjøvik.'

'Is that where you're from?'

'Close. I'm from Skreia.'

'Skreia,' Dokken repeated, as if the place itself were important. 'When was the last time you visited him?'

'I don't remember.'

'Was it before or after you were in prison?'

'Before,' Blix answered quickly.

'When was the last time you spoke to him?'

'I don't re—' Blix stopped himself. 'It's been a while.'

Blix noticed that the psychologist now had deep frown lines between his eyebrows.

'Perhaps you should take another trip,' he said. 'If for nothing else, then to—'

'No,' Blix interjected.

Dokken gazed at him for a while.

'Why not?'

'I don't want to.'

Silence descended again.

'What was your relationship like with your mother?'

Blix sighed. 'Good,' he said. 'Let's talk about something else.'

Dokken scrutinised him a while longer. Sat back in the chair and crossed one leg over the other.

'Let's get back to what we started this session with,' he said. 'What it means to you to feel pretty good. After all, that's what we're all aiming for, mostly. Each day, and throughout our lives.'

He drummed his fingers on the notepad, seeming to weigh his next words.

'You were in prison, Alexander, for almost eight months. But you were acquitted in the Court of Appeal. And you've now been a free man for a little over two months.'

'It depends on what you mean by "free",' Blix objected. 'I'll never be completely free from what happened, or from what I've done. None of that ever goes away.'

'No, but that's the same for everyone,' Dokken said. 'We carry everything we've ever done and experienced throughout our lives with us, whether they be short or long. That's just a part of us. We can't go back and change any of it. It is only you, me – we – who can do anything about our own future.'

'So I just have to get over it? Is that what you're saying?'

'Not at all,' Dokken replied, unfazed by Blix's raised voice. 'What you have experienced will always affect you. But what we're doing here isn't trying to patch up your wounds so they stop bleeding. Rather, we want to do the opposite: we want to open them up and let the blood run as long as is necessary. In the long run, we want to try to train your body and brain to just let it bleed without you thinking too much about it, or feeling the pain to the same extent.'

'That doesn't sound abstract at all,' Blix said sardonically.

'But it's actually *not* abstract,' Dokken replied. 'There are a number of specific techniques that have proven to be very effective for people struggling with major trauma or deep grief.'

He waited until Blix looked at him then said: 'Have you heard of EMDR?'

Blix shook his head.

'EMDR stands for Eye Movement Desensitisation and Reprocessing. It's a way to stimulate the brain in order to make it easier to live with negative experiences.'

Blix raised an eyebrow.

'When we experience something traumatic,' Dokken continued, smoothing out a crease in his sky-blue shirt, 'our ability to process emotions and memories can be completely thrown out of whack. It's all simply too overwhelming. The pain is too great. What we do with EMDR is reprogramme the brain to process stress and trauma without activating the same strong emotional reactions.'

Blix could hear Dokken go into more detail about exactly how this worked, but his mind drifted back to the man in the green raincoat.

'We can try something called EFT too,' Dokken said after a while. 'Or tapping. Which is another technique. That's something you can do at home too, on your own.'

Blix stroked his chin but said nothing.

'You have said before...' Dokken cleared his throat '...that it goes against your own sense of justice that you are no longer in prison. Because you shot and killed a man.'

'It was an act of revenge,' he said quietly.

'You prevented him from harming, or even killing, Emma Ramm.'

'True, but I was primarily thinking about punishing him, not saving Emma. And that's the honest answer.'

Dokken watched him.

'I shouldn't be here,' Blix said. 'I don't mean *here*, specifically, in your office. I mean ... out. I should have plead guilty and taken my sentence like any other offender.'

'And you feel guilty about that.'

Blix looked up at him. 'Yes.'

Dokken drummed the pen against the notepad.

'But so what if there was an element of hatred, revenge or punishment involved?' he said. 'Who wouldn't react the same way to a man who took the life of one's own child?'

Blix looked down. Said nothing.

'That doesn't make you a bad person.'

'Perhaps not,' Blix said. 'But it does make me a bad policeman.'

'Is that what defines you as a person?' Dokken asked. 'The kind of policeman you once were?'

Blix had no answer.

'And another thing – would it make your life better if you hadn't stopped him? If he had gone ahead and killed Emma Ramm too?'

Blix continued staring at the floor.

'In a way, you've actually been given a second chance.'

'Not really,' Blix responded. 'I can never work as a policeman again.'

'No, but it's not beyond the realms of possibility to think of this freedom as a gift. It's happened before, and with people who have done worse than you. It is possible to do something with that freedom. That gift.'

Blix stared at him. 'Like what?'

'*I* can't give you the answer to that. That is something you have to find out for yourself.'

Again, silence.

'May I make an observation?' Dokken asked after a while.

Blix looked up at him. Waited.

'It seems like you're flogging yourself,' Dokken began. 'First and foremost because you failed to save your daughter, but also because you killed a man and are now free. You even visit your old workplace every day. So you can remind yourself of what you did and what you've lost. That is a brutal thing to do to yourself.'

Blix didn't answer.

'Right now,' Dokken continued, clearing his voice, 'your own head is your worst enemy, because your mind is going in circles. You won't get anywhere like that. You're like a dog trying to bite its own tail.'

Blix listened but had nothing to say.

'But,' Dokken said, 'you keep coming here, even after your previous experiences with people in my profession, and you do so voluntarily. That tells me that deep down you want to get help. That you do want to feel better. It shows a strength of character. And I would like to help you, Alexander. But you have to let me.'

Blix glanced up at the clock on the wall. Dokken followed his gaze. It was quiet again.

'In psychology, we have a concept we call self-compassion,' Dokken began. 'It's about being kind to yourself. About acknowledging that yes, I am in pain right now. And at the same time saying that yes, it's perfectly okay to feel that pain. It's important to take care of yourself. And it's important not to make things worse than they need to be.'

'So I should walk somewhere else?'

'That might be a good place to start,' Dokken said. 'And, as I've said before: get a dog, if you're not allergic. Dogs are wonderful companions.'

Dokken spent the next few minutes sharing some anecdotes from his own life with his own four-legged friends, and what enrichment they had brought in difficult times. As the clock approached 11:45, he signalled for them to wrap up the appointment.

Blix stood up, sweat between his shoulder blades, glad the session was over. Dokken accompanied him out into the hall. After Blix had pulled on his still-wet jacket, Dokken said:

'You should see your father. Even if you don't feel like it. *He* might need it. And who knows,' he said. 'Maybe you need to see him too.'

Blix bent down to tighten his shoelaces, even though he had just finished tying them. When he stood up again, he said nothing.

'Do it,' Dokken repeated. 'Because one day, maybe soon, it may be too late.'

Blix buttoned up his jacket and reached for the doorknob.

'Thanks,' Blix said, without looking at him. 'Enjoy the rest of your day.'

3

It didn't take more than a couple of minutes before Emma Ramm realised what a mistake she had made. It was by no means a disaster though, to enter the Botanical Garden without the slightest knowledge or interest in shrubs and plants. She had always appreciated the aesthetic things in life, but when her walking partner had four legs and a level of curiosity about every single thing happening around them that was a little more than the average, then the experience suddenly became a lot more frantic.

Terry was a Tibetan terrier who she had been told was a 'laid-back' dog, but could also be a lively, friendly little guy with 'many charming traits'. He was supposed to be both outgoing and smart, and not particularly aggressive or difficult to deal with. But – and this was the big but – he could also be 'not quite as loyal to strangers'. Which, really, was what Emma was to him.

Be firm, she told herself, almost like repeating a mantra. Regardless, it was Terry who pulled her to the right, yanked her to the left – desperate to experience all the exciting smells and traces of something or other across every nook and cranny of the Botanical Garden – which probably had more nooks and crannies than anywhere else in Oslo.

When she eventually managed to get Terry to take a breather at the top of the hill, or rather on a bench where she could look out over the upper Grønland district, she wondered what the previous owners had done with him. The only thing she knew about him was that he had been adopted from a shelter.

Emma checked her watch.

Blix was late.

She passed the time by scrolling through the news sites on her phone. It was a wonderful feeling to be able to do so without the fear that her competitors had discovered a case she should have covered herself, without having to think of all the angles she should tackle a story from as soon as she read an item she knew would dominate the news for the next few days.

It had taken time to shake off those old habits, those old ways of thinking. It had taken time to get used to detaching herself from her old routines too, such as getting up early in the morning to exercise before the work day began. Now she could sleep in until half-seven before hopping on her bike or sliding into her running trainers and taking to the streets to try to keep up with the city's light-blue trams.

Emma's phone vibrated in her hand.

It was a number she didn't recognise. She usually let unknown callers ring through to voicemail – she hated talking to telemarketers or people wanting her to take part in some dull market research. This time though, she answered, seeing as she still couldn't see any sign of Blix.

'Is that... Emma Ramm?' The voice on the other end sounded like it belonged to a young girl.

'It is?'

'Hello. I...'

A prolonged silence. 'My name is Carmen,' the girl eventually said. 'I'm sorry that I...'

She stopped again. Emma straightened up and planted both feet on the ground.

'I was wondering if I could have a chat with you?'

Emma frowned. For a school assignment, perhaps, she thought. A student who had found her name in an article about the topic of whatever project they were doing. It had happened before.

'Sure you can,' Emma replied. 'What about?'

'I'd rather not say over the phone. I...'

Again, silence on the other end.

'Sorry,' she said. 'I'm not very good at talking over the phone.'

Emma felt a wave of sympathy for the young girl. 'Do you want to talk in person?'

'Yes. Or, no. Um, yes. If that's okay. If you have time?'

Emma glanced at her wristwatch, even though she knew that time itself wasn't a problem.

'Can I ask why you want to talk to me in particular, Carmen?'

'Because...'

The seconds ticked by. Emma heard a sniffle on the other end. Then another.

'Forget it,' she said abruptly. 'Sorry for bothering you.'

And the next moment, the line went dead.

Emma looked at her phone. A quick online search revealed that the number of the girl who had called her was registered to a Victoria Prytz.

'Whoa,' Emma said out loud.

The next moment, Terry sprang to life. Emma immediately understood why – Blix was walking up the hill towards them. Terry charged at him, hauling Emma up from the bench. She had to hold on tightly to the lead in order not to be dragged along the tarmac after him.

Blix bent down as Terry jumped up at him, tail wagging back and forth. Leaping at his face, then back to the ground, doing a spin, before leaping up at Blix's face again with an eager, soaking-wet tongue. Blix received the love, joy and the biggest welcome in the world with a gentle smile.

'Hi,' he said to Emma when Terry finally finished the welcoming ritual.

'Hello.'

Emma released a heavy sigh. Blix, she saw, had even darker bags under his eyes than when she had seen him earlier that day. The skin beneath his chin looked flushed.

'How did it go?' she asked.

Blix looked around quickly. 'You know that those sessions are confidential?'

'Um,' Emma said. 'It's only the psychologists who have to keep their traps shut. You, on the other hand, can run your mouth all you want. Especially to someone who's looking after your dog.'

She winked, sent him a smile. Blix took the dog lead from her. Terry had calmed down a bit, was now preoccupied with an invisible trace of something along the edge of the tarmac.

'Everything go okay?' he asked, nodding towards the dog.

'Yeah, all fine,' Emma lied. 'We've had a great time together.' She tried not to roll her eyes.

They walked down the hill, towards Jens Bjelkes gate.

'What're you up to for the rest of the day?' she asked.

He glanced up at the clouds. It wasn't long before it would start raining again. 'I'm ... heading home, I think.' He studied his surroundings. Followed a car with his eyes as it drove towards Sofienberg.

'I'll walk with you.'

They continued towards Tøyengata.

Emma thought of the young girl who had called her. Carmen, who by all accounts seemed to be the daughter of Victoria Prytz and therefore the stepdaughter of Oliver Krogh. Emma was about to tell Blix about the phone call, but could see that he was lost in his own thoughts.

'You're not going to tell me then?' she asked.

'About what?'

'Um, hello?' Emma said dejectedly. 'You were there for three quarters of an hour.'

'Yes, but...'

He looked away.

'Have you heard of EMDR?' he finally asked.

'What's that, a new country in Eastern Europe?'

There, a slight movement in his smile lines. Emma almost felt like patting herself on the back.

'No, never heard of it,' she said. 'What is it?'

'Just something,' Blix said, shaking his head.

'Just something?'

'Yeah, some ... psychobabble nonsense. Nothing I'm going to try.'

But you still mentioned it, Emma thought.

They made their way down Tøyengata. A red bus drove by in the opposite direction. And a few minutes later they arrived outside number nineteen, where Blix lived.

'Thanks for looking after Terry,' he said with a long sigh, glancing down the road. 'He ... doesn't do well, being home alone.'

'You're welcome.' She looked at him. Suddenly burst into laughter.

'What is it?'

'No, it's just funny, that's all,' she said. 'You're probably the last person in the world I would have thought would get a dog.'

'What makes you say that?'

She looked down at Terry, who had plonked himself down on the ground beside Blix. His tongue lolled out of the side of his mouth. It looked like he had a heart rate of 350.

'I didn't think you even liked dogs.'

Blix glanced quickly over Emma's shoulder, as if scanning the area for something. She turned to look in the same direction, but saw nothing of note.

'And then all of a sudden this guy moves in with you. Something completely dependent on you to survive.'

Blix said nothing.

It hit her then, that perhaps it was just as much the other way round.

'You're a stimulating conversation partner, Blix. Informative and inclusive.'

'Sorry,' he said with a faint smile. 'I'm just a little tired.' Again he glanced over her shoulder.

'Are you expecting a visitor or something?'

'No, no,' he said. 'I just...' He looked down.

Emma scrutinised him. 'You do know I can read you pretty well at this point, right?'

Blix sighed but didn't answer.

'Is something going on?' she asked.

'No, no. It's nothing,' he said.

'Are you sure?'

'Yes.'

He looked at her and shook his head. Emma didn't believe him for a second.

'Okay,' she said anyway. 'I'll leave you be. You'll tell me one day.'

Blix seemed disconcerted as she bent down.

'Thanks for today, Terry,' she said, patting the dog on the head. 'It's been a pleasure.'

Terry tried to nip her hand in return.

4

Standing at the post boxes in the hallway was Holger Evensen, a man a few years younger than Blix, who had moved into an apartment at the back of the building in the spring. Despite the fact that it was now cold out, Evensen was only wearing a white T-shirt and a pair of well-worn joggers. He gave Blix an exasperated look when Terry lunged over to say hello.

'You know you have to apply to the condominium for permission to have a dog here, right?' There was a hint of disdain in his voice. With irritated movements, he took out his mail.

'He's a rescue dog,' Blix tried to argue.

Holger Evensen snorted and started up the stairs as he leafed through his letters, his slippers slapping on the dirty steps.

Blix's post box was half full of junk mail and bills. A couple of envelopes of a more personal nature had also found their way in. There was sender information on the back of two of them – R. Nakstad from Honningsvåg and Alma Söderqvist from Uddevalla.

Sweden now too, Blix thought. That's a first.

He walked back out into the courtyard, kept two bills and threw the rest into the paper recycling bin.

He heard the sound of a door opening and slamming shut on the floor above. Blix hurried back to the front door, unlocked it and made for the stairs. Once on their floor, Terry abruptly planted himself on the carpet in the hallway. His ears were pushed back and his snout twitched, as if he could smell something new, foreign. Blix had to prod him forward with his foot until they were finally inside the flat and he could close the door behind him.

'What is it?' he asked, unclipping his lead.

Terry strolled off, unconcerned. Claws click-clacking against the wooden floor.

Blix hung up his jacket and followed him into the kitchen.

He put down the post and filled Terry's water bowl. Warmed up the leftovers from yesterday's stew and tucked in with two dry slices of bread. The clock on the wall steadily ticked away, like an eternal reminder that life goes on.

Terry settled down at his feet. Blix considered whether he should get some sleep himself, but could feel in his body that he wouldn't be able to. Instead he went into the small study and sat down to work on one of his flies. The Antron yarn which, with some difficulty, would become the fly's tail, had twisted itself around the hook shaft.

He took a deep breath, untangled it, and began again, until he was satisfied. It looked better this time.

He had just finished weaving two peacock feathers into the attachment point above the barb when his phone rang in the kitchen. Blix remained seated, concentrating on his work. With each ring, he became more and more irritated. Whoever was calling finally gave up.

He finally managed to attach the feathers to the hook eye when the ringing started anew.

'Goddamn it,' he muttered, and stood up.

The movement was a little too sudden. His lower back throbbed. He limped into the kitchen. The display showed no number, just the word 'unknown'. He answered with a grumpy hello.

'Took your time,' a distorted voice answered on the other end. It sounded muffled, as if a piece of cloth had been placed over the receiver.

'Who is this?' Blix asked. 'Who am I talking to?'

No answer. Instead, the voice said: 'I would like to make a confession.'

Blix moved the phone to his other ear. It sounded like the caller was purposely lowering his voice by a couple of octaves.

'What do you mean?' Blix asked.

'I would like to make a confession,' the man repeated.

Terry had woken up. He got up from his blanket and lay down under the table.

Blix wasn't sure if the person on the other end meant he simply wanted to admit to some error, or he was talking about confessing to something more serious.

'If you really mean it,' Blix began, sitting down. 'If you want to confess to a crime, then you've got the wrong person. I no longer work for the police.'

'I put it in your post box.'

'Huh?'

'My confession. I put it in your post box. But...' He paused. '...It's no longer there.'

Blix glanced over at the bills he had brought in. Felt his heart pounding.

'You shouldn't just throw away what people send you, Blix,' the man continued. 'It's rude.'

The motor in the fridge kicked in and made a steady hum. Blix swallowed, unsure whether, or how, he should continue the conversation. It didn't matter – in the next moment, the connection was cut.

Blix sat with the phone in his hand for a few moments. Then pushed himself up and walked towards the door. Terry followed, but Blix shot him a stern look and held up a flat hand: 'Stay!'

Terry obediently laid back down. Blix hurried out of the door and down the stairs. In his haste he forgot both his phone and keys, but there was always a door wedge downstairs he could use to prop the front door open.

There were lights on in several of the windows around him. A brief movement behind the curtain of a window on the first floor, but otherwise, he didn't see anyone.

He opened the recycling bin, glad that the bin lorry wasn't due today. It only took a moment before he found the stack of letters he had thrown in there. He filtered through the junk mail and found the envelopes. Opened the letter from R. Nakstad first.

There was a picture and a handwritten letter inside. The R stood for Regine. Blix quickly realised that she was just a lonely woman. He crumpled the paper up and looked around again. Two boys walked by on the street, each with a gym bag slung over their shoulders, but neither of them paid him any attention.

He tore open the next envelope. Alma Söderqvist would like to invite him to Uddevalla. That letter was also thrown back into the bin as soon as it was opened.

The last envelope had no name on it, neither for the recipient nor the sender. It really just looked like generic, unaddressed advertising.

He squeezed it to check its contents. A photograph, it felt like.

Tentatively, he slid his index finger under the edge of the glue and popped open the envelope.

'Jesus,' he muttered to himself.

It was a Polaroid picture of a woman.

Elisabeth Eie.

The mother who had been missing and presumed dead for almost two and a half years.

5

Emma was sitting on a bench dappled with damp spots. From the top of St. Hanshaugen park, eighty-three metres above sea level, she could see well into the Oslo Fjord. A cruise ship curved its way through the narrow inlets, heading for Skagerrak's open waters. The cloud cover was dense. There was a chill in the air.

It was 5:30pm.

Carmen Prytz was still nowhere to be seen. Emma opened her phone messages and quickly scrolled through the brief communication they had had earlier that day. Curiosity had prompted her to get in touch and say that of course they could meet – *just choose a time and place and I'll meet you there*. She hadn't expected to hear back, but a response came anyway, a good hour later. Just a time – 5:30 – and a meeting place. Nothing else. It was now approaching 5:40. Still no sign of Carmen. Emma texted her to say she was there, adding a smiley face. No response.

It had been just over two months since Emma had quit her job as a journalist. She had been sure that she would use all this free time to figure things out and make a start on something new, but she still had no idea what to do next. It had been a great feeling at first, having no responsibilities. Everything was possible, open. She had even considered going back to university, but for what? What would she do?

Emma had thought that the right career path would materialise for her one day, as if there was a place in the universe meant just for her. Perhaps it was an overly romantic and childish idea. In the meantime she took each day as it came, making the effort not to worry too much. This did make her everyday life easier, in a way, but it also made it more difficult. More boring. Emptier. Work out, eat, sleep, read a bit, fix a few things in the apartment, take a trip to IKEA. Spend time with Irene and Martine – her sister and niece – go out with a couple of friends. Go back home with a stranger, but never spend the night.

Not exactly sustainable in the long term.

She had to make money, too. The book she had written had been well received, but had been nowhere near a bestseller.

It was now 5:45.

Carmen had obviously got cold feet.

Emma stood up with a sigh and straightened her trousers a little. And was about to head off when she caught sight of a girl approaching with tentative steps. She was wearing an oversized black hoodie and was looking nervously in Emma's direction.

Emma recognised Carmen from her Instagram thumbnail. Her account was private, so that was all she'd been able to see – and basically all the public information Emma had been able to find about the girl she was going to meet.

Emma waved.

Carmen slowly came closer. Emma met her with a smile and an out-stretched hand. Carmen reciprocated nervously. Her thin fingers were warm.

'Sorry I'm late,' she said. 'My mum, she...' Carmen stopped herself.

The girl in front of Emma had long, light-blonde hair and a round, full face, badly afflicted by skin problems. It looked like she had a rash around her mouth. On other parts of her face, slightly larger spots had dried up and left angry, dark-red crusts. The teenage years, Emma thought. A terrible, merciless time, in so many ways.

'That's okay,' she said gently. 'Shall we sit?'

Emma gestured towards the bench she had just got up from. Carmen sat down and put her hands in her lap. Squeezed her fingers a little, brought one of them up to her mouth. Started biting her nail. Took it out, examined it.

'Thank you for agreeing to meet me,' she said without looking at Emma. 'I ... wasn't sure if I should come.'

Carmen seemed shy and unsure of herself. Emma had met many girls just like her back when she was a young girl herself – not least when she had looked in the mirror.

'What can I do for you?' she asked.

The teenager waited a few moments.

'Do you know who I am?' she asked, shoving her hands deep inside the pockets of her hoodie.

Emma nodded. 'Kind of.'

'Then you've also seen what's going on with my stepfather, Oliver Krogh?'

'It's been hard to miss,' Emma said.

Oliver Krogh was in custody, suspected of having killed a childhood friend. At the end of July, Bull's Eye – Krogh's hunting and fishing store – had burned to the ground. It was first assumed that Maria Normann, who worked for him, was inside, and that Krogh had set fire to his own shop.

Maria Normann had still not been found, yet a few days after the fire, Krogh was arrested.

Whatever his motive was, the media hadn't yet been able to find it. So far no charges had been brought against him, but everything seemed to indicate that they were imminent.

'He's innocent.' Carmen took out a round, dark-blue tub from one pocket and unscrewed the lid. Dipped her little finger into it and rubbed the moisturising balm over her lips. 'My stepfather couldn't have killed anyone,' she said, putting the tub back.

'What makes you say that?'

'He's just not like that.' Carmen shook her head.

Emma could see that the girl was on the verge of tears.

'What does he have to say about what happened that day?' Emma asked.

'He denies it, of course.'

'Does he have any idea who might have done it, then?'

She hesitated a little, then shook her head. 'We ... talked to the lawyer about hiring a private investigator, but Mum ... didn't want to.'

'Why not?'

'She ... said it would be too expensive. But the most important reason was probably that...' Carmen lowered her head. Started to cry quietly. She sniffed and apologised.

'Oh, hun,' Emma said, placing a hand on her arm. 'There is nothing to apologise for.'

Carmen wiped her cheeks. 'They were drifting apart, I think, even before all this happened. And afterwards, after he was arrested...' She shook her head. 'It didn't take long before she said that she wanted a divorce. I think she was glad to have someone to blame. It made it easier, or something.'

'Easier to leave him, you mean?'

'Yes.'

'So she doesn't believe him either?'

Carmen sighed. 'I don't think so.'

They both fell silent for a while.

'So ... your mother doesn't know you're here?' Emma asked. 'She doesn't know you've contacted me?'

Carmen looked up at her. Shook her head.

'Are *your* parents still together?' Carmen asked after another minute's silence.

Emma pondered how best to answer her. The fact that her mother was shot and killed by Emma's father was not something she usually spoke freely about to just anyone. She merely shook her head.

'Carmen, before we go any further: You know I'm not a journalist anymore, right?'

'Yeah, I ... read that.'

'But still you wanted to talk to *me* about this?'

A couple of seagulls were squabbling over a meal on a patch of grass a small distance away. It was difficult to say who was winning.

'No one will help him,' Carmen said. 'The police seem convinced he did it. He's all alone.'

Emma suspected that the young girl had been in contact with other, more high-profile journalists before her.

'I read about you online,' Carmen continued. 'It said that you'd received an award for your work. That you weren't afraid to work on difficult, unpopular cases.'

Emma felt a little uneasy, but had to admit that Carmen's call and Oliver Krogh's case had piqued her curiosity. As a journalist, she had always been sceptical of overwhelmingly one-sided media coverage. But that didn't mean it was wrong, or that she could do anything to balance the voices proclaiming the man's guilt.

'I know I'm asking way too much,' Carmen said. 'And I have nothing to pay you with either. I just don't know who else to ask.'

Emma didn't know what to say. Now having agreed to meet the girl, it felt wrong to turn her request down.

'The police have been searching for Maria Normann, but haven't found her,' Emma said. 'However, your stepfather is still in custody. Do you think the police might have some sort of evidence or indication that is telling them he's guilty?' Emma hadn't found any suggestion of this in the media. 'Have you, his family, heard anything like that?'

Carmen stared straight ahead. 'We've only been told a little,' she said. Emma waited for the girl to continue.

'They ... found some blood,' Carmen went on. Her voice was weak.

'Blood?' Emma asked.

'Maria's blood,' Carmen explained. 'They found traces of her blood in the ruins of Oliver's shop.'

6

One of his neighbours met him at the door and tried to say hello, but Blix walked straight past her, up to the second floor. Terry was waiting for him back in the apartment. Blix ignored him, just continued into the kitchen and grabbed his phone.

Another missed call from an unknown number he couldn't call back. He cursed, slumped into a kitchen chair and dropped the picture and envelope on the table. In the middle of the picture there was a small hole, as if it had been attached to a board with a pin or thumbtack. The point had been slotted through Elisabeth Eie's head.

He stood up again, went to the cupboard under the sink and looked for a pair of rubber gloves. Found none, so took two plastic food bags with him and slipped the envelope into one and the picture into the other, without contaminating them further.

The Eie investigation had been his.

It had been a special case from the start. Two officers had come out of the Oslo Courthouse building one day and found a large envelope underneath the windscreen wipers of their patrol car. Blix's name and job title had been written on the outside, along with a note stating that the contents were private and that delivery was urgent.

Blix had received it an hour later. The simple message had been written on a large, white piece of paper: *Something is wrong with Elisabeth Eie*. Her address and date of birth were also provided, so there would be no doubt as to whom the note was referring.

Blix had sent a patrol car to check her address. The apartment had been empty. Seven hours earlier, she had dropped her daughter off at the nursery and had then met with a case manager from child-welfare services. And that was the last time Elisabeth Eie was seen alive.

Blix found himself standing again, leaning on the table, palms down, staring at the photo of her. Her hair looked as if it were flowing around her. Her eyes were wide open. The skin on her face had a blue tinge.

Everything indicated that she was dead, but he couldn't tell from the photo exactly how she had been killed.

Whatever surface she was lying on was dark. Maybe brown. It could be a basement floor, Blix thought, or a carpet. There were no other details in the photograph that could help him determine where she was when it had been taken.

He straightened up, flipped the picture over and looked at the back. In the middle of the smooth surface, a black marker had been used to draw a cross where the pin had punctured the Polaroid. Surrounding that cross were three smaller crosses. This meant nothing to him.

Elisabeth Eie had been from Lillestrøm, but had moved about a bit. She had worked as a substitute teacher in a primary school. Her daughter was called Julie and after Elisabeth's disappearance she had been taken into care by child welfare. The child's father was a man in his forties who received disability benefits and was not considered fit to care for her.

He had a strange first name. Skage. Skage Kleiven.

Initially, much of the routine investigation had been focused on him, but Kleiven's sick father had passed away two days before Elisabeth Eie disappeared. In the following days, Kleiven had been busy organising his father's affairs and funeral. Among the places he had been seen around that time, one was the funeral home, where he attended several appointments.

Blix moved the picture into the light from the window and looked at it more closely. Elisabeth Eie had light-blue eyes and long, curved eyelashes. Thin, arched eyebrows and a prominent, powerful nose. Her mouth was half open. In the picture, it looked like she was gasping.

He jumped when the phone rang.

Again, an unknown number.

Blix replied immediately, stating his full name this time.

'You found it,' the gravelly voice said.

Blix went to the window and glanced out. 'Who are you?' he asked.

'You think I'm just going to tell you like that?'

'You said you wanted to confess.'

'That's true,' the man said, as if he was surprised at himself. 'I did say that.'

'I don't work for the police anymore,' Blix said.

'I know.'

'You'll have to take this up with them.'

'No.' The man dismissed the idea. 'This is between us.'

Blix thought for a moment.

'Was it you who wrote the letter back then?' he asked. 'The envelope with my name on it?'

No answer.

'Is the picture real?' Blix continued.

'Does it not look real?' The man on the other end seemed taken aback.

Blix didn't answer.

'I took it the morning I killed her,' the man said.

Blix took a sharp breath in.

'Why did you do it?' he asked. 'Why did you kill her?'

The answer came without a second's pause: 'Because she deserved it.'

'Why?' Blix repeated. 'What had she done?'

Silence on the other end.

'Who are you?' Blix pressed. 'What's your name?'

He heard a sound somewhere on the other end, behind the silence, but was unable to identify it.

'How did you know Elisabeth Eie?'

The man still didn't answer.

'How did you kidnap her?'

No response.

'Where...' Blix had to clear his throat again. 'You say you want to confess,' he said, trying a new approach. 'But you're not telling me anything.'

'Oh, I think I've told and shown you quite a lot,' the man eventually retorted.

Blix flipped the picture over. 'What do the crosses mean?' he asked.

'I can tell you that later,' the man replied. 'If necessary.'

'What do you mean?'

No answer.

'Why are you coming forward about this now?' Blix continued. 'And why is it so important for you to confess to *me* exactly?'

The man remained silent.

'Are you the one who's been following me?'

Silence. A long silence. The thought of the man in the green raincoat made Blix feel clammy.

'I saw you earlier today,' Blix said. 'You saw me too – that's why you ran. Into the underground.'

He didn't deny it.

'Okay,' Blix said and returned to the window. He realised he was getting nowhere. 'What do you want me to do with what you've told me?'

'That's for you to find out for yourself.'

Blix took a deep breath. It was like talking to Krissander Dokken.

'A picture won't do,' he said. 'I need to know where she is.'

'You shouldn't just throw away what people send you, Alexander.'

'Yes, you said that.'

'If you hadn't, you would have also seen the other pictures I've sent you.'

A chill ran down Blix's spine.

'What do you mean, *other* pictures? Do you mean other pictures of Elisabeth, or do you mean...?' Blix swallowed. 'Or have you sent me pictures of others ... you've...?'

There was no answer.

The line went dead.

Blix needed a few seconds to compose himself, to run through everything he had been told. His pulse was still high when he called Nicolai Wibe's number, but the police investigator didn't answer. Tine Abelvik didn't pick up either.

'Oh, come on,' he said irritably, and sent them both a text telling them to call him back. *It's about Elisabeth Eie*, he added. *I have new information.*

He took pictures of the photograph, both front and back, and sent them those too. This time, it was only a matter of seconds before Tine Abelvik called him back.

'Blix,' she said. 'Hello.' Her voice sounded tired. Drained.

'Hello,' he said.

'How ... are you?'

'Did you get the pictures I just sent?'

'Um, yes.'

Blix spent the next thirty seconds recounting what had happened. He spoke quickly, barely taking a breath.

'Do you remember that case?' he asked when he was done. 'It was all we worked on for a while.'

'Sure,' Abelvik answered. 'Of course I remember it.' There was something measured about her answer, as if she hadn't quite caught on or understood the seriousness of what he had just told her.

'I think it's the same guy,' Blix went on. 'The same one who wrote the letter that started the investigation when she disappeared.'

'You didn't recognise him?' Abelvik asked. 'I mean – had you heard his voice before?'

Blix shook his head. He had tried but failed to place it.

'His voice was distorted,' he explained.

Abelvik hesitated a moment.

'Okay,' she said. 'We have to analyse the photo and see if we can verify it.'

'It seems genuine to me,' Blix said. 'Why would anyone make up something like this?'

'That whole thing with the anonymous letter – it was widely reported in the media at the time,' Abelvik replied. 'You were the face of the investigation, before everything else happened. You're even more well known now. Celebrities often attract unwanted attention, often from people with no perception of reality.'

Blix wasn't sure if he had heard her right. 'You have to take this seriously,' he protested.

'We will,' Abelvik assured him. 'But what's most likely here – that a murderer has suddenly decided to come forward and confess, or that this person is ... a little muddled?'

They might not be mutually exclusive, Blix thought.

'So what are we going to do?' he asked. 'Nothing? Should we just wait and see what happens or...?'

'I'll send a car,' Abelvik answered. 'We'll come pick up the photograph.'

Some random patrol officer, Blix thought. She didn't want to come herself.

'I can bring it in,' Blix said. 'It'll be easier. Faster too.'

'You needn't do that,' Abelvik responded. 'Stay home for now.'

Blix looked down at Terry, who was staring up at him innocently.

'Okay,' he said with a sigh. 'How...'

Again he stopped himself. He didn't want to know how she was. He didn't want to know how any of them were.

'Talk soon then,' he said instead. And hung up.

With a forceful movement, he slammed the phone back down on the kitchen table. Terry stood up, as if in protest at the sudden loud noise.

Blix walked over to the window and looked out. A taxi drove past. Someone was standing on the other side of the road, looking down at their mobile phone.

Next to Blix, the clock on the wall ticked away steadily. Tick, tock, tick, tock. Disgruntled, he tore off the glass that protected the hands and dial, and removed the battery. The silence that followed was deafening.

7

'But ... how is that possible?' Emma asked. 'Blood ... I mean, wasn't everything destroyed by the fire?'

'Not everything,' Carmen replied, and shifted her foot slightly, placing the sole of her shoe parallel to the joint of one of the slabs in front of them. 'Gun cabinets aren't flammable. They found the blood on one of them, in the crack of the door.'

Emma thought about it. This strengthened the case against Oliver Krogh considerably.

'And there's no possibility that the blood could have found its way there earlier?'

'I ... don't know,' Carmen replied. 'The lawyer didn't say anything about that.'

'The lawyer,' Emma said. 'Is that Leo van Eijk?'

'Yes.'

A man in running leggings and a jacket passed by, steering a pram in front of him as he navigated around the puddles. The sound of a leaf blower could be heard in the distance.

'I think I'd like to walk a bit,' Carmen said after a while. 'Can we?'

Emma was more than willing. It was starting to get cold.

They stood up at the same time. As they did, Carmen's phone fell out of the large pocket on the front of her hoodie. It landed screen-side down on the paving slabs in front of them. Carmen cursed and bent to pick it up.

She inspected the damage. The screen was covered in nicks and scratches. She sighed and shoved the phone back into her hoodie.

Emma let her lead the way.

Carmen appeared to be familiar with St. Hanshaugen. Without hesitating, she headed straight onto the path that led down towards Geitmyrsveien.

'Did you know her well?' Emma asked. 'Maria?'

'I wouldn't say I knew her *well*,' Carmen replied. 'But I'd see her every now and then, when I stopped by the shop.'

'How often was that?'

'I actually worked there myself from time to time. When my step-father needed help.'

'What kind of impression did you get of her?'

Carmen thought about it. 'Maria was nice, straightforward. Although she'd clearly had a tough life.'

Emma knew what Carmen was referring to. In the days and weeks after the fire, the newspapers had been heaving with material about Maria's life. They did little to hide the fact that she had once been a drug addict and had spent parts of her life living on the street.

'Why did he hire her? She didn't have much experience with either hunting or fishing, I gather?'

'They were childhood friends,' Carmen answered. 'So he wanted to help her, I guess. Help her get back on her feet or something. Which he did. She was doing well. Was quite good with customers eventually. Oliver was very proud of her, at least.'

'She had a child too, right?'

'Yeah,' Carmen said. 'Jonah. Cute kid.' She looked sad again. 'He's only four,' she added.

She took out the little round tub once more and spread the balm over her lips.

Emma's perception of the girl beside her had changed in the little time they had spent together. From first seeing her as an insecure child, she now appeared to be much more grown-up. As if she just needed to talk a little to come out of her childlike shell.

They walked on, passing a birch tree. Its yellow leaves had fallen off and settled on the ground. Carmen took out her phone and quickly checked for any messages, then put it back.

'Tell me more about your stepfather,' Emma said. 'How long has he been in your life?'

'Since I was seven,' Carmen said. 'My actual father lives in Abu Dhabi. He's been there since I was two.' She rolled her eyes. 'I mean ... Oliver is my *real* dad. At least he was the one who taught me stuff,' Carmen continued. 'Skiing and skating, those kinds of things, y'know.

Normal parenting stuff. Plus, things were so tiring and difficult for Mum.'

A car drove slowly towards them. Carmen looked away as it passed.

'What do you know about the day the shop burned down?' Emma asked.

'Not much, really. It was a Sunday like any other. Oliver left at some point. Said he was going to work.'

'On a Sunday?'

'Yeah, but that was normal. He'd go in to get ready for the week, that kind of thing. There were always a thousand things to do.'

'Was he going to meet Maria there?'

Carmen paused before answering.

'I don't know.'

'But she was probably there, right, given that the police suspect him of killing her? Surely they must have something that indicates that?'

Carmen shrugged.

Emma had several questions on the tip of her tongue. One of them she hesitated to ask, but decided to go for it anyway.

'What did your mother think of Maria?'

The question made Carmen laugh. 'I mean, she wasn't happy about Maria coming into our lives, that's for sure. She had her suspicions about them both.'

'And by that you mean...?'

Carmen continued to smile. 'The same thing everyone else is thinking. A marriage on the rocks, a new woman comes into his life, he perks up, seemingly out of nowhere, despite the fact the shop's going downhill ... It's not difficult to jump to conclusions. Two plus two equals sex.'

'But you don't know for sure? You're just assuming?'

Carmen closed her eyes for a few seconds.

'I don't know for sure, no. But I'm not stupid.'

'Did you talk to your mother about Maria?'

Carmen shook her head. 'Mum, she ... Well, it's not that easy to talk to her about *anything*, really. She can be a bit hysterical.'

Carmen steered them further onto Bjerregaards gate. A van was parked up on the pavement with the side doors open.

A man pulled out a box with *Kitchen Utensils* written on the side.

'I guess you'll be heading home from here?' Carmen said.

They were almost at the junction. Ueland's gate was at a standstill. The traffic stretched back in every direction.

'Yes,' Emma said, still thinking through everything she'd heard.

There was so much she wanted to ask. So much she was curious about.

'How about this,' she began. 'I'll see if I can find out any more about what happened. And for now ... we can keep in touch?'

Carmen looked at her gratefully.

'I can't promise anything,' Emma added. 'And I don't know how much time I can spend on this either.'

'I understand. I'm just glad that—'

'And I have no idea how much pushback I might encounter,' Emma continued. 'If you're right, that someone else *did* kill Maria Normann and set fire to your stepfather's shop, then it won't be as easy as just finding out who did it and proving it.'

'Thank you anyway,' Carmen said. 'For agreeing to meet me.'

She wrapped her arms around Emma, who gave her a warm squeeze back.

'Stay positive,' she said. 'Keep your head up. Don't be afraid to look people in the eye.'

Carmen smiled meekly.

'You haven't done anything wrong,' Emma added.

Carmen didn't answer.

But when they parted, Emma could see that there were tears in her eyes.

8

'Jonathan, no. *No*, I said. And you, Tom-Erik, keep up with the others.'

Grethe Nordby sent a stern look at them both. The little buggers giggled, a sure sign that she was going to have to tell them off again. Had they ever just done as they were told, without her having to yell at them or threaten them with a good smack?

'Are we there yet?'

'I'm hungry.'

'Do we *have* to go on a walk?'

'My shoes are wet.'

'Mine too.'

Their voices blended together – one long, uninterrupted stream of nonsense, shouting, bickering, chaos. They hadn't even reached the path before the first complaints poured in. They had left school too late, and Grethe hadn't even finished her coffee before rushing out of her door that morning.

Activity days had to be the work of the devil, she thought and closed her eyes – hell's little prank on those who had actually dreamed of doing something good in teaching, something more than just shouting commands and stern admonitions at the next generation of hopefuls.

In theory, she knew that it was a good idea to take the children out into nature – there was a lot you could teach six- and seven-year-olds about trees, and plants, and animals and deer tracks, but there wasn't a single child in front of her who looked up from the ground or who took time to marvel at all the beauty and wonder surrounding them. Not in her class, anyway. Perhaps she shouldn't expect too much, but it was tempting to think that activity days were something politicians had invented so that they didn't have to drag their own offspring into the forest for a day out themselves.

You've taken the wrong turn in life, Grethe told herself. You should have done something else, become a glassblower or a yoga instructor. You should have found your *ashtanga vinyasa* or whatever the hell it's called, so you could find some inner peace, so everything around you could be calmer too.

Instead, there was just a never-ending din.

If she had been able to afford a smartwatch, her health alarm would have been pinging on her wrist every forty-five minutes. It didn't help that she had her very own homo sapiens specimen at home, not even two and a half years old, who still couldn't sleep through the night, who would always wake them up, especially her, for some reason – as if she were the only one who could find the baby's lost teddy bear or do something about the damp patch on the bedsheet. And Martin, of course, he could fall asleep again twenty-six seconds later and wake up at seven the next morning refreshed. Meanwhile, she wasn't even sure when they last had sex, or what day of the week it was.

Was this what life was supposed to be like at thirty-two?

There were actually supposed to be three teachers on the trip today, but Kenneth was 'off sick', leaving just Grethe and Turid. Up front, Turid looked to be in control – she turned around at regular intervals and did the same as Grethe, checking that everyone was there.

But not everyone was there.

They were missing Tom-Erik and Jonathan.

Oh my god, Grethe said to herself and scanned both sides of the path, through the trees, turning every which way. They were here just a minute ago.

A dawning panic grew in her chest. She called out to Turid, shouting that they had to stop. Turid didn't hear her, because of the racket the other kids were making, but when Grethe screamed, they all fell silent.

'Has anyone seen Tom-Erik and Jonathan?'

The children in front stared up at her. Some of them exchanged glances. Turid ordered those at the very front to stand still while she moved her way back along the long, restless line of children – twenty-six of them usually. Now only twenty-four.

'They were here,' Grethe said, she could hear the shrill tone in her own voice. 'And then they were gone, just like that.'

There was no reproach in Turid's gaze. Not yet, anyway, but Grethe blamed herself – she shouldn't have zoned out, she should have been more alert. But this was so bloody typical of Tom-Erik and Jonathan. They were wild at heart, those two, and it could very well be that they were just trying to mess with her. It was probably Jonathan who had convinced Tom-Erik to do it.

'No one leaves the path,' Turid said to the others, in a firm, authoritative voice. 'Tom-Erik?' she shouted. 'Jonathan?'

There was no answer.

Both Grethe and Turid scanned the area, but saw no abnormal colours or movement among the trees. They continued to shout, some of the children also joined in.

Grethe walked away from the path and into the forest, ducking under branches and stepping over bushes, all while continuing to shout, a growing distress in her voice. She went back in the direction they had come from, but the boys could be anywhere at this point. Hell, she told herself, if only she could get hold of them...

Another, much worse thought started to form – that something could have happened to them, that there had been another person in the woods with them, someone who had taken them, had done something to them. It would have been her fault in that case. She should have been looking after them, keeping an eye on them. She imagined the police tape, the blue lights sweeping across the car park, the questioning afterwards, for *years* afterwards. How the hell could she live with herself if it turned out that—

There.

Between the branches: the red of Tom-Erik's jacket. And there, Jonathan standing or sitting beside him, she couldn't quite tell. Grethe was relieved at first, then the anger re-emerged.

She stormed towards them, cursing because her feet were now soaking wet. She could see, even from a distance, the steam of their breath puffing out of their mouths. A branch whipped her in the face.

Grethe wanted to scream, wanted to fillet the two of them, the bastard kids, but stopped with a jolt just behind them. A thin gasp escaped from between her lips. Around them, the sound of the moss and leaves crackling. The first raindrops hit the top of her head and shoulders, but she ignored it.

She walked up to Tom-Erik and Jonathan and put her hands over their eyes. Although she knew it was already too late.

9

The most difficult part about tying fishing flies is getting the wings right, so that the work assembling them doesn't damage them.

Blix pulled out two small, golden-brown pheasant feathers. He moistened his left index finger on his tongue and pressed the tip against the feather so that it stuck. He then did the same with his right index finger, so he ended up with a feather affixed to both fingers.

It was an exercise in concentration.

He took a breath in and moved the feathers over to the little fishing hook, currently held in the vice.

The investigation into the Eie case had been intense. She had disappeared during a period in which they had been understaffed. Blix had had both tactical responsibility for the case and was first point of contact for the next of kin. The answers failed to materialise, and eventually the investigation was scaled back. He was left alone on the case, when Sofia Kovic, his closest colleague, had been shot dead.

That was the beginning of the end of his career in the force. Blix doubted that anyone had even looked at the Eie case since.

One of the feathers slid out from between his fingers. He sighed and started again.

He had thought a lot about Tomine, Elisabeth Eie's sister, and had wondered if he should write to her from prison, but never did. Blix glanced over at his phone. He still had her number saved.

He considered calling her, but decided he should wait until he had heard from Abelvik. He felt that so far the police had been dismissive and handled the matter unprofessionally. He didn't understand why they hadn't taken him in for questioning, tracked his phone, or checked for prints on his post box.

Presumably the issue was him – the fact that they were unsure how to act around him.

He concentrated on the fly again. He carefully let go, in order for the small pheasant feather to move down his finger until the wing tips reached as far back on the hook bend as they could go, and then pinched them together with his fingers. Now came the hardest part: attaching it all in one go. He eased the binding thread in a loose loop around the hook and gently tightened it.

He had the radio on in the background. He hadn't caught the beginning of the morning news, but had enough to understand that the police had cordoned off a wooded area near Leirsund. A dead body had been found. The newscaster's voice was sombre. The police were reticent, but the body allegedly showed signs of having been there for a while.

One of the pheasant feathers slipped and lay askew along the fish hook. Blix released his grip and let both feathers fall to the table.

Leirsund, he thought.

Not far from Lillestrøm, where Elisabeth Eie was from.

Blix got up and took his phone with him into the kitchen.

Terry came padding after him.

The discovery of the body was plastered across the front page of the major news websites, but there was little information of note. Nowhere did it say whether it was a man or a woman, but *VG Nett* had reported that the body found had been partially buried.

Blix scrolled down the screen with his thumb and found Abelvik's number. She didn't answer.

'Damn it.'

Terry looked up at him. Blix looked out the window. He had nothing better to do.

'Come on then,' he said to Terry.

The dog, tail wagging, followed him into the hall. On his way out of the building, Blix checked the post box. It was empty.

It was warm enough, but the cloud cover was thick and grey. Blix let Terry mark one of the park trees along the street, and then pulled him over to the car. Terry had a blanket in the back seat and his own seat belt.

The car radio was tuned to a channel that played music from the eighties. Blix absent-mindedly tapped a finger on the steering wheel as he drove.

Leirsund was a residential area without a town centre. Two women walked by on the other side of the road, each pushing a pram. Blix drove past, turned around and pulled into a bus stop. He opened the door to ask if the women knew where the body had been found, but as he went to step out, a patrol car drove by. Blix pulled the door shut and followed in pursuit.

They crossed the river, drove past a community centre and turned left at a primary school. The road passed a sports complex. People and cars were gathered on a gravel car park at the edge of the forest. The patrol car he had been following drove right up to the police tape. Some photographers from the press raised their cameras.

Blix parked a short distance away and let Terry out. The dog stood there stiffly and took in the unfamiliar terrain before lowering his snout to the ground.

Behind the cordon was a wide path that led into the forest. It was blocked off with police tape, mostly to mark the area of investigation. If you wanted to get a look at the burial site, you could easily walk into and through the forest from another entrance.

Terry padded towards a group of onlookers. A woman in hiking clothes stood with a light-brown mixed-breed dog. It had spotted Terry and pulled on its lead. The woman followed.

'Are they okay saying hi?' she asked, nodding down at the dogs.

Blix nodded. The two dogs eagerly sniffed each other.

Blix noticed her eyes lingering on him for a moment.

'Have we met before?'

'I don't think so,' he replied without looking at her. 'Do you know what happened here?' Blix nodded towards the police presence. 'I heard something about a body being found?'

The woman shivered. 'Some school kids found her. Poor kids.'

'Her?'

'Yes, a woman, I believe.'

The dogs circled each other. Their leads twisted together. Blix untangled them.

'Did you hear anything else?' he asked.

'Someone said that the body was wrapped in plastic and that she looked like she had been dug up. But I don't know how true that is.'

Terry began to pull on the lead. Blix loosened his grip.

'We should get going,' he said.

The woman pulled her dog back.

'It's really awful,' she said.

Terry tried to pull him over to the path and the cordoned-off area. But Blix led him instead towards an information board with a map.

EIKSMARKA HIKING AREA was printed in large, blue letters.

The terrain seemed varied, covering woodland, marshes and mountains. Several hiking trails criss-crossed the park. Some of them were marked different colours, depending on their length.

Blix thought about the back of the photo that had been delivered into his post box. He searched for the picture he had taken of it on his phone and held the screen up in front of the map trying to see if the crosses matched any features, but it didn't help.

Terry was itching to head into the trees. Blix held him back as he studied the map. In the photo, it looked as if Elisabeth Eie had been lying indoors somewhere. She must have been carried into the forest after she was killed. The burial site was probably not far from the car park. If he made his way into the forest at an angle, he would reach the path some distance from the cordons at either end.

He glanced over at the police tape. The officer standing guard there was busy with something on his phone.

Blix quickly made up his mind.

'Yes, go,' he said, and let go of Terry's lead.

The forest was dense, with the tall trees blocking out the light. Terry jumped over broken branches and ducked under felled trees. Blix hung back, pushing rogue branches away from his face and trying to keep an eye on where he put his feet. The terrain became rough and forced them to turn north. Terry seemed to have found an animal track and continued onwards, his muzzle to the ground. A leafy thicket prevented Blix from leading them towards the path he had seen on the map, and by the time they found their way around it, they were well off course.

He picked up Terry's lead and held him back while he tried to get his bearings. Somewhere to their left he heard the hum of a motor, as if from a generator.

'This way,' he said, pulling Terry in the right direction.

He followed the sound. It grew louder. Soon he could smell exhaust fumes.

He stopped again and looked back. The car park was probably about five to six hundred metres diagonally behind them.

Terry was impatient. Blix let him lead the way. It wasn't long before he noticed glimpses of light through the tree trunks. He crept ever closer before squatting down and pulling Terry close. It had to be the burial site.

Spotlights on tripods illuminated a sectioned-off area. Technicians in white overalls were working on something on the ground.

Blix took out his phone, opened the map and marked where he was. The site was around fifty metres north-east of his location. The hiking trail ran between him and the area in which the crime-scene investigators were working.

He looked at the back of the picture again. Blix had to assume that the large cross marked the burial site, but there were no clues as to which other areas corresponded to the markings. And there was nothing to indicate which way round the picture should be held or how great a distance there was between each cross.

Terry was getting restless. Blix stood up slowly and put the phone back in his pocket. None of the white-clad technicians had noticed him. He stepped onto the path and followed it back towards the car park.

The policeman at the entrance to the forest turned abruptly on him.

'Where did you come from?' he asked.

'The forest,' Blix replied, ducking under the barricade.

Another police car drove into the car park, a tired-looking unmarked station wagon with additional lights on the grill.

'This area is currently off limits,' the officer told him.

'Sorry,' Blix said. 'I came in from another path.'

The unmarked police car swung round the car park in one big curve, and pulled up with the front facing back the way it came. Blix recognised the car. Holding number 106. He used to drive it himself. He had spent the night in it once, in a lay-by in Dovre, when an unexpected assignment had dragged him to Trondheim and back.

The doors opened. It was Tine Abelvik, alongside a younger man Blix hadn't seen before. A new colleague.

Abelvik pulled a pair of wellies from the car boot. Blix walked diagonally across the car park to meet her. She looked up at him in surprise.

'Blix? What are you doing here?'

'Walking the dog,' he replied. 'What about you? You're outside your usual district.'

Abelvik stared at him.

'Is it Elisabeth Eie?' Blix asked with a nod towards the forest.

Abelvik's young colleague approached them, but remained silent.

Blix turned his back on the photojournalists and lowered his voice. 'It *is* Elisabeth Eie, isn't it?'

Abelvik sighed. 'We're not doing this here,' she replied and looked at her watch. 'Can you meet at the police station in two hours?'

She slammed the boot shut.

'Two hours,' she repeated. 'I'll meet you downstairs.'

10

Even though it had been two months since Maria Normann disappeared, she was still listed as a resident at an address in Sagene. Emma didn't quite know what she had expected when she rang the doorbell, but of course no one answered.

She tried the flat next door instead. She could hear the sound of a loud, foreign radio station coming from inside. A brass sign hung on the red door with the name *Gunhild Faldbakken* engraved on it. Below the doorbell on the adjoining wall was a handwritten note which read: *Doesn't work*. Emma clenched her hand into a fist and rapped her knuckles on the wood. Had to do it a second time, before the radio inside the apartment was turned down.

An elderly woman with long grey hair opened the door cautiously and poked her head out.

'Hello,' Emma said, then introduced herself with her full name. She stopped herself from adding, out of habit, that she worked for news.no.

'I'm here about your neighbour,' she said instead. 'Maria Normann. I'm trying to find out a little bit about ... her life. I'm thinking of writing about her,' she added, blushing at her own lies. 'As I'm sure you're aware, she's been missing for a while.' Emma's words echoed down the walls of the narrow hallway.

'Yes,' Gunhild Faldbakken said hesitantly. 'She ... has.'

Behind her, a grey cat meowed. It slowly crept up to the woman's ankles. Emma thought about the news alerts that had appeared on her phone earlier in the day. The discovery of a dead body in Leirsund. It could be Maria.

'How long have you lived here?' Emma continued. 'If I may ask?'

The woman thought about it.

'It must be nearly twenty-six years, I think.'

'Wow. Ages then.'

She regretted her choice of words, but the woman didn't seem to care.

'What about Maria?' Emma continued.

'I think she lived here a couple of years, maybe. It's a council flat,' she added.

Was there a hint of derision in her voice? Emma wasn't sure. Anyway, there was nothing to indicate that the woman was going to invite her in.

'Did you know her well?' It occurred to Emma that she was referring to Maria in the past tense, as if it were a fact that she was dead.

Gunhild Faldbakken shook her head, simultaneously nudging the cat back into the apartment with one foot.

'But we bumped into each other from time to time,' she said. 'As you do when you live next door.'

'What was she like?'

The woman thought for a moment.

'She ... kept to herself, really. Didn't try to make friends with anyone, even though she had a wee chatterbox of a child who wanted to say hi to everyone.' The memory made her smile. 'But his mother wasn't very sociable. That's how things are here, sadly. It's been like that for years. People don't look at you when you pass them.'

'Do you know if she had a lot of visitors?'

'She'd have people come by from time to time. A regular amount, I'd say.'

Emma was silent for a moment, and Gunhild Faldbakken took hold of the door handle and started to pull it closed.

'Just one more question,' Emma asked. 'If you don't mind? You mentioned her son. Jonas, correct? Do you know where he is now?'

'I have no idea,' Faldbakken said. 'But I know he has a kind grandmother. She was one of the people who would stop by and look after him. Maybe he's with her?'

'Do you know where she lives?' Emma hastened to ask.

'No clue. But I think her first name was Hildegard. It probably wouldn't be that hard to find her.'

✳

Faldbakken was right – it only took Emma a couple of seconds to find the information online for a Hildegard Normann, registered as living at an address in Smestad. The road she lived on was called Gullkroken and was only a stone's throw from Hoffselva. Before Emma got back in the car, she called Hildegard and asked if she was willing to talk to her about her daughter Maria.

'Why?' Hildegard Normann asked cautiously.

Again, another instance where it was difficult for Emma to justify her curiosity.

'I'm a freelance journalist,' she forced out. She was now thinking of writing a feature article on the circumstances around Maria's life, but only if she could actually find something new worth telling.

'I'm about to take a walk around Smestaddammen,' Hildegard Normann replied. 'You're welcome to join me, if you want.'

She mustn't have heard anything from the police today, Emma reasoned. So the body found at Leirsund couldn't have been Maria's.

It was the middle of the day, so it took no more than twenty minutes to drive out to Smestad. It never ceased to amaze Emma how little time it took to get from the hubbub of Oslo city centre up to the city's residential areas with their houses and gardens. The Hoffselva river itself was narrow here, its banks dotted with trees that had sprouted up right down at the water's edge. Everywhere Emma looked, birds were either taking flight or landing on the surface of the water in elegant, gliding perfection.

'The doctor says I have to stay active,' Hildegard Normann said with a slight smile, after they had introduced themselves. 'Even though there are other things I'd rather be doing.' She slowly pushed a walker in front of her.

Hildegard Normann looked much older than she probably was. When she walked, her back was bent over like a hook, and her head had a slight tremor when she spoke.

'Did you know that the pond here is a resting place in the spring and autumn for migratory birds?'

Emma shook her head.

'It's mostly because of the water plants here,' Hildegard Normann informed her, pointing. 'There are a lot of benthos around as well.' Hildegard stopped for a moment. 'That's beneficial bacteria and other organisms,' she clarified. Then she carried on walking. 'Not much in the way of fish, but further down the river there you'll find brown trout and sea trout. Isn't that wonderful?'

'Yeah,' Emma said. 'It is.'

They moved on slowly.

'There aren't that many people who care about Maria now,' Hildegard Normann said. 'Isn't it strange how quickly people forget?'

She didn't seem bitter about it.

'There's so much else to worry about, I think,' she continued. 'People have enough on their own plates.'

The gravel crunched under their feet as they walked.

'What about the police – do you hear from them much?' Emma asked.

'Not as much as I would have liked,' she said. 'But he'll be punished one day. I just wish they could find her. Do you understand what I mean?'

Emma nodded. That was probably the most important part to the relatives – to find an answer, a conclusion, so that they could at least try to move on – carry on with their lives.

'I don't quite know what it is I want to know about Maria,' Emma said. 'But maybe you could start off by telling me a little bit about her, in your own words?'

The question made Hildegard Normann think.

'It's odd,' she said with a sad smile. 'When I try to think how I can summarise her entire life, it's like every memory of her just disappears.' She shook her head. 'But Maria,' she said with a heavy sigh, 'let's say she wasn't an easy child. She was the first of my two – she came one year and ten months before Oda. She was quite the tomboy, our Maria. Liked climbing trees and play fighting and stuff like that.'

'So did I,' Emma said, smiling.

'Did you also struggle with mood swings?'

Emma didn't have time to answer.

'Maria wasn't particularly interested in school, apart from P.E. and the more hands-on classes. Nothing else appealed to her, not when she was younger anyway. That changed when she started chasing the boys. It wasn't just her either. Oda too, she...' She looked away. 'We ... lost Oda,' Hildegard Normann said quickly. 'When she was young.'

She said it bluntly, as if it were pure factual information with no emotional weight.

'It hit Maria hard, of course. Same with all of us, really. Her father ... he couldn't be here. And I mean *here*, quite literally. He wound up in Cyprus in the end, where he's probably still licking his wounds and dousing them with red wine to this day. That's if he's not dead by now too. I've no idea.'

She paused.

'But what's clear is that growing up in an environment like that...' Hildegard Normann shook her head. 'You grow up too fast.'

Emma knew all too well what Maria's mother was talking about.

'How old was she when it happened?'

'When we lost Oda? Maria was fifteen.'

'The worst age,' Emma said. 'For a lot of reasons.'

'Oh yes. And I ... I had so much going on myself, you could say. And with that, on top of everything else, Maria must have found it difficult to cope. That was probably when things really started to go downhill for her. Drinking, drugs, and ... well, you've probably seen everything they've written about her.'

Emma nodded. 'Thank you for telling me all this,' she said. 'It can't have been easy for you.'

Hildegard Normann turned her head to look at Emma full on, a sad but grateful smile on her face. 'Jonas is with me most of the time,' she said. 'A lawyer helped me. Made sure I was appointed his guardian. Jonas is actually with my brother today though, but Geir-Arne can't have him for that long. You know how it is – it's quite demanding looking after young children.'

She paused before continuing:

'I don't know what will come of him in the future. None of us will be able to take care of Jonas full time. Least of all *me*,' she said, gesturing to the walker. 'I'm only getting worse and worse.' She put a hand on her back as if to emphasise the point. 'But I can't bear the thought of him ending up in some foster family.'

Emma wanted to tell Hildegard Normann about her own grand-parents, who had taken care of her and Irene for years after they were orphaned. Wanted to tell her to find the strength from somewhere, even though it was a huge commitment, and an even bigger sacrifice. But it was not a gift everyone was able to give.

'How is he – Jonas?' she asked.

'Oh, you know. Children are so adaptable. He's happy, mostly, but sometimes he asks about his mother – where she is and when she'll be coming home and the like, and well ... I don't always know how to answer.'

They walked round a clump of trees, so the water's edge almost dis-appeared from view. A woman pushing a pram approached them. She didn't look up as she passed, just continued gazing down into the pram.

'So there's no father in the picture, I take it?'

'No,' she said, scoffing. 'I'm not sure if Maria even knew who the father was.'

Emma didn't feel like digging any further into that particular matter.

'I heard that Maria was best friends with Oliver Krogh when they were young?'

Hildegard Normann glanced at Emma. It was clear that the mere thought of Maria's employer and possible killer enraged her. Then her expression softened somewhat.

'Yes,' she said. 'I guess they were. As long as it lasted.' She shook her head. 'That man has destroyed our family ... I've often wondered how everything could go so wrong. He was such a nice boy and ... his family were the same. We spent a lot of time together back then, all of us. Especially Maria and Oliver – they were inseparable, in nursery, in school, after school.' Hildegard Normann seemed to disappear into her memories. 'I can't speak for him, but I think that was probably the best time in Maria's life. It didn't seem to matter then if you were a boy or a girl. Everything was untainted by the influence of friends, shops dividing the children's sections into blue and pink, societal norms for everything. But then ... then they grew up, and well...' She shrugged.

'...They lost touch?' said Emma.

'Yes, as you do I guess, as a teenager.'

Emma remembered what that was like.

'Oliver popped back up again when Oda...'

Hildegard Normann looked away. It took a few moments, then she continued.

'It came as a shock to us all, I think, when Oda told us that she was dating Oliver.'

Emma had to control her expression and stop herself from reacting to this news. She just kept her eyes on the face of the woman beside her.

'I thought they were way too young – she couldn't have been more than thirteen when they started ... seeing each other. Isn't that what they call it these days? But I remembered Oliver was a nice boy, a good boy, so I wasn't too anxious about ... you know. But...'

Again, she needed to take a moment.

'Oda was ... a special girl. Had a propensity for the dark and the melodramatic, perhaps. Seemed to become a teenager quite young, if you know what I mean. She became *very* infatuated, very fast. It was Oliver this, Oliver that. It was Oliver over her grades and everything else, you could say. And Maria ... she probably got a little jealous, I think.'

'Was she in love with him too?'

'No, I think it was more about Oda sort of taking what was hers, in a way. Girls can be odd.'

That made Emma laugh. Hildegard Normann smiled too, but soon grew serious again.

'It was a very intense relationship – for Oda at least. And when he ended it, that's when...'

She stopped, completely, covered her mouth with her hand. A dry hiccup escaped her. A man with a long beard came jogging towards them. By the time he passed, Hildegard Normann had managed to pull herself together.

'Sorry,' she said. 'But ... now they're both gone. And both because of...' She bit her lower lip.

'What do you mean?' Emma asked.

'Oda took her own life,' Hildegard Normann said and tried to straighten up a little, but in the next second her body seemed to sag again. 'After that ... or, it *was* that which...' She paused and glanced quickly at Emma. Sighed heavily.

'It's been a long time,' she said. 'My god, a lifetime, even. You never forget, of course, but as the years go by, it starts to hurt a little less. But then, all this, it all comes back to you, the wounds open again, you know. Your own children...'

She shook her head. A tear trickled down her cheek. Her face muscles tightened.

'I hope he burns in hell,' she said. 'I hope Oliver Krogh suffers every single day for what he has done to my girls.'

11

Terry stood up in the back seat, clearly keen to go with him.

'Not this time,' Blix said, pushing the car door closed.

He pulled his jacket tighter around his neck, rounded the block and stared up at the large, grey police station. His gaze slid along the row of windows up on the sixth floor.

Two hours had passed. He walked with slow steps up the walkway towards the main entrance, bowed his neck and entered.

He hadn't been back here since just after Iselin died and he came to confront Gard Fosse.

Nothing had changed. The large entrance hall seemed to hum with all the voices and noise. Open corridors wrapped around the staircase. Up on the seventh floor, a uniformed man was leaning over the railing, looking down. Others hurried past.

A security guard got up from the counter and glanced over at him. Blix came to, realising that he had been lost in thought for a moment. He nodded to the guard, who he could tell had recognised him.

He pulled out his phone and fired off a message to Tine Abelvik to say that he was waiting downstairs.

A woman stood up from the nearest bench and went up to one of the passport counters with the waiting slip in her hand. Blix remained standing.

A familiar face appeared in the area behind the security gates. Nicolai Wibe. He and Abelvik were the investigators Blix had worked most closely with.

He walked over to the railing that separated the public and staff area and called to Wibe.

Wibe seemed surprised, uncomfortable. 'It's been a while,' he said.

'I'm just waiting for Abelvik,' Blix explained. 'I'm here to see her about the Elisabeth Eie case. Are you working on it?'

Wibe shook his head and didn't seem to be aware of the fact that the killer had been in contact with Blix. 'I'm working on the Oliver Krogh case.'

Blix had only heard the basics. 'Maria Normann,' he said.

Wibe nodded. 'Missing for two months. He's hidden her well.'

The lift doors opened behind Wibe. He moved towards them. 'Good seeing you,' he said.

'Likewise.'

Wibe entered the lift and raised his hand to wave goodbye, before the doors slid shut.

Blix lifted his chin to look up at the sixth floor. A few minutes later, Abelvik appeared over the railing. She looked down, located him and headed towards the lift. Blix moved back to wait by the security gates. The lift doors slid open. Abelvik came out, swiped her access card and let him in.

'Thanks for coming,' she said, turning back to the lift.

Blix walked in with her.

'You found her?' Blix tried to confirm. 'It's definitely Elisabeth Eie?'

Abelvik met his gaze. 'You know how this works,' she replied. 'Identification takes at least a day.'

'But you're not sitting around waiting for the autopsy and DNA results,' Blix pressed. 'You're working from a theory about who it is.'

Tine Abelvik hesitated. The lift passed the fourth floor.

'There was a handbag with the body,' she said at last. 'The papers inside indicate that it belonged to Elisabeth Eie.'

The lift stopped and the doors opened.

'Anything else?' Blix asked. 'Have you traced the phone he called from?'

Abelvik gestured to the open lift door. 'We'll deal with that later,' she said.

Blix walked ahead, towards the homicide department. Before letting them in, Abelvik stood for a moment, the key card in her hand.

'Things are different here now,' she said. She seemed to be searching for the right words to explain what she meant. 'You have friends here,' she continued. 'And I consider myself one of them, but there are also those who believe that the way you acted after Iselin's murder was wrong – regardless of whether the courts thought you a criminal or not.'

Blix met her gaze. 'What are you trying to say?'

Abelvik sighed. 'The whole story has had a detrimental impact on the reputation of the police.' She swiped the key card.

'Is this something *you* are saying, or are you just repeating Gard Fosse's spiel to the press?' Blix asked.

'What I'm trying to say is that you'd be wise to lie low,' Abelvik replied, and opened the door. 'Just ... don't try to tell anyone how to do their job. You're here to provide a witness statement.'

He followed her down the corridor and into the large, open-plan office. The room was half full. It looked the same as before, yet felt different. Some looked up curiously from their workstations, others made themselves busy. 'Tobias Walenius will be the one interviewing you,' Abelvik said, and nodded towards the innermost corner. 'Probably for the best. He's new here.'

A young man with a turtleneck jumper and a shaggy beard stood up from what had once been Blix's desk. It was the same man Blix had seen alongside Abelvik at Leirsund.

'Was he given my old job?' Blix asked.

'There have been a few internal moves,' Abelvik explained. 'He used to work in the family violence unit, but there's a limit to how long you can stay working in child abuse.'

The new-hire investigator came over to them, introduced himself and held out his hand. Blix shook it. Tobias Walenius appeared to be in his early thirties. He had an inflamed pimple on the right side of his forehead.

'We've met a while ago,' he said.

Blix cocked his head but couldn't place him.

'You held a few lectures back when I was at the Police University College,' Walenius said with a smile.

That meant he had graduated about ten years ago. He was young enough to be Blix's son.

'I've reserved interrogation room two for us,' the young investigator continued. 'You can follow me.'

Blix looked over at Abelvik. 'Can't we just do this around a meeting table?' he suggested. 'I think it'd be more fruitful.'

'The intel you have must be officially included in the case,' Abelvik replied. 'We can talk afterwards.'

Her phone went off. She glanced at it and put an end to the discussion by saying she had to take the call.

Blix followed Walenius to the interrogation room. He closed the door behind them and gestured for Blix to sit in one of the two chairs. Walenius sat down on the edge of the chair opposite and spent a good while getting the cameras and voice recorder set up. When the red recording light came on, he formally noted the time and place. He then requested that Blix provide his full name, social security number and address.

'Job title?'

Blix hesitated. He had had several meetings with various public agencies to clarify the situation. So far, it had only resulted in modest financial support and routine talks with a psychologist.

'I am not currently in work,' he replied.

Walenius jotted that down.

'As a witness, you are not obliged to talk to the police,' he continued. 'If you are willing, you must be made aware that it is a criminal offence to lie or withhold information.'

Blix closed his eyes and nodded.

'Furthermore, you do not have to answer questions that could expose yourself or close family members to punishment by law,' Walenius continued.

Blix had interviewed hundreds of witnesses. Maybe a thousand, but didn't say anything, just nodded.

'Are you willing to provide a statement?' Walenius asked.

It sounded like a staccato reproduction of the instructions found in a police training textbook. Blix struggled to hide his irritation.

'Yes,' he answered.

'Okay,' Walenius said, leaning back a little. 'Then I want you to talk freely about why you contacted the police yesterday.'

Blix took a deep breath in and felt his chest rise.

'I called the police because until twenty-two months ago I was employed as an investigator here in the homicide department and was responsible for the investigation into Elisabeth Eie's disappearance,' he answered. 'Yesterday I was contacted by a man who wanted to confess that he had killed her.'

Walenius straightened up a little and scribbled something down in his notebook.

'Can you tell me exactly what happened?' he asked. 'I understand that the interrogation situation may be uncomfortable for you, but we need an official record. It's the alpha and omega in a case like this. I'm sure I don't need to tell you that.'

Blix nodded, and started by explaining how he had just come home from walking the dog. From there it took almost an hour before Walenius seemed satisfied they had covered all the circumstances surrounding what had happened.

Walenius changed his position in the chair and leaned back. 'If this is the murderer,' he began, 'why do you think he contacted you in particular?'

Blix looked down at the table. He had pondered the same thing himself. Not just over the last twenty-four hours, but ever since Elisabeth Eie had disappeared. The anonymous warning had arrived before anyone could report her missing. It was as if the perpetrator specifically wanted Blix to handle the case. Then Iselin's murder and his own stint in prison got in the way. But there was a lot that pointed to the man having waited until Blix was out again, before resuming contact.

'I don't know,' is all he said.

'It must be someone you know,' Walenius thought aloud. 'The fact alone that they contacted you through your private phone number limits who it could be.'

Blix nodded and explained that they had had the same discussion two and a half years ago. Trawled through his relationships and looked at cases he had investigated, without coming up with any real suspects.

Walenius had a few more questions before he considered the job done.

'Thank you,' he finished and stopped the recording. 'I'll tidy up your testimony and get in touch so you can check through it.'

Blix stood up.

'I'll show you out,' Walenius offered.

'I need a word with Abelvik first,' Blix said. 'I'll let myself out from there.'

Walenius was first at the door. 'I'll walk with you anyhow,' he said as he opened it.

Blix turned left, scanned the office landscape, but didn't see her.

A familiar face emerged from the copy room. Ella Sandland.

'Hi,' he said.

She returned his smile.

'Have you seen Tine around?'

Ella Sandland hesitated. 'In Fosse's office, I think.'

'Thanks.'

Blix strode towards the office belonging to the head of the department, with Walenius behind him. The door was ajar. He pushed it open. Gard Fosse and Tine Abelvik were sitting on either side of the large desk. Fosse stood up. Blix closed the door behind him, so Walenius was left on the other side.

'So nice of you to pop in, Alexander,' Fosse began. 'I heard you were about.'

'I received a call from Elisabeth Eie's killer yesterday,' Blix started. 'I expect you'll have traced where the call came from by now?'

Neither of them looked like they wanted to answer.

'Strictly speaking, we don't know whether the telephone call has anything to do with the case,' Fosse replied.

'He put a photo of the body in my post box,' Blix retorted. 'Who made the call?'

Fosse's gaze wavered. 'What is important to me, and to the police leadership team, is that we do this the right way,' Fosse said.

Blix cocked his head to the side. 'And what does that mean?'

Fosse let out a sigh. 'You have to let us deal with this from here,' he replied.

'I'm involved,' Blix said. 'I have been from day one.'

The head of department nodded, but said nothing.

'I don't think you understand what this is all about,' Blix continued. 'There could be more like Elisabeth Eie.' He swallowed. 'He said he sent me several letters, other ... photos.' He moved his gaze from Fosse to Abelvik. 'Did you see the crosses on the back of the picture?' he asked. 'Have you checked whether there are more bodies in the forest in Leirsund?'

Gard Fosse made a gesture with his hand. 'This case has the potential to garner a lot of media attention,' he said with a serious expression. 'But the media could easily get the wrong idea. It won't do the investigation any good if the press start digging into everything again, with all that's happened to you since Elisabeth Eie disappeared.'

Blix's mouth went dry.

'You're a civilian, now,' Fosse continued. 'I understand your commitment and we appreciate the information you have provided, but beyond that we cannot discuss the case with you.'

'What's the matter with the two of you?' Blix asked, swallowing. 'The killer is communicating with me. He's probably following me. It won't be long before he makes contact again, surely.'

'We are ready to handle whatever comes up,' Fosse assured him, looking over at Abelvik for support.

Tine Abelvik nodded, her gaze fixed to the floor.

Blix took a step back. 'Fine,' he said with a curt nod.

He turned to the door and left it open so that Abelvik could follow him out.

12

Emma sat in the car and thought through everything she now knew about Oliver Krogh. Nowhere had it been mentioned that he'd also been in a relationship with Maria's sister, even though that was many years ago now. Judging by Maria's mother's tone and expression, it seemed as if she blamed, or at least suspected, Krogh for Oda's death too.

She had not pressed Hildegard Normann about it. The question was whether it was even relevant. If any reason for Maria Normann's disappearance could be found in this old relationship.

You only got involved in this to help Carmen, Emma reminded herself. Instead, you may have found something that strengthens the suspicion against her stepfather.

As soon as Emma had started sniffing around the case, she had realised that she would have to talk to Oliver Krogh's lawyer at some point. It was a conversation she was not looking forward to. Emma knew that her name was not at the top of the list of people Leo van Eijk sent Christmas cards to, especially not since, a little over a year ago, she tracked down a witness in a narcotics case who effectively torpedoed the defence of a client van Eijk was representing. The fact that a guilty man was convicted did nothing for the lawyer's dislike of people like her.

Emma knew there was no point in calling him directly or leaving a message – the lawyer would never call her back. But she found out via his secretary that he was in court that day, between twelve and three o'clock. Emma parked in a car park nearby and ate a quick lunch in the hotel restaurant across the street from the courthouse. While she waited she searched for more information on Oliver Krogh, but only found the same websites she had already visited.

He was a handsome man, she thought. Seemed to have a three-day stubble situation going on in pretty much every picture she found of him, with a little sprinkling of grey here and there, especially around the ears. His hair was always cut short, his face weather-beaten. In the photos, he was always dressed in outdoor clothing, which made it easy to picture him in a canoe or under an open night sky. It wasn't hard to imagine him at his happiest out there in the elements, chowing down on some fresh catch he'd caught and grilled over a fire pit himself.

Victoria Prytz seemed to be his exact opposite – in all the pictures Emma found of her, she was dressed to the nines and photoshopped. Her hair was always styled and elegant, and her make-up was painstakingly perfect – pretty, but not over the top. Emma couldn't help thinking Victoria and Oliver made for an awkward couple, although there were also pictures of them together on big game hunts.

Prytz Eiendomsutvikling, of which Victoria was the owner and general manager, bought homes, renovated them and sold them off at a great profit around Eastern Norway. On the balance sheets for the Oslo municipality the previous year, she was listed with a fortune of just over sixteen million Norwegian kroner. She could most likely afford to pay a private investigator, so, as Carmen suggested, it was probably more a question of whether she wanted to.

She looked tough, Emma thought. Beautiful, but sharp and angular – a bit like she had a 'my way or the highway' attitude. She wasn't looking forward to reaching out to her. If she was going to do so at all.

Noticing the minute hand was approaching three, Emma paid for her meal and went to stand outside the main door of the Oslo District Court. Every time it opened, she readied herself to pounce on Leo van Eijk, but it seemed the lawyer was making her wait. Eventually, Emma walked inside. She was afraid she might run into one of her old colleagues, but it didn't seem like there were any high-profile cases scheduled for the day.

At 15:31, Leo van Eijk finally appeared, heading towards the exit. His steps were determined, his eyes fixed on his phone as he walked, as he did his best to appear preoccupied. But Emma stood in his way, waiting to smile when he had to slow down and look up at her.

A grimace crossed his face. 'Emma Ramm,' he said with a sigh. 'And here I was, thinking you had stopped bothering people like me.' His tone was tired, arrogant.

'I have a couple of questions for you about Oliver Krogh.'

'Yes, I'm sure you have,' the lawyer said with another sigh. 'I'm on my way home. It's been a long day.'

'I'll walk you to your car,' Emma said. 'We can walk and talk.'

'Do I have a choice?' he said.

'You can try to walk faster than me, of course, but I don't think you can. And believe it or not, I'm here to try to help your client.'

'Is that so?'

Leo van Eijk opened the large, heavy door and stepped out into the afternoon. Emma followed close behind, annoyed that he didn't hold the door open for her.

'How's he doing?' she asked.

'How do you think?' Leo van Eijk parried and hurried down the steps. Continued to the right. A tram came gliding towards them from Tullinløkka.

'If he's innocent,' Emma said, 'I'd imagine he's in pretty bad shape.'

The remark made Leo van Eijk laugh.

'It may surprise you,' he said. 'But there are quite a few guilty people who are also having a terrible time.'

'Which category does Oliver Krogh belong in?'

'Nice try,' the lawyer said with a fake laugh this time. 'But you know perfectly well that I cannot comment on my client's guilt or innocence. He'll be getting the best defence he deserves, regardless.'

It was the usual legal rigamarole. Emma had heard it a hundred times before.

'I'd like to believe he's innocent until proven guilty,' Emma said, fully aware that she was answering his platitude with another, but it was no less the truth. 'Right now, everyone else is thinking quite the opposite.'

'And you don't?' Leo van Eijk grinned mockingly.

'Why is he in custody if the police haven't found Maria Normann?' Emma asked. 'Why do they think he's the one who killed her?'

'You'll have to ask the police that.'

They crossed into the car park. Emma followed.

'You're not giving up, are you?' van Eijk asked.

'If I'm going to assist your client,' Emma said, 'it would help me to know what evidence he's facing.'

'Why do you want to help him?' van Eijk queried over his shoulder. His dress shoes click-clacked against the floor.

'Because...' Emma thought about it. 'Because his stepdaughter thinks he's innocent.'

The lawyer stopped and turned around. 'You've contacted Carmen?'

'Carmen contacted *me*,' Emma corrected him. 'Wanted help to prove that Oliver was innocent.'

He stared into Emma's eyes, as if trying to determine whether she was telling the truth or not.

'Christ,' Leo van Eijk said finally.

'Yeah, I was surprised too,' Emma said. 'A girl in her mid-teens who wants to help her stepfather when no one else in the whole of Norway will.'

The lawyer had no answer to that.

'And believe me,' Emma said. 'I have other things to spend my time on than running around, trying to find answers that no one wants to give me. But I promised Carmen I'd give it a try, if nothing else. That's why I'm here. Oliver Krogh is *your* client. Perhaps it might be in *your* interest to try to help me?'

Emma saw that her little speech had given him something to think about.

'Emma,' he said, taking a step closer. 'For your own sake, but mostly for Carmen's, I would recommend you leave this alone.'

Emma frowned. 'Why?'

He looked around quickly, clearly uncomfortable talking about this, then lowered his voice and said: 'I am trying to avoid the details of my client's private life becoming public.'

'What do you mean? Are you trying to get him to agree to a plea deal?'

The lawyer hesitated to say anything more, and Emma realised she was right: he wanted his client to confess and take the plea deal, no matter whether he was guilty or not.

'His private life, you said. What does that mean?'

Leo van Eijk sighed. 'I can't go into that.'

'And your client – what does *he* think of your proposal?'

Again, no response. Leo van Eijk started walking again.

'Let me guess,' Emma said. 'He's refusing to confess.'

The lawyer didn't answer. Emma followed him all the way to his car – a sleek black Porsche Cayenne that looked like it had come straight from the factory. The lawyer unlocked the car with one click, opened the door, turned to her and said:

'The matter is complicated enough as it is, Emma. I don't need people like you rummaging around in it.'

'So all this preaching about the best defence for your client – it's just bullshit? You're not interested in turning over as many stones as possible to help him?' Emma realised her voice was raised. 'You can at least tell him that you spoke to me and that I'll be trying to look into the matter from his side as well. That, I think, you are obliged to do.'

'What I am obliged to do,' he said in an instructive voice, 'is what I can for him within the framework and rules of the law.' Leo van Eijk put one foot inside the car. 'You can't ask for much more than that.'

'So you're not even going to tell him that we spoke?'

He lowered himself into the driver's seat and looked up at her.

'Have a good day,' he said with a sigh and closed the door.

13

Blix knew he should eat something, but he couldn't bear going into the shop or any of the restaurants in the neighbourhood on his way home from the police station. He just wanted to get home, go inside, and sit down with an ice-cold beer. Crawl into his lair and let the silence settle between the walls.

As soon as they entered, Terry dashed to his water bowl and slurped down a few mouthfuls while Blix prepared some kibble, tripe and dog sausage in a bowl for him.

The day had been exhausting. Blix could feel it in his whole body. It had been a long time since he had been active like that, but the physical exhaustion wasn't the half of it. A sense of unease ran through him – a nausea, a vague sensation of something unresolved, some detail or other he should have thought of or remembered.

He needed to do something.

The person who killed Elisabeth Eie hadn't allowed her to live more than her thirty-three years. A child of four had become an orphan. Little Julie would be six now. Maybe seven.

Did she still remember her mum?

It was Tomine, Elisabeth's sister, who had been the police's primary contact within the family at the time, and in the years that followed too. They had probably been notified by now, Blix thought, and his stomach clenched at the thought of it.

He should have been the one to tell them. He was the one who had led the investigation at the time. He had been in contact with the family, with Tomine.

In the beginning, he had been in touch with her several times a day. Gradually, there had been fewer reasons to call or ask her to stop by, but sometimes he did so anyway, even when there was nothing new to tell her. His reasoning at the time had been two-fold: both to give her, as a representative of the next of kin, the feeling that the case still had the highest priority, and to assure them that the police were leaving no stone unturned to solve the case. But there was a third reason as well, which Blix had not wanted to admit to himself at the time.

He had liked her.

He had enjoyed being around Tomine. She had a pleasant disposition: a warm and gentle voice and a friendly expression, so unlike the many relatives who had looked at him over the years with a kind of expectation or annoyance in their eyes, as if he had insulted them personally by not solving the case immediately.

Tomine had always understood that the police had several leads to pursue, that it took time to collect all the relevant data and follow up on it, act on the tips that came in, question people. In the first phase after Elisabeth disappeared, they had worked around the clock.

He had also seen Tomine angry – and scared, and she could be dejected and frustrated, sad. Once she had cried in his arms – he had just stood there and held her, not quite knowing what he should or could do, even though the protocol was obvious. You did not enter into any kind of intimate contact with the relatives. Which was probably the reason why Blix had always shied away when she had asked him questions of a slightly more personal nature.

It had been a long time since he had been in contact with her. Not since before Iselin was killed.

Blix pulled out his phone and scrolled through his contacts. Stopped at Tomine's number. He sat and stared at it for a while, then put the phone down and went to the toilet. On his way to the bathroom, he passed the open door to his small study, where he kept his fly-tying equipment. And stopped.

He stepped inside and moved over to the bench. A cold shiver ran through him.

The fly was finished.

It had not been finished when he left it. He was sure of that.

Or was he?

Could he really have forgotten that he had finished it? Was he losing it already, just like his father?

No.

He hadn't finished it. He couldn't have done. He would have removed it from the vice and put it aside. Packed it away in a hard plastic container, where all the other completed flies lived.

Someone had been in his apartment.

Someone had finished the fly for him.

Why?

What the hell?

Blix quickly looked around for other signs that someone had been there. Perhaps someone was there right now – he hadn't been into the bedroom or bathroom since returning home.

He looked around for a weapon, anything he could use if he ended up in an altercation. The only thing nearby was a pen on the table next to the fly-tying equipment. He grabbed it. Held it as if ready to stab someone. Walked towards the bathroom. Stopped and listened, put his ear to the door. With a sudden movement he swung it open, the door slamming and rebounding off the wall, but he knew within seconds that no one was hiding inside the small bathroom.

Blix stepped out of the doorway. Moved silently on towards the bedroom. He could feel his pulse throbbing in his neck. With another, sudden jerk, he yanked open the door and stepped in, ready to attack, his eyes quickly scanning the room.

There was no one on the bed.

No one underneath it either.

Blix opened the wardrobe, although he knew it would be unlikely that a grown person would be able to hide in there, in all the mess. He went out on the balcony too, but saw no sign that anyone had been there since he had last spent a few minutes on one of the folding chairs.

There was one room left.

Iselin's, where she had lived for a while a few years back. Blix had barely been in there since she died.

He didn't want to go in there now either, but he had to. He couldn't go to bed later without knowing whether or not he was alone.

Blix stopped in front of the door and took a deep breath. Closed his eyes. He didn't remember what she had left in there, if anything.

She might have taken everything with her when she moved, he wasn't sure.

Carefully this time, he pushed down on the door handle. Pulled the door towards him slowly.

It was as if a wind tried to blow him over, a scent of stale air and dust. The walls, the floor, the ceiling, the bedding, the carpet, the white dressing table that had also served as a desk – all were bare now. Blix realised instantly that no one had been in here either, not for a long time. There were no footprints in the dust on the floor. He closed the door immediately, before he could think too much about what the empty room represented.

He turned toward the living room and caught his breath – *tried* to breathe, but the air was now trapped somewhere below his diaphragm. He had to close his eyes and concentrate to regain some kind of balance. When he opened his eyes again, he met Terry's reassuring gaze and found that it helped calm him down.

Blix bent over and ruffled the dog's fur. Krissander Dokken had been right – it did help, having the company of a four-legged friend.

He took a few deep breaths and tried to form a conclusion. Someone had been inside his apartment. He couldn't imagine it was anyone other than the man who had called him and sent him the photo of Elisabeth Eie. The fact that he had finished tying the fishing fly for him had to be some kind of message. A kind of greeting, as if he were mocking him or wanted to scare him. Part of his sick plan.

Blix walked to the main door. Opened it and inspected the lock, but found nothing wrong with it. If some home invader had managed to get in, they would have had to get through two locked doors – the front door on the ground floor and the door to his apartment. Although, it was possible to slip through the front door downstairs on the ground floor whenever any of the other residents came or went, for his flat you'd need a key.

Blix knew where all his keys were. At least he thought he did. He had one on his key chain. He checked the dresser drawer in the hallway. The spare key was where it should be. Iselin had also had one. Merete had taken it when—

Merete, he thought.

It was Merete who had looked after his flat when he was in prison. She had never returned the key, nor had he asked for it. Maybe he should call her and check if she knew where it was?

He dropped that idea. At least for now. But he would make sure to change the lock as soon as he woke up in the morning.

It was too late to do it now.

His phone rang on the living-room table.

Terry jumped up and started growling. Blix walked over to it. The display told him the call was from a restricted number.

'Hello?' he said, hearing for himself how weak he sounded.

'Good evening, Blix.'

It was him.

The man.

Blix swallowed.

'What do you want?' he asked.

'They've found her,' the voice stated at the other end. 'But you already know that, of course.'

Blix moved the phone away from his ear and looked at the screen. If Abelvik had been able to track down the number the man was calling from, they would have had to set up communication surveillance on his phone. At least, that's what he would have done, if he had been in charge. They were probably listening to the conversation right now.

'Are there more?' he asked.

It seemed as if the man on the other end was taking his time formulating an answer:

'There are many like Elisabeth,' he said in the end.

Blix went to the window. It was getting dark out.

'What do the crosses mean?' he asked.

'It's not that difficult to understand,' the man replied.

'They don't make sense,' Blix said. 'They're just scattered around on a blank piece of paper. Impossible to know what's up or down.'

'I see,' the man replied. 'So they didn't let you see her. See how she lay.'

Blix didn't understand what he meant.

'I'm guessing you don't know about the drawing either?'

Blix frowned.

'What do you mean? What drawing?'

The voice on the phone rang with laughter.

'I'm sure they found it, but of course they didn't say anything. Not to you, anyway. Now you're not one of them.'

'What kind of drawing are you talking about?'

The man didn't answer.

'Does it hurt?' he asked instead. 'Being on the outside?'

'I think you should turn yourself in,' Blix said – stuttering and feeling himself start to sweat. 'We could meet somewhere, and then I could … go with you to…'

'How's your father?'

Blix froze.

'What do you mean?'

There was something malicious, something sinister about the voice. 'Your father,' the man repeated. 'How is he?'

Blix swallowed. 'Why do you care about my father?'

'Because fathers are important,' he said. 'Some say that mothers are the most important people in a person's life, but I have a soft spot for dads.'

'What do you know about my father?'

There was no answer. Just a kind of mirthless laugh.

'You should visit him,' the voice said. 'It must be lonely in that nursing home.'

Blix opened his mouth.

But the next moment, the connection cut out.

Terry stared up at him. Blix remained standing there, the phone in his hand. His mind raced.

He should call Abelvik. The number was still on his speed dial, but something was holding him back.

He returned to the window and looked out, without fixing his gaze on anything. He could hear a siren in the distance.

Gard Fosse had made it clear that they didn't want him involved. And Abelvik gave the impression that they had full control of the situation.

Blix looked down at his phone again. The call had lasted forty-two seconds. He envisioned the surveillance room down on the fourth floor of the police station, where all traffic on tapped phones was logged and positioned. Abelvik was probably busy sending out units to the man's location.

He went to the kitchen table, sat down and typed out a text instead of calling. Just a short note that Abelvik need only shoot him a message if she thought there was anything he could contribute.

The indicator at the bottom of the message log showed that the message had been delivered, then read. But he received no answer.

14

Emma had sent Blix several messages throughout the day, mostly because she wanted to know if he had slept, if he had eaten, and if he had gone for a walk with Terry. Blix hadn't answered. Even when she texted him after her brief meeting with Leo van Eijk, she still didn't hear back.

Which is why she now found herself standing outside Blix's apartment block, looking up at the windows. There was a light on in his flat. She made her way into the courtyard and rang the doorbell.

He didn't answer.

Emma tried one more time, just in case the doorbell had stopped working. The exact same result. She sighed and called him instead, but after eight rings and no response, she hung up and sent him another text:

Hello. I'm outside. Trying to get hold of you. Starting to worry.

She sent it, adding:

Also, it's freezing out here.

She wasn't joking either. An icy wind whipped between the walls of the buildings. Emma regretted leaving her gloves in the car. Her hands always got so cold and dry when autumn arrived.

She called him once more and pressed the bell at the same time. Held her index finger against it this time. It took a few seconds, then finally: the intercom on the wall panel came alive.

'Sorry,' Blix said. 'I... don't really feel like having company just now.'

'Two minutes, I promise,' Emma said. 'There's something I need to talk to you about.'

'What's that then?'

Emma could hear from his voice that he was tired.

'And you think I'm going to stand out here at your front door and shout about it so the whole block can listen in?'

She heard him sigh.

'Does it have to be now?' he asked.

'It doesn't *have* to be now,' Emma replied. 'But it'd be nice.'

She waited. Could picture him as he closed his eyes, weighing up whether he could bear her company. Emma didn't consider letting him off lightly this time – he needed a little nudge every now and then. You couldn't always take the easy way out.

A few seconds later, the door clicked. Emma smiled and pulled it open before he could change his mind. On the second floor, the door to his apartment stood ajar.

Emma walked in. 'Evening.'

Terry came trotting towards her, tail wagging, happy steps. She bent down and ruffled the fur on his back. It didn't take more than a second and a half before he grew bored and sloped off back to his bed in the living room.

Emma kicked off her shoes and socks. Her feet were icy cold. It wasn't until she'd hung up her coat that she looked up at Blix, who was standing there, looking back at her with tired, red eyes.

'Jesus,' she said. 'What's happened?'

His face was colourless and drawn. But he didn't just look exhausted. There was a disquiet to him. A fear.

'Tell me,' Emma demanded. 'What's going on? And don't say it's nothing – I'm not blind, and I'm not stupid.'

Blix exhaled heavily through his nose and gestured for her to sit down.

'Do you want something to drink?' he asked. 'Tea or anything?'

'Yes, but we can do that later. Speak, now.' She sat down on the sofa and waited.

Blix stayed standing, gazing down at her.

'You remember the Eie case?' he asked, finally sitting down too.

'Elisabeth Eie,' Emma nodded. 'You never found her, nor the man who sent you that anonymous message.'

She hadn't written about the case, but she remembered it well. An anonymous letter had appeared on the windshield of a police car outside the Oslo District Court, and had been their best lead. Through a combined video and telephone operation, the police had mapped people's movements around the courthouse, but had never managed to trace the sender.

'He's reached out again,' Blix said.

Emma pushed herself forward on the sofa. 'What do you mean?'

Blix folded his hands in his lap and told her the whole story, starting with the anonymous phone call. Emma listened without interrupting.

'But ... what the hell,' she said when he had finished. 'That's just, completely...'

She didn't know what else to say.

'You'll have to change the locks,' she said.

'I ... haven't thought that far ahead yet.'

'But Blix, what if this isn't the first time he's been in here, what if—'

'I know,' he said, holding up his hands. 'I'll do it ... It's just that everything feels like such a huge task. Just going to the shop can be too much sometimes. You know what I mean?'

Emma sighed but didn't answer him.

'Why do you think he's calling you?'

'I don't know,' Blix answered. 'No idea.'

'Well, it's clear that he knows a lot about you,' Emma said, hearing in her own voice how upset she was. 'He even mentioned your father.'

Blix nodded.

'I didn't even realise you *had* a father, much less that he's in a nursing home. We've never talked about him.'

Blix lowered his gaze. 'No, I guess we haven't.'

Emma wondered why they hadn't – maybe the two of them weren't as close as she had thought. Or perhaps the absence of a mother and father in her own life had made her take less interest in other people's.

'Where is he?' she asked in a gentle voice.

'Hm?'

'Your father,' Emma said. 'The nursing home he lives in. Where is it?'

'Just outside Gjøvik,' Blix said.

She nodded slowly. 'How many people know that he's there?'

'Not many.'

'But this guy, who in all likelihood killed Elisabeth Eie and who has been in your home and finished off your fishing ties, *he* knows that?'

'It's not exactly classified information,' Blix said. 'And we don't know with one-hundred-percent certainty that it was him who was here.'

'No, sure, but don't you think it's a little concerning?'

'Yeah,' Blix said. 'I do.'

They sat and looked at each other.

'Have you called him?' Emma asked eventually.

'Who?'

She looked at him, exasperated. 'Your father.'

Blix shook his head.

'Why not?'

He didn't answer immediately.

'I've ... been busy.'

'Busy?'

'Yes, he called just before you arrived. The man, I mean.'

'Your phone wasn't busy when I called,' Emma argued. She felt herself getting irritated. 'Don't you think you should call the home and check, at least? See if everything is all right with your father?'

Blix stared down at the tabletop. Didn't answer.

'How do you interpret what he said about your father?'

'I don't quite know,' Blix said.

'No alarm bells going off after everything that's happened over the last few days? You don't think there's any point in finding out if everything's okay?'

Blix rubbed his hands together. Still didn't look up. Emma waited for an answer. It took a long time to come.

'I don't have much to do with my father,' he said at last.

'So it's not that worrying, is that what you mean?'

Blix didn't answer.

'You have to call him right now,' Emma said. 'You ... have to go see him. Call the police.'

'There's no point going there now,' Blix protested. 'It'll be night by the time we get there. At least for him.'

'Then call the nursing home, damn it. Get them to check that everything is okay.'

Emma looked at him. When he didn't act, she said:

'Give me the number. I'll call them myself.'

15

He sat high, he sat comfortably.

It was an experience to drive this car. The tyres elegantly resisted the pressure from the vehicle's 2,138 kilos. The car almost floated over the asphalt.

His eyes glanced at the phone in the passenger seat. Every lamppost he passed was reflected on the screen. He reached out and flipped it over so that it was face down. Smiled at the thought: it was impossible to trace. They were probably trying, but they would never be able to connect it to him.

He straightened up in his seat and stared ahead. Enjoyed the feeling of control over engine and machine. He had always enjoyed driving. Alone, with no sound in the car other than the whistling of the tyres on the road, the engine humming, the rustle of his clothing when he moved or turned. Driving was almost like a form of meditation to him, a kind of trance that helped him breathe easier, think more clearly.

Over the years it had become increasingly important for him to find small moments of peace and quiet, so that he could quell his heartbeat and find a sense of balance. That's why he never had the radio on or listened to an audiobook in the car. The experience should be completely silent.

But there was a sound in the car now, a creaking or vibration some-where, creating a steady, low-frequency hum. He moved the keys and coins in the centre console around, but it didn't help. He stretched his hand around the back of the seat he was sitting in and felt to check if there was anything on the floor that might be the cause of this nightmare sound. But no.

There were some papers in the map pocket on the driver's side door. He shuffled them about. It didn't help. He hit the steering wheel, leaned over the seat next to him – there must be something underneath or in the pocket on the passenger-side door making this infernal noise. He quickly looked up at the road and realised that he had veered over the line into the next lane. He managed to pry his hand into the compartment on the other side and grabbed everything he could and tossed it all into the seat next to him.

The sound didn't stop.

He sat up abruptly, a movement he carried into the steering wheel so that the car jerked all the way into the opposite lane. The light of an on-coming vehicle hit him square in the face – the long beep of the other car's horn made him grab the steering wheel with both hands and wrench the car back onto the correct side of the road, and just in time. A mere second later and the honking car whizzed past.

'Christ,' he said out loud, blinking a few times. His heart was pounding hard in his chest. He tried to regain control of his breathing. Grabbing the Coke bottle he had chucked onto the seat next to him, he unscrewed the cap with his teeth. Took a long sip. When he could no longer hear his own ragged breaths, he also noticed that the sound had stopped.

The bottle, he muttered.

Fuck's sake, it had to be the bottle.

He put it back on the seat next to him, just as it had been, with the spout resting against the seat belt buckle. After a few moments the same sound started again.

He shook his head and smiled. Moved the bottle so the sound stopped.

That had been a close one.

A small detail like that, one thoughtless moment, and *voilà* – it could all be over. But that was life, he thought. Everything could be taken from you in an instant. That is, if you weren't paying attention and didn't see the signals. If you hadn't planned ahead.

Alpha and Omega.

He never stopped right outside the house.

Parked in the car park of a nearby shop, on the other hand, no one would pay any attention to his car. It did mean he had to walk a bit, but it always felt good to stretch his legs after a long drive.

He retrieved the hat from his backpack. He should put on gloves too, and cover up other exposed areas of skin, but that could wait until he was indoors.

There were lights on in some of the neighbouring houses.

He could see some of the people in them too, but they were busy sitting in front of flickering TV screens.

At the back of the house, he let himself into the cellar with a key he had found the first time he had been there. Once in the hall, he took off his shoes and put down his bag. Pulled out a pair of dark-blue plastic shoe covers and wrapped elastic bands around his ankles so the covers would stay in place. He also took out a pair of disposable gloves and pulled the ends over his jacket sleeves. Stretched a rubber band around each wrist, so that nothing could get in or out.

Without flicking on any of the light switches, he made his way up to the ground floor.

In his youth he had often snuck into the houses of people he knew. He enjoyed the thrill, of being inside the homes of his teachers or fellow students. Enjoyed seeing how they lived and what they filled their days with. How they really felt. It never ceased to amaze him how alike everyone was. How they had the same things on their window sills or on the wall, as if there was a formula for how to decorate. Maybe they had seen something they liked in a weekly magazine or at the neighbour's, he'd thought, and so they wanted the same thing themselves.

He had wanted the same too.

He would have settled for something completely and utterly average – he didn't need anything extravagant or over the top. A friendly look or a kind comment would have been enough. A meal prepared with love, not seasoned with sighs and groans. To be treated in a way that was nice, kind, decent. Fair. It wasn't difficult. It was just a matter of wanting to treat him like that, and doing it.

In the living room, a dark blue, otherwise nondescript blanket lay folded over the back of the sofa. The remote controls were placed on the table next to a crossword puzzle. A candlestick with four prongs, each with the remains of a purple candle, was gathering dust in the centre of the table. A wooden bowl that looked like a child had made it was placed further along, close to the edge.

On the floor not too far away was a dry pot plant. He saw several, in fact, all nearly dead. Above the sofa hung a painting depicting a mountain landscape somewhere or other, with a crystal-clear fjord in the foreground and seagulls circling a fishing boat. There were pictures of a married couple on the wall, taken some time in the seventies. He saw no photos of the child, not even on the mantelpiece.

In the kitchen, he stopped in front of the fridge. A magnet shaped like a ladybird held a letter in place: a notification of an overdue check-up at a GP surgery that had long since expired. A deposit slip worth twenty-three kroner hung at an angle next to a pad of lined paper, on which a note was written in neat handwriting: *Whole milk, apple juice, butter, lamb cutlets.*

He took a deep breath and opened his backpack again. Pulled out the plastic folder and looked through the contents. Smiled, and removed the magnet, using it to place the paper next to a child's drawing that was hanging front and centre on the fridge. As if it was some special place of honour. In the bottom right corner, a child had written: *Iselin, age 7.*

He took a step back.

Perfect.

Before going out the same way he'd come in, he filled a large kitchen glass with water and gently emptied it in each of the living room's parched pot plants. The plants didn't deserve to die, he thought. They hadn't done anything to anyone.

16

Blix woke up to Terry trying to get onto his bed. He pushed him away and swung his legs out.

The night before he had gone to bed with a tight knot in his stomach and a pressure in his chest that stabbed at him when he breathed. He had thought of his father, and of Emma's angry expression when she looked at him as she spoke to Anette, one of the nurses at the nursing home. After Emma had been assured that nothing was out of the ordinary, neither with Blix's father nor the ward, she had thanked her and said that they would come to visit tomorrow morning.

'I'll pick you up at nine,' she said to Blix after hanging up. Then she had left, without saying bye.

✳

When Blix met her outside on Tøyengata a few minutes past nine, her rage had seemingly dissipated, but there was still a kind of reservation or aloofness to her that he couldn't remember having been on the receiving end of before. She said a few words to Terry as they strapped him into his seat belt, but it was several minutes before she spoke to Blix.

'What's wrong with you, honestly?' she asked. 'Someone threatened your father's life, and you're not even interested in finding out whether he's still breathing?' She shook her head. 'Isn't that callous?'

Looking at it in isolation, she was absolutely right, but he didn't comment on it.

'Aren't you going to say anything?' she asked.

'There's not much to say,' Blix replied.

Emma snorted and slammed on the brakes behind a Ford that had suddenly stopped.

'Now, I don't know much about what it means to have a father,' she said. 'But I know that if it could have been a matter of life and death, then I would have tried to move heaven and earth to … to … I don't bloody know.'

Up ahead, the traffic light changed to green. The cars in front of Emma were slow to react. She pressed down hard on the horn. The driver of the car in front raised a crooked hand in the air and extended a middle finger.

'Yeah, screw you too,' she snapped and gripped the steering wheel so hard that her knuckles turned white.

Drop it, Emma, Blix wanted to say. There is so much you don't know.

The worst of the morning traffic had passed. Emma kept a steady pace out of town.

'It's been a long time since I had anything to do with my father,' he said after a while, looking out of the window. A grey colossus of a building to the right of the road seemingly housed an indoor ski slope. 'It's just how it is,' he added.

'No,' Emma disagreed, shaking her head. 'Things don't just happen like that. They become that way because something happens.'

Drop it, Blix repeated like a mantra to himself. Let it be.

They drove on.

'We never got along well,' he said. 'For as long as I can remember.'

'How so?'

'I don't know,' he said, shrugging. 'It's a long story.'

'Well,' Emma said, 'it's a long drive.'

Terry lay down in the back seat. It didn't take long before the hum and shaking of the car lulled him to sleep.

Emma looked over at Blix. 'I understand it can be difficult to talk about,' she said. Her voice had softened. 'And I do feel guilty that I never asked you about your parents.'

'We had other things to talk about,' Blix said.

They drove in silence for a while.

'Speaking of which,' he said. 'What was it you wanted to talk to me about?'

'Huh?'

'Yesterday,' Blix explained. 'You came by last night saying you needed to talk to me about something.'

'Ah,' she said, seeming a little embarrassed. 'It was about Oliver Krogh. You've heard of him, I presume?'

Blix nodded.

Emma gave him a quick outline of the case, as she understood it, and what she had done since Carmen Prytz contacted her the day before.

'I thought you'd quit being a journalist,' Blix stated when she had finished.

'Yeah, I thought I had too,' Emma said. 'But there might be a good story there. Have you ever had anything to do with his defence lawyer before?'

'Leo van Eijk,' Blix said with a sigh. 'The prosecution's nemesis.' He rolled his eyes. 'Infamous for his theatrics – and he really does manage to evoke some deep and genuine indignation on behalf of his clients.'

'I'm not so sure he bothered to do that in Oliver Krogh's case.'

'Then he's probably guilty.'

'Yeah, that's what everyone seems to think,' Emma replied.

'But not you?'

'It's a bit early to say really. I'd like to see what evidence they have. And by "they" I mean your old colleagues in the police.'

'And you'd like me to help you with that?' Blix said. 'They're not all that keen on me down at the station, I'm afraid.'

'There's no one you could ask? Not everyone feels that way, surely?'

Blix thought about it. 'I don't know.'

He looked out of the window again. They crossed the bridge over the Nitelva river. There was almost no movement in the dirty brown water.

'But you can help me run through a few ideas,' Emma said after a short while. 'If he *is* responsible, and he has killed and dumped Maria Normann somewhere – why would he, and what kind of direct or even circumstantial evidence could they have against him?'

Blix shrugged. 'There could be a lot.' He thought for a moment. 'But there must be something that indicates some kind of conflict between the two of them. Emails or text messages. Maybe they had a relationship on some level that one of them wanted out of. Or they'd had a falling out about something or other.' He mulled it over some more before continuing: 'A secret that had come to light, perhaps. Something one of them had done to the other.'

This made Emma look over at him, as if she thought he was on to something. But she didn't comment on it.

✳

Almost an hour later, they arrived at the nursing home. Before they pulled into the car park in front of the low building, Blix told Emma that he wanted to go in alone.

'By all means,' Emma said. 'I'm just the chauffeur. You probably can't take dogs in either.' Then, before Blix could say anything: 'I'll take Terry for a sniff round the block. We'll probably find a good few trees he can mark as his own.'

After Emma had attached his lead, they strode off, away from the white building. Blix raised his shoulders high and slowly lowered them again. Walked towards the main entrance. The doors slid open. He entered. Looked around. Immediately got the sense of an institution – of old age, death. It even smelled like deterioration in there, despite the fact that the care home looked perfectly clean and like it had been refurbished not that many years ago.

Blix took a few steps further inside. Spotted the reception desk and approached. Behind the glass partition, a woman looked up at him nonchalantly as he said hello.

Then she lifted her chin abruptly and said: 'Whoa.'

Blix didn't know how to reply. He ended up offering another cautious 'hi'. Then: 'My name is Alexander Blix.'

'Yes, I'm aware of that,' she said. 'I mean, of course I know who you are.'

'I'm ... Gjermund's son.'

'I know that too,' she said, laughing. It took a few more moments before it dawned on her that he was there for a reason.

'Sorry. Wait here a moment, I'll call for Petter.'

Blix waited while the woman behind the glass put the phone to her ear. It only took a few seconds, then she said: 'If you'd just sit over there for a minute, Petter will be with you in a jiffy.' She pointed towards a set of sofas with stiff, red cushions that looked like they had been taken straight out of an IKEA brochure from the nineties. Blix did as he was told. Sat down, put his hands in his lap. Straightening his back, he glanced at the woman, who continued to stare at him with a poorly hidden smile.

A man in his thirties came walking towards him with quick, energetic steps. The name tag attached to his shirt made it easy to figure out who he was.

'Petter Thaulow.'

Half standing, Blix received Thaulow's outstretched hand.

'Just sit, it's fine,' Thaulow said. 'We can have a quick chat here first, I think.'

Blix agreed.

'It was nice to put a face to the voice,' Thaulow began. 'Or, I mean, I've seen your face before. Of course. Just...'

Just not here, Blix thought to himself.

'But I was very glad when I heard you were coming today,' Thaulow went on. 'And Gjermund will be too, I'm sure.'

I'm not so sure about that, Blix thought.

'I haven't told him you're coming,' Thaulow added.

'How ... how is he?' Blix asked.

'Ah, you know, the usual ... Well, he did throw up after breakfast this morning.'

'So is that not usual?'

'No. But it's not exactly that unusual here either,' he said. 'The people who live here, they're not exactly...'

Healthy, Blix wanted to finish for him. If you ended up in a nursing home, it was usually your last stop. That would never be Blix's fate. Never.

'I'm guessing he doesn't have many visitors?' he asked instead, clearing his throat.

Thaulow shook his head. 'There is someone called Magnar who comes by once every two weeks or so. Magnar is an old—'

'I know Magnar,' Blix interrupted. His old teacher who would come by every Saturday to watch the match of the day with his father.

'Beyond that...' Thaulow shrugged.

'Okay,' Blix said with a sigh. 'Is he in his room?'

'If I know Gjermund, he's probably in the TV room. Arguing with Birger over whose turn it is to have the remote, no doubt.'

Probably not the most productive argument when you can't remember much of anything, Blix thought, glad that he didn't say it out loud.

'I ... guess I should go and say hello then,' he said. 'Now that I'm here.'

'I think that'd be a good idea,' Petter Thaulow said, standing up. 'I'll walk with you.'

17

Blix followed the carer through the corridors. With each step he felt the tension building in his body. His hands grew clammy.

He passed rooms with open doors, beds with people in them – half asleep, half alive. Members of staff who walked by, nodding at him with reserved smiles.

Words came out of Petter Thaulow's mouth as they walked, but Blix didn't catch any of them.

He thought about the last time he had seen his father.

Gjermund Blix had been brought into the Østre Toten district sheriff's office after he had been found wandering around in a dressing gown and slippers a good distance from home. A local officer had contacted Blix and told him what had happened. Blix had got straight into his car and driven from Oslo to Lena, where the sheriff's office was located. He had picked up his exhausted father and driven him home without a single word being exchanged.

For the entire night, Blix had just sat in the kitchen of his childhood home, staring at the walls. He had listened to the sounds of the house, had let the memories wash over him – let his mind wander back to a time in his life he had tried hard to forget.

The next morning, his father had come shuffling into the kitchen and looked at Blix as if he were a ghost. The old man wouldn't believe a word of what happened the night before. They ate a silent breakfast of toast, rancid butter and stale jam. They drank coffee from his parents' old cups.

'You need to get checked out,' Blix finally told him. 'Next time you might end up freezing to death.'

'Pah,' his father said. 'There's nothing wrong with me.'

Then, with a snort he stood up and said:

'Go back to Oslo. There's nothing for you here. You made that choice a long time ago.'

Blix looked down. Took a sip from the coffee cup and looked at his father one last time before he cleared the breakfast table and left.

With the exception of Merete and Iselin, no one in his life knew anything about his father. Or his mother. There were certain aspects of his childhood that he had not even shared with his then-wife. Merete had, nevertheless, understood that his relationship with his parents had been difficult. She had always told him to let the past be the past: 'There is a lot of power and strength in being able to forgive, Alexander. Regardless of what happened between you.'

But Blix had never been able to let go.

He didn't think he ever would be able to either.

Petter Thaulow pointed towards the TV room, where a man was staring at the screen attached to the wall, an apathetic look on his face. Petter smiled at him, then turned to Blix.

'I'll be out here if you need me.'

Blix thanked him and stepped into the TV room. Gjermund Blix hadn't noticed that someone had entered the room. Neither had the man sitting in the chair next to him, staring up at what Blix quickly realised was a news broadcast. The channel was showing brief clips from various events around the world. The volume was turned all the way up. Blix was glad that they weren't talking about Elisabeth Eie.

He tentatively approached. The sound from the screen was deafening. There was barely a metre between them when Gjermund Blix turned his head and looked up at him. He looked into his eyes for a long time but said nothing. He didn't need to either – Blix saw what he always saw in his father's eyes, what he had tried to escape from his entire adult life.

Contempt.

Anger.

And even more now: reproach. It wasn't hard to understand why. It was Blix who had contacted the local healthcare service and quietly ensured that his father was being checked up on. After he fell from a ladder and broke his upper femur six months ago, there had been no other option than the nursing home.

'Hi, Dad,' Blix said. 'How—'

The question got stuck somewhere in the back of his throat. He could see for himself how he was. His father must have lost at least ten kilos since they last saw each other. His eyebrows were bushy. His hair grey and thin. As for his face, his skin hung in loose folds from his cheeks. It had obviously been a few days since he had shaved. Or rather, since someone had shaved *him*.

Gjermund Blix was wearing a light-blue tennis shirt that Blix hadn't seen him in for probably twenty years. Although he was thinner everywhere else, his stomach had gotten bigger. Rounder. He was wearing a pair of dark-blue woollen slippers with two holes in the left shoe.

'Hi,' Blix repeated – it was all he could think to say.

Gjermund Blix continued to stare back at him. A few hairs fluttered inside one of his nostrils – the fluttering seemed to increase in pace and intensity. And then, without opening his mouth, he turned his head back towards the screen.

Blix stood and stared down at his father.

For how long, he had no idea.

Until he eventually turned and left.

18

While waiting for Blix, Emma took refuge in the shelter of a nearby bus stop. It had started raining again – a hard, splashing storm that drummed against the wooden roof. Terry snuggled against Emma's leg as he lay down on the cold asphalt.

Emma texted Carmen, just to let her know that she had started doing some research but hadn't gotten far yet. There was still a lot to get to grips with, she noted, which wasn't just a way to avoid Carmen asking further questions.

Emma added: *Do you think it's okay to have a chat with your mum?*

It took a few minutes, but then Carmen answered:

I'd rather you didn't.

Emma couldn't help but ask: *Why not?*

To which she didn't get a response.

Instead, the phone rang. It was Blix.

'I'm done,' he said brusquely. 'Where are you?'

Emma told him that they were just a few minutes away. She dragged a reluctant Terry back out into the rain. It helped that they were running – the little guy seemed to think it was a fun game. When they got to Blix, Terry grew even more excited. But Blix ignored the dog and instead went straight towards the car.

'It went that well, huh?' Emma asked.

He didn't answer. Simply fastened Terry's seat belt and got in. Emma started the car and put it in gear.

'So how did it go?' she asked timidly.

'Good,' Blix said. 'In the sense that it was just as much a waste of time as I thought it would be.'

There was a note of anger in his voice. Emma could feel it. Probably with some of it directed at her, given she was the one who had forced him to go on this visit. She saw his eyes wander out of the window.

'But no reason to worry then?' Emma asked.

'I stopped by his room.' Emma saw him shake his head weakly. 'There was nothing there to indicate ... anything. The carers weren't worried. All a waste of time,' he repeated. 'Damn nonsense,' he added, his voice a little lower.

Emma pulled out onto the motorway. Decided to wait a moment before asking her next question.

'How ... was it seeing him again?'

Blix gave her a sharp look. He had always been a man of few words, but it had rarely been harder to get something out of him than now. Which only made Emma even more curious. She did, however, understand that this was not the time to push him.

They drove on.

'Was it round here, where you grew up?' she asked after a while.

Blix nodded.

'Could you be a bit more specific?' she said mildly.

He looked at her again. You really hate me asking, she thought. Well ... good, that means it's even more important to keep going.

'It's a large county,' she said. 'Lots of towns, villages.'

Blix hesitated, then said, 'Skreia. I grew up in Skreia.'

'Skreia,' Emma repeated. 'Gotcha.'

'Do you know where that is?'

'No.' She laughed.

'You're not missing out.'

'In other words, it wasn't exactly great growing up here?'

Again he looked abruptly at her. She didn't expect to get an answer. So it was surprising when he eventually said:

'No.'

He lowered his gaze. Emma was quite the aggressive driver, but she was driving slowly now.

'It was alright,' he said. 'I had friends and stuff. School.'

Emma didn't say anything, even though the words were dancing on her tongue.

'And then there was football,' he continued. 'For a while anyway. Off and on. That ... helped.'

'I didn't know you played football,' said Emma. 'Were you good?'

'So, so,' he said. 'I quit when I was seventeen.'

'Why did you quit?'

He shrugged. 'It got too serious.'

They continued in silence.

'What did your parents do?' Emma asked. 'For work, I mean?'

A long moment of silence passed.

'My mother ... didn't work. My father was a joiner.'

'So a lot of banging and hammering went on at your house, in other words?'

Emma tried to smile, but Blix just stared ahead without saying anything.

'What was her name, your mother?'

The tyres whistled against the wet asphalt, creating an ambient noise in the car. Terry had gone to sleep. The only other sound was the windscreen wipers.

'My father,' Blix said suddenly – Emma jumped at the sound of his voice. 'He was never interested in being a dad. And after Mum died...'

He stopped. Looked down at his lap.

'My dad pretty much stopped giving a shit about anything after that. Work, food. Me. Just a whole load of self-pity and self-medication.'

Unconsciously, Emma slowed down a little more.

'I was sixteen when my mother died,' he said. 'Stomach cancer. I eventually moved in with my grandmother, and then after that, by myself. Got a job. Worked while studying. In Gjøvik first. Then moved to Oslo and started at the Police University College.'

'Wow,' Emma said. 'That's impressive. After such an upbringing.'

'I don't know about that.'

Emma hoped he would open up even more now that he had started.

'So you cut off contact with each other?'

Blix nodded.

'You never called, never came for a trip home?'

'There was no point.'

The journey continued for a few minutes in silence. Emma tried to make eye contact with him intermittently, but Blix either stared straight ahead or out of the window.

'I tried a couple of times,' he said after a pause. 'Called. Always seemed to catch him when he was drunk and ... mean.'

'Mean?'

'Yeah, he ... said things, cruel things.'

'Like what?'

Blix put both hands up to his face and massaged his cheeks. Opened his mouth wide a few times, as if he needed some extra air.

He didn't answer her.

Emma swallowed. 'You didn't get back in touch or anything after you started a family either?'

'No,' he said. 'Well, a little.'

'He wasn't at your wedding then?'

The idea made Blix laugh. 'Oh yeah, that'd have gone well.'

'What about Iselin?'

Blix blinked. 'What about her?'

'Did *she* ever have anything to do with him?'

'Not directly,' Blix said. 'But I know that Merete would send him Christmas cards and the like. Letters from Iselin, some of her drawings. She thought it was sad that he didn't have any contact with his grandchild.'

'Sure. I can understand that,' Emma said.

'I guess. I don't know if Iselin had any contact with him herself, as she got older. She never said anything about it to me if she did. I have no idea if he even knows that she ... that she's dead.'

Emma nodded slowly. 'Didn't you ever ask him why he wasn't interested in being a father to you?'

Blix sighed. She could tell that he was tired. 'Let's talk about something else.'

❋

It was past one when they got back to the capital.

'What do you think I should do next?' Emma asked as she stopped outside the apartment block Blix lived in. 'What would you do next, if you were investigating the Oliver Krogh case, but didn't have access to the case files and police records?'

Blix thought about it for a few moments.

'I would look into Maria Normann,' he said. 'Try to find out what she was doing on the day she disappeared, and the days leading up to it. And then I would visit the scene of the fire.'

'You would?'

'It was something I often did as a police officer,' Blix said. 'When we'd get stuck on a case, I'd go back to the crime scene, just to be there, spend some time there. Preferably at the same time of day as when the crime took place. Just ... to look around a bit, take in the atmosphere, feel if the place spoke to me in a way it hadn't before.' He looked at her. 'It may sound strange,' he said. 'But I found it useful. Not every time, of course, but ... surprisingly often.'

Emma nodded. 'Thanks for the tip,' she said. 'You don't want to come with me, then?'

Blix shook his head. 'No, thank you. I have to get that lock on my door sorted.'

19

Rainwater had collected in a puddle in front of the main door. Terry stopped for a drink. Blix let him lap up the water while he found the key. He let them in and checked the post. The only thing in there was advertising. Behind them, the door creaked to a close and the lock clicked into place.

Terry pulled on his lead. They made their way up to the second floor. When they had left that day, Blix had stuck a small piece of paper between the door and the frame, so it wasn't visible. As he opened the door, it fluttered down to his feet.

He took off his jacket and shoes in the hallway, went into the study and checked the fly-fishing equipment. Everything looked as it had that morning, but he still compared it to a picture he had taken before Emma picked him up. The kitchen table and coffee table were also untouched.

'Okay then,' he said aloud to Terry. 'What shall we do now?'

The dog waddled away and lay down on the rug under the living-room table. Blix sat down with his phone and searched for an electronics website. Surveillance cameras were both high quality and affordable these days. He could click and order a pack of three wireless security cameras for just under seven thousand kroner. They could be picked up at Elkjøp in the Storo shopping centre in an hour. 'Motion detection, night vision and easy installation', he read. If he aimed one of them out of the window, just right, he could capture the foot traffic coming in and out of the courtyard.

He lived on monthly welfare benefits, but the payments were divided into a number of smaller instalments throughout the month. His lawyer believed it wouldn't be long before he reached a settlement with the state – compensation for the time he had spent in prison. A payment would come before Christmas, the lawyer had hinted.

Blix was just adding the cameras into the digital shopping cart, when the phone rang in his hands. Tine Abelvik. He let it ring twice more before answering.

Abelvik started by clearing her throat. 'Did he call you again?' she asked.

Blix stood up. 'Aren't you tracking his number?' he asked, taking a few steps across the floor.

Abelvik hesitated.

'Are you at home?' she asked.

Blix confirmed he was.

'I'm outside,' Abelvik said. 'Can I come up?'

'You know where the bell is,' Blix replied.

He hung up, went to the door and pressed the buzzer to unlock the main door downstairs. Terry came padding over as Blix opened the apartment door. He blocked the way out with his foot, so the dog couldn't get past. Together they stood and listened to the footsteps making their way up the stairs.

'Hello,' Abelvik smiled.

Blix nodded back and stepped aside to let her in. She squatted down and greeted Terry.

'Coffee?' Blix asked, without answering.

'I won't stay long,' Abelvik answered and stood up.

'I'll put a pot on,' Blix said anyway and went into the kitchen.

She followed him. Terry just behind; he plonked himself down under the table.

'He's calling from a Dutch number,' Abelvik explained while Blix measured out the coffee grounds. 'An unregistered pay-by-cash subscription.'

'No surprise there,' Blix commented. 'And what about wiretapping?'

'You know I can't confirm that,' Abelvik replied.

Blix had stopped counting, but thought he'd added at least seven spoonfuls.

'He called you yesterday, after you finished giving your statement,' Abelvik continued. 'What did he want?'

Blix didn't answer, just busied himself filling the pot with water. Abelvik pulled out a kitchen chair and put her bag on the table.

'We didn't get approval until this morning,' she said and sat down. 'The number was connected three hours ago, but now it's dead. The SIM card has either been removed from the phone, or the phone is turned off.'

Blix leaned against the kitchen counter and crossed his arms.

'Historical traffic data shows that only three calls have been made from that number,' Abelvik continued. 'All three were to you. The last call was yesterday at 5:22pm.'

The coffee maker started to hum. Blix dropped his arms and put his hands in his pockets. 'He was wondering if you found the drawing,' he replied.

Abelvik looked down.

'Maybe I could get something more out of him if I knew what he was talking about,' Blix continued.

'It wasn't my decision to keep you out of this,' Abelvik said. Her gaze wavered. 'And I don't agree with it.'

'What kind of drawing are we talking about?' Blix asked.

'It was found with the body,' Abelvik replied. 'A simple, folded A4 sheet with a child's drawing. It looks like a child drew it, in any case. We'll get someone to look at it to assess whether it was drawn by a child or whether it's just supposed to look like that.'

'What's on it?' Blix asked.

'A red house, a sun and a blue sky,' Abelvik replied. 'The kind of thing children like to draw.'

'Do you have a photo of it?' Blix asked, nodding towards her bag, where he assumed she had her phone.

Abelvik shook her head.

'It must mean something,' Blix continued, eager. 'Can you send me a picture of it?'

'I've already said too much,' Abelvik said.

'But he called me and asked about it,' Blix objected. 'Maybe I could see something in it if I could just look at the thing. Something the police wouldn't be able to interpret.'

'I'll have to consult with Fosse first,' Abelvik answered.

Blix pushed himself off the kitchen counter, walked over to the window and back.

'Had the drawing been there with her all along, or was it put there recently?'

Abelvik hesitated, took a deep breath in before answering.

'It definitely couldn't have been there as long as she was,' she replied. 'Otherwise the paper would have dissolved.'

'So he dug her up and then put the drawing there?'

Abelvik waited a moment.

'A lot seems to indicate that, yes.'

'So there's a very specific point he's trying to make with that particular drawing,' Blix went on. 'There must be a message.'

Abelvik considered his point.

'Yes. I mean, maybe.'

'Why else would he put it there?' Blix argued. 'And why ask me about it afterwards?'

Abelvik said nothing.

'What about the body?' Blix asked. 'Did you get anything from it?'

'It's too early to say,' Abelvik replied.

'Come on,' Blix said. 'You're talking to me like I'm a journalist. What condition was it in?'

Abelvik hesitated again.

'She was wrapped in plastic,' she replied. 'So the coroner is optimistic.'

'Have they said anything about the cause of death?'

'Not yet, but there were no external injuries. No signs of violence.'

'What position was she found in?' Blix asked.

'What do you mean?' Abelvik asked.

'In comparison to the crosses on the back of the picture?' Blix replied.

Abelvik stared at him. 'I don't understand...'

'Neither do I,' Blix replied. 'I asked him about the crosses, if it meant that there were more victims.'

'And?'

'He didn't answer, but said something to the effect that I wouldn't understand what the crosses meant given I hadn't seen how she was buried.'

Blix glanced at the coffee pot. Almost ready. He retrieved two cups from the cupboard and placed them on the table.

'How long's the list?' he asked.

'Which list?'

'The list of women who have gone missing over the past three years,' Blix replied. 'Who haven't been found.'

Abelvik moved the cup in front of her.

'Blix...' she said, seeming flustered. 'There's no point in making this any bigger than it is.'

Blix let out a slow breath, dejected. If the phone had been tapped, Abelvik would have heard the man himself, would have a different understanding of the situation.

'Have you started a search with dogs?' Blix asked. 'The cadaver dogs?'

Abelvik shifted in her seat and shook her head almost imperceptibly.

'Did he say anything else?' she asked.

Blix realised he was getting nowhere. He glanced through the doorway, towards the hallway and the room with the fishing flies. Considered whether he should say that he thought the killer had been inside his home, but Abelvik would probably think he was being paranoid. Which would make her even more sceptical of anything else he said.

'He asked how my father was,' he said instead.

'Your father? Why?'

'No idea.'

Silence.

'How is your father?' Abelvik asked.

'Fine,' Blix replied, turning back to the kitchen counter. The coffee was done.

'Have you spoken to her sister?' he asked, pouring them each a cup. 'Tomine?'

'She's been notified,' Abelvik answered. 'But we don't have a confirmed ID yet.'

Blix sat down and looked at his former colleague. She blew on the coffee before taking the first sip, as she always did. Then she smiled.

20

Emma followed the directions from the map on her phone and left Oslo city centre behind. She liked this stretch of road, out towards Ingierstrand, where the route passed close to the Oslo fjord.

There was little movement on the water. No wind today, which made the surface smooth as glass, brushed with a mixture of grey and white lacquer.

Gamle Mossevei wound its way through the landscape.

Emma had cycled this road countless times, out to Tusenfryd, where she would always stop and turn around, but she had never taken particular notice of Oliver Krogh's hunting and fishing business. It was located on the edge of a small commercial plot for shops that required extra space. There was a tile outlet next door and a business that sold sun-shade products. Beyond that, it appeared to be mainly warehouse space.

Bull's Eye was situated a little way off, by itself, right next to the edge of the forest. When Emma parked up, she couldn't see anything of Lake Gjersjøen, but she knew it was close by. She got out, stiff from spending so much of the day in the car. She interlocked her fingers and stretched her hands above her head, pushing her shoulder blades back. Her knuckles cracked.

All that remained of the shop was a shell – the foundations and charred support beams, as well as some scattered, blackened remains of what were once wooden planks. The whole place was still surrounded by police tape. Emma took a few random pictures with her phone, primarily to give herself an overview and something to study more closely when she got home.

She glanced back at the road before ducking under the tape. There was a rancid smell in the air – ash and stale smoke. It must have been weeks since the police finished their investigations. Emma had no illusions that she would find something they had overlooked, such things simply didn't happen, but that didn't stop her from looking more closely at the ground and turning over objects in the foundations, even though they could have ended up there at any time after the fire.

There was a tarp at the very back of the ruins. Emma manoeuvred her way towards it, pushed aside one of the concrete bricks holding it in place and peered underneath.

The covered area looked no different from the rest of the remains, but she realised that it must have been where the back door was. And that the police must have found something there.

She took a few more pictures before putting the tarp back down. There was nothing else in the building that seemed of any interest.

Emma tried to imagine what could have happened. An argument that got out of hand? Had they been inside the shop, where no one could see them, and a heated discussion had escalated? Either way, the perpetrator must have panicked, Emma surmised, since he set fire to the shop afterwards – presumably to cover his tracks.

But would Oliver Krogh have set fire to his own shop? He'd been its proud owner for eight years.

If you were going to go as far as setting fire to the business you've spent your life working on, you had to be doing it for money or to destroy evidence. The latter was assumed to be the motive here.

She took a few steps forward.

Maria Normann must have been carried out of the shop and then away somewhere, without anyone having seen it happen. Her body must have been dumped somewhere where it couldn't be easily discovered. A lot of moving parts had to go right, Emma concluded. But the perpetrator *had* made it happen.

Emma stepped out of the ruins and scanned her surroundings. A path led into the trees at the back of the plot. A gust of wind caught her scarf, so she tightened it around her neck. She decided to follow the trail into the forest.

It was narrow. Impossible for more than one person to walk along at a time. With every step, she could feel the stones and roots of the forest floor digging into her shoes.

A couple of minutes in, Emma spotted a clearing in the trees ahead.

Lake Gjersjøen.

It was wide and dark – the ideal place to hide someone, she thought. But it would require someone to wrap up the body and attach a heavy weight to ensure it remained in the lake's muddy depths. She didn't know exactly where the divers had searched and how meticulously they had done so, but with local knowledge, she thought, you could probably make the police's work extremely difficult.

All that required planning, she thought. In which case it was intentional. A premeditated murder, not a 'crime of passion'.

She stopped at the water's edge and looked out. Spotted a swan in the distance. The path continued on around the lake. A little way away she noticed stones stacked up in a circle with black lumps in the middle. The remains of a coal barbeque. It did look like a nice place to go for a swim or to fish.

There was also a path heading in the opposite direction. Emma decided to follow it.

She had been walking along the water for a few minutes when she noticed a red canoe that had been pulled up onto land and now lay behind a tree. From a distance it appeared new. She toyed with the idea that it might have been one of Oliver Krogh's last sales.

Emma pushed through some heather and bushes to get to the vessel, which was turned upside down. She flipped it over with her foot, surprised by how light it was.

The canoe was empty.

Emma looked around. There were no oars nearby. She turned the canoe back into its original position.

A snap of a twig nearby made her turn sharply. Prick up her ears. In the distance – the screeching of a car's tyres against the still-damp asphalt. A call from a bird close by disappeared in the whistling from the branches – the rustling of the leaves increased, pushed into motion by another gust of wind.

Emma peered into the trees. She couldn't see anything, neither animal nor human. Nevertheless, she hurried back to her car.

21

The din that greeted him as he opened the door made Blix feel a pressure; it started deep in the pit of his stomach, quickly moved up to his chest and seemed to push him back.

Too many sounds and people. Voices moving over and into each other, glasses clinking and cutlery rattling. Blix stood in the entrance, unable to focus on any of the details of the interior. For a moment he considered turning and walking back out, but then he spotted a raised hand waving to him a little further inside. That made him focus and he then saw her stand. And smile, gently.

Blix set his legs in motion again, even though they didn't even feel like they belonged to him. He slowly made his way past chairs and tables, brushing against people's jackets and avoiding the seated customers and the excessively large bags they'd placed on the floor. Until finally, he was standing in front of her.

'Hello, Alexander.' Tomine Eie's voice was low, but it still penetrated the cacophony.

'Hello, Tomine.'

She hesitantly took a step closer. Then it was as if she finally made up her mind and embraced him, pulling him into a hug. The contact with her cheek lasted a split second, but it still sent a jolt of warmth through him. She smelled good – a soft, sweet perfume.

'So nice to see you again,' she said into his ear and took a step back, as if to take in his appearance. Blix couldn't look her in the eye – instead, he started fumbling with the zipper on his jacket.

'You too,' he said.

The moment seemed to stretch out, neither of them seeming to know quite what to say. Tomine sat down again. Blix took a few moments to get the jacket to hang properly on the back of the chair. As he sat, he lifted his head. Looked at her.

Her hair had grown longer. She had developed rather becoming wrinkles at the corners of her eyes. She was wearing jeans and a bright-yellow blouse. Around her neck, she had a loosely tied pink silk scarf.

'It's been a long time,' she said with a smile.

'Yes,' Blix said. 'It has.'

She put her hands on the table and leaned forward a little.

Blix mirrored the movement. 'Have you ordered anything?' he asked.

'No, I was waiting for you.'

He nodded, looked around. 'It's nice here,' he said.

'It is.'

Tomine's phone was lying on the table. A news alert made the display light up. Blix noticed the time.

'I thought *I* was early,' he said, feeling the corners of his mouth tug upwards. The smile fully developed when he saw the same happening on the opposite side of the table.

'I wasn't quite sure where it was,' she said with a nervous laugh.

Blix had sent her a message as soon as he found out that Elisabeth Eie's next of kin had been notified. Tomine had responded to his condolences with a thank-you and an emoji showing a heart split in two. Just a few seconds later she had asked how he was, a question he felt was too difficult to answer in just a few sentences. That is, if he was going to tell her the truth. That's why, acting on impulse, he asked if they should get a coffee sometime soon, *to catch up*. Tomine had answered yes immediately, and suggested that they might as well do it then and there, if he was free?

Blix had needed a few minutes to respond. His vague, non-committal and timeless proposal had in no time become something very real and not just that: imminent. He regretted being so direct. But then he too answered yes, and added *why not?*

'How are you?' he asked. 'Stupid question, I know, on a day like this.'

The thought made her smile – a sad smile. 'Not too bad,' she said. 'We already had come to terms with the fact that Elisabeth was probably dead, but of course, when you finally get confirmation...' She shook her head. 'It's a bit like losing her all over again. Does that make sense?'

Blix nodded.

'And then you start feeling guilty for having carried on with your life in the meantime,' she continued. 'At least to a certain extent. With work and friends and ... TV shows. And then you suddenly start laughing at things again, and in a sober moment a little later you feel like the worst person in the world. Of course, you're not, but you can't help but think it.'

Blix didn't know what to say.

'But we're glad you found her,' Tomine Eie said. 'As horrible and painful as it is, it's also a relief.'

You.

She said 'you', in the same way that he still thought of himself as an investigator. He considered correcting her, but let it go. He was unsure how much she knew about the circumstances surrounding the discovery of her little sister. But he didn't say anything about that either.

'I was actually happy when you texted me,' she continued. 'Maybe "happy" is the wrong word. But...' She shook her head, ashamed of herself. 'What I'm trying to say is that it was nice to hear from you again, despite the fact it was because of Elisabeth.'

She smiled.

'Maybe I should have called you instead,' Blix said. 'But I wasn't sure ... if you would *want* to hear from me.'

That made her laugh. 'Why wouldn't I want to?'

'Oh, I don't know. Because...' He looked down.

'Because you were in prison?'

Blix waited a moment, before lifting his head to look at her. Saw that there was a hint of green in her brown eyes.

'Something like that, yeah.'

She leaned in a little closer. 'There can't possibly be a single person in all of Norway who sees you as a criminal, Alexander. You stopped a man who wanted to kill someone. You did the world a favour. It would be remiss if you weren't acquitted, you who had already lost—'

She stopped and put her hand over her mouth.

'Sorry,' she said immediately. 'I didn't mean to say that so ... outright.'

'It's fine,' Blix assured her.

'Christ,' she added. 'How insensitive of me. Jeez.'

'Don't worry about it. It really is fine,' Blix said. He meant it too. 'But thank you,' he added. 'I'm glad you see it that way.'

She smiled again.

Neither of them said anything for the next few seconds.

'They have food here too,' she said.

It was only then that Blix noticed the appetising scents wafting round the room.

'If you're hungry?' she added.

'Are you?'

She considered it.

'A little, maybe.'

'Let's eat something, then,' Blix said, as his mind wandered back to Terry, who was alone at home in the apartment.

Tomine ordered the creamy 'catch of the day' soup. Blix chose the duck confit that came with carrot puree, green beans and Borettane onions. He couldn't remember the last time he had eaten a meal out like this. It struck him that it might have been with Iselin.

'Maybe we should have some wine too,' Tomine suggested as the waiter stood beside them.

Blix hesitated for a moment, but nodded and accepted the waiter's recommendations without really listening.

His last dinner out with Iselin had been at a French restaurant on the far side of Grünerløkka. Iselin had also ordered wine. Iselin who had always been his little girl and who, all of a sudden, was sitting there in front of him, an adult who drank wine. He had wondered when and how that could have happened.

The first glass he enjoyed with Tomine settled into his cheeks – a deep, good heat that made him sink a little further into his chair. It was Tomine who spoke the most, who told him about the interior-design business she ran, independently, and about everything she wanted to fix in the apartment, about where she wanted to travel – if only she had a little more money. Blix enjoyed listening to her. There wasn't much to say about his own life from the last months and years. When she asked what he was going to do next, he answered truthfully – he didn't know.

'You'll figure it out,' she said.

'Yeah,' Blix said. 'Maybe. How's Julie doing?'

Tomine took a sip of wine. Put the glass down slowly.

'Quite well, I think,' she began. 'She's started school now, but it's hard to say how she's really doing. She looks happy at least, when I've seen her, anyway. Her foster family also seems quite normal and nice. Positive, kind people. And that's ... good.'

Blix noticed a sad expression cross her face.

'I do wish that ... that she could be with me, but ... there's something about having a mother and a father, I'm sure. Stability, you know. And I'm ... alone, and spend far too much time at the shop.'

She quickly glanced up at him, as if she had said something inappropriate.

'What about Julie's father?' Blix asked, clearing his throat. 'Is he still in the picture?'

'Skage?' Tomine rolled her eyes. 'He's still trying to get custody, poor thing. He's got no idea it's a battle he's never going to win.'

'What makes you say that?'

'Because he's not fit to be a father.' She made a circular motion with her index finger on the side of her temple. 'And because he's never been a regular presence in Julie's life. It would be strange and traumatic for her if he suddenly became one now, after she's settled in with a new family.'

Blix nodded slowly.

They had almost finished eating when he said:

'It's been a few years since Elisabeth disappeared. Is there anything you see, now, in retrospect, that the police should have looked into at the time?'

Tomine lifted the napkin to her mouth and lightly wiped her lips. She took a few moments to answer.

'I don't quite know what else you could've done,' she began. 'You turned over every stone you could at the time.'

Blix pushed the plate aside and lowered his voice again. 'Did the police say anything else when they contacted you today?'

Tomine slowly shook her head, thoughtful.

Blix lay his hands flat on the table in front of him. 'They didn't indicate whether they had any suspects or anything?'

'I didn't ask anything like that,' Tomine admitted. 'I couldn't really gather my thoughts at the time.'

She studied him.

'Have they said anything to you?' she asked.

He shook his head. 'But...' He hesitated, wondering how to phrase it.

'What is it?' she asked.

Blix touched his face. 'Elisabeth and Julie ... If I remember correctly, your sister had quite a few children's drawings hanging on the fridge and the walls at home?' He said it like a question.

'Yes...?'

'Do you remember if there was a specific motif Julie liked to draw? Or if there was one drawing that held a special meaning to Elisabeth in one way or another?'

'I'm ... not sure I understand what you mean.'

Blix took a moment.

'I ask because a drawing was found where ... your sister was found. With her.'

Wrinkles had formed on Tomine's forehead as he spoke.

'And that drawing – it was a child's drawing?'

Blix nodded. 'I haven't seen the drawing myself, but it supposedly depicts a red house and blue sky.'

Tomine thought about it for a few seconds.

'That doesn't mean anything to me at all.'

'That's okay.'

Neither of them said anything for the next few seconds.

She suddenly looked up at him. 'How do you know all this? You're not part of the investigation anymore, are you?'

Blix took a deep breath. 'The person who ... took your sister ... contacted me.'

'What are you saying?'

'Or, well, at least I think it's him.'

Blix told her what had happened over the last few days – how the man on the phone had confessed to him, how he had previously sent Blix a photo of Elisabeth.

Tomine looked at him with her mouth agape. She put down her cutlery and stared blankly ahead for a few seconds.

'A few days ago,' she said finally. 'I also got a letter in the mail.'

'What?' Blix straightened up in his chair.

'It's not unusual that people have got in touch over the years, primarily to express their sympathy and compassion. But that letter, it was ... different.'

'In what way?'

'Well, I don't remember exactly what it said, because I threw it away immediately, but ... there was something about Elisabeth getting what she deserved, and how Julie is much better off now.'

'Julie?' Blix asked. 'He mentioned Julie, specifically, by name?'

Tomine nodded. 'It was disgusting, really.'

'What else did it say?'

'I don't remember.'

'That was all, just two sentences?'

'I...'

'Try and think back,' Blix urged. 'Try and visualise it, if you can.'

Tomine closed her eyes. Blix waited for her to open them again.

She shook her head.

'Was the letter signed in any way?'

'No.'

'And you threw it away immediately, you said?'

'Yeah. I thought it was probably just some lunatic who likes messing with people. They must exist, right?'

Blix didn't answer that question.

'Was it a handwritten letter?'

'No. Typed out.'

'What about the envelope – did you notice anything special about it at all?'

'No, it was a perfectly normal envelope, I think. White. Standard size.'

'Do you remember if it had a stamp, or if it was just put in your post box?'

'Oh, I don't know. I didn't think to look.'

'Tomine, have you mentioned this to the police?'

'No.'

'And you didn't talk to them before today?'

'Correct. And today we only had a very brief conversation. I didn't think of that letter until you told me about yours, just now.'

They fell silent.

'You have to tell the investigators,' he said. 'I can do it for you, if you want?'

Tomine didn't seem to know what she wanted.

In the next moment, Blix felt his phone vibrate in his pocket. He let it ring. After a short pause it started ringing again. For a second, Blix thought it might be the man in question. He pulled the phone out and looked at the display.

Tine Abelvik.

'Take it,' Tomine said. 'It might be important.'

He slid his thumb over the display.

'Blix,' Tine Abelvik said. 'Where are you?'

'I'm ... at a café.'

'We have a hit on the children's drawing. A fingerprint. How quickly can you be here?'

Blix looked up at Tomine, who was paying close attention to the conversation.

'Quite quickly, if necessary. Whose fingerprints?'

It only took a moment before Tine Abelvik said:

'Yours.'

22

In the car on the way back to the city centre, Emma thought of Carmen, and of her mother, who ran a property-development company in Oslo. The company's head office was located on Thomas Heftyes gate in the Frogner district.

From the outside, it looked like any other estate agency – screens between the large windows with images of housing projects, each one grander than the next. Central to all the digital prospectuses was the company's logo – the framework of a house with a delicately designed monogram of the initials VP inside. No one would doubt that Victoria Prytz had a hand in everything the company did.

Emma stepped into the premises with no little unease, given that Carmen didn't want her talking to her mother about her stepfather's case. That in itself suggested that Victoria Prytz might not be the most cooperative person. If she wasn't interested in helping her husband, it was unlikely she would welcome any prying questions from Emma. Still, she had to try.

Giant advertising posters hung from the high walls inside the premises of Prytz Eiendomsutvikling, showing projects that were either under development or were well along the way to completion. 'The people make this city', Emma read. 'We take a people-first approach with our housing'. Apparently, the aim was to 'create attractive neighbourhoods' and 'make the city better'.

Victoria Prytz obviously wasn't the only person making all this happen. In the entrance alone, Emma counted four other employees, all exquisitely dressed in suits and freshly ironed, toothpaste-white shirts. The boss herself was nowhere to be seen.

Emma approached the nearest available customer-service representative and asked if it would be possible to have a word with Victoria Prytz.

'She's currently occupied,' the woman – or rather, going off the name-plate on her desk, Monica Rogne – answered. 'Is there anything *I* can help you with today?'

'Could you tell her that I'd like to talk to her? My name is Emma Ramm. I'm a ... former journalist. I have some questions that I hope your boss can help me answer.'

There was a slight change to Monica Rogne's expression. As if she were automatically suspicious, immediately guarded.

'Do you have an appointment?'

'No. But it won't take long.'

Monica Rogne stared at her. Ice-blue eyes. Her eyelashes arched upwards, grazing her eyebrows.

'Normally you would have to make an appointment,' she said, and stood up. 'But, give me just a moment. I'll find out if she has time to see you.'

Emma felt her face redden. While Monica Rogne disappeared into the room behind her, Emma looked round. Met the gaze of one of the other employees, who immediately looked away.

Emma checked her phone while she waited. Irene had sent her an Instagram reel, which she swiped away with a quick flick of her thumb. Nothing from Blix. She wondered what he was doing. How he was feeling. Not least about the situation with his father.

It took a while before Monica Rogne returned.

'You can come with me,' she said.

Emma was escorted into Prytz Eiendomsutvikling's inner chambers, where Victoria Prytz herself sat waiting in a conference room. Her phone was on the table next to her, the screen facing down. She stood up when Emma entered, and mechanically extended her hand, but did not meet Emma's gaze when they introduced themselves.

'Thanks, Monica, that'll be all. Close the door behind you, please.'

Victoria Prytz walked back to the chair she had been sitting in and gestured for Emma to sit on the opposite side of the table.

'Thank you for taking the time to see me,' Emma began. 'Without an appointment.' She tried for a smile. Prytz didn't bite.

'Can I offer you something to drink?' The words came out of Victoria Prytz's mouth as if on autopilot. 'Tea? Coffee? Water?'

'No, I'm fine, but thank you,' Emma said.

Victoria Prytz poured herself a glass of water, and set the jug firmly back down on the table. She was a slender woman in her early forties. Her face was heart-shaped, her hair gathered in a tight ponytail. The room smelled of an aroma Emma recognised but couldn't place. A body lotion, perhaps. Or a strongly scented perfume.

'So,' Victoria Prytz started, clapping her hands. 'What makes a former journalist such as yourself turn up at my place of work, unannounced?' Her face was focused, expectant.

'I'm trying to get some insight into the case your husband is involved in.'

'Is that so?' Victoria Prytz said. 'And why is that, may I ask?'

'Mostly, I would say, because there aren't that many voices advocating for his innocence.'

Emma wanted to add that that seemed to apply to Victoria herself too, but restrained herself, not wanting to be too confrontational.

Victoria Prytz narrowed her eyes. She seemed self-assured, Emma thought, but also ready for battle. A little aggressive.

'Who has asked you to do that?'

'Er, no one really.'

Prytz smiled. 'Well, you must have been employed by someone. Surely you have no vested interest in spending time on this, now that you're no longer a journalist?'

Emma didn't know how to answer that.

'Can you tell me why you think your husband is guilty?' she asked instead.

'With all due respect,' Victoria Prytz said, 'you're not a person I need to say anything to.'

'That's true,' Emma replied. 'And I—'

'I don't want to hear it.'

'Okay, I understand. But, regardless, if I ... Do you think your husband did kill Maria Normann then?'

A wrinkle appeared at the bridge of Victoria Prytz's nose. Her eyebrows sloped downwards into a frown. She unconsciously stroked her ring finger. She had several rings on her fingers, but none on that one.

'I don't know who you think you are to come waltzing in here, demanding to talk to me about ... our family's worst tragedy.'

'I haven't demanded anything, I'm just asking—'

'You were behaving threateningly towards Monica.'

'Threateningly? I—'

'You scared her.'

'What? That ... wasn't my intention at all, if that is the case,' Emma argued – her cheeks were burning. 'And I'm really sorry if I...'

She didn't know what else to say. Victoria Prytz wiped away something invisible from the corner of her mouth.

'Sorry,' Emma repeated. 'I understand that this is a difficult time for you. And I—'

'Do you?' Victoria Prytz stared at her with contempt. 'You obviously think you have some kind of right to dig into other people's private lives.'

'Not at all, I—'

'And you won't even be honest with me and say who you work for. Which is both rude and disrespectful.'

'I work for Carmen.'

Emma cursed inwardly and closed her eyes.

'What did you say?'

Emma didn't answer.

'Did you say ... Carmen?' Victoria Prytz stood up. 'Did *Carmen* ... Have you spoken to my daughter about this?!'

'She ... she came to me about it.'

'So...'

Victoria Prytz seemed at a loss for words. She put one hand on her hip and the other to her forehead as she continued to stare in horror in front of her.

'She seems to believe that your husband is innocent.' Emma could hear the quiver in her own voice. 'And I'm not trying to—'

'Get out.' Victoria Prytz pointed at the door. 'Out. Now!'

Emma held her hands up and slowly stood.

Victoria Prytz came around the table from the other side and jabbed a trembling index finger at her. 'How dare you,' she said. 'Taking advantage of a teenage girl like that.'

'Honestly, that's not what I—'

'Carmen,' Victoria Prytz interrupted. 'She's not...'

She closed her eyes, as if having to pull herself together so as not to blow up.

'She has always been close to her stepfather. Only natural, perhaps, given her biological father left us when Carmen was just two. She ... well, she *hopes* that Oliver is innocent, of course, but that...' She shook her head. 'It's just wishful thinking. A fantasy.'

'How can you be so sure?'

'Because...' Victoria sighed heavily. 'That's none of your business, and you'd better get out of here before I call the police.'

'The police? But—'

'Out,' Prytz demanded, pointing at the door again. 'Get out. And stay away from us, especially my daughter.'

23

Rainwater trickled between the cobblestones on the footpath up to the police station. Blix stepped aside for a woman pushing a bicycle. Behind her, a man strode towards him with a large, black umbrella. He lifted it and glanced at the road ahead.

Blix met his gaze. It was Roger Kvande from child-welfare services. He had dealt with the reports of concern regarding Elisabeth Eie's daughter and was one of the last people to have contact with her before she disappeared. He was the one who had later made the decision to place Julie in a foster home.

He stopped a few feet away and they greeted each other with curt nods.

'Are you here because of Elisabeth?' Kvande asked.

Blix nodded in confirmation. 'You too?'

'Yes', Kvande answered, but seemed uncertain. 'You're not back on the force again?'

'No,' Blix replied. 'But I was the lead investigator,' he continued, clearing his throat. He didn't want to say anything about the real reason why he was there. 'I guess they need to go over some practical stuff with me.'

Kvande nodded. 'A terrible case,' he said. 'I'll have to inform the foster family. Julie will have to be told that her mother is dead.'

'You're still in touch with her?'

'I've made a few home visits,' Kvande answered.

'How is she?'

'There have been a few challenges,' Kvande replied. He didn't seem altogether comfortable talking about the details of the job.

A police siren started up in a side street nearby.

Kvande half turned towards the station behind him and fixed his gaze on the upper floors. 'Do you know if they have any suspects?' he asked.

'No,' Blix replied.

Kvande was about to say something more, but stopped.

'Here comes Skage Kleiven,' he said then, and nodded towards the entrance with a stifled expression. 'He's probably been briefed too.'

Blix narrowed his eyes at the police station. A man about Blix's age was standing outside the massive doors. He was holding his jacket in one hand and his phone to his ear with the other. Blix recognised him as Kleiven. He seemed a little plumper than Blix remembered from the investigation. The fact that Julie was going to be placed in a foster home had led to a heated conflict between him and Kvande. At one point, Kleiven had even threatened Kvande's life, all because he hadn't been given custody of his child.

'Sorry, but I should be getting off,' Roger Kvande said.

Blix nodded a goodbye and moved on. Skage Kleiven was standing under the eaves of the entrance and seemed to be dialling another number on his phone. He looked up and around when Blix said his name.

'Yes?' he replied, frowning, as if unsure who Blix was and what he wanted.

Blix introduced himself. 'You've been informed about Elisabeth Eie, I gather?' he said. 'I was investigating the case when she disappeared. We met then, several times.'

'Yeah, that's right,' Kleiven replied. 'Of course, yeah. I remember.'

Blix gave him a half-smile. 'Maybe we'll finally get some answers now,' he said. 'Find out what really happened.'

'Maybe,' Kleiven said. 'Who knows what she got herself into.'

'It's awful, either way,' Blix said.

Skage Kleiven slid the phone into his trouser pocket. 'I'll be off,' he said and started pulling on his jacket.

'Me too,' Blix replied.

Tine Abelvik was waiting for him in the lobby. Blix followed her through the security gate.

'Are you sure?' he asked. 'They're definitely my fingerprints?'

Abelvik waited until they were alone in the lift to answer him.

'A manual comparison has been made in addition to the machine search,' she replied and pressed her finger on the button for the sixth floor. 'It's a positive identification.'

Blix looked down at his hands. His fingerprints had been in the register since way back when he was a patrol officer. The forensics technicians had entered them into the database after he had rushed to a bloody crime scene where all officers had primarily been focused on saving lives, not securing leads. Forensics had taken his prints to separate them from the perpetrator's. The victim had been pronounced dead at the hospital that evening. The killer had been given thirteen years and was long since out.

The lift signalled that they had arrived on the sixth floor.

'I met Roger Kvande and Skage Kleiven outside,' Blix said as they stepped out. 'Did they have any new information?'

'It's an ongoing investigation,' she replied, instead of saying that that was information she couldn't share with him.

Blix nodded and was ushered down a corridor.

'We can go in here,' Abelvik said, pointing to one of the meeting rooms.

'No interrogation this time?' Blix asked.

'I'll be talking to you myself,' Abelvik replied, and let him in before following herself.

The room was all set up. A folder with case documents was at one end of the table, along with a notebook and voice recorder. There were cups and glasses, but no pot of coffee or jug of water.

They sat down. Abelvik started the recorder and read out the usual statement. She pulled out a photocopy of the drawing that had been found on the body of Elisabeth Eie. There were purple spots and stains on it from the chemical examination. He could see hints of several fingerprints that had been steamed out. At the bottom of the page, a ring had been drawn around one of them with a grey pencil.

'A thumbprint from your right hand,' Abelvik explained.

Only parts of it were visible, a few loops and arches, but with enough checkpoints for identification.

Abelvik pulled out another piece of paper. It was from the back of the drawing. Four finger marks were circled in a similar manner as the thumbprint on the front.

Blix pulled the drawing towards him and carefully lifted it up. His right thumb rested over the copy of his thumbprint, the other four fingers supported the sheet from beneath. At one time or another he had held the drawing in his hand, in the same way as now, but he had no recollection of having done so.

Blix cleared his throat, slowly shaking his head. 'I can't say I've seen it before,' he said without taking his eyes off the drawing.

Almost the entire page had been coloured in. The green grass, a red house, a big yellow sun against a blue sky. Next to the house was a garden, where a child was sitting on a swing, but facing away.

The lines were controlled and the various elements were precisely placed, but it was obviously drawn by a child, not by an adult who wanted it to look that way.

'Could the drawing have been done afterwards?' Blix asked. 'I mean, could the paper have been blank when the fingerprints were deposited?'

'No,' Abelvik answered. 'It was done with wax crayon. So the prints are set in the colours.'

'What about the other prints?' he asked, putting the drawing down. 'There are more here.' Abelvik left the drawing on the table between them.

'They have not been identified,' she replied.

Blix tried to collect his thoughts.

'The only thing I can think of is that it's one of Julie's drawings,' he said, but couldn't quite make it all make sense.

'Elisabeth Eie's daughter?' Abelvik said, glancing at the recorder.

Blix nodded. 'Yes,' he said. 'Her room was full of them. We went through the whole house after Elisabeth disappeared. We used gloves, but I went back there with Elisabeth's sister as she wanted to collect a few things for Julie to take with her. Julie was living with her for a period, before child-welfare services relocated her.'

He pulled the drawing towards him again. Julie had been four when her mother disappeared. The colourful drawing seemed a little too advanced for such a young girl. The arms and legs of the child drawn in the image were proportional. The windows in the house had panes, and there was a chimney on the roof.

He looked up at Abelvik. 'You should talk to Elisabeth's sister again,' he said. 'Tomine. I met with her before you called. She had received an anonymous letter, some kind of hate mail about Elisabeth. The letter mentioned Julie. Something about how she was better off now, without her mother.'

'Oh?' Abelvik said, putting her pen to paper.

'Yes, just a few days ago,' Blix added.

Abelvik noted something down. 'Just the one letter, or several?'

'Just the one I believe. She threw it away.'

'But no one's called her?'

'No.'

'Okay. Then maybe it's not that important. Or dangerous, for that matter.'

Blix could see that the information had given her pause. Abelvik's train of thought had given him something to think about too. It hadn't occurred to him that the perpetrator might have some kind of plan for Tomine as well.

His gaze was drawn to the children's swing in the drawing.

'Have you examined the paper itself?' he asked. 'Do you know anything about how old it is? How long my prints could have been there?'

'I did ask forensics about that,' Abelvik answered. 'It's difficult to determine. There are so many factors at play – humidity and the like. At least a couple of years though, but they said it could be much older.'

She let the silence linger.

Blix bit the inside of his lower lip as his thoughts raced. His daughter had loved drawing when she was little. He couldn't remember what her drawings had looked like, but imagined that they were probably all of animals.

Merete might have taken them all. He had none himself.

A knot tightened in his stomach. Perhaps Iselin had kept some, in her room?

'Who do you know who has small children?' Abelvik asked, interrupting his train of thought.

Blix lay one hand on the armrest and straightened up in his chair.

'Emma Ramm has a young niece,' he answered. 'I've met her a few times, but never seen her draw.'

There weren't any others, really.

'There are some kids that live on my floor,' he thought aloud. 'But I've never found any drawings of theirs lying about. I don't even know their names.'

'When was the last time you saw a child's drawing?' Abelvik asked.

Blix swallowed.

'In prison,' he answered. 'Some of the cells were full of them, but it can't have come from there. I never touched any of them.'

He sat with his eyes fixed on the drawing. It was a photocopy, but there appeared to be a mark from a pin or needle at the top of the sheet. He looked at the copy of the back of the paper. The pinhole was more obvious there.

'Has anything more come out of the investigations at Leirsund?' he asked.

Abelvik looked down at the case file, straightened it on the table and played with the corner of the top sheet.

'The investigations have been completed,' she replied.

'In the surrounding area as well?' Blix asked. 'Have you figured out what the crosses mean?'

There was a scraping sound as Abelvik pushed her chair backward.

'I'll get us something to drink,' she said, standing up. 'Coffee?'

'Yes, thank you,' Blix nodded.

Abelvik grabbed the recorder. 'Pausing the questioning at 18:23.'

She walked towards the door, stopped and turned to him.

'I've got Fosse to conduct a search with the dogs tomorrow,' she said. 'Milk or sugar?'

Blix smiled. 'Black is fine, thank you,' he said.

Abelvik nodded and closed the door behind her. Blix put his hands in his lap and looked over at the folder with the case documents. He sat for a while, then suddenly leaned forward, pulled the stack of papers towards him and spun it around.

The first documents were old, and several of them he had written himself. Attached to one of the reports was a copy of the anonymous letter that had set the whole investigation off two and a half years ago. No fingerprints or DNA were found, either on the letter or the envelope.

Almost at the bottom of the pile was what he was looking for: the folder of photographs from the discovery site. It contained maps of the area with accompanying photos. Elisabeth Eie had been wrapped in a grey plastic sheet. A series of pictures showed how the crime-scene technicians had worked to unwrap her. The child's drawing appeared to have been folded up and tucked under one of the folds of plastic.

The grave appeared to be about eighty centimetres deep, but there was nothing about the hole or the way Elisabeth Eie was placed that seemed to have any kind of significance.

He glanced at the door before pulling out his phone and taking photos of a few of the pictures, then quickly turned the pages.

Most of the paperwork involved routine steps in the investigation. The children and the teacher who had found the body had been questioned, and some witnesses had come forward with observations from around the area. This had led nowhere.

At the very bottom of the pile of documents were print-outs of the recent police statements given by Skage Kleiven and Roger Kvande. Blix took pictures of them but didn't take the time to read or look any further. He closed the folder and pushed it back across the table. It was a while before Abelvik returned.

'Sorry to keep you waiting,' she said, placing the coffee pot in front of him.

Blix poured himself a cup.

'I have some other questions for you as well,' she continued, and started the recorder again. 'I need an account of your movements over the past seven days.'

'My movements?' Blix repeated. He understood what Abelvik was after, but it still irked him. 'Why?' he asked.

'To rule everything out,' she answered.

Blix took a sip from his cup. 'You want to know if I have an alibi?' he asked.

Abelvik fixed her eyes on him. 'Your fingerprints were practically found on the body,' she replied. 'I have to ask.'

'Am I a suspect, Tine? Do you think I killed her?'

'Please, Blix ... Don't make this difficult.'

He took another sip of his coffee.

'Do you know when she was dug up?' he asked.

'Probably no more than four days before she was found,' Abelvik replied.

Blix leaned back. He tried to think through where he had been and what he had done, and concluded that he had mostly been home alone. He told Abelvik as much.

'With Terry,' he added.

Blix went on to tell her about his appointment with the psychologist and about the short trip to his father's nursing home in Gjøvik.

'Have you been to the Leirsund area before?' Abelvik asked. 'I mean, before yesterday?'

Blix shook his head and answered no. 'And I was never closer to the crime scene than maybe thirty or forty metres.'

She questioned him as to his other movements – where he'd been, what route he'd walked, who he'd seen, which shops he'd been in. Finally, she thanked him and stated the time when she turned off the audio recording.

Blix stood up.

Abelvik glanced at the folder she had left behind while he was alone in the room.

'Let me know if you come up with anything or figure anything out,' she requested.

'I will,' Blix replied, and paused before adding:

'Thanks.'

24

Emma took a careful sip of the hot chamomile tea and set the cup down on the living-room table.

'I made a list of missing women,' Blix said, returning to the living room with a sheet of handwritten notes. 'This is based on what I've managed to find online and in the newspapers.' He handed Emma the document. 'There could be more though.'

Emma took the paper from him and studied it.

'How far back have you gone?'

'Three years. I thought I'd start with that anyway.'

Emma counted six names. Only one of them caught her eye.

Maria Normann.

'Do you think he might have taken her too?' she asked, pointing her index finger at the name.

Blix shrugged. 'I don't quite see how or why,' he admitted. 'The police have a man in custody, and it's unlikely to be Oliver Krogh who called me.'

The remark made Emma smile. It was good to hear him make a joke, even about something as serious as this. She noticed a change in him. There was more of a spring in his step, a little more warmth in his voice. Maybe he needed this, she thought – something to work on, something to occupy his thoughts.

They had enough questions to be going off anyway, both together and individually.

'I think he's killed more, though,' he added.

'What makes you say that?'

'It just ... it doesn't really make sense for him to contact me in this way, if there isn't more behind it. And he's delivered on what he's said so far.'

'But he hasn't been specific that he's killed more, has he?'

'He made an effort to imply it,' Blix replied. 'On top of that...'

He took out his phone and found the picture of the crosses from the back of the photo the man had sent him.

'There must be some purpose behind these,' he said, showing her the screen. 'A code or something that he wanted *me* specifically to see. Why else would he have put them there?'

'He could be messing with you, Blix.'

'Perhaps. But more important than the game itself must be the reason for why he's playing it. And why with me, exactly?'

Emma didn't have a good answer.

'I think he's just getting started,' Blix continued. 'Or that he's been at it for a while and these crosses mark where he's hidden his other victims.' He looked at her. 'I feel like going out and searching.'

Emma glanced up at the clock.

'Not *now*,' Blix added. 'When it gets light.'

'But where?' Emma asked. 'It's just a few crosses, nothing more.'

Blix enlarged the picture of Elisabeth Eie on the stone floor.

'If you look, you'll see there's a little hole in the picture, right through her head,' he said. 'The middle of her forehead, give or take.'

Emma examined the photo. Blix swiped to the image of the back of the photo.

'On the other side you'll find the same hole in the middle of the biggest cross,' he explained, swiping back and forth on the camera roll.

Emma saw and understood what he meant.

'I think we're meant to start from the largest cross and look at it like a kind of hub. And then...'

He swiped to the next photo, which showed how Elisabeth Eie was found in the forest.

'How did you manage to get this?' Emma asked.

Blix ignored the question.

'If we imagine that the other crosses are based on how Elisabeth was buried,' he continued, 'a cross directly above her head in the picture means that we have to look directly above where her head was located when she was found. We can use how her body was positioned to navigate.'

He obviously had a clear picture as to how this could all be connected, but Emma wasn't sure if she understood what he meant. 'I'm not sure I see how this all comes together, Blix.'

'Maybe it doesn't,' he said. 'But it's worth a try.'

'Well, if nothing else, we'll have a nice walk in the forest.' She winked at him.

Blix didn't answer, just kept staring at the pictures on his phone, swiping back and forth, back and forth. He looked almost obsessed, Emma thought.

'How did you manage to take a photo of the case file?' she repeated.

Blix looked up at her, a wry smile on his face. It took a few seconds to explain what had happened when Tine Abelvik left the meeting room at the station.

'Oh my god,' Emma laughed. 'You're worse than me.'

Blix smiled.

Emma took a sip of her tea.

Silence settled over the table. Emma looked at the clock again. It was getting late. She was glad that Blix had called and asked her to come over. It was obvious he saw the value in debating the case with her. Emma enjoyed verbally sparring with him too. They'd become quite good at it.

'I should be getting home,' she said and stood up.

Blix did the same. Yawned but didn't seem tired. Emma gave him a hug. Blix seemed surprised, but put a hand on her shoulder.

'Try to get some sleep now, Sherlock,' Emma said.

'In a bit,' Blix said. 'The boy needs a walk first.'

Terry barked and jumped up.

25

As the sound of Emma's footsteps disappeared down the stairs, Blix went back to the living-room table and picked up his phone.

No messages from Tomine.

When he had left the police station a few hours earlier, he had tried calling her, as their parting at the café had been so abrupt. He hadn't been able to bring himself to say anything about the fingerprints at the time, primarily because he hadn't understood what it all meant himself. But she hadn't answered his call, nor had she responded to the message he had sent her soon after.

Blix searched for her number again. Went out into the hall as he waited for an answer. It rang and rang. He put on his jacket. Terry came padding towards him. Blix held the phone between his ear and shoulder as he attached Terry's lead to his collar. No response on the other end.

Had something happened?

Blix hung up and sent her another message:

Just checking to make sure you're okay. Blix.

He dropped his phone in his inner jacket pocket.

'Shall we go for a walk?'

Terry grew even more eager.

Outside it was autumnal and cold, but no wind. But somehow it felt there was movement in the air, like something was vibrating around him. It was a strange sensation. As if something in the city had changed.

It was approaching 9:45pm.

Terry sniffed everything he came across. Lifted his leg here and there. Blix inhaled the evening air as he thought about the letter Tomine had received, the message written inside. He would like to have seen the exact wording. The essence of the letter – that Julie was better off without her mother – indicated a certain grudge against Elisabeth Eie. If it was the killer who had sent Tomine that letter, everything pointed to a personal motive for taking her sister's life.

But why tell Tomine about it?

Blix took his phone out again. Still no reply or confirmation that Tomine had read his message.

He opened the camera roll and found the photos he had taken of the new police statement made by Roger Kvande. The interview transcript covered three pages and clearly followed routine procedures. The first part was a straightforward retelling of when he had last seen Elisabeth Eie. She had disappeared just a few hours after her appointment with him in his office at child-welfare services.

It was difficult to read on such a small screen, but Blix picked up the main points as he walked.

Roger Kvande had been thirty-six at the time. Two and a half years later and he was still single, still living at Stovner. In the original investigation, Elisabeth Eie's phone activity had shown a level of contact between herself and Kvande that seemed to go beyond the purely professional. Kvande had denied it, when questioned at the time, but admitted that they had met once outside of office hours. The meeting had been of a casual nature, although they had ended up going for a coffee together. He repeated the same explanation now.

The last part of the transcript was an account of his movements in the last few days. His everyday life seemed quite empty. In addition to work, he had been to choir practice. He had been to Leirsund a few years ago, but had never visited the forest around Eiksmarka specifically.

Kleiven had also been called in for another round of questioning. Blix read that Julie's father was still out of work and was still living in the same place.

When asked if he knew where Eiksmarka was, Kleiven replied that he thought there was a place with that name out in the Bærum area. He had driven past Leirsund many times, he had said in the interrogation, but never had any business there. He described the relationship with Elisabeth as a mistake. It had ended early, well before Julie was born, and he claimed to hold no grudge against the child's mother over the fact it hadn't worked out.

Blix and Terry headed down the pedestrian street towards the Botanical Garden. There were few cars on the roads and not many people out either. Blix alternated between reading through the case documents and casting quick glances at the road ahead. Suddenly the image on the screen disappeared and was replaced by Tomine's name, illuminated against a black background. Blix felt a moment of relief. Happiness too, and a jolt of excitement.

He swiped his thumb over the answer option.

'Hey,' he said, barely breathing. 'There you are.'

'Hey.'

Her voice was soft, quiet. Blix felt his heartrate calm immediately.

'Sorry I had to run off earlier,' he said. 'It was...' Even now he couldn't bring himself to explain.

'It's fine,' she helped. 'I knew it must've been important.'

'Where are you?'

'The shop,' she said. 'I went for a walk after you left. Started cleaning up a bit. You know how it is, once you get started...'

Blix nodded and turned his head at the same time, back in the direction they had come from. Terry veered off the curb.

Blix heard Tomine say something, but didn't catch what.

He turned back again.

On the corner to Tøyengata was a man, standing close to the traffic barrier. When Blix had first seen him, his outline against the wall of a house, he had only appeared as a silhouette. Now, the man had moved a little, and the green of his jacket was illuminated beneath the light of one of the street lamps. He had a hood pulled over his head. Blix wasn't sure if it was a raincoat, but he was pretty sure that when he stopped, the man did the same.

'Are you there?' Tomine's voice broke through his concentration, but Blix had his eyes fixed on the man and in the next moment began to walk towards him. Terry protested at the sudden change in direction, but quickly relented. Blix pulled him along and started running as well.

'What—'

'I'll call you back,' he said and hung up.

The man in the green jacket turned back in the direction he had come from – slow, hesitant steps at first, then he increased his speed until he was hurtling down Tøyengata. The surrounding blocks of flats meant that he could quickly disappear from view.

Blix ran as fast as he could, looked both ways and crossed the street. Terry led the way, periodically turning his head to check where Blix wanted to go and what he was running for. His lungs tightened, and he began to lose power in his step.

Once at the barrier he stopped and looked down the street. A figure strolled at a leisurely pace, his phone in front of him. The screen illuminated his face. The man in the green jacket was not there. But he couldn't have gone far.

It was some distance to the nearest side street, two hundred metres at least. Had he managed to get that far? He could have disappeared into one of the building's courtyards too, Blix reasoned, or was hiding in the shadows.

Blix gasped for breath as he scanned every inch of his surroundings. No sight of him.

A woman came out of a shop that sold Somali textiles. She closed up and locked the door behind her, after what must have been a long day's work.

Terry pulled on his lead. Blix scouted for any other movement, ready to set off again at a moment's notice. The woman from the shop pushed something into her ear and pulled her bag higher onto her shoulder. Started walking in the direction of the city centre. A car drove into the street from the other end. The headlights lit up the asphalt and pavement. Blix couldn't see any shadows.

Arriving at his own apartment building, Blix stopped again. Stood on the threshold and looked left and right. The street was shrouded in darkness. It felt as if someone was watching him. He felt like calling out to the man in the green raincoat, to dare him to approach.

Instead, he pulled on Terry's lead and headed into the courtyard.

There was still movement in the air.

As Blix let them both in, a breath of ice-cold air hit the back of his neck.

It made him shiver.

26

The worst of the morning traffic was over. Blix peered through the rain-soaked windscreen and looked up at the sky. There was nothing to indicate that the weather would be improving.

Emma was wearing waterproofs and waiting outside the café. Blix pulled over. She got in, handed him a take-away cup of coffee and glanced at the empty back seat.

'No Terry today?' she asked.

Blix drove off with one hand on the wheel.

'The police will be up there with the dogs today,' he answered before drinking. 'It'll be easier without him.'

'Is there anything new?' Emma asked. 'Have you spoken to anyone?'

Blix bit the lid of the coffee cup. He had shared more with Emma than with the police and wanted to continue to be open with her.

'I think I saw him yesterday,' he replied.

Emma twisted round in her seat to face him. 'The intruder?' she asked. 'The murderer?'

Blix told her what had happened after she had left, during his evening walk with Terry.

'Have you told the police?' Emma asked. 'If he's following you, they'll have the opportunity to catch him.'

'They think I'm imagining things already,' Blix replied.

'Not Abelvik, surely?'

'No, maybe not, but Gard Fosse calls the shots.'

Emma drank from her coffee, but quickly swallowed, seeming to realise something. 'Wait – did you bring any shovels? Just in case?'

Blix nodded and rested his arm on the side window.

As they continued the conversation from the night before, and tried to come up with various hypotheses as to what the perpetrator wanted, the city disappeared behind them. Blix drove the same route he had taken two days earlier.

'It's just over here,' he said, pointing as they passed the primary school.

They turned off the road and drove up towards the edge of the forest. The front wheel hit a pothole along the gravel road. Emma placed her empty coffee cup in the centre console.

'Doesn't look like there's anyone here,' she said as they approached.

Blix sighed, annoyed. It seemed Abelvik and Fosse hadn't taken him seriously. He hated that feeling.

'Maybe we're too early?' Emma suggested. 'Or maybe they're waiting for the weather to improve?'

'Maybe,' Blix replied.

He drove across the open lot and parked at the entrance to the forest. The police tape had gone. The low trees swayed in the wind.

His phone rang.

Blix pulled it out from his inside jacket pocket. He didn't recognise the number, but answered anyway.

'Good morning, Blix, it's Krissander Dokken. Am I interrupting anything?'

'No, no, it's fine.'

'Great. Something's come up – can we move tomorrow's session to the day after? Preferably at the same time, if possible?'

Blix had completely forgotten that he was meant to be seeing the psychologist again tomorrow.

'Oh, no problem, sure,' he replied.

'Excellent. Thank you.'

They hung up.

Blix noticed Emma's gaze on him. He didn't bother explaining.

They got out, zipped up their raincoats and headed into the forest. The canopy shielded them from most of the rain. Blix led the way. After a few hundred metres, a newly trodden path sloped off to the left and up to the burial site.

The grave had been filled in again. A bunch of twigs had been laid over the freshly turned soil in an attempt to disguise the site from any onlookers.

Blix took out his phone and pulled up the pictures from the case file. A wide-angle shot showed Elisabeth Eie in the grave, after the plastic sheet had been pulled back. Her head was a metre's distance from a young oak tree with a smooth, grey trunk. Blix looked up from his phone and over to the tree. It had a notch in the bark, a half-overgrown crevice, as if someone had brought an axe down into it at some point.

The killer, Blix thought. In order to get down into the soil, he would have needed an axe to cut through the roots.

Emma glanced over his shoulder at the phone. On the back of the Polaroid picture he had taken, a cross had been drawn to mark the body of Elisabeth Eie. The exact spot they stood in now. Directly above the top of the picture was a slightly smaller cross.

'We have to go that way,' Blix said firmly and pointed ahead.

Emma forged on, pushing her way through a dense thicket.

'How far do you think we have to go?' she asked.

Blix caught a branch that recoiled backward. 'Impossible to know,' he replied, looking back to keep his bearings. 'We need to look out for anywhere you could bury a body, a spot that looks like it may once have been dug up.'

The terrain opened out a little. Blix walked up to stand next to Emma, and they continued side by side with a couple of metres between them.

'It may be covered with twigs,' he added.

In some places the forest floor was soft with moss, in others it was firm, with tree roots trailing along the ground. It was just a matter of weeks or days before everything would be covered in the autumn leaves.

After a hundred metres they came out on a narrow path.

'I think we've gone too far,' Emma said, 'Should we go back and try again?'

Blix agreed. This time they walked with an even greater distance between them. Emma would occasionally veer out of his sight, but she was never so far away that he couldn't hear her.

They were almost back to the burial site when Emma called out:

'There might be something here!'

'Coming!' Blix shouted back.

She was standing by a clump of trees. The ground in front of her was grassy. Much of it had lost its colour.

'It looks a little elevated,' she said, nudging one of the tufts of grass with the toe of her boot.

She was right. A section of the forest floor stood out slightly from the surrounding vegetation, but it was no more than a metre wide in one direction and a little narrower in the other.

'What do you think?' Emma asked.

Blix considered it. He didn't think the place seemed worth investigating further, at least not without the cadaver dogs having marked it.

The rain picked up. Emma retreated under the trees.

'It's the best spot we've found,' she said.

Blix was about to suggest that they go to the car, when he spotted something. On one of the tree trunks nearby, there was a gash in the bark, at about head height.

He went over and traced a finger over it. It was almost a centimetre deep and five centimetres long. The straight edges made it seem manmade.

'Could it be some kind of symbol?' Emma asked.

'There was a similar mark in one of the trees where Elisabeth Eie was found,' Blix replied.

He pulled his hand away and looked down at the ground. 'I'll get the shovels,' he said.

Emma stayed behind while Blix went back to the car. He had found two shovels down in the basement of his apartment block. A rusty spade and a snow shovel – not exactly ideal. He brought them both back, along with two pairs of work gloves.

'Wait. Let me take a picture first,' Emma said, pulling out her phone. She photographed both the ground and the marked tree, before Blix thrust the spade into the earth and tipped out the top layer of soil. He did the same again until he had carved out a square.

The soil underneath was loose. The spade disappeared deep into the forest floor. Emma helped him, using the shovel to scoop away the soil.

'If someone has been buried here, it's unlikely to be Maria Normann,' she said. 'It's way too overgrown. She's only been missing for a couple of months.'

Blix straightened up and leaned on the shovel. Cold rainwater dripped onto his neck as he bent over. It ran down his back.

'You're right,' he said.

The list he had made of missing women went back three years. The site they were digging in had been untouched for much longer than that.

He continued to dig. The spade suddenly cut through something soft. Blix bent down and plucked it loose with his fingers.

Black plastic.

'Shit, there's something here,' Emma said.

A dog barked in the distance. Another responded. The sounds came from the parking lot.

'The police are here,' Blix said.

'Should we go and meet them?' Emma suggested.

Blix had no desire to stop now. He knelt down and started digging with his hands. Rainwater had washed down from the sides of the square he'd dug and was turning the soil into mud.

The spade had pierced a black plastic sheet. Blix removed the surrounding soil and made the opening larger.

A foul smell hit him.

Inside the plastic was a piece of cloth. A blanket or bed sheet. It ripped when Blix tried to untangle it. He removed the dark rags to reveal pale-grey knuckles.

Emma let out a gasp.

The bones looked so small.

27

Apartment buildings, he thought, were basically a kind of plague.

Too many people lived in them. Too much could go wrong. At any moment he could run into a neighbour suddenly opening their door. You never knew who might be trying to catch your eye, mentally noting details of your shoes or clothes, maybe even taking in what your face looked like. You could never be sure.

He came to recognise each of them eventually.

There was the woman with long, dark hair who always walked with short, quick steps, and was always alone. She never looked up when she arrived or left the first floor of Tøyengata 19. Next door was home to a young, childless couple, who often argued, usually before they had even entered the apartment.

On the floor above lived a single, gay man who worked as a personal trainer at a gym connected to Oslo Spektrum. He was one of those people who said hello to everyone, who smiled at everyone, but never authentically. A family of five lived on the same floor, of which the youngest child was about four years old.

Next door to Alexander Blix on the third floor lived a grumpy forty-something-year-old teacher. Above him – a single, older woman with short, grey hair who practically never left the apartment but who was often visited by her children and grandchildren. The neighbour upstairs was fifty-one. He lived with a flight attendant. And at the very top, on the fifth floor – a married couple in their mid-thirties with a two- or three-year-old child who was reluctant to go to nursery in the morning, but who was tired and grumpy in the afternoons. Sometimes the parents enticed him upstairs with the promise of a tasty dinner, or ice cream or lollipop. Sometimes nothing helped. The cry was like a siren going off in the stairwell.

Tøyengata 19, he thought.

A cross-section of Apartment Block Norway.

He checked his phone. Blix had left home at 9:00am. Midday, as it was now, was an auspicious time. It was the mornings and afternoons that the block of flats saw the most traffic going in and out. But, of course, there were always surprises.

He rummaged around in his rucksack and found the key ring. As always, he carefully opened the door and held it open for a few seconds. Stood still for a moment, listened. Ears attuned to the noises around him, he let go of the door and turned around. When it was quiet, as it was now, he would hurry upstairs, always on high alert, ready to turn and get out of there at a moment's notice. This time, he met no one on his way up to the second floor.

Normally it was quiet in Blix's apartment, but he heard noises as soon as he entered. He'd expected them this time. Paws clicking against the parquet floor.

The dog approached him, slowly, his eyes fixed on the strange man. He took off his backpack. Opened it. The last thing he wanted was for the mongrel to start barking.

Luckily he had gloves on.

He put one knee on the floor, and tried to speak softly and calmly to the dog as it came closer, started to growl.

The memories flooded back.

The dogs of his childhood.

He hadn't liked them either.

After he had done what he came to do, he took out his phone and saw that it was 1:22pm. Time to leave.

On the landing of the second floor he came to an abrupt stop. The sound of the front door opening downstairs.

Cautiously, he peered over the railing and caught sight of a figure that was easy to recognise.

Fuck.

For a few moments he stood there frozen, weighing up what he should do.

Then he turned, gingerly putting his foot on the step, then the other. Blix checked the post downstairs. Excellent, that gave him a few extra seconds.

The door downstairs slammed shut.

He took two steps at a time, quickly heading back up, trying to put his feet down as gently as possible, continuing on past the door of the apartment he had just left, further up to the top floor.

Blix had started his ascent up the stairs.

Try to match the same rhythm, he told himself, stick to his pace. He just about managed it. He had made it up to the fourth floor. There were peepholes in the doors on both sides. He pulled the hood even further down his forehead. The heat from Blix's apartment had turned into sweat. His armpits had gone clammy. As had his scalp beneath the hood.

He stopped halfway between the fourth and fifth floors. Clung to the grey wall. Further down the stairs, he could still hear Blix making his way up.

He stopped. The sound of keys jingling.

And then, sounds coming from the floor above.

A door on the fifth floor opened.

28

With the key ready in hand, Blix walked up to his apartment.

His feelings were jumbled, but leaned most towards frustration.

A dog?

The remains had appeared old. It was impossible to tell whether they had been there for three years or twenty. An autopsy might be able to suggest something about the breed, but they were unlikely to find any other answers.

Emma had been relieved to have confirmation that they were not human remains. For Blix it was the opposite. The missing women were dead. If they had found at least one of them, it would have been a positive development. It would have given a family an answer, moved the investigation forward and increased the chances of the cases coming to a conclusion. But all they had found was the remains of a dead dog.

Abelvik had suggested that it could be a family dog whose owners had given it a final resting place among the oak trees. Blix wasn't so sure. The marking on the tree indicated that the same person had buried both the dog and Elisabeth Eie. He had pointed out the marking to Abelvik and explained its location in relation to the crosses on the back of the photo.

It had made her think.

Before Blix and Emma were asked to leave the forest, Abelvik had assured him that they would look for more of the same carvings.

Someone was coming down from the top floor. The toddler's blonde mother who always looked tired. Her gaze slid over Blix's drenched clothes.

'Bad weather out there,' he commented. 'And the wrong clothes.'

The rain water had soaked through his shoes and jacket. He longed for a hot shower, but had to feed Terry and take him out for a walk first.

The woman just smiled in response. Blix considered asking if she had seen any strangers in the hallway lately, but before he could say anything, she had hurried on.

The hinges of the door creaked as he let himself in. The apartment was strangely quiet.

'Terry?' he called.

No reaction. Blix walked in with his boots on, calling out for the dog again.

This time he heard the claws hitting the floor as Terry jumped off the couch. He came running out of the living room with his tail wagging from side to side.

Blix crouched down, scratched him behind the ear and talked to him for a bit. They were interrupted by his phone. He felt a tightening in his diaphragm when he saw that the call was from an unknown number.

'Yes?' he answered.

'Hi there, it's Petter Thaulow from Furulia nursing home,' said the man on the other end.

Blix checked the phone again. The number for the care home in Gjøvik was saved on his phone and usually appeared on the display. They must have several lines.

'Hi,' he replied, not without relief, although he realised the call must be about his father. 'Is something wrong?'

'No, nothing unusual,' Thaulow replied. 'I mostly wanted to find out how your visit went yesterday. I didn't get a chance to talk to you again before you left.'

Blix heard the sound of traffic in the distance. A siren howling.

'It ... went well,' Blix said, not wanting to go into details. 'Why do you ask?'

'Just to follow up,' Thaulow said. 'I spoke to Gjermund a little earlier this morning. He was a little ... riled up. More restless than usual.'

'Oh?'

'Yes, but nothing to worry about.'

Blix walked over to the kitchen cupboard where he kept Terry's kibble.

'I'll take some of the responsibility for that though. I should have prepared him for your arrival. I realise things haven't been great between the two of you.'

Blix didn't know what to say to that. He filled the measuring cup.

'I'm actually calling mostly to say that if you're thinking of popping in again soon, please let us know in advance. Then we can prepare him.'

'Got it,' Blix said. 'Will do.'

He went to the dog bowl, but stopped, confused. Terry's food bowl was full.

He looked over at the dog.

Terry had eaten his breakfast, hadn't he?

'In that case I won't disturb you any longer,' Thaulow said. 'Have a nice day.'

Blix didn't respond.

Thaulow ended the call.

Terry went over to the bowl, sniffed the dry food and chomped down on a mouthful of what was already there.

Blix walked around the apartment with the measuring cup of dry food in hand. Nothing seemed amiss. The fly-fishing equipment was untouched.

He went back into the kitchen and poured the dry food back into the bag.

Terry was almost done eating. He looked up at him with round eyes before gulping down some water.

Blix leaned against the kitchen counter, arms out to either side along the top. That's when he noticed it.

A child's drawing hanging on the fridge.

29

Emma was sitting at her regular table on the second floor at Kalle's Choice, when the phone rang. In front of her: a bowl of Caesar salad and a large latte.

When Emma saw who the call was from, she hurried to find her ear buds.

'Leo van Eijk,' she said, frantically trying to finish chewing. 'This is a surprise.' She laughed in an attempt to start the conversation on a light note.

'Is this a good time?' Oliver Krogh's lawyer asked, completely unfazed by Emma's attempts to lighten the mood.

'Of course,' Emma replied, swallowing hard.

She took a quick sip of her coffee.

'My client has ... asked me to get in touch. To give you a better picture of the situation surrounding his case. He is ... grateful that you're showing an interest in this.'

'Thank you,' Emma said, smiling. 'You can pass on my regards to your client and tell him I appreciate his time, and that he's willing to be open about his case with me.'

'Well,' van Eijk scoffed. 'Whether this is a sensible use of his time is another matter.' The lawyer spoke in a haughty tone, as if he were her superior. 'Do you have something to write all this down? Forget I asked, actually. I'm sure people like you always do.'

Emma didn't, actually. Her laptop was at home, and it was too much trouble to go downstairs and ask one of the café's employees for a scrap of paper. She decided to stay put and just jot it all down on the notes app on her phone.

'I'm ready,' she said, quickly checking that the phone had enough battery.

'Okay,' Leo van Eijk sighed.

The lawyer began by telling her that the fire in Bull's Eye, Oliver Krogh's shop, had probably started a little before 3:00pm on Sunday,

31st July. The alarm was triggered at 3:02pm. It was connected to the fire station's warning system. So, eleven minutes later, two fire trucks were on the scene.

'Oliver wasn't too far away when the alarm went off,' van Eijk continued. 'I'll get back to that in a moment. He arrived a few minutes after the fire brigade. One of the firemen told the police that Oliver was visibly upset – which was understandable, because his life's work was on fire, but he was also afraid that Maria Normann might be inside. It proved impossible for the firemen to get in – the building was already ablaze. All that was left were a few stumps from the infrastructure, as well as some remnants of the gun cabinets and a couple of planks here and there. None of the shop's products could be salvaged. Everything went up in smoke.'

Emma heard the lawyer raise a glass to his mouth and take a sip. He put it down and shuffled some papers.

'After the flames were finally extinguished, they couldn't tell with the naked eye whether Maria Normann could have been in there. At the time, it was impossible for the police to investigate further, they had to wait until—'

'Can I stop you there for a moment?' Emma asked.

The lawyer exhaled hard, seemingly unhappy at the interruption.

'Why was your client worried that Maria might be inside?'

'Because he thought she was there. He was absolutely sure of it, in fact, because her car was still parked outside. I'll come back to that,' he said again.

'Okay. Sorry for interrupting.'

Leo van Eijk went on to tell her how Maria's mother, Hildegard Normann, had reported her daughter missing later that evening after she had not returned home when she said she would.

'She was supposed to pick up her son at 6:00pm. Her mother started calling and texting her about half an hour later. At 8:38pm she called the emergency services, as it was unlike her daughter to not answer her calls or pick up her son.'

'Hildegard Normann hadn't heard that there was a fire in the shop?'

'No, she had been busy looking after her grandson. The police updated her on what had happened, but also said that there was nothing to indicate that Maria could be in the ruins. Her mother kept Jonas at her house that evening and dropped him off at the nursery the following day. At that point, Maria still hadn't appeared, nor had she contacted anyone.'

The lawyer spoke as if he were reading the table of contents from a book – dry, slow, uninspired.

'On the same day, the police – led by investigator Nicolai Wibe – conducted the first interrogation with Oliver Krogh. He was asked to account for his movements the day before, which he unfortunately did without being one hundred percent transparent. In addition—'

'What do you mean?'

'Hm?'

'Sorry for interrupting again, but what was he not being honest about?'

The lawyer cleared his throat. 'Oliver said that he arrived at the shop for the first time that day after the fire started. That ... turned out not to be true. But I'll get back to that.'

'Okay. Sorry. Again.'

The lawyer sighed. 'Further to that point, during the first interrogation, Oliver was asked if he knew where Maria Normann could be. He replied that he did not.'

Emma could hear Leo van Eijk flipping through some documents.

'Oliver didn't want to speculate where she might have gone either. The police then wanted to know why Oliver was so close to the shop when the fire started. Oliver first explained that he, like Maria, was on his way to work. It was not unusual for them both to work for a few hours, even on a Sunday. The police began their routine investigations, which eventually included Maria Normann's telephone and other digital data. That made Nicolai Wibe curious about Oliver's communication activity as well, since Oliver and Maria had been in contact with each other a lot.'

'Not so strange, is it?' Emma wondered aloud, 'given that they worked together?'

'Yes, true ... but it...' He exhaled hard. 'Their call history went back a few months. It started with text messages, then it moved to various apps. On one of these apps, they had no contacts other than each other,' van Eijk said. 'And there ... the communication was of a slightly more explicit nature.'

'They were in a relationship.' Emma said it more as a statement than a question.

'Yes. There is no doubt about that, based on the content.'

'Could you be a little more specific?'

He was breathing hard. 'There were pictures, videos, voice notes – all of a, how can I phrase this? uh, spicy nature. I'm sure you understand what I mean without my needing to go into detail.'

'Yep. Sure.'

'Perhaps it is beginning to dawn on you why I am trying to keep this case away from the media,' he added. 'Why I am trying to spare Oliver's wife and stepdaughter from, uh, airing his dirty laundry, which will undoubtedly end up on the front page of every newspaper if this gets out. That's why I was also strongly opposed to us having this conversation, you and I, but I'm doing what my client has asked of me.'

Emma said nothing. She understood.

'It turned out that Oliver and Maria had agreed to meet that Sunday, in the shop, "to chat" as Maria apparently told him. About what, she didn't specify. But they were supposed to meet at 2:00pm. In other words, just under an hour before the place burned down.'

This didn't bode well, Emma thought.

'All digital evidence, be that from their cars or phones, supports this: they met at the store at 2:00pm. Confronted with this evidence, Oliver had to admit that they had met earlier than he had explained in his first interrogation, and that they had a relationship of a sexual nature. The fact that Oliver had withheld this information from the beginning, and had even lied about what time he got there, was, of course, very unfortunate. And it only gave the police even more reason to believe that he had something to do with her disappearance.'

'What does Oliver have to say about this meeting? What did she want to talk to him about?'

'He was also reticent about that ... At least to begin with. He said it was private. But he admitted that they had had sex that day – meaning in the shop – and that later he had needed to go for a drive.'

'Go for a drive?'

'Yes it...' The lawyer sighed. 'I'm going to play you a recording,' he said. 'Maria tried to call him after he got into the car. When she couldn't get hold of him, she didn't text him but sent him a voice note.'

Emma could hear that Leo van Eijk was sitting in front of a computer. 'I'll turn up the volume a bit,' he said. 'Let me know if you can't hear it.'

A few clicks of the mouse later and the recording began.

'Hi ... it's me.'

Emma gasped. It was surreal, hearing Maria Normann's voice. Emma had imagined Maria to have a rough, almost masculine voice. Instead, her voice was light, airy, cautious and raspy. Maybe also a little anxious.

'Sorry,' Maria Normann continued. 'I know this is all a bit sudden. I'm just as shocked as you. I didn't quite know how to tell you either. I'm sorry I couldn't tell you straight away.' She sighed, heavily. 'I know it's not ideal, and ... god knows it wasn't planned either. I mean it's not too late to ... end it. I think. I can book an appointment or something.'

Heaven and hell, Emma thought.

Maria was pregnant.

30

Blix checked the clock. Fifteen minutes had passed since he hung up on Abelvik. He went from the window in the living room, then back to the kitchen and looked at the drawing again. It was an outline of a stubby child's hand, drawn in tan-coloured pencil. That was all.

He still felt it in his body, the shock of finding it. His breathing was laboured. He had to concentrate on inhaling properly.

The perpetrator had been back, had let himself in. Had made himself at home.

It had been a long time since he had been this upset. His whole body vibrated with a pulsating restlessness.

'Damn it,' he cursed.

He should have changed the lock, installed those surveillance cameras.

His pulse finally began to slow. Blix took a little more time to collect himself, then picked up the phone and called Merete.

His ex-wife answered immediately. Not wanting to worry her in any way, he began the conversation by asking how she was. He heard the scepticism in her voice.

'Is something wrong?' she asked.

'No, no,' Blix hastened to assure her. 'I've just misplaced one of the keys to the apartment. I've got another, but I wanted to check if you had one too?'

'I do,' Merete confirmed. 'Do you want it back?'

'No, there's no rush,' Blix said. 'As long as I know I can get it.'

'You can get another one cut, right?' Merete suggested.

'I can,' Blix said. 'But you're positive you definitely have it? Could you please check?'

Merete didn't answer right away. He heard her pull out a drawer.

'It's here,' she said.

'Okay. Great,' Blix said.

He rounded off the conversation with a few of the regular phrases before hanging up and losing himself once more in his own thoughts.

He had lost his keys during a visit to Tomine Eie's home once – he presumed that they had fallen out of his jacket pocket while taking off his shoes or putting them back on, but that was the only time he could think that he'd ever misplaced them. She had found them behind a pair of trainers and called him the next day.

A heavy vehicle passed outside on the street. The vibration penetrated the walls. Blix went to the window and looked out. He stood for a while before turning back to the fridge.

The drawing was held up by two magnets. One on the top and one on the bottom. They were something Iselin had brought home one day. Magnets of small apples, pears, bananas and other fruits.

Abelvik had asked him not to touch anything. Blix went to the kitchen drawer, tore two plastic bags from a roll and slid one over each hand. Carefully, he pulled off the pineapple keeping the top attached to the fridge, flipped the paper over and checked the back.

Nothing there.

He put the magnet back in place, pulled off the plastic bags and studied the drawing again. The paper seemed old. It was stiff and faded. The hand could belong to the same child who had done the drawing they found his fingerprints on.

Terry padded across the kitchen and took a drink from the water bowl. The water dripped from his chin as he walked over to Blix and plonked himself down at his feet.

In almost every case Blix had worked on, the perpetrator had gone to great lengths to stay hidden. This was different. He sought some kind of attention, as if there was something he was trying to convey. There was a message in his actions. Either that, or he was dealing with someone utterly off their rocker. Or both.

His phone rang.

Abelvik.

'We're here,' she said.

Blix let them in via the buzzer, stepped out onto the landing and looked down. He heard two pairs of feet making their way up the stairs. The head of Tobias Walenius appeared behind Abelvik. Both greeted him with short nods and stood on the threshold of the apartment, squinting inside, as if unsure whether they should enter.

'Come in,' Blix said.

He led them through the hall. At the door to the kitchen he stepped aside and pointed to the fridge.

'There,' he said.

The two investigators both remained in the doorway, before Abelvik cautiously entered the room. Walenius followed.

'I've never seen it before,' Blix said. 'Someone placed it there while Emma and I were at Leirsund.'

The young investigator seemed sceptical.

'And you think it's the same person who called you?' he asked. 'The one who sent you the photo of Elisabeth Eie?'

'Her killer,' Blix stated with a nod.

Walenius moved a little closer to the drawing.

'How did he get in?' he asked.

'I've no idea,' Blix replied. 'But I think he's been here before. At least once.'

Abelvik's eyebrows furrowed into a tight frown.

'When?'

Blix felt like sitting down, but settled for holding on to the back of the nearest kitchen chair.

'On Tuesday,' he answered. 'When Elisabeth Eie was found.'

'How do you know that?'

He told them about the fly that had been finished when he got home, and how someone had been following him, surveilling him.

'Why haven't you mentioned this before?' Walenius asked.

The answer was in his sceptical tone, but Blix didn't say anything, opting to shrug instead.

Abelvik also seemed exasperated.

'Does anyone else have access to a key?' Walenius asked.

'Only Merete,' Blix replied.

'Could she have—'

'No,' Blix interrupted him. 'She wouldn't have loaned my key to anyone, and no, she wouldn't have used it herself. We're divorced, Merete and I, but we are not enemies.'

Walenius seemed to accept his answer.

Blix changed the subject: 'There is a connection here,' he said. 'You found a child's drawing on Elisabeth Eie's body, and now whoever it is has left another drawing, a child's hand, here in my home.'

A thought formed as he spoke. That the case may not have been about Elisabeth Eie, but that for the perpetrator, it was about her child. About Julie.

He kept the thought to himself.

'He could come back,' he said. 'We should install hidden cameras, or have the police here next time I go out.'

He saw that Abelvik was considering the proposal.

'I've called in forensics,' she said. 'They're already on their way. If what you say is true, it has only been a short time since the perpetrator was here. So any traces should still be fresh. We have to act fast.'

'But this is an opportunity to catch him,' Blix objected. 'To lure him into a trap.'

Walenius spoke before there was any further discussion. 'Do you have anywhere else you could go tonight?' he asked.

Terry shuffled about restlessly. He should have been out and back from his walk ages ago.

'For how long?' Blix asked.

'It takes the time it takes,' the young investigator replied, glancing around the room.

'Perhaps you could ask Merete?' Abelvik suggested.

Blix ran a hand over his face. Staying the night with Merete was not an option. The suggestion made him think of Tomine, but that wasn't something he could ask of her either. His only option was Emma.

'I'll figure something out,' he said.

'It'd be good if you could pack as little as possible,' Walenius added. 'And that you limit how much you walk around.'

Abelvik's phone rang. She answered and received a short message.

'The technicians are downstairs,' she said.

Blix sighed, walked out of the kitchen and found a bag. Walenius accompanied him around the apartment while he packed toiletries and a change of clothes for the next two days.

Terry didn't seem entirely happy, but came padding over when Blix reached for the dog harness. Abelvik opened the door as he went to leave. Two technicians in all-white boiler suits came in, each carrying a large suitcase.

'We need a key,' Abelvik said.

Blix pulled out his key chain and removed it.

'I need my phone charger,' he remembered.

Walenius stood in his way.

'I can get it,' he said. 'Where is it?'

Blix rolled his eyes but didn't protest.

'In the living room,' he explained. 'Next to the sofa.'

Walenius disappeared inside. Abelvik's phone rang again. She checked the display and answered curtly with her name. Blix saw her eyes widen when she heard what the person on the other end had to say.

'Are you absolutely sure?' she asked, half turning her back to him.

Walenius returned from the living room. He too perceived that something must have happened.

'Here,' he said, handing over the charging cable as he looked at Abelvik.

Blix coiled it up and stayed to have a few last words with Abelvik, but she was still busy on the phone.

'We'll let you know as soon as the technicians clear the apartment,' Walenius said, as if to indicate that he wanted Blix to leave.

Blix pulled an extra jacket from the coat rack and pushed down the door handle.

'Get them to check if it's Julie's hand,' he ordered, nodding towards the technicians in the kitchen. 'There must be fingerprints on the paper, from a child's hand.'

Walenius nodded.

Abelvik returned, put the phone in her pocket and smiled briefly at Blix. 'I'll call you later,' she said.

Blix picked up his bag, gave her a nod and left.

31

Maria Normann's voice rang in her ears. Emma sat up a little.

'I know we were careful, but...'

Maria paused.

'I know things haven't been easy at home,' she continued, 'and you've said before that you don't want to be a father, that it's more than enough with ... but ... it's something else when it's your own child.'

Emma heard her taking a deep breath.

'I understand that this is a lot to process. There's a lot to think about, with your wife and ... everything. But ... just ... come back. Please? So we can talk more about it? We need to agree on this – together – figure out what we're going to do. About the baby and ... everything else.'

A long pause followed.

'Come back,' she begged. 'Please.'

The voice note ended. Emma heard Leo van Eijk make a few clicks with the computer mouse.

'So that's why Oliver needed to go for a drive,' he said. 'To process everything.'

'What time did she send him that voice note?' Emma asked.

'2:38pm.'

'Okay, well, in that case,' Emma began, 'this speaks very much in Oliver's favour, wouldn't you say? I mean, if he wasn't there at that time, twenty minutes before the fire started, then he can't have been there to kill her either. He would have had to have been remarkably quick if so: have time to kill her, transport her somewhere, and then come back by about quarter to three.'

'That's one argument,' Leo van Eijk said dryly. 'The problem for Oliver is that his phone was registered at the same cell-phone tower when the voice note was sent and then again afterwards.'

'How does he explain that?'

'He forgot his phone,' van Eijk said. 'After finding out about the pregnancy, he was so worked up that he left without thinking about taking his phone with him.'

'So the phone was left in the shop?'

'Correct.'

'Meaning that it was destroyed in the fire?'

'Partially. The police found it in the ruins. They were able to extract data from it, amazingly.'

Emma scratched her temple. 'What does *he* say he did after Maria told him that she was pregnant – in his own words? Where did he go? And how long was he gone?'

'He said he was just driving about with no destination. Past Tusenfryd, out towards Mysen. Oliver knew that Victoria had her suspicions that something was going on between him and Maria. He didn't like going behind his wife's back, and he also said that before that fateful Sunday, he had thought about ending his relationship with Maria. But ... it wasn't that easy.'

'Why wasn't it?' Emma asked.

'He was in love with her on some level, I suppose. I didn't push him for details.'

'Was he thinking of leaving Victoria at any point?'

'Yes, they talked about it, Maria and Oliver. Both via the apps and most definitely in person.'

Emma thought it through.

'If he didn't have his phone with him when he drove off, does that mean he didn't get to hear Maria's voice note until later?'

'Correct. He also had no idea about the fire until he returned to the store. And then, as I said, it was already too late.'

There was a momentary pause over the line.

'What makes this even worse for Oliver,' Leo van Eijk continued, 'is that Maria's blood was found at the crime scene, in the crack of a gun cabinet door. Which suggests that something happened to her inside the shop.'

Emma thought back to what Carmen had said.

'But exactly when it happened, you don't know?'

'Nope.'

'In other words, the blood could have found its way there on another day?'

'Unlikely,' Leo van Eijk stated. 'Maria's mother hadn't noticed any injuries or the like when Maria handed Jonas over earlier that day.'

'She might have covered it up,' Emma suggested.

'Maybe.'

Emma could sense that the lawyer didn't believe that line of thought.

'What do the police think happened then?'

'They believe that Oliver came back long before he said he did, meaning after the drive, and that they had an argument inside the shop that escalated. They say that he smashed her head into the gun cabinet, hard enough to kill her, and then carried her outside and set fire to the shop to cover his tracks. After that, they suggest he drove off, again, with Maria, to dump or hide her body somewhere, and to give himself an alibi. They believe he left the phone on purpose.'

'Oliver denies all this, I assume?'

'Vehemently.'

Emma considered it.

'What does he think happened, then?'

'Oliver thinks someone must have come after he left.'

'So that person took advantage of the small window that occurred sometime between 2:38pm and 3:00pm?'

'Yes.'

'That's not much time to beat someone to death,' Emma objected, 'carry her out, drive off, and dump her body. And do all that without being seen, in broad daylight on a nice summer's day.'

'It certainly isn't.'

'So, in that case, there must have been someone waiting for an opportunity, who saw Oliver leave and knew that Maria was left in the shop, alone.'

'Something like that,' the lawyer admitted.

'In other words, we're talking about someone who knew they were going to be there.'

'That's what Oliver believes.'

'So ... who else knew then?'

Leo van Eijk took a deep breath. 'His wife,' he began. 'Oliver believes that she is behind this, somehow.'

'Oh?'

'Because of his relationship with Maria. Oliver thinks that she must have found out and wanted revenge on both of them. Victoria would never have done it herself, Oliver insists, but ... that she had someone else do it for her.'

'A hitman, you mean?'

'Indeed. He has mentioned this to the police as well, but it isn't a line of inquiry they're putting much stock in.'

Emma's mind raced.

'They've questioned her too, I assume?'

'Repeatedly. But she was, according to her own statement, at work that afternoon. A viewing in Smestad. Although I don't know how precisely the police followed up on the information she gave them.'

'How did she find out about what had happened?'

'The police called her, I think. It wasn't Oliver, anyhow.'

The café owner, Karl Oskar Hegerfors, came walking up the stairs to where Emma was sitting. He smiled as always and gestured to see if she had finished her food. Emma shook her head.

She thought about hitmen. Dangerous people who, if they were smart enough, never communicated with their employers via phone or any other devices that could leave a digital footprint.

'You've not looked into this then, I'm guessing?'

'What, the possibility of Victoria having something to do with it?'

'Yes?'

Leo van Eijk laughed. 'I'm a lawyer, Emma, not a private investigator. My job is limited to defending my client within the framework and rules of the law. I'm sure you understand that.' The lawyer couldn't sound more condescending.

'The matter was raised at the time,' he continued, 'as to whether Victoria would hire an outsider to help her husband, but ... she was unwilling.'

Her reluctance to do so made sense to Emma, now she had heard the details of the story. And Oliver Krogh probably couldn't afford to pay for a private investigator out of his own pocket.

'If we look away from Victoria Prytz for a moment,' she said as Karl Oskar disappeared down the stairs, 'who else would know that Oliver and Maria would be in the shop that day?'

'Well, we can't know if Victoria told anyone,' Leo van Eijk replied. 'Oliver didn't mention it to anyone. And it's unlikely that Maria did, given what she wanted to talk to Oliver about. But one possibility is that she may have told someone that she was going to work. Of course, Maria's mother knew. Otherwise ... I have no specific names for you.'

Emma felt her phone vibrate on the table, but she didn't bother to check who the message was from.

'I saw that the police have been looking for Maria. They've searched Lake Gjersjøen, and other places. The surrounding forests.'

'Yes. They're concentrating on the areas close by. Primarily those that Oliver could have managed to drive to.'

'They'll have checked his car too then, I assume, for any possible traces of her?'

'Of course. They didn't find anything.'

'Did they track down what other vehicles were seen in the area?'

'I would think there were quite a lot.'

'So they haven't?'

'I have nothing here to indicate that they did, no,' the lawyer replied dryly.

'It wouldn't be an option for you to point out to them that they should go down that route?'

He sighed. 'Yes. Maybe.'

The line went silent.

'Thank you for telling me all this,' Emma said, thinking of poor Carmen. 'I have to admit – there's a lot to indicate that the police have a good case against him.'

'That's what I've been trying to tell you.'

'Yeah, but ... still. Look, I know it'd be hard to organise, but I'd really like to talk to him myself.'

Silence again.

'Talk to who?'

'Oliver.'

An even longer silence this time.

'You're joking, I hope?'

'No.'

'He's in custody, Emma. With a ban on any letters and visitors. I, as his lawyer, can't even take my own phone in with me when I talk to him.'

'I know, but—'

'So how exactly do you think you'll get him to talk?'

When Emma didn't answer, the lawyer started laughing.

'Dream on, Emma. It's not going to happen.'

She knew he was right.

'So now you know more or less what the situation is,' van Eijk continued, 'how do you think you can help Oliver?'

Emma thought about it.

'I don't quite know,' she began. 'It's not so easy when the burden of proof and the evidence points in one and the same direction, and especially when we still don't know what actually happened to Maria. I'd like to believe him, and I'd like to help, if it's even possible. If Oliver has any suggestions as to where I can look for her, or who I should talk to ... to see if there is anything to his claim about his wife's possible involvement in this, that would be great.'

'I'll ask him.'

'Thank you,' she said. 'I really appreciate you taking the time to do this.' They hung up.

Emma took a sip of her latte, now stone-cold. She thought about everything she had learned and what she should do next. If anything. It was clear Oliver had an issue explaining his whereabouts, and yet he had still requested that his lawyer contact her, a complete stranger, and reveal his most embarrassing and private details of his life. Is that something you would do if you were guilty?

Emma unlocked her phone with a swipe of her thumb. The message had been from Carmen:

Hi Emma. I don't want you looking any further into my stepfather's case. There's no point. Sorry for contacting you and for wasting your time on this.

'Carmen,' Emma said aloud to herself. 'Poor girl.'

She didn't for a moment doubt who had made the fifteen-year-old send her that.

32

The trees in the park had started to drop their leaves. The wind dragged them along the grass.

Terry backed up into position by a bush. Blix pulled a poo bag from his pocket, and realised as he did so that he hadn't brought any food for Terry with him from the flat. There was a discount shop on one of the side streets near Emma's. He pulled Terry with him and tied him to a post outside.

The selection in the store was minimal. They had the same type of food that Terry usually ate, but not the same treats he liked to have in the evening. Blix picked up a few things and headed over to the till.

A boy of primary-school age was kneeling in front of the shelves of comic books, leafing through one of them. A woman cut in front of Blix with her trolley. She tore the book out of the boy's hands.

'How many times do I have to tell you? You can't have it!' she said angrily and rammed the comic book back onto the shelf. 'Come on.' She grabbed his arm and hauled him up. 'Do you think I'm made of money?'

The boy squirmed away and sat back on the floor. His mother cursed and told him off some more, then she pulled the trolley back before shoving her son with it.

'Ow!' the boy complained.

The mother pulled the trolley back again. When it looked like she was going to push it into the boy again, Blix took a step forward and stood in between them. For a moment he looked into her eyes. She seemed offended at first, then resigned. She seemed about to say something, but instead manoeuvred the trolley towards the till, as if she was afraid of losing her place in the queue.

'Just sit there then,' she snapped at her son.

The boy scrambled to his feet and followed his mother. He stood behind her and looked sideways at Blix while the woman put her shopping on the conveyor belt.

'Hello,' Blix said softly, trying for a smile.

The boy didn't reciprocate, just continued staring at him. There was something painful and recognisable in the child's eyes. A heavy, heavy loneliness. A feeling of not being loved, not even liked. A fear of when the next jab, the next cruel word, would come. A desperation for his mother to notice him. Talk to him normally.

'And twenty of the Princes,' the woman said, nodding at the shelf behind and rummaging in her bag for her purse.

The clerk turned to the cupboard behind the till and found what she asked for. Blix put his shopping onto the belt.

'That'll be four hundred and eighty-two kroner,' the shop assistant said, having scanned through the cigarettes.

The woman pulled out her card, but dropped it on the floor. Blix bent down and picked it up for her. It was in his hands just long enough to see that it belonged to Turid Nyjordet, before she plucked it out of his fingers and huffed at him. She held it against the card machine, but it didn't seem like she had enough to cover the cost.

Blix looked past the woman, towards the sliding doors. Terry was now lying down with his head resting on his paws.

'Put this back,' the woman said angrily, quickly picking out some items: a box of cereal and a bag of apples.

The shop assistant took some time to register the returns, which was enough for the payment to go through. The woman asked for two bags and stuffed the items inside while Blix paid for his purchases.

Terry stood up as he came out. The boy from the magazine aisle wanted to pet him, but was dragged away by his mother. Blix stood and watched them go, feeling a pang of sorrow somewhere deep within. He untied the lead from the bollard and let Terry smell the shopping bag before they walked over to the car.

Blix found a free parking space near one of the junctions close to Emma's building and they headed up to her flat.

Emma crouched down and greeted Terry as they entered. 'What's going on?' she asked.

Blix hadn't had time to explain over the phone, beyond the fact that they needed a place to spend the night. He updated her as they moved into the living room and sat down on the couch. Emma was full of questions, but Blix had no satisfactory answers.

'I can stay a few nights in a hotel though,' he said. 'But it would be a great help if you could take Terry.'

'No, it's fine, I've got room for you both,' Emma said. 'I can get the spare room sorted for you,' she assured him.

Blix smiled. 'Thanks.'

She called for Terry and patted the sofa cushion next to her a few times, trying to get him to jump up and sit beside her, but Terry just rolled his eyes and lay where he was.

'I think I should check in on Tomine,' Blix said. 'She needs to know what happened.'

The corner of Emma's mouth tugged upward a little.

'I'm worried about her,' he added. 'And I want to know more about the letter she was sent.'

'And you can't find that out via a text?' She winked at him. 'Just go – go on. I'll look after Terry.'

He looked at her, embarrassed. 'Thanks.'

33

Emma had never had a dog in the apartment before. Blix had left in-structions, 'in case he was late', but for now there was little trouble in having a four-legged friend of Terry's calibre in her home. He was mostly asleep. Looked a bit dishevelled, Emma thought, but maybe that was the way dogs were.

She put the kettle on. While it was boiling, she went into the guest room to put on a new set of sheets. It was a bit messy in there, she real-ised, after Martine's last sleepover.

Emma peeled off the duvet cover and stood with it in her hands as she examined the pillow and sheet. The tufts of hair her niece had left behind.

She felt a knot in her stomach tighten.

Unconsciously, Emma reached for her own head, to the wig she had picked out today. It wasn't long before Martine would see the first signs in *her* hair, the bald patches that would soon appear. As large as coins.

For Emma, it had started in eighth grade. She remembered it well, that autumn when she could tear off whole handfuls at once, with no idea what was happening to her. Her grandparents didn't know what it was to begin with either, nor what they should do about it.

In the second year of high school, she began to lose the rest of her body hair as well: eyelashes, brows, the hair under her arms. That's when things took a turn – she suddenly looked sick, and those around her started asking questions, talking about her when they didn't think she could hear them. With no eyelashes or eyebrows, she was almost unrec-ognisable, and she hated looking at herself in the mirror. Gradually she came to terms with the fact that she would always look like this. That that was who she was now.

It took quite a while before Emma was able to like herself though, before she believed with conviction that others could too. As she found new bedding for Blix, she thought about how the disease had shaped her as a person. Her hard, outer shell that could sometimes hide both her anxiety and her nervousness, and which meant that she rarely let anyone in. At this point in her life, Blix was the only exception.

The water had long since boiled by the time Emma was back in the kitchen. She made herself a cup of chai and sat down at the living-room table with her laptop and phone.

She read the message from Carmen again.

It was tempting to reply and ask if her mother had forced the young girl to tell Emma to drop the matter, but she decided against it. There was no point. Besides, things had gone too far now for her to just give up. After the conversation with Leo van Eijk, Emma was left with a good picture of the case material. The questions about what had happened in Oliver's shop that day, and not least what had happened afterwards, were all lined up and ready to be answered.

Emma opened Facebook and looked up Maria Normann's profile. The last thing Maria had done was update her profile picture. The change had happened on the 17th May a few years ago. In the picture, she was wearing a beautiful, traditional Norwegian dress, pushing a pram and seemed happy and content with life.

Emma opened another tab and looked up the Bull's Eye website.

As she assumed, the page was still active – plastered with images and offers for various products. She scrolled down. In the middle of the page, she stopped at a large advert for canoes. It was some kind of campaign, and seemed to include canoe trolleys.

If it was true, as the police assumed, that Maria was killed inside the shop, Emma reasoned, then there couldn't have been more than a few minutes between the time she sent that voice note to Oliver Krogh and her murder. The building was engulfed in flames before the fire brigade arrived. Whoever was responsible must have acted quickly. Which made it more likely that it was a planned attack, which in turn only strengthened the theory that a hitman was behind it.

Emma thought of Victoria Prytz's sharp, furious gaze. Her harsh, un-friendly tone. The accusations, the exaggerations. The hold she had over her daughter.

Maria's Facebook page was full of messages – people reaching out, worried, begging for any sign of life. Some were furious at Oliver Krogh and the police for not having found her. A Helle Lindqvist had posted a lot of pictures of Maria, including photos of the two of them: together, out on a walk, in the forest, sitting around a firepit.

They looked like best friends.

Emma continued scrolling. Stopped on an old photograph of a girl – she couldn't have been more than eleven or twelve years old when it was taken. Underneath the picture, Maria had written: 'Gone, but never forgotten'.

Oda.

Maria's sister.

How awful for a life to end like that, Emma thought. When you were young, emotions could be all-consuming and so destructive. She recalled how she had felt at times, how she had hurt herself, cut herself with her grandfather's razor until the blood started to trickle. In her darkest moments, she had wanted to end it all too – she couldn't understand why life was so unfair, why so much shit had landed in her lap.

Emma couldn't remember what had made the dark thoughts disappear, but it hadn't been just one thing, one event. She hadn't read a self-help book or been told anything by anyone that had turned her outlook upside down. She hadn't taken any tablets either. For her, it was just about waking up the next day, and the next day, and then the day after that, again and again.

Emma clicked on Helle Lindqvist's profile. There were even more pictures of Maria there – she had posted news articles, updates on how the search operations had gone, rallying people, urging everyone to keep looking, keep notifying the police of anything new.

Emma found her number, put in her ear buds and pressed call. While she was waiting for an answer, a news alert popped up on her phone. In small print, at the top of the display, it said:

Police have cordoned off a new area of forest near Leirsund, where the body of missing Elisabeth Eide was found on Tuesday.

34

The street lights came to life just as Blix stopped outside Tomine Eie's apartment building. He looked up at the windows and felt an unfamiliar feeling. A kind of trembling sensation emanating from his body.

Emma was right – he could have just texted or called Tomine to update her. But he wanted to see her. Be with her, be near her.

He stepped towards the door to ring the bell, when it was suddenly pushed open and he found himself looking into a familiar face.

Skage Kleiven seemed just as surprised as Blix.

They nodded to each other.

'Have you been to see Tomine?' Blix asked.

'Yes. No one tells me anything,' Kleiven answered grumpily, straightening his cap a little. 'The mother of my child is found dead and I have to read about it in the papers.'

'You were at the police station yesterday though,' Blix pointed out.

'Yeah, but they didn't say anything then,' he replied. 'At least not to me.'

He took a step, as if to head off.

'Do you know if they have any suspects?' he asked.

Blix shook his head. Skage Kleiven scrutinised him.

'Are you going up to Tomine's?'

The question made Blix flustered.

'I thought I would,' he replied. 'I don't have anything to do with the case now, but we were in contact a lot about it, back then.'

He saw no reason to elaborate.

'Good,' Kleiven said. 'It's good you're out again. It was shocking, what happened to you.'

Blix thanked him.

Kleiven left without another word.

Blix approached the door and rang the bell. It only took a moment before Tomine answered on the intercom. He said his last name, feeling immediately like he was being overly formal. She didn't reply, but the lock on the front door clicked open. Blix pulled it towards him.

Tomine lived on the fifth floor. Once he had finally reached her door, he could feel his legs and lungs burning.

'Sorry,' Tomine said with an understanding smile. 'I should have warned you about the stairs.'

'It's fine,' Blix said, returning her smile as he tried to hide his laboured breathing.

They hugged – a brief embrace. She smelled good.

'Come in.'

Blix followed her inside. The scent he was met with was a mixture of something good from the kitchen, and a candle with notes of something mild and smoky. He took off his shoes.

'I just bumped into Skage Kleiven outside,' he said.

'Yes, he stopped by,' Tomine nodded. 'Was wanting to know if I knew anything more about Elisabeth.'

She moved some jackets around on the pegs so that Blix could hang his up.

'I feel bad for him,' she added. 'Some have to put up with more shit than others.'

Blix agreed.

'Sorry, it's a little messy in here,' she apologised.

'Then you should see my apartment,' he replied with a laugh that felt fake.

Tomine turned to him and smiled. 'Do you want something to drink?' she asked. 'I have coffee, tea. Wine. Or I have beer as well, if you'd prefer?'

Blix took a few seconds to decide.

'You're a beer man at heart, aren't you?' She walked towards the kitchenette.

'Eh ... it depends,' he said.

'On what?'

'I ... actually don't know.'

His answer made Tomine laugh.

'I'll have whatever you're having,' he said.

'Great, you take a seat.'

She pointed to the dark-grey sofas in the living room. As well as this room and the small kitchen, Tomine's apartment consisted of an office and a corridor leading to what he assumed were a bathroom and bedroom.

Blix sat down. Two candles were lit on the coffee table in front of him. The wall behind him was bare, while the one opposite was decorated with vintage art-deco posters. The TV was placed at an angle in the corner of the room, on top of a tired, pink table.

'What've you been up to today?' she asked, opening the fridge. Blix watched as she took out a wine bottle, its cork firmly lodged halfway down the neck. She struggled a bit to get it out.

'I was in Leirsund,' he said, and went on to tell her why, and what he and Emma had found. 'And if that wasn't bad enough...' He went on to tell her about the children's drawing on his fridge door.

Tomine stared at him with wide eyes.

'That ... was why I wanted to talk to you,' he added.

She needed a few moments to digest what he had said.

'But that's absolutely insane,' she said finally.

'Yes.'

'He didn't leave any message besides that?'

'No.'

'No letter, no text or anything?'

Blix shook his head.

'But what does it mean?'

'I don't know.'

Tomine came back over, wine glasses in hand. She sat next to him on the sofa. Handed him a glass.

'Thank you,' he said.

She shuffled a little closer. Blix swirled the wine around in the glass. Took a tentative sip. There was something familiar about the cold, sweet taste.

'That letter you received...' he began.

'What about it?' He could tell that she was a little wary.

'Do you remember anything else about it?'

Blix watched as she tried to think back.

'The wording was quite unique,' he said, as if to try to help her recall. 'That your sister got what she deserved, and that Julie was better off for it, or whatever it said.'

'Yes.' Tomine had fallen into deep thought.

'There must have been a point in saying it, and to you specifically,' he continued. 'Otherwise, what was the point?'

She didn't have a good answer.

'Some kind of morbid memento?' he suggested. 'To remind you of what happened? But that doesn't quite make sense either. And the fact that he used Julie's name – it must mean that he knew her. Or was familiar with her. At least knew about her on some level?'

Blix watched Tomine's pensive face, and decided to rein himself in a little.

'I wonder if it could be one of Julie's drawings,' he continued cautiously. 'That it might be her hand on the drawing at my house.'

'What?'

'It's just a thought,' he added, not to concern her any more than necessary. 'The police are checking for any fingerprints. So it should be possible to find out when the hand was traced onto the paper.'

Tomine opened and closed her mouth, as if she needed time to formulate her thoughts.

'If you're right, that would mean whoever was responsible was very close to them,' she said. 'Someone who would have been able to get hold of it.'

Blix nodded. 'How did that letter you received begin – do you remember? Was there a hi or a hello, or was it just straight into—?'

Blix stopped. He could see that Tomine had now landed on something.

'It did say something...'

She thought some more.

'It was a quote, I think,' she said. 'Good god, how could I have forgotten?'

'Do you remember what the quote said?' Blix asked.

She shook her head. 'Not everything. But I remember the beginning.'

'What did it say?' Blix urged.

Tomine looked at him. 'I think it was "All that I am, or hope...", but there was something else after that.'

Blix patted both his pockets, but realised he had left his phone in his jacket. Tomine understood what he was thinking and grabbed hers, which was lying on the table in front of them.

'Type what you said into the search engine,' he requested.

Tomine did as she was told. Just a few seconds later, her eyes widened. She pressed a link and turned the display towards Blix.

'That was it,' she said.

Blix read 'All that I am, or hope to be, I owe to my angel mother'.

'Abraham Lincoln,' he said aloud, taking in what was written beneath the quote.

The late American president had used those exact words when talking about his mother who had died when he was only nine years old. Although he had only known her for a short time, he remembered her for her warmth, compassion and love.

'What the hell is that supposed to mean?' Tomine asked. She shook her head. 'I can't believe I didn't hold on to that letter...'

'There was no reason to think it could be important,' Blix said. 'But, there was nothing else in it?'

'No.'

'And you're absolutely sure of that?'

'Yes.'

They sat in silence for a few moments. Tomine took a sip of her wine. Blix gazed at her eyes. The yellow flames of the candles glowed in the dark-brown irises. They looked as if they were concentrating on something, contemplative.

'Where is Julie right now?' he asked.

'I've no idea,' Tomine replied. 'Safe at home with her foster parents I'd imagine.' She raised her head towards him. 'Do you think she could be in danger?'

'There's no reason to believe that,' he answered quickly.

'But you asked.'

Blix pleaded guilty. It seemed likely that Julie might play an important role in all this.

He thought of the Lincoln quote. In a letter of that nature, one so short – there had to be a definite meaning in every sentence, in every word. In essence, he was thanking his mother for making him who he was.

So what kind of person was the perpetrator?

'I'm glad you're here,' Tomine said suddenly.

He looked at her. Smiled.

'I ... feel safer,' she added.

'Were you scared?' he asked.

'No, not scared, but ... I don't quite understand what's going on. I guess I'm a little ... anxious, maybe. Tense. I felt better once you arrived.'

Neither of them said anything for the next few seconds. She extended her hand a little closer to his. Held his little finger, stroked it a little.

'Do you have a place to sleep tonight?' she asked gently.

Blix nodded and told her that Emma had a spare room.

'You could always ... sleep here, if you wanted?'

They looked at each other. Blix felt his pulse begin to rise. She took his hand in hers. Blix squeezed it back. Tomine moved a little closer. Placed a hand on his cheek.

He closed his eyes, felt something let go inside him – it started in his shoulders, a tension suddenly punctured, slipping away, disappearing from his chest, down towards the stomach. It suddenly felt easier to breathe, and a calmness came over him, as if she had pushed an invisible button. A sound made him open his eyes again.

Tomine took his wine glass and set it down. In the next movement she cupped his face with her hands and pressed her lips to his. Blix kissed her back – it was as if he had suddenly become someone else, a person he did not know existed. When he felt the tip of her tongue against his, how she placed one hand on the back of his neck and stroked the other over his cheek, down to the top button of his shirt and began to tug on it, Blix couldn't help but let out a gasp.

35

Terry lagged behind. He didn't seem particularly happy to have been taken out for an evening walk. Emma stopped on a street corner and checked her phone. Blix hadn't responded to any of her messages.

The media coverage from Leirsund had erupted. Every online newspaper had reporters stationed at the forest, even though they couldn't currently report anything other than the fact that there was an ongoing police operation. She would have liked to have been there herself, along with Blix.

Emma pulled Terry along with her.

They arrived at the café that Helle Lindqvist had suggested, close to Birkelunden. Emma coiled Terry's lead around a drainpipe a few times and checked that it wouldn't come off on its own, or with force.

'There,' she said happily to Terry, who looked up at her as if wondering whether she was really going to leave him out here.

'I'll be as quick as I can,' Emma promised. 'I'll bring you a bowl out.'

She bent down and quickly stroked the dog's head. He looked very unhappy, she thought, like he was in pain. She felt a bit guilty.

Helle Lindqvist was already inside, sitting at a table in the far corner. Emma was grateful that they were a good distance from the nearest occupied table. After they had introduced themselves and Emma had fetched them both a cup of coffee, they exchanged a few polite phrases about the café, how nice Grünerløkka was and other pleasantries.

Helle Lindqvist was a short woman. Even though they were sitting indoors, she had a military-green beanie on her head. Around her neck she wore several chains in various colours and sizes. Her black T-shirt, which bore the name of a heavy-metal band, revealed strong, sinewy arms tattooed with various figures and symbols. Her hands were covered in rings. As she spoke, Emma noticed that she had a tongue piercing.

'I run my own salon,' she said, running a finger over her tattoos. 'Let me know if you're interested and I'll sort out a good deal for you.' She winked.

Emma smiled. 'Thanks for the offer.'

She had considered getting a tattoo once, but never really understood what it entailed. She said as much to Helle, who spent the next few minutes outlining all the pros and cons. Helle was a real chatterbox, Emma realised quickly. Discreetly, she turned her head to check on Terry. He had flopped down outside, his head resting on his paws.

'Maria Normann,' Emma finally cut through. 'I understand you were one of her best friends?'

Helle Lindqvist grabbed the coffee cup with both hands and stared down at the table.

'Yes,' she said with a deep sigh. Having appeared so open and happy, she had suddenly become sad and thoughtful.

'As I said on the phone earlier,' Emma continued, 'I'm trying to find out what happened to her.'

'It's pretty obvious what happened.'

'Is it?'

Helle Lindqvist looked up at Emma. 'Oliver was arrested.'

'He vehemently maintains his innocence.'

That made Helle smile. 'Yes, I guess they all do.'

Emma took a sip of her coffee. 'You knew Oliver too, I'm guessing?'

'I wouldn't say I knew him, but ... I was aware of who he was, from my childhood. Maria and I have known each other since we were little. We talked about everything. So of course she told me about—' She stopped herself, as if realising she had said something she shouldn't.

Emma put down her cup. 'I know they were in a relationship,' she said. 'It was quite serious too, as I understood.'

Helle Lindqvist released her shoulders. 'Well...' She considered what to say next. 'I don't know about that.'

An older woman arrived at the next table. Emma flashed her a quick smile, realising that she would need to choose her next questions a little more carefully.

'Tell me about Maria,' she said instead. 'She was your friend. But how much did she mean to you?'

The lady at the table beside them struggled to take off her jacket, but finally managed to shrug it off. Then, with great difficulty she sat down.

Helle Lindqvist flipped her phone over and checked the display, then turned it back. 'I was actually best friends with her sister at first, but then...' Again she lowered her gaze.

'Yes, I heard about what happened to her.'

'You *are* well informed,' Helle said, looking up at her with a sad smile. 'So many tragedies in that family. It's no wonder that Maria ended up how she did.'

She took a sip of her coffee before continuing:

'She really looked after me back then, Maria. After Oda died, I mean. I was devastated, utterly devastated, perhaps more so than Maria herself. Or maybe she just hid it better, I don't know. Seemed like it, anyway.' She looked down. 'Everything that happened back then brought us closer. At first, she was like a big sister to me, while I maybe became the little sister she had lost. You know what I mean?'

Emma nodded.

'Did you ever meet Maria?' Helle asked.

'Not that I know of.'

A smile curled around Helle's lips. 'Trust me,' she said. 'You would have remembered. Maria was the kind of person you never forgot. She made an impression on people. She was impossible not to like. There was ... something magical about her.'

A pain clouded her eyes, making Emma wonder if the relationship between the two of them had ever been more than just friends.

'She *saw* people,' Helle continued. 'Really saw them. Deep, deep down, saw them for who they were. Does that make sense?' She didn't wait for Emma to answer. 'She had this special ability to get people to open up, to look inside themselves, you know. Really examine themselves and who they wanted to be. She could have been, what's it called, a lifestyle coach or a mentor or something? She had a talent for that kind of thing.'

'But she never did anything about it?'

'No, she didn't bother, I guess,' Helle continued. 'And then she ended up doing ... other things, and all that took over her life. I was never involved in that kind of stuff myself and I'd say we drifted apart a bit during that period. But we bumped into each other now and then, and after Jonas was born ... she tried to get her life back on track.'

'Do you know who the child's father is?'

Helle gazed at Emma for a while.

'It could be anyone,' she said, with a sad tone again. 'Not all of her customers...' she glanced at the next table '... liked to be careful.'

Emma understood what Helle was insinuating, and now formed a clearer and slightly different picture of Maria Normann.

'Jonas was her salvation in many ways. Or a way out, at least. But of course, with both feet firmly planted in addiction hell, it wasn't easy. She lived with me for a while. Jonas too. I tried my best to take care of her – of *them*. Without patting myself on the back too much, I think that period was probably pretty important to her. And then she reconnected with Oliver, and...'

Emma waited for her to go on. Helle grabbed her phone again with one swift movement. A message had arrived, which she quickly read and answered with lightning-fast thumbs. The partially broken screen made Emma think of Carmen.

Helle put the phone down.

'It went as expected,' she said. 'Pretty fast. As I said, everyone falls in love with Maria.' There was a note of bitterness in her voice. 'And for Maria, Oliver was the knight in shining armour himself, wasn't he; the one who came riding in to save her ... At least, that's how she saw it. *Completely* forgot that...' She looked away. 'Maria wasn't really a city girl, like me. She loved animals and nature. In Oliver, perhaps, she found something safe, something she had missed ... and cherished,' she added. 'It was nice that he gave her the opportunity to work and to learn something new, but ... it quickly turned into so much more. At least for him.'

'Are you saying that she wasn't in love with him?'

Helle Lindqvist snorted. 'If she was, she never said anything about it to me.'

Maybe she hadn't wanted to, Emma thought. The voice note Maria had sent to Oliver had an air of desperation to it – she had *wanted* him to come back. Emma considered whether she should mention the pregnancy to Helle, but concluded that she couldn't be sure that Helle even knew about it. And Emma didn't want to make her pain any worse.

'I was actually supposed to be with her that day.' Helle looked down again. 'But, as usual, she texted me and cancelled. Said she had to work. I knew what that meant.'

'What did that mean?'

Helle let out a short laugh. 'Well, that they'd be getting down to business, so to speak. Obviously. There was no good reason why she needed to go to work on a Sunday.'

Emma quickly glanced over at the neighbouring table. The elderly woman had taken out her phone and seemed engrossed in it.

Helle shook her head.

Emma used the moment's silence to check her own phone. There was another news alert from *VG Nett:*

Police confirm the discovery of another body in Leirsund.

Blix was right.

She was unsure how much further she wanted to push Helle Lindqvist, and was thinking about rounding off their conversation, when Helle suddenly said:

'Let me know if you'd like to get a glass of wine or something one evening. We can get to know each other a little better.'

Emma was taken aback by the remark, and by Helle's inviting smile.

'Oh,' Emma said. 'Yes. Uh, I will.' She thanked her a little sheepishly for having come to meet her, and started to move towards the exit.

Just then, a woman entered the café and shouted: 'Whose dog is that lying out here?'

Emma immediately raised her hand in the air. 'He's mine,' she said, worried. 'What is it?'

'It's just lying there,' the woman said, a look of panic on her face. 'It looks like it's...'

Emma hurried past her and out the door. Terry was lying on his side and staring straight ahead. In front of him: a pool of bloody vomit.

36

Afterwards, when Blix looked up at the ceiling of Tomine's bedroom and at the lamp emanating a faint yellow glow, Iselin appeared in his mind.

As a rule, she was always there in one way or another, but suddenly – as he felt Tomine's steady, soft breath against his chest – it was as if Iselin occupied everything. A brutal wave of pain and grief hit him in the diaphragm, and he had to push himself up and forward to catch his breath.

Tomine quickly pulled away, allowing him space.

Blix narrowed his eyes and put his hands in front of his face.

'What is it?' Tomine asked. There was concern in her voice.

Blix tried to swallow away the hard lump that had become lodged in his throat. 'Sorry,' he stammered. 'It's...'

He shook his head. He took a deep breath, but it was as if a sharp, icy object had pierced his lungs.

'Just ... give me a moment,' he added.

Tomine sat up next to him. Blix struggled to compose himself. When he was finally able to breathe normally again, he decided to tell her the truth. He couldn't bear pretending, not with Tomine. He knew that she was aware of what had happened to Iselin.

It only took a moment to explain. His voice cracked as he spoke his daughter's name, and he needed a few more seconds, afterwards, to collect himself.

Tomine placed a hand on his back. Stroked it carefully, slowly.

'Sorry,' Blix added, 'I didn't think something like that would happen ... *here*. Now.'

'Love,' she said tenderly, 'it's absolutely fine.'

He removed his hands from his face and turned to look at her. Her eyes were filled with tears.

'I often have ... episodes like this,' he said, 'but I'm usually alone.'

Tomine pulled him close. They remained half sitting, half lying down like that for a long time.

'I'm sure you must feel so much guilt about it,' she said after a while, still tenderly, softly.

Blix pushed himself up and looked at her.

'For allowing yourself to live a little, here, with me,' she added. 'For letting yourself enjoy a good ... moment. Your body is probably full of endorphins still, and you probably haven't felt that for a long time. Or, so I'd imagine.' She smiled.

Blix laughed. Felt how good it was to laugh, even just a little.

Tomine immediately became serious again.

'Your subconscious is probably telling you that it was wrong to feel that way. Like you're not *allowed* to feel anything good again.'

He let himself be captured by her brown eyes. He stared into them, the tiny hints of green.

'You haven't done anything wrong, Alexander,' she said. 'On the contrary.'

She took his hand.

'For once, maybe your heart was a little less broken, but you shouldn't feel guilty about that.'

Blix pulled her close again. Resting his head against her shoulder, he allowed himself to give space to Iselin again, completely. His tears flowed uninhibited, freely.

He missed her so much.

So terribly, so intensely.

※

Blix had no idea what time it was, but it had been dark outside Tomine's windows for a long while. He thought about her suggestion of staying the night, but as tempting as it was, it felt wrong to leave all the responsibility for Terry to Emma.

You should check your phone, he told himself, but he didn't want to move an inch from Tomine's bed.

His mind wandered.

Again, Iselin came to him, but slightly less painful this time.

'Skage Kleiven,' he said.

Tomine was lying on her back next to him, staring up at the ceiling.

'Does he have any contact with his daughter at all?' Blix asked.

'I don't think so,' Tomine said.

'Poor man. It can't be easy.'

Tomine didn't answer that.

'There was a period where he texted me quite a bit,' she said, 'wondering if I could help him with the custody case and stuff like that. He wanted me to vouch for him. But I couldn't, of course – I didn't know him.'

Blix turned to look at her. The duvet was large, and soft and comfortable.

'There was a year he wanted help delivering a Christmas present,' she continued. 'I agreed – it would have been heartbreaking, saying no.'

Blix waited for her to continue.

'It's just far too sad that the child's own father – regardless of what you might think about how capable he is or what else he's done in his life – can't have the opportunity to see his own child,' she said. 'Or at least to give his daughter a present on her birthday or Christmas.'

'I agree.'

'But, he never asked me again, so ... if he's continued to buy her gifts, then he must have had someone else help deliver them.'

Silence fell between the pillows. Blix thought of the brief meeting he had had with Skage Kleiven and Roger Kvande outside the police station. The animosity between them. The history.

'What impression do you have of Roger Kvande?' he asked.

The answer came without hesitation. 'The child-welfare guy? I don't like him.'

'What makes you say that?'

'I don't know really. I just have a bad feeling about him. I think he's a little ... creepy.'

'In what way?'

'I...' She thought about it. 'He was kind of, going after Elisabeth. Or rather ... I thought he showed a bit of an unhealthy interest. Was a bit too personal when he spoke to her, and ... I thought there was something a bit predatory about how he looked at ... well, us. At girls. Women. I'd like to see his internet history, put it that way.'

'You think he has abnormal tendencies?'

She gave a quick shrug. 'I don't know really. It's probably foolish of me to speculate. Especially to a policeman.'

She caught his eye and smiled. Blix liked that she still thought of him like that.

'I don't know about you,' she said, pushing herself up. 'But I'd really like to finish that glass of wine.'

'Mm, that sounds perfect.'

She smiled and slowly got out of bed.

'Would you mind grabbing my phone too?' Blix asked. 'It's in my jacket pocket.'

'I'll be right back.'

Blix lay his head on the pillow as he listened to the sounds of the apartment. Tomine's steps across the floor, the wine glass in the living room that clinked against something on the table.

It had been a long time since he had found himself in an unfamiliar bed like this. The light-green walls gave the room a warmth.

He liked being there. Enjoyed it very much, actually. And he liked *her*, liked everything about this new ... whatever it was and where it would lead them.

It took a couple of minutes before Tomine returned, still naked – the wine glasses in one hand and Blix's phone in the other. She leaned down towards him. He accepted the phone and his glass. Immediately saw that the display was full of messages and missed calls. Many of them from Emma.

'What now,' he said quietly to himself.

'Hm?' Tomine came around to the other side of the bed.

'Jesus Christ.'

Blix read the last message Emma had sent.

'What is it?'

Tomine put the wine glass down on the bedside table and climbed back under the covers. Blix stared vacantly ahead of him for a few seconds.

'I'm so sorry, Tomine,' he said, turning to her. 'But I have to go.'

37

Emma was lucky – there was a twenty-four-hour veterinary hospital in Nydalen. A vet was ready when she walked in with Terry in her arms.

'The owner is on his way,' Emma explained.

When Blix finally got there, Terry was still in the treatment room.

'How is he?' Blix asked.

'I don't know,' Emma said. She felt on the verge of tears.

'Where is he?'

Emma pointed to the room where the examination was taking place. Blix knocked, and didn't wait for an answer before pushing the door open.

Emma followed him inside. Terry was lying on a cushioned bench, his eyes blinking slowly.

'He's my dog,' Blix explained.

The vet nodded. 'Come sit by him,' he said, wheeling his chair over to the computer screen.

Blix pulled a visitor's chair up to the bench and lay a hand on Terry's back. Emma stood at the door.

'Do you know what he ate today?' the vet asked.

'Nothing out of the ordinary,' Blix replied. 'Just his usual plain kibble and water.'

'It looks like he's ingested something he couldn't tolerate. He has quite a high fever. As you can see, he's also tired and lethargic. With vomiting and diarrhoea on top of that ... classic symptoms of poisoning.'

Emma glanced over at Blix. She could see that his mind was racing.

'The fact that his body has gotten rid of some of it by itself is a good sign,' the vet continued. 'What we need to do now is see if we can get the rest out. If there's anything left, that is. I'm afraid you'll have to be here a while.'

'But he'll be okay?' Blix asked.

The vet gave him a sympathetic smile. 'I think there's a very good chance.'

The vet stood up.

'You two stay here with him. I'll be right back.'

He pushed his chair over to Emma, and she sat down next to Blix. Terry's breathing came in short gasps. Blix stroked his head gently. The dog closed his eyes. A clock ticked on the wall.

A few minutes passed without either of them saying anything.

'Earlier today,' Blix finally said, 'when I got home...' He shook his head. 'I didn't quite understand ... but it looked like Terry hadn't ... I mean, there was still food left in his bowl. And water. I thought I had...'

He stopped himself.

'What are you saying?' Emma said.

'It could be that Terry ... I saw him drink and eat it.'

'Oh my god...' Emma groaned and leaned back, her head resting against the wall.

At the same time, Blix's phone rang. Emma was sitting close enough to see that it said *ABELVIK* on the display.

'Put it on speakerphone,' she asked. 'I'll listen.'

Blix gave her a sidelong look.

'Come on, it's just us. And you're going to tell me what she says afterwards anyway.'

He hesitated a moment, answered and did as she asked.

'Hi Tine,' he said.

'Blix,' Abelvik replied. 'Hello.'

'Thanks for calling,' Blix said.

Emma could see that he hesitated momentarily, before saying: 'I'm at the vet's in Grünerløkka. Terry's taken a turn. The vet believes he has ingested poison.'

There was a moment of silence on the other end.

'Poison?'

'He hasn't had anything to eat or drink today other than what he's had at home,' Blix continued.

Emma nodded to confirm.

'Is he okay?' Abelvik asked.

'The vet thinks his chances are good, but ... Are forensics still in my apartment?'

'Yes, they're still there.'

'Tell them to check Terry's water bowl and his food. Send samples to toxicology.'

'I'll let them know. We'll look into it.'

'Thank you,' Blix said. 'Oh, one more thing...' He cleared his throat. 'I heard another body has been found in Leirsund?'

Emma heard Abelvik breathe hard into the phone.

'Correct.' She didn't say anything else.

'Is it someone from the list of missing women?'

'The person in question has not been identified,' Abelvik replied.

'Okay, is it a woman or a man?'

Abelvik hesitated.

'A woman,' she answered.

'Age?'

'An older woman. Over sixty, I would guess.'

'Is there anything that indicates how she was killed?'

'No. And Blix, that's not why—'

'Was she found far from Elisabeth Eie?'

Abelvik sighed. 'About a hundred metres. In terms of direction, it might match one of the crosses on the back of the photo you were sent.'

'So that means there's one cross left,' Blix said. 'In other words, another body to find.'

Abelvik waited a moment.

'We'll go out and continue the search when it's light again tomorrow. But I didn't call you to update you on that, Blix. I'm calling ... because of the fingerprints from the drawing on your fridge.'

'Yes?'

'We have a hit. But they don't belong to Elisabeth's daughter, Julie Eie.'

There goes that theory, Emma thought.

'Okay, so whose are they?' Blix asked.

Abelvik didn't answer immediately.

'The fingerprints belong to your daughter, Blix,' she said at last. 'They belong to Iselin.'

38

He saw her long before she saw him.

She staggered out of the toilet, her hands still wet. She finished drying them on her jeans and headed back to the bar. Leaned against the counter and grabbed hold of the beer glass as if it were a good, old friend.

A man stood beside her and spoke to her occasionally. It looked like he was the one paying. He was the one who ordered at least, but there was no caress or closeness to suggest that they knew each other well. Good, he thought; then maybe she wouldn't go home with him, but maybe something would develop. The night was still young.

Every so often, she would have to stumble back to the toilet or go outside for a smoke. As a rule, she never took more than four or five drags from the cigarette. Didn't want to lose her place at the bar.

He hated the smell of smoke.

It stuck to his clothes, to the walls. At home, the smell had been everywhere. It had almost become part of the furniture. It had been especially foul when it leaked from her mouth. When she stood over him, shouted at him.

Whenever he smelled cigarette smoke, he had to close his eyes and push the thoughts away, banish the memories. He had a lifetime's worth of them. It hadn't helped, all the talking about it, the trying to process it. Moving wouldn't have helped either. The memories were etched into him like a burn, like he'd been branded.

What he was doing now helped.

This was processing it.

He felt lighter, better. Revived. He should have done this a long time ago.

Planning. Accounting for every circumstance, attending to every detail. But now he was in the midst of it all – everything he started – those circumstances and details weren't the same. So now he just had to carry on, changing along the way, adapting, implementing. Completing. Blix was finally fully invested in this, as he had to be, but there was nothing to indicate that he *understood*. Not yet.

He had to do something.

More.

Which was exactly why he was right here, right now, with a beer on the table, even if it was mostly for show. The pub buzzed with voices and the sounds of one of the country's stadiums, from which some sports game was being broadcast. Doors opened, doors closed. People flooded in, and eventually trickled out. The room slowly emptied. She persevered, he'd give her that. The man next to her had left. She had finished off his glass too.

Seeing her start to put her jacket on, getting ready to go home, he went outside. It was late, but there was still a fair amount of traffic on the road.

He took out the pack of cigarettes and lit one, even though it made him want to vomit. He kept the lighter in his hand. Waited.

The door opened.

She stopped outside, as he had assumed she would. He took a drag and blew the smoke out quickly, so she wouldn't see that this was something he didn't usually do. She fumbled around with her handbag. Stumbled to the side momentarily. Her eyes were unfocused. Her eyelids moved slowly.

She struggled to get the purse latch open.

'Need a smoke?' he asked, and stepped closer. Smiled.

She looked up at him. Her eyes found him before the rest of her body followed suit. She needed a few seconds to focus. On him, and understanding what he said.

With untrained fingers he pried out a cigarette, about halfway through the pack. He held it up to her in an alluring motion. Took a few steps closer.

She grabbed hold of the cigarette. Took two attempts to put it between her lips.

'Thanks,' she said.

He lit the lighter, held it to her mouth. She leaned into the flame and inhaled deeply. Closed her eyes and exhaled slowly. This time she took the time to enjoy the moment. There was no glass to rush back to.

'Thank you,' she said again. She sounded sad, almost.

He didn't want to stand in the light of the streetlamp for too long, so he pulled back a little, closer to the wall.

'Heading home?' he asked.

She nodded. The movement made her sway.

'To your husband and kids?'

She snorted. Took another drag. Her eyes flickered disapprovingly at the cigarette, as if to see what brand it was.

'Come on, you can't say a woman like yourself doesn't have a kid or two,' he said, dropping his cigarette to the ground. He stepped on it and smiled at her.

She looked over at him. As if she were trying to figure him out. 'Have I seen you here before?' she asked.

'First time,' he said. 'I just moved here. I live on Bergstien.'

'Are you fucking with me?'

'No.'

'That's where *I* live.' She looked at him like she couldn't believe it.

'Then you can ride home with me.'

There it was. The moment. The first step. There was never any certainty that it would work. She could say no, could insist on walking. In the middle of Oslo, he wouldn't be able to do anything about it. He would have had to come up with something else. Adapt. Maybe find someone else. But she was the best option here.

She staggered a little again. 'You ... drove here?'

'Yeah, straight from work,' he said, knowing it was a poor lie. 'Had no beer in the fridge. New apartment and all that,' he went on, as if that explained it. 'Had to have a beer after a long day at work, didn't I? Sometimes you just have to, right?'

He wasn't sure if she was listening. She could barely keep her eyes open.

'Come,' he said. 'It's just a few minutes' drive. It's cold out too.'

She hesitated a moment, but eventually followed. He helped her across the street, as if she were an old lady. He talked as they went, in a light, jovial tone. He told her all about a job he didn't have, about an apartment that didn't exist, about how there were so many advantages to living in the big city. The lies came easily. Everything was so much easier when he didn't have to be himself. When he could be someone else, play a role. Pretend.

Back at the car, he unlocked it and looked around. Opened the door to the passenger side. No one seemed to take particular notice of them. They were just two people going somewhere, driving somewhere. Home. Away. To Leirsund, perhaps.

Once she had fastened her seat belt and he'd driven off, he said:

'It'll be good to get some sleep.'

She didn't answer. Just closed her eyes, slowly.

'Mattias may have fallen asleep by now.'

She blinked, a little faster.

'Or maybe not.'

She pushed herself up a touch. Turned her head towards him. He simply stared straight ahead at the road. Manoeuvred the car slowly and surely through the city streets. He could see in his peripheral vision that she was a lot more lucid now, but she hadn't yet realised that he had locked all the doors.

'Mattias,' she said. 'How...?'

'Oh, I heard you,' he replied. 'Talking about him, in the pub. You said to that guy standing next to you that the boy was home alone. Seemed like you were bragging about it, kinda.'

She didn't answer.

'How old is he? Eight? Nine?' He shook his head. 'And you just left him at home, alone, all evening.'

She gripped the seat belt with one hand as she looked out of the window at the apartment buildings passing by. The cars on the road, the lights coming towards her, piercing her eyes.

'Stop,' she said. 'I ... I want to get out. Stop the car.'

Her previously glazed eyes had suddenly become alert, sharp. The adrenaline had kicked in. Fear. And for a moment he thought of Elisabeth, who had had the same look on her face when she realised that he might be intending to do something to her. It was the look they all had.

'Please don't hurt me.'

He pushed his foot down on the accelerator and took one hand off the wheel. Tucked it into his jacket pocket as he thought about Blix's father. How frail he looked now. How easy it would have been to end his life too.

With trained movements he grabbed the anaesthetic pen he had ready. With one quick, precise stab, he thrust it into her thigh and pushed down. She screamed, just like the others. First out of shock, then fear and horror. She flung herself away, against the car door, flailing her arms. The screaming became more hysterical. She hit out at him, but the contents seemed to work quickly – it only took a few seconds before she lost both her strength and her voice. He yanked the needle out and dropped it into the footwell in front of her.

Her hands relaxed.

Her head hung limp against her chest.

He breathed more slowly.

It was going to be a nice drive.

39

Terry lay on a blanket next to Emma's spare bed. Blix carefully sat up and put his hand on Terry's back. His breathing was deep and heavy.

Slow movements, just rising and falling.

Normally, Terry would have been awakened by Blix's touch, but he was still asleep. The dog's body had been through a tough night. It would take a while before he would be back to normal. The fact that he was breathing and sleeping was the most important thing. They had plenty of time.

His phone was on the bedside table. Blix pulled it over to him. Tomine had sent him a message at 2:23am. Had wished him goodnight. That was all. Blix texted back, wishing her a good morning. Added that Terry seemed to be over the worst of it, but that they were going to take it slowly today. He promised to call after he had been to the police station. The meeting with Abelvik and the others was set to begin at 9:00am.

Blix let Terry sleep, and got up himself. It was unusual to wake up in a different apartment from his own. Not even half a day ago he had thought that maybe he would be getting up at Tomine's place. Big changes in a short amount of time, he thought, and headed into the kitchen, found a jar of instant coffee and put the kettle on.

Emma was up before the water had boiled.

'Good morning,' she said. 'I have a coffee maker, by the way.'

'Instant's fine for now, but thanks,' he said.

'Sleep well?'

'Yes,' he lied. 'You?'

'Kind of. But that's normal for me.'

The truth was that his mind had been racing throughout the night, about everything that had happened over the last few days. He had tried to figure out where the perpetrator could have obtained a drawing with Iselin's fingerprints on it. Whoever it was had obviously been in his flat several times, so the most likely thing, he had concluded, was that he himself had had a picture lying around at home. But where? There wouldn't have been any drawings in the drawers in her room, or in his. The next option was the communal attic, in one of the boxes he kept up there, even though he couldn't remember having ever put anything like that in them. If the perpetrator had a key to his apartment, it wasn't beyond the realms of possibility that he would have managed to get into the attic as well. Although you needed a different key to get in.

They ate a quick breakfast together, discussing Terry and Maria Normann. Emma wanted him to go over to Bull's Eye with her, to the scene of the fire.

'Why?' Blix asked.

'I'd like your opinion,' she said. 'You, as a policeman, have more training than I do in thinking like a perpetrator.'

Blix realised she had something specific in mind but didn't want to push her.

'I don't know how long they'll need me at the station,' he said. 'But maybe we can go for a walk after? Terry might need some fresh air by then.'

She smiled. 'I'll look after him until you're back.'

Blix swallowed some more coffee and got ready. Put his shoes on in the hallway. Terry came padding out of the bedroom, his tail between his legs. His movements were feeble.

Blix bent down and gave him a good fuss.

'I'll be back soon,' he said. 'Then we'll go for a walk.'

Terry licked his palms.

'Is it cold out today?' he asked Emma, standing up.

'It's supposed to be colder than yesterday, apparently,' Emma replied.

Blix grabbed the thick jacket he had brought from home. Put it on. Slid the keys into the pocket. He was about to put his phone inside the inner pocket, when he felt something else. An envelope.

His jacket had been hanging in his hallway at home, untouched, since the last time it was this cold, last winter. He had no memory of putting an envelope there.

He took it out.

There was something square inside.

His mind immediately went to the photograph he had received a few days ago. The Polaroid of Elisabeth Eie. The man who had later called him and said: '...you would have also seen the other pictures I've sent you.'

Emma came closer. There was a look of concern in her eyes.

Blix could tell that she understood that he hadn't left the envelope in there himself.

'Do you have tweezers or something like that?' he asked. 'And some disposable gloves, maybe?'

'Give me a minute, I'll check.'

Emma disappeared into the bathroom. She was back a few moments later with tweezers. Blix held them in his right hand, the envelope in his left. He carefully pried open the flap – it hadn't been glued down – and gripped the edge of what was obviously a photograph.

'I'll need to put this down somewhere,' he said.

'The kitchen table,' Emma replied.

Blix followed her. 'Do you have any baking paper or similar?'

Emma found a paper bag and placed it flat on the kitchen table.

Blix pulled the picture out completely.

And gasped.

He couldn't stop his hand from shaking as he lay the photo down.

It was an old photograph of a teenager with short, messy hair. The boy was standing in a garden in front of a swing. In his hand: a Norwegian flag.

'Who is it?' Emma asked.

Blix didn't answer, just stared down at the shy boy.

'It's ... me,' he said.

He remembered the moment the photo had been taken.

He remembered who had taken it too.

'You?' Emma gaped. 'But ... why is that picture in your jacket pocket?'

Blix had no idea. But it seemed obvious that the perpetrator must have put it there during one of his visits to his apartment. And for a reason. But the more important question, it struck him now, was how the perpetrator had got hold of the photo in the first place. Blix knew that he'd never had that photo in his own home

Which meant it could've been taken from one of two people.

Merete being one of them. That was assuming she'd come across it at some point in their married life. The other option, Blix thought and swallowed hard, was that it must have been taken from his father's house.

40

'You do realise that this is not a sane person?' Blix looked at Abelvik first, then at Walenius, then back to Abelvik again.

She picked up the picture, turned it over, looked at the back. Blix had already checked – there were no crosses or other markings on it.

Walenius was the first to sit down. He pulled his bottle of water towards him and unscrewed the cap. 'What do you think he's looking to achieve with this?' he asked, taking a sip and leaning back casually.

'I don't know,' Blix replied. 'It has to make sense in his head somehow.'

'Photos and drawings that keep on popping up around you,' Walenius continued. 'It all brings you right back into the middle of the action, doesn't it?'

He said it as if Blix were enjoying what was happening around him, almost insinuating that Blix was looking for attention.

Abelvik put the picture back onto the table. The unaddressed envelope was in a separate transparent bag next to it.

'Where could he have got it?' she asked, sitting down.

Blix threw his hands out and shrugged before sitting down as well.

'It is, as I said, Iselin's hand on the drawing from your fridge,' Abelvik went on. 'The forensic technicians found a print from each finger. They matched prints that were taken from her case.'

Blix nodded.

'Which gives us reason to believe that the child's drawing found on Elisabeth Eie's body could also be Iselin's, since it had your fingerprints on it.'

Blix understood their thinking and muttered a reply that they were probably right, but he had no explanation as to where the drawings could have come from.

'Have you finished in the apartment?' he asked.

'Not quite,' Abelvik answered. 'We'll need it for another day, I think. Are you doing okay?'

Blix nodded.

'Where are you staying?' Walenius asked.

'At Emma Ramm's,' Blix replied, his mind still focused on the child's drawings. Merete had kept more from Iselin's childhood than he had. Following the divorce, their daughter had lived with her.

Walenius leaned forward a little. 'Have you had problems with vermin?' he asked.

'What do you mean?'

'Vermin, like mice or rats?'

'No.'

'Never?'

Blix shook his head. 'Why do you ask?'

'The technicians found a box of rat poison in the cabinet under your sink.'

'Rat poison? What are you...'

'We're testing the water in Terry's bowl and his food,' Abelvik interjected. 'But as your vet said, his symptoms seem consistent with poison.'

Blix shook his head. 'It's not mine,' he said.

'A box of old-fashioned rat poison,' Walenius explained. 'It was old and almost empty. Placed right at the back, by the drain pipe.'

Blix shook his head. 'I've never bought or used rat poison,' he said.

Walenius made a note of something and flipped back and forth in the notepad on his lap.

'You're seeing a psychologist, is that right?' he asked.

The room was silent. Blix opened his mouth, but couldn't say anything. Walenius checked his notes again. 'Krissander Dokken, correct?'

Blix's mouth went dry. He could feel the heat of his forehead. 'What the hell does that have to do with anything?' he asked.

'It's only natural to ask why you might be seeing him,' Walenius continued. 'You are of course free to answer, or not, if you so wish.'

Blix had to control himself.

'You know what I've been through,' he said and looked over at Abelvik. 'It's a rehabilitation scheme provided by NAV.'

Walenius made a movement with his head that was probably supposed to give the impression that he understood.

'Have you had any delusions after everything you've been through?' he asked.

'What the fuck is this?' Blix snapped. 'Do you think I made all this up?'

It was impossible to read Walenius's face.

'You have lived a policeman's life in the centre of it all,' he said calmly. 'You have been through traumatising events and then, suddenly, it all stops. This is the kind of thing that can create dramatic personality disorders—'

Abelvik interrupted her colleague. 'That'll do,' she said sharply.

Blix had already stood up.

'The damn...' was all he could force out.

'This whole case started with you and it continues with you, after you were acquitted and released,' Walenius said. 'It raises some questions that need to be answered.'

Blix reached for his head. 'Do you think I made up those corpses in Leirsund too?' he seethed. 'Or ... do you think *I* killed them?'

Walenius didn't answer.

Blix turned and walked towards the door.

He heard Abelvik get up: 'I'll escort him out.'

Blix had already gone some distance down the hall when she called out and told him to wait.

He stopped and turned around. 'What the hell was that?' he asked, pointing towards the meeting room. 'Some disturbed lunatic has killed several people. And yeah, it has something to do with me, but I'm not the bloody...'

He stopped himself.

'I'm sorry,' Abelvik said. 'Walenius ... he's missing some antennae.'

Blix strode over to the lift. Abelvik followed him in.

'Who did you find at Leirsund?' he asked after the doors slid closed.

Abelvik hesitated.

'The name will be released later today,' she said. The lift started its descent. 'So keep it to yourself until further notice: Lina Marie Jansen. She was sixty-eight when she disappeared.'

'How long ago was that?'

'Three years, approximately.'

Blix repeated the name to himself. There was something familiar about it, but she wasn't on the list of missing women he had compiled.

'It was the Innlandet police's case,' Abelvik clarified.

That explained why Blix hadn't included her.

The lift doors opened. They stepped out.

'Whereabouts in Innlandet was she from?' he asked.

'Gjøvik,' Abelvik answered. 'She was a retired psychologist.'

'Any relation to Elisabeth Eie?'

Abelvik shook her head and let them out through the security barriers. 'Nothing that would indicate that thus far,' she said in a low voice.

'Any clues at the burial site?'

Abelvik didn't answer.

'We'll need to take your jacket,' she said, pointing to it.

Blix peered out at the overcast sky outside.

'Because of the picture,' Abelvik added. 'The forensics will need to have a look at it.'

Blix started to take it off.

'No, that's okay, I'll come with you to the car,' Abelvik said. 'Then you won't freeze.'

They walked around the block in silence.

'Did you find anything on the body?' Blix asked again when they got to the car.

Abelvik hesitated.

'A drawing,' she finally answered.

Blix lifted his hand and ran it through his hair.

'We haven't found any fingerprints on it yet.'

'What was the drawing of this time?'

'A small child, hand in hand with an adult. Obviously drawn by a child again.'

A typical motif a child would draw, Blix thought. He pulled his jacket off. Abelvik took it. It seemed like she was considering whether or not to say something.

'What is it?' Blix asked.

'I'm worried...' Abelvik began. 'About this whole situation, about what we can expect.'

'You and me both,' Blix said, opening the car door.

'I've asked that all new missing-persons cases be reported to us,' Abelvik continued, but paused momentarily before finishing: 'And it's not certain that there is anything. But...'

'What?' Blix asked. He immediately felt the chill without his jacket on.

'An alert came in this morning,' Abelvik explained. 'A thirty-two-year-old woman who has an eight-year-old son. When the boy woke up this morning, she wasn't at home. The neighbour reported it.'

'Where?' Blix asked.

'Here in Oslo,' Abelvik replied.

'Any connection to Elisabeth Eie or the psychologist from Gjøvik?'

'Doesn't seem like it, but we're working on it as we speak,' she answered. 'What we do know is that her name is Turid Nyjordet. She receives disability benefit.'

Blix felt his stomach clench. The woman from the shop. The one who hadn't had enough money. He opened his mouth to tell Abelvik about her, but held back, afraid of further inflaming Walenius's suspicions.

'When was she last seen?' he asked instead.

'The neighbour said that they had seen her going out at about nine o'clock last night,' Abelvik answered. 'The boy doesn't know about any of that. He's in care for the time being.'

Blix swallowed. That was only a few hours after he had seen her at the shop. He had been lying in Tomine Eie's bed at the time. And then at the vet's.

'Be careful,' Abelvik told him, turning away. 'And call me if anything happens.'

Blix stayed where he was and watched her walk away before getting into the car.

41

Emma realised straight away that something must have happened.

Something *else*.

Blix had been pale and short of breath when he entered the hallway. The words that had come out of him made no sense.

She understood that the police had launched an investigation into a new missing-persons case, but it had taken a minute for Emma to realise that Blix had actually met the missing woman at the shop the day before.

He shook his head.

'It could be a coincidence, of course,' he continued. 'The fact that her ... that she's the one who's gone missing now. And it doesn't mean that anything might have happened to her ... she could turn up at any time. But ... what if she *doesn't*?' He looked at her. 'What if she's been taken too? By the same man?'

'You think he saw you interacting with her? And *that's* why—?'

'I mean, I think he's been following me ... everywhere,' Blix said. 'It wouldn't be that odd if he had seen all that yesterday too.'

'But why would he take her specifically? You're not connected to her in any way, are you?'

Blix thought about it.

'I don't know.'

'But if that is the case,' Emma continued, 'that he's still following you, or saw you there ... then that means he might know you're here too. Now. With me.'

The seriousness of what she just said seemed to dawn on Blix as well.

'I ... didn't think of that,' he said. 'That by coming here, I've potentially directed his attention onto you too. I've put you in danger, just by being here.'

Emma gave him a brief smile. 'Well I'm used to that,' she said, winking at him. 'It'll probably come to nothing. You're here now anyway. And so's Terry.'

She turned to the dog, who slowly stood up. Only now did he seem to realise Blix had come back. Which made the dog pick up speed. Blix bent down and stroked him a while.

'Let's take that trip you talked about,' he said. 'To the scene of the fire by Lake Gjersjøen. I need to think about something else. And Terry may need a bit of a walk.'

'Fine. But you need something warm to wear,' she said. 'Wait there.'

She went into the bedroom and found a roomy, high-necked woollen jumper. Blix pulled it over his head. It was a bit tight, but it would at least keep the autumn chill at bay.

It was overcast, but the clouds had settled low in the sky. Blix looked both ways before they walked to Emma's car. Emma turned twice herself before they climbed in.

As they drove out of town, Blix updated her on the latest discovery at Leirsund.

'I'm not meant to say anything,' he began, 'but her name is Lina Marie Jansen. Retired, former psychologist. I can't see any common denominators between her and Elisabeth Eie. Nothing obvious at least. They're far apart in age. Didn't come from the same place.'

'Where was Lina Marie Jansen from, did you say?'

'Gjøvik.'

Emma glanced sideways at him. 'Gjøvik ... is not that far from Skreia, where you grew up.'

'Yes. I'm aware.'

'You ... don't think that's important?'

'I don't know. I'm not the only person from Gjøvik. It's a big place.'

'But given that you seem to be at the centre of all this,' Emma continued, 'Lina Marie Jansen must also be about you, don't you think?'

Blix thought it through.

'I really don't know,' he said finally. 'I've no idea.'

For the last stretch, they were stuck behind a cluster of competitive cyclists, who kept up a good pace. The group continued south on Gamle Mossevei, while Emma turned off and parked in the same place as last time – just outside the remains of Oliver Krogh's hunting and fishing business. Terry was a little more difficult to get out of the car than usual, but once he was attached to his lead, he immediately started pulling and sniffing everything he could.

Blix encouraged him over towards the ruins of the shop.

'What I've been thinking about,' Emma began, 'is how Maria Normann might have been transported away from here and where she might have been dumped. That's if we're assuming she's dead, of course. Either way, we know that she left a voice message for Oliver Krogh at 2:38pm, and that the fire alarm went off twenty-four minutes later. A little over twenty minutes is not a lot of time to kill someone, hide them somewhere and then set the whole place on fire, regardless of the order in which those things happened. At least not if you have time to drive as far as Oliver Krogh did. But that's what the police believe happened here.'

Blix nodded.

'Okay, so, if we're *here* and we don't have much time, but we have to dispose of a corpse. Where would we do it?'

Blix looked around.

'There's the forest over there, of course. And then we have the lake. But we've already searched in there,' he said. 'I mean, *they* have. The police.'

'Yes, but they can't have ... Hang on, come with me.'

Emma led him onto the path down to the water. She remembered the eerie feeling she had felt the last time she was there. As if someone has been staring at her, watching her. Even though it was broad daylight, she was glad to have Blix and Terry there.

It only took a couple of minutes and they were down at the water's edge. A cold wind howled across the lake.

'What do you reckon,' she asked, 'if you're trying to think like a suspect? This is the fastest way to the water, but it's not particularly deep from here. There isn't much in the way of a current either. I've checked.'

Blix gazed out over the surface of the lake, looked around.

'With a boat, you can get pretty far out, and quickly,' he said. 'But it wouldn't be easy to dock here, especially if you're alone.' He pointed to the area closest to the water's edge, where the reeds were thick. 'But that may have been how the perpetrator got away, of course.'

Emma smiled.

Blix noticed. 'What is it?'

'You said "perpetrator." Not "Oliver Krogh".'

Blix thought about it.

'I've been spending too much time with you.'

They smiled at each other.

'This way,' she said, leading them away from the wider path onto a narrower one that cut through tall thickets and bushes. A few minutes later they were out in a clearing. Pulled quite far up on land, poking out from behind a tree, was the red canoe Emma had seen the last time she was there. It didn't look like anyone had moved it. It was still lying as it was, with the keel facing up.

She said nothing until Blix spotted it. She noticed a pensive look cross his face.

'A lot seems to indicate that the police are locked into the idea that Maria Normann was taken away in Oliver's car,' she said. 'Even though they *say* that they've looked for alternative transport options, I doubt they actually have. When they realised that Oliver had lied in his explanation, they put the blinkers on and bet everything they had on finding clues that matched their suspicions.'

Blix moved toward the canoe. Lifted it slightly.

'It's very light,' he said. 'It wouldn't be difficult to pull this down to the water.'

He turned. There was a small opening towards the shore of the lake.

'Or out of it, for that matter.'

'I saw an ad for canoes and canoe trolleys on the Bull's Eye website,' said Emma. 'This one looks pretty new.'

'You think it's from the shop?' he asked, walking around the other side of it.

'I mean, it could come from anywhere,' she said. 'But Oliver Krogh sold these canoes, and the shop is, after all, just a stone's throw away. It was probably quite easy to get hold of one of these inside the shop as well. Then with the trolley, it'd be fairly easy to transport something that weighs quite a lot. A human body, for example.'

'Which would be hidden from most people in a canoe,' Blix commented. 'That's a good thought.'

She felt herself swell with pride.

'But if that is the case,' he said, 'why didn't the perpetrator get rid of the canoe afterwards? Why just leave it here?'

'Isn't that quite common?' Emma asked. 'Canoeists just leaving their canoes lying along the water? If you spend a lot of time on the lake, I mean?'

'Don't ask me,' Blix said. 'I have no idea. But the time aspect is important here. Right after the murder, a canoe isn't the easiest thing in the world to get rid of. So if it *is* commonplace to leave a canoe lying on the bank, then I guess it wouldn't necessarily be something you think twice about if you saw it.'

He thought a moment longer.

'Help me turn it over,' he said. 'Hold on to the very tip of it, if you can. Avoid touching it too much, although any fingerprints on the outside will have been washed away by now.'

She followed his instructions. Just like last time, the canoe was empty.

'I wonder where the oar has got to,' she said.

'Again,' Blix replied. 'I have no idea what canoeists usually do. Maybe that's how they prevent people from stealing them? By taking the oar with them.'

Emma wasn't convinced.

'You mentioned the amount of time,' Blix said. 'That no one could kill someone, wheel them out here, paddle out into the water, dump them, and then go back to set the building on fire, all in a little over twenty minutes.'

'Unless the body was dumped *after* the person set the shop on fire,' Emma suggested. 'He killed Maria first and put her in the canoe so she was ready to wheel out. He then set the fire and transported her down here after. Paddled out while the firemen and police did their thing. And, at that point in time, they weren't thinking about looking for someone. The perpetrator could have come back again later, pulled up the canoe and walked off that way,' she said, pointing to the path that continued along the water. 'That might actually be perfect.'

Blix agreed.

He studied the canoe.

'If I were to place a body in here,' he said. 'I would put it *under* the seats. That way you wouldn't risk the body falling out. There would have been no risk of an arm or leg dangling out either.'

Blix bent down and looked even closer at the canoe.

'But that means that you would expect to see some blood,' he said. 'Contamination. Even if he had time to wrap her up. And this canoe seems to be squeaky clean.'

He tried to look under the seats, but it wasn't easy. As if on a whim, he took out his phone. Emma couldn't see his screen, but understood immediately – Blix leaned into the canoe, careful about where he put his hands, and turned the phone in his hand so he could photograph the underside of the bar. He moved his hand along the side of the boat as he continued to take pictures. Did exactly the same all the way down.

Finally, he seemed satisfied. He stood up and opened his camera roll. Emma stood beside him to watch.

The first picture was grainy.

The second – a little better. All they could see was a dark surface. Blix tried to zoom in, but Emma couldn't see anything abnormal.

'What are you looking for?' Emma asked.

Blix didn't answer, just continued to scroll through the pictures he had taken.

Then stopped.

Zoomed in on what looked like a dark spot.

'This,' he said, turning the screen towards her. 'This is what I was looking for. If you're going to wash a boat or a canoe,' he explained, 'it's easy to forget that clothes and bodies can end up in places you wouldn't expect. That could be blood,' he said eagerly, pointing.

They looked at each other.

'We have to call Nicolai Wibe,' Emma said. 'Get them to come and test it themselves.'

42

He dreaded growing old.

In many ways it was like becoming a child again – unable to take care of yourself. This was life for the residents of Furulia.

It was a sad sight.

Maybe he should go to Switzerland, he thought as he strolled through the main entrance, whenever he realised his life was coming to an end.

Euthanasia.

Assisted dying.

One fatal injection, and then sit back and let the long sleep take you. Avoid being humiliated on life's home stretch, alongside people you don't know, people who are more or less left to themselves and their thoughts, their memories, just like you. It was much better to just get it over and done with, on your own terms.

The busiest time at the nursing home was in the morning, when the residents needed help getting washed, dressed, being given their breakfast and medicine. Now, after lunch, the care duties were more as and when. The carers didn't necessarily have to be available all the time. The residents were mostly left to their own devices while the staff retreated to the staff room and used the time for administrative tasks.

Gjermund Blix was in the TV room.

One of the other patients was also there. Her gaze was apathetic, as if she had entered a trance.

'Hello, Gjermund.'

He jumped. It wasn't ideal, having the TV up so loud – it meant the staff had to shout to get anyone's attention.

Gjermund looked up at him blankly, lost in a haze of confusion. No sign of recognition.

'How are you today?'

Gjermund said nothing, just shifted his gaze back to the TV – an old British series that looked straight out of the seventies.

'Shall we go for a drive?'

The question made Gjermund turn to look at him again.

'We can take a trip to the cemetery. Visit Elinor's grave.'

Gjermund blinked a few times. 'Elinor,' he said. His gaze had suddenly become more alert.

As with Turid Nyjordet, there was a certain risk associated with such a pointed question. That was the decisive, the essential moment. And it was something that the patient next to him might just notice, might remember for later too. Or one of the other staff might overhear.

The thought of Elinor seemed to make Gjermund restless. He got up and muttered something about having to go home.

'I can drive you. It's a nice day for a drive. It'll be especially nice in the cemetery today, too.'

For a moment Gjermund stood as if in shock. He reached out one hand, as if he needed something to lean on, something to ground him in reality, but ended up clinging to the back of the chair.

'You don't need a jacket. It's nice and warm outside.' That wasn't true, but Gjermund wouldn't remember that. It was more important that they avoid suspicion just now. If Gjermund was wearing a jacket, someone might think he was going somewhere.

But there was still a lot that could go wrong. They could be seen; they could be stopped. Gjermund could expose them – he could tell passersby that he was going home, that he was going to see Elinor, that they were just going for a ride.

That is why he stayed a few metres behind, but made sure that Gjermund found the lift and got into it. So far so good.

Downstairs, he let Gjermund leave first. He followed close behind, but at a good distance, ready to retreat if someone called out for the old man. If it didn't work this time, he thought, maybe it could work another day. He wasn't in a rush.

43

They got back into the car to wait for Nicolai Wibe. He had estimated that he would be there within the hour.

Blix lifted Terry into the back seat and was about to climb into the front himself. But Emma had walked back over to the ruins and was now beckoning him over.

The yellow-and-black police tape flapped in the wind. Grasping it with one hand, Emma lifted it up and crouched underneath. Blix remained on the other side. A few steps in was an area covered with a thick plastic sheet. Presumably what the crime-scene technicians thought was the actual crime scene.

'Looks like there was a back door here,' Emma said, pointing.

She took a few steps further in, accidentally stepped on something loose beneath the rubble and had to lean against a blackened wall.

'Be careful,' Blix warned her. 'There's a reason why the barricades are still here.'

'Come look at this,' Emma replied.

Blix glanced back at the road before ducking under the tape himself. The charred remains of the building crunched beneath his feet as he made his way over to her.

'I think this used to be the part of the shop where the canoes were kept,' she said, pointing.

Blix nodded in agreement. Hard, melted plastic covered the ground around them. Red and green lumps from what might have been canoes or kayaks.

Emma lifted up some twisted metal bars. 'This could be from one of the trolleys advertised on the website,' she said.

Blix nodded again, turned and looked towards the edge of the forest. It was a short distance from this part of the shop to the back door and then on to Lake Gjersjøen.

'Do you think the technicians could find out how many canoes would've been here?' Emma asked. 'Or trolleys, for that matter?'

'Shouldn't be a problem,' Blix replied, looking around again. 'The fire doesn't seem to have totally obliterated everything.'

'If he has data from the shop saved on a server, they could always check the inventory and see if a red canoe is missing?' Emma suggested.

Blix smiled. He allowed himself to be impressed by her creative thinking, but didn't say anything. His phone vibrated in his pocket. He pulled it out. Merete was calling, rather than replying to the message he had sent her about Iselin's old drawings. He walked a few steps away from Emma, heading back to the car. He felt a little uncomfortable talking to Merete, after what had happened with Tomine. Felt like he had been unfaithful, despite the fact his relationship with Merete had been over for years.

'Don't you have any drawings yourself?' she asked.

Blix climbed in behind the wheel.

'No.'

'I have a few in a box in the attic,' Merete continued. 'You're welcome to come by and go through them.'

Blix thanked her.

'And none of them have gone astray?' he asked.

'Gone astray?' Merete repeated. 'What do you mean?'

'Could any of her drawings be kept elsewhere?'

It didn't seem like Merete had understood what he meant.

'It's been many years since she did that sort of thing,' she began. 'She drew a lot back in kindergarten and at school, but she didn't bring everything home with her. But I doubt anyone cared that much to keep them. My parents may have saved the ones they received. I can't speak for Gjermund though.'

'For ... my father?' Blix asked.

Merete hesitated.

'Yes, we sent some to him,' she said. 'Iselin and me. On his birthday and Christmas and the like.'

It disturbed him, the thought that Iselin's drawings may have been taken out of his father's house.

'What kind of drawings?' he asked. 'Do you remember?'

'It's been so long,' she replied. Then changed tact: 'Can't you ask him yourself? Maybe he did save them.'

Blix let his gaze move to Emma, who was still walking around inside the ruins.

'Why do you ask?' Merete continued. 'Is there a particular drawing you have in mind? One you're looking for? I can go up to the attic and have a look for you.'

'No need,' Blix replied. 'I'll come by myself soon and explain.'

'That'd be nice,' Merete replied. He could hear the smile in her voice as she said it, hear that she meant it.

'Great,' he said.

Movement in the rearview mirror made him turn around. An unmarked patrol car swung onto the car park.

'I've got to go,' he said, glad they could end the conversation on a positive note.

Blix pushed open the car door and noticed that Emma had appeared back on the other side of the barrier. Terry sat up in his seat. Blix told him to stay and went to greet Nicolai Wibe. He had an older woman from forensics with him who seemed concerned at the sight of Blix.

'We're heading in that way,' Blix explained, pointing to the path.

No one said anything as they walked.

'Oliver Krogh sold canoes like this in his shop,' Emma said when they arrived.

Wibe nodded, but seemed sceptical.

'Where did you find the blood?' he asked, glancing over at Blix.

'I don't know if it is blood,' Blix clarified before pointing to the spot under one of the seats.

'We'll get an answer to that soon,' the technician replied.

She knelt down and opened the small plastic briefcase she had carried through the forest with her.

'Can you tip it onto its side?' she asked.

Blix and Wibe grabbed each end of the canoe and vaulted it towards her, making it easier for her to reach the spot. She used a spray bottle and squirted a chemical compound under the seat. She then soaked a strip of paper in the solution and held it up for the others to see. The moist part of the strip took on a clear green tinge.

'Human blood,' the technician confirmed.

Blix exchanged glances with Emma.

'I'll take some samples with me for DNA analysis,' the technician continued, looking at Wibe. 'Then you can send someone to bring in the canoe.'

Wibe nodded and looked out over the grey lake. Blix could tell that this discovery was making him rethink the case. The fact that Maria Normann's body might not have been driven away somewhere, but rather, taken out into the lake.

'There's a wide cove right around the headland there,' Emma said, pointing. She stood with her phone in her hand, looking down at a map. 'It's over fifty metres at its deepest, and completely out of sight from any roads or buildings.'

'You'll have to conduct a new underwater search,' Blix said.

Wibe still didn't say anything. The technician cut out part of the seat cover and put it in a labelled bag.

The wind rustled through the trees around them.

The slightly tense atmosphere was broken by Blix's phone. He felt a pang of fear in his chest when he saw that it was the nursing home in Gjøvik.

'Hello?' he answered. 'Alexander Blix speaking.'

'This is Petter Thaulow from Furulia nursing home,' the man on the other end began. 'It concerns your father.'

'Has something happened?'

Thaulow hesitated.

'He's not on the ward,' he replied. 'Doesn't seem to be here at all, actually. We wanted to speak to you before contacting the police ... You haven't heard from him or anything, have you?'

Blix swallowed and looked over at Emma.

'How long has he been gone?' he asked.

'It's probably been a few hours,' Thaulow replied.

'Then you have to notify the police,' Blix said.

He started walking back to the car.

'Now,' he insisted, trying to keep his voice steady.

44

The narrow road meandered through the forest. Emma kept a firm grip on the steering wheel, glad the road was dry. A quick glance at the dashboard revealed that she was driving well over the speed limit.

Blix sat in the seat beside her, the phone to his ear. He couldn't get through to the nursing home. The local sheriff's office had several patrols out searching. They had also posted a message on Twitter, but so far no one had seen a man who matched the description of Gjermund Blix.

'Shit,' Blix cursed, and hung up.

They drove on in silence. Emma could see that Blix was tired. His cheeks were red and he had deep bags under his eyes. His gaze was nevertheless focused, as if he were calculating something. There was a fear in his expression that made Emma think of Iselin.

'He's wandered out alone before, hasn't he?'

Blix barely turned his head. 'Yes,' he answered quietly.

'So he might have done it again, now,' Emma suggested.

He didn't seem convinced.

They emerged out onto a wider road, so Emma could put her foot down. She thought of Lake Gjersjøen, of the police. It would take time before the blood sample would be conclusively analysed. The divers wouldn't be there to start their work for a while either. And Gjersjøen was big.

The police had done a poor job last time. The searches had been carried out on the assumption that Maria Normann was likely to have been dumped from the edge of the water, because Oliver Krogh wouldn't have had time to do anything else. And it was assumed that the body could not have drifted far from the bank. In a canoe, however, it would be easy for the perpetrator to row further out. If, on top of that, he had planned the whole thing, it was not improbable that he had scouted out a suitable place to dump her in advance.

Emma felt unusually excited.

It was to her credit that the police now had to carry out the new search. It gave new hope to Maria's mother, and to the rest of the family, that she would be found.

They drove over the Arteid bridge. It wasn't until they were approaching Kløfta that Blix said:

'That picture that was in my jacket – it couldn't have been kept anywhere but at my father's house.'

'Do you think...?'

He shook his head. 'My father has nothing to do with this. Other than as a way to get to me. But he may still know something. He may know who has been to the house, for example – he might have had some home nurses or the like go in before he ended up in the nursing home.'

'We can't be sure that he will remember that,' Emma commented. 'Or that he'll be so easy to communicate with, for that matter.'

'I know. And we have to find him first.'

Emma flew past an airport bus.

'Was there anything special about that particular picture?' she asked.

'What do you mean?'

'There have to be plenty of photos of you from your childhood,' she explained. 'But that picture ... looked like a celebration or something?'

'Constitution Day,' he said. 'And I'd just turned thirteen.'

They passed the exit to Jessheim, continuing north.

'My mum took that picture. Insisted on me wearing that exact outfit. I wanted to wear something else, but Mum ... refused. I remember thinking I looked stupid.'

He looked away. Didn't say anything for a long time. Emma didn't push him.

'Thirteen,' he said. 'I didn't care about Constitution Day back then. Didn't even know what we were celebrating. All I remember was the hot dogs and games at school. That's all I cared about. That and the ice cream.'

'Same here,' Emma said, smiling. 'I was allowed as many ice creams as I wanted. My record was seven, I think.'

Blix shook his head. 'I didn't like parties.'

'Why not?'

He waited a moment. 'Because ... it meant a lot of drinking at home. And if there was drinking, then there'd be arguing. It was only a matter of time. And they never considered taking their rows elsewhere, away from me.'

They approached the exit to Dal and Råholt.

'It ... can't have been comfortable.'

Blix didn't answer.

'You were thirteen, you said? In the picture?'

'Yes.'

'So ... was your mother already ill by then?'

He twisted slightly in his seat to face her. 'What do you mean?'

'You said before that she died when you were sixteen. Some people end up living with cancer for quite a while before they ... die.'

Blix stared down into his lap. Pretended to be preoccupied with the phone.

'Sorry,' Emma said. 'I didn't mean to dig—'

'She was sick long before that,' Blix said. 'But it wasn't just cancer.'

Emma looked at him and was about to ask what he meant, when Blix suddenly sat up in the seat.

'What is it?'

He said nothing, just stared ahead. His eyes were wide open.

'I've just remembered where I know the name Lina Marie Jansen from,' he said.

'The psychologist from Gjøvik?'

'Yes.'

He continued staring out of the front window.

'Where?' Emma asked.

Blix didn't answer.

The next moment his phone rang. Emma saw an unsaved number come up on his screen, but he answered anyway and put it on loud-speaker.

'Blix speaking.'

'Hi, I'm calling from the Lena sheriff's office,' the voice said. 'We've found your father.'

Emma eased her foot off the accelerator slightly.

'He is sitting in bed at home.'

'Oh? How did he get there?'

'He says he was driven there.'

'Okay ... driven by whom?'

'We haven't been able to figure that out yet.'

Blix's forehead had creased into deep wrinkles.

'But he's okay? He's not injured at all?'

'He doesn't seem to be.'

Blix looked over at Emma.

'Okay,' he said. 'We're on our way.'

45

Tall, slender tree trunks flickered by on either side of the car. Blix was glad Emma was the one driving. His mind raced, each thought immediately replacing the one before.

It was afternoon by the time they arrived. The cloud cover had split into different layers and colours. Emma's car had been nice and warm, but as soon as they got out, the autumn chill crept in.

A dirty police car with a dent on the front fender was parked outside the house. One of his father's old neighbours was watching what was going on from their kitchen window. A young couple in gym clothes had stopped. The man appeared to be filming on his phone.

A uniformed officer met Blix on the stairs.

'Where is he?' Blix asked.

'In the bedroom,' the officer replied. 'He refuses to come down.'

Blix was about to enter, but could not bring himself to lift his foot over the threshold.

Looking inside, everything was as it always had been in his father's old home. The doors and windows were the same, the floor in the hall, the hooks on the wall. It even smelled the same: a whiff of old, roast coffee. Tobacco. Textiles in need of a wash. The smells of his childhood immediately released a flood of memories: his mother cooking, the dinner table around which few words were exchanged, his father forcing him to eat, regardless of what was on the plate. They couldn't afford to throw food away, shame on you, think of the children in Africa.

The hours spent in his childhood bedroom, where he had to stay. Where he had to be quiet too, he couldn't disturb them, because his father was tired, and his mother was ill. If he played music, he had to do it through his headphones – small, uncomfortable ones that scratched against the thin skin of his ears. Always had to go to bed at nine o'clock. It wasn't until he became a teenager that he was most graciously allowed to stay up an hour longer. And then he always had to drink a glass of warm milk before bed – it was something his mother had seen on TV, and she always spoke in such a soft voice when she explained how good this was for him.

There was no point saying that he thought it tasted a bit strange, or that he didn't even want it, that he couldn't finish it all. Because then she would get angry and sad, because milk was expensive, and so was the honey she had put in it.

Blix forced his legs to move, one after the other. Nodded to an investigator he had met before but whose name he couldn't remember. There was sympathy in the man's eyes. Compassion.

Blix noticed the empty shoe rack in the hallway. His father could, of course, have walked straight in without taking his shoes off, but that was unheard of. They always had to take their shoes off. Wipe them off on the doormat and then put them on the rack. His father's shoes on the top row, his mother's in the middle, Blix's on the bottom. When he had left his backpack or hat or gloves behind, he occasionally forgot, or pretended to forget, the rule and hadn't bothered taking off his shoes – he was just running in and out quickly anyway. If his parents were home, he'd get an earful. Especially from his father. He would get an earful about something or other anyway. But, back then, he hadn't even thought about the fact that dirty shoes leave footprints.

You're doing it on purpose, aren't you?

The parquet creaked as Blix stepped inside. As if on autopilot, he bent down to untie his shoes, but he stopped and straightened up. In front of the wardrobe with mirrored doors, he paused for a moment and stared at himself. He was pale. It looked like he had developed a few more wrinkles around his eyes.

Emma followed behind him. She said hello to the others in the room.

'I'll wait here,' she said.

Blix nodded.

Took a step further into the hallway, towards the bedrooms. His was on the left, next to his parents' room. There was a bathroom on the opposite side of the hall. A study further in. A solid layer of dust lay on the skirting boards. The house was freezing.

His father was sitting upright in bed with his bare feet atop an old rag rug. He looked at Blix, his mouth agape at first, as if he couldn't believe he was really standing there, his own son. Then he pursed his lips and tightened his jaw muscles.

'Hi, Dad,' Blix said.

He was surprised at the gentleness of his own voice. He stopped just inside the door.

'So this is where you came, is it.'

It was a statement more than a question. He didn't receive a response either way. His father just stared at him, as he had at the nursing home, with a mixture of anger and contempt in his eyes.

He was a pitiful sight. His face hollowed, the bottom half covered in stubble. Grey, thin, unkempt hair. Eyes that blinked at him, bloodshot, faltering. Maybe he remembered more now that he was back here, Blix thought, at home in his own surroundings. Or maybe not.

He waited for a few seconds and walked a little further in, even as his father's suddenly angry voice sounded in his head: *You have no reason to be in here!* He was strictly forbidden from rummaging through the drawers and cupboards of his parents' bedroom. On Sundays, they would emerge from the room a little later than on weekdays, and when they did, his father's cheeks would always be redder than usual. In the meantime, Blix would have been elsewhere. Usually he would lie down in the living room, after waking up with a pounding headache and nausea that would never go away. A general condition that gradually got worse and worse. His mother had lavished him with concern and care, and would often cry too, on his behalf. She would have loved to have taken away his pain and made it her own.

'The doctors can't work it out,' she told anyone who would listen. But it wasn't true – they never went to the doctor. Not with him at least. And when his mother herself became ill – really, seriously ill – then his own ailments were no longer important. She 'had enough on her own plate'. She did stop insisting that he drink warm milk with honey before bed though. And as the cancer ate away at her and she wallowed in all the sympathy she received from friends and acquaintances, Blix slowly started to recover.

'What are you doing here?' he asked now.

'What kind of question is that?' his father retorted. 'I live here. What are you doing here?'

'How did you get here?' Blix asked.

His father looked at him. 'He drove me.'

'Who drove you?'

'Him...' He searched for the words. 'I don't remember his name.'

'But it was someone you know?'

His father snorted, but did not answer.

'Who was it, Dad?' Blix pressed.

'I ... I don't know,' he snapped angrily.

'Was it the same person who let you in here?'

'What are you talking about? I *live* here.'

'Where's your key?'

The man's old eyes darted around the room. 'It's where it always is.'

'There's no key on the chest of drawers in the hall, Dad.'

'No, well. Then it's probably somewhere else.'

As a child, Blix had wanted to become a joiner too. He wanted to be with his father at work. He wanted to learn how to cut, saw, nail, hammer. He had loved the smell of sawdust, of wood oil, that accompanied his father home after the day's work. 'The smell of creation,' his father had once said. 'Of craftsmanship. You need to learn to use your hands, boy.'

Blix had been particularly fascinated by his father's work van, which was full of tools and equipment. But he had never been allowed to touch any of it or look around in there. His father's tools were sacred.

Once in a while his father had taken him on a fishing trip somewhere or other. Mostly because his mother needed time to herself to 'recover'. His father had never said much on these trips. They had simply stood next to each other and cast – his father with a fly, Blix with a spinner or small lure. His father had shown him, once, how to tie fishing knots. After that, he had to manage by himself. The same was true of the fish they caught – if they were to keep them, he would have to kill them himself. Gut them, eat them. 'You have to watch. Observe.' The advantage here being that Blix learned how to learn. He never had to ask for help.

But why didn't *you* observe? he wanted to ask his father as he sat in the double bed, muttering to himself. How could you not see what was happening? Or maybe you did see but didn't care. Questions that had haunted Blix since a teacher filed a report with the child-welfare services, and later made him reluctantly go to see Lina Marie Jansen.

Blix tried to steer the conversation back to who had driven his father home, but the old man wasn't going to say another word. Blix left the bedroom, passing Emma standing in the hallway outside, but didn't say anything. He knew she would have heard what little had been said.

Blix continued into the kitchen, where the two police officers were talking to each other. They stopped when Blix entered. One of them glanced at the oven. The door was open.

On a rack in the middle of it: his father's walking boots.

Blix turned the tap on and found a glass from one of the upper cabinets. As he drank, slowly, sip by sip – which didn't do anything to rid him of the tight knot that had formed in his chest – he noticed that the potted plants in the room all seemed green and healthy.

His gaze halted at the refrigerator.

There was something on it.

Several pieces of paper, he realised, as he took a few steps closer. One of them was a drawing. A child's drawing. A big, yellow sun in the middle of a bright-blue sky. There was a house in the foreground with crooked windows and a chimney, from which thick brown smoke rose in spirals. And in the bottom right corner:

Iselin, age 7.

Blix would have continued staring at it, and only at it, had it not been for the lined A4 page hanging next to it. A handwritten letter that made him narrow his eyes and approach with slow steps. The top line read:

To Alexander

46

Emma stood in the living room and looked at the books that Blix's parents had acquired over the years. Knut Hamsun's complete works. André Bjerke. Aksel Sandemose. Sigrid Undset. Scandinavian classics that all looked like vintage editions. Almost no modern books.

Only two photographs sat on the bookshelves: the wedding of what must surely be Gjermund and Elinor Blix, taken some time in the early seventies. The other was of an elderly woman, sitting on a veranda with her feet in the grass, surrounded by a bed of flowers. She had a cigarette in her hand, and it looked like she didn't enjoy being photographed.

Emma could recognise some of Blix's features on her face. His grandmother, probably.

There were no pictures of Blix.

Maybe because they had been put away, or because there weren't ever that many, possibly. None worth framing, at least.

Emma felt sad on Blix's behalf. She had grown up without parents, but those who had taken care of her growing up – her mother's parents – had shown her and her sister endless amounts of love, for everything they did. There was none of that between these walls. It felt as if the ghosts of the past ruled over the house she now found herself in, ghosts that were angry, disappointed, sad, grieving. The worst parts of their life here had been given the most space.

Emma imagined Blix walking about this home on eggshells – a subdued, reserved boy. She could see it in him now too, that it bothered him to be here. A withdrawn expression clouded his face, a passivity she didn't recognise in him. As if the past had suddenly become the present. And she wondered if this was where it all began, the key to everything that had happened recently. Whether it had all begun in Blix's life a long, long time ago.

Emma's phone buzzed. She took it out of her jacket pocket, despite the fact she didn't want to talk to anyone just then. A quick glance at the display made her change her mind.

'Hi, Emma speaking.'

'Leo van Eijk here,' the voice announced on the other end. 'Am I interrupting anything?'

'No,' Emma lied. 'It's fine. Are you calling because ... Have they found Maria?'

'What?'

Emma realised that Oliver Krogh's lawyer mustn't have been informed of the latest developments in the case. She quickly told him that the police had sent out a new diving team in Lake Gjersjøen, and that they were analysing a blood sample that had been found in an abandoned canoe.

'That's ... encouraging news,' Leo van Eijk replied. 'I...'

He stopped himself. Emma was about to ask what he wanted to say, when the lawyer continued:

'I have spoken to my client. He wanted you to know that he would like to help in any way he can. You seem to be getting somewhere yourself with this, but there is one more thing that you might find useful. Do you have something to write this down on?'

'Er...' Emma looked around for a pen or paper nearby. She found an old crossword puzzle and pencil on the shelf beneath the coffee table. She sat down in the leather chair next to it, and asked Leo van Eijk to continue.

'My client has given me the password to his wife's email,' he said. 'He cannot, of course, check it himself. There may be something in his wife's communications with ... someone who may be able to tell us a little more about what she did in the weeks and days before Maria Normann disappeared.'

Emma listened closely as the lawyer spelled out both the username and password.

'And if a four-digit code is needed somewhere, she always uses 2005. The year her daughter, Carmen, was born.'

'Okay,' Emma said, underscoring the information with two quick lines. 'This is very helpful, thank you.'

'I guess it goes without saying, perhaps, but ... you didn't get this information from me.'

'Of course not. Thanks again. I'll see what I can find.'

Emma hung up.

She was tempted to use the password right away and see if she could find anything out, but decided it was better to do that on her laptop, back home.

A chair in the kitchen scraped against the floor. The two officers who had been in there walked out. One of them pulled out his phone and put it to his ear. The other sent Emma a quick smile, before he too busied himself with something on the phone.

Emma scrolled through her contacts. It had been a while since she had communicated with Nicolai Wibe, but now, after what she had set in motion out by Lake Gjersjøen, she felt confident that he would answer if she called.

He didn't. The first call went straight to voicemail. He might still be out at the lake, Emma reasoned. She sent him a message instead, asking if the blood sample had been analysed yet. She added that it was Emma Ramm, thinking that Wibe might not have her number saved.

A little over a minute later there was a reply: *DNA won't be back until tomorrow at the earliest.*

Emma replied: *Has the search started at Lake Gjersjøen yet?*

Not long after, she received a thumbs-up emoji. He added: *Found a canoe oar. Could be connected. Otherwise, nothing.*

Emma continued: *Can you notify me if the search is successful? I'll be happy so long as I don't have to find out about it online.*

Again she got the same answer: a thumbs-up. Good, Emma thought. Although she was no longer a journalist, she did still enjoy being ahead of the game.

'Emma?' Blix called out to her from the kitchen. She hurried in, eager to share the news. Then stopped when she saw Blix sitting at the kitchen table. He looked up at her. His face was, if possible, even more anaemic.

On the table before him: a sheet of paper and a pair of tweezers.

'Read,' he said quietly. 'Use this to turn the sheet.' He handed her the tweezers.

Emma walked over to the table. Took the tweezers and sat down next to him.

And started reading.

47

To Alexander

I don't know if you know who I am, but we meet occasionally on Wednesdays. We even played football against each other once too. You won 5-1. I don't play anymore.

I wasn't sure if I should write to you or not. But I thought I'd at least try, start with a letter, and then see. I like to write. I've written letters to many famous people. The king, for example. Ronald Reagan. David Bowie. But I never sent them. I enjoyed it though. It was like they were my friends, sort of.

I'm not very good at connecting with people in real life. It's like I don't know what to say. It's a shame we don't go to the same school, because then I could just put a letter on your desk or in your bag when you weren't looking. We are quite similar, I think. You and me. Maybe we can become friends. If you want. You can come and play computer games with me. Dad lets me play all the time. He's pretty cool like that. He lets me watch horror films too. Maybe we can go to the cinema one day? Dad could drive us.

I don't like seeing the psychologist. She's strict. She always asks such difficult questions. About the same things, just in a different way. Does she do that with you too? I don't understand why I have to go. I don't want to. But Dad says it's for my own good.

Maybe it's because I dream so much. I have a lot of strange dreams. Last night I dreamed that the place I was staying in was suddenly flooded, and then the door to our house was locked. I saw Mum in the window. But she wouldn't open it for me. She just stared at me as I yelled and screamed and pounded on the glass. And then I woke up.

I've kept some of your drawings, by the way, that you did while you were waiting for your appointment. You can have them back, if you want. The psychologist had just thrown them away. Dad says we have to take care of things. He keeps hold of everything. You never know when you might need something, he says.

I don't like dogs. One time when I was out hunting, two German Shepherds charged at me. I was only five or something. Thought they were going to have me for dinner. They weren't on a lead. Luckily, Dad was nearby and chased them away. You should have heard him yell at the owner afterwards.

What more is there to say about me? I have a guitar that I play a little from time to time. I'm not good at anything, even though Dad says I am. Do you play an instrument? Maybe we can play together sometime. Start a band. That would be cool. I like A-ha. I don't understand people who don't like A-ha. I want to be as cool as Magne Furuholmen. He's my favourite.

I should stop writing now.

Maybe I'll see you on Wednesday. Then I'll try to say hello.

48

'It's not signed.'

Blix had been lost in his own thoughts while Emma read. Her voice made him flinch. She carefully turned the letter over again.

'He never sent it,' Blix said. 'But he obviously kept hold of it.'

'What do you mean?'

'I never received it. I would have remembered. Which means he has been here and put it on the fridge himself. For me to find.'

Emma put the paper down and turned to face him. 'Do you know who it could be?'

Blix shook his head. 'I have no idea.'

'But how—?'

'I remember that there was usually someone else sitting in the waiting room, but I never socialised with any of them. I just wanted to get out of there.'

Emma turned her gaze back to the letter. 'You were both ... patients,' she concluded. 'Seeing Lina Marie Jansen. The murdered psychologist.'

Blix hesitated a little, but said finally:

'Yes.'

'When was this?'

'For me, I saw her from the age of fifteen, about, until ... well. It was a few years, I think.'

'But...' Emma searched for the right words. 'It's obvious that he knows who *you* are,' she said.

Blix nodded.

'But you don't remember who it could be?'

'No.'

'Try and think carefully,' she pleaded.

'I *have* thought about it carefully,' he argued. 'I really have no idea who this is.'

'But, someone must know,' Emma continued. 'There must be patient records or something.'

Blix nodded but didn't answer.

'He must have been here several times,' he said after a moment, looking around. 'To have found Iselin's drawings and that photo of me from one of the photo albums.'

Blix sat in thought. The boy who had written the letter had to be the same person who had driven his father from the nursing home to here, the same person who had been at his flat, and who had killed Elisabeth Eie. Who had likely also killed Lina Marie Jansen.

He needed to tell Abelvik that the name of the murderer was to be found in the retired psychologist's patient files, that they had to go through his father's house in search of fingerprints and other clues.

One of the local police officers interrupted his train of thought.

'Will you be driving him back?' he asked.

Blix looked up at him.

'Your father,' the police officer clarified. 'We've been called in for another job. It's probably best if you take him back yourself.'

Blix thought about what his father had said about the driver, the man who had let them in. *I don't remember his name.*

'Of course,' he said, standing up.

He took his father's shoes out of the oven and carried them into the bedroom with him. His father was still sitting in bed, a blank expression on his face. When he spotted Blix, his gaze hardened.

'Dad,' Blix said, trying to be firm, 'do you remember Lina Marie Jansen?'

Gjermund Blix stared up at him.

'In the mid-eighties,' Blix continued. 'You took me to see her sometimes. Mum couldn't do it. Couldn't take me.'

His father mumbled something Blix didn't catch. He wanted to ask if his father remembered another boy in the waiting room, but realised that there was no point right now. He seemed tired and confused.

'Come,' Blix said. 'We're going.'

'Going?'

'We'll drive you back.' Blix walked over to the bed. 'Your shoes,' he said, holding them out for him. 'You put your shoes in the kitchen.'

His father shook his head.

'Are you stupid?' he said, looking out at Emma in the hall.

Blix didn't answer, but instead held out an arm for his father. 'You must be hungry. It's almost time for dinner.'

The thought of food seemed to make the old man more compliant. He slowly pushed the duvet aside and put his feet on the floor. His socks were falling off. Blix bent down and pulled them onto his feet properly. It made him think of Iselin when she was little. Iselin, who had sent drawings to her grandfather, even though she couldn't have possibly known what he even looked like.

It was a thought that made Blix unspeakably sad.

He put his father's shoes on for him. Helped him out of the house and into the back seat of the car with Terry.

His father pulled his hands away when the dog moved closer to say hello.

'He's friendly,' Blix assured him, fastening his seat belt.

'What do we do about the house?' Emma asked. 'Do you have a key?'

Blix glanced up at the old building.

'We'll just leave it unlocked,' he said and climbed into the passenger seat.

Emma manoeuvred the car back out onto the road. The world passed by outside the windows. Fields, houses, buildings he recognised, buildings he didn't.

Blix clutched his phone in his hand, turned it over and over. Tomine had sent him a message, but he didn't open it. There was too much to digest, to think about. He didn't have room for more. They were chasing a killer. Or maybe it was the opposite? Blix felt like a piece in a game he still didn't understand. It bothered him. Annoyed him. But he was in detective mode again – unavoidable. In one way or another, this was all about him, so *he* would have to be the one to get to the bottom of it.

Blix had dropped the letter into a clear plastic bag and taken it with him. He saw no point in calling Abelvik yet and sharing the finding with her. The letter itself was not particularly useful, apart from the fact that it was the voice of a young boy who had obviously been disturbed over the years. He could give it to her when he returned to Oslo. By then he might have something more to tell her.

Emma steered the car onto the main road, only to get stuck behind a tractor.

'It must be someone who lives, or at least *lived,* in the area,' she said in a low voice. 'Since you went to the same psychologist, I mean. You even played football against each other once.'

'Yes,' Blix said.

He turned to look into the back seat. Terry had put his chin in his father's lap and was lying there with his eyes closed. His father stroked his hand over the dog's fur in a slow, steady motion.

Emma pulled out into the opposite lane and accelerated past the tractor.

'It's a shame you didn't go to the same school,' she said. 'Otherwise we might have found him in one of your old school photos or something.'

Blix turned to look at her again.

'We may still be able to do that, but we'd have to talk to all the schools in the area.'

'And not every school even had photos,' Emma said.

'We'd need the correct year too.'

Emma sighed. 'The old needle in the proverbial haystack,' she said. 'Annoying that he didn't sign the letter.'

'He probably wouldn't have hung it on the fridge if he had. This is a game to him – all of this. He doesn't want to make it easy for me. At the same time, it *is* clear that he wants me to know that it's him.'

She drove on.

Blix received another message from Tomine. He didn't open that one either.

'Alexander,' Emma said, glancing briefly in the rearview mirror. 'If I may ask, why ... why did you have to see Lina Marie Jansen?'

Blix had known she would ask. He had almost invited the question by letting her read the letter.

'It was one of my secondary school teachers,' he said quietly. 'Her name was Hege. She saw that I ... wasn't doing well. She submitted a report to the child-welfare services. So that's...' He paused and thought of his father's fury when the letter from the agency had appeared in the post at home. 'That's how I ended up seeing the psychologist,' he finished. 'After a lot of back and forth.'

'Didn't you remember that you had been to see her?'

'Sure,' said Blix. 'Of course. But her name ... things back then, it's all a little hazy to me. I didn't really want to go either. It was primarily about ... getting my health back.'

'Your health?'

'Yes...' Blix couldn't bear to go into details about it just now.

'You killed her,' a voice said from the back seat.

Blix turned to look at him. 'What did you say?'

'*You* killed her. Your mother.'

Blix sat and stared at him, speechless. He didn't know where it came from, this ability his father always had to make him mute, even now, well into adulthood. But he couldn't bring himself to say a single word. Couldn't correct him, couldn't confront him about what had really happened.

They pulled off the main road at the sign for the Furulia nursing home. The light from the sunset broke through the layers of clouds. The rays bathed the surrounding fields. The dewy grass sparkled.

Emma pulled up outside the main entrance. 'Do you want me to come in with you?' she asked.

'No, it's fine,' Blix assured her.

He got out, walked around the car and helped his father out of the back seat. The old man stood hunched over and looked around. His eyes were misty, empty. Somewhere in there may be the key to all this, Blix thought, but right now there was nothing his father could help with.

49

You killed her.

Emma couldn't get Gjermund Blix's words out of her head. During the short drive, she had stolen a few glances in the rearview mirror, just to get a closer look at the man who had been so formative in Blix's life, in one way or another. She had felt a bit like an intruder, like she was a part of something that wasn't meant for her. But what had his father meant, really? Blix's mother died of cancer. At least that was what he had told her.

There were people who had grown up in difficult circumstances, but who had nevertheless become outstanding, successful adults – a description she felt applied to Blix.

She checked her email as she sat and waited. Read a couple of newsletters and deleted some junk mail. She had no idea how long Blix would need to talk to the staff, so she decided to use the time to do some searches on Lina Marie Jansen. The online hits were mostly reports about the psychologist's disappearance just before the autumn holidays three years ago. According to one of her neighbours, she was on her way into the forest to pick some blackberries, but she never came back. Whatever happened to her was a mystery, given the police and search teams had combed every inch of the forest. Considering what they now knew, Emma thought she most likely met her killer near a car park on the outskirts of the forest, and she must have been transported away from there somehow, and without anyone witnessing it.

Emma found an article Jansen had written in *Aftenposten*, in which she advocated that children have just as much responsibility as their parents for how their lives turn out. 'Stop blaming your parents', she wrote. The chronicle formed the starting point for a TV debate – *Nature versus Nurture* – for which the psychologist had been invited to speak.

Emma didn't have the patience to read it just then. Instead, she swiped over to Facebook and looked up Victoria Prytz. It had been a while since

Carmen's mother had posted anything new. Probably because of the arrest, Emma reasoned. Social media could be a dumpster fire.

She decided to see if she could log into Victoria's email. There was no point waiting until she got home.

In the email app, she entered the address and password given to her by Leo van Eijk, and pressed enter.

She was in. That was easy.

Emma straightened up in her seat and looked around before she started scrolling.

Victoria Prytz had twenty-six unread emails – junk mail advertising trips abroad and beauty products, a newsletter from Oslo Concert Hall, a digital receipt from a furniture shop. She had received a notification from a fitness app as well – someone had sent her kudos on her 'PT session with Johan'. Emma scrolled down the list, careful not to click on anything that hadn't already been read.

All of little interest. She found no correspondence suggesting that Victoria Prytz had anything to do with Maria Normann's disappearance. But she'd had a glimpse into who Victoria Prytz was as a person, at least, and what she spent her time on.

Emma's gaze moved over to the margin, to see if Prytz had set up any interesting folders. Nothing abnormal, Emma noted. The usual sent items, deleted items. Emma quickly scrolled through them anyway.

Several of the deleted emails were from a website Emma had visited from time to time: *Womensaid.no*.

She opened one of the emails and saw that it was some kind of confirmation for a post on a discussion forum, with a link to the post itself.

Emma clicked on it and was taken through to the website.

The title of the post was 'Mentally ill child'. It was created by someone posting as AnonymousUser, Emma read:

Mentally ill child

I have a fifteen-year-old child who is extremely difficult to deal with. I think there's something wrong with her. She's in so much pain all over

her body, she's tired and she's sick, but the GP can't find anything wrong
with her. I suspect the problem is between her ears, but I can't say that
to her, because then she'll get even angrier than she already is. Every
day is like living in a war zone. She slams doors, rolls her eyes at me
and says things to me with pure hatred. Sometimes she breaks things
too, in a blind rage. Throws things. Nice, expensive things.

The last thing she wants is to go to a psychologist. I suggested it to her
once. After that she didn't talk to me for two weeks.

I am so tired.

I'm so afraid of what she might do. I feel like a bad mother, and I
probably am. But I can't take it anymore. I'm actually starting to get
scared that she's going to hurt herself. Or me.

Has anyone here experienced something similar, or does anyone have
any good advice?

Emma read some of the replies to the thread. There was an outpouring
of sympathy and praise for being so brave as to share this. Many recognised the situation themselves – she was by no means a bad mother; on
the contrary. Some suggested that it might be ADHD. Had she had her
child tested for this?

AnonymousUser replied to every comment and thanked them for
their help and sympathy – she felt better, safer, knowing that there was
a community out there, that she wasn't alone. Some made suggestions
about where she could seek advice and help from various services.
AnonymousUser thanked them for their input, but wrote back that her
own experience of the healthcare system was that they never understood
her, or her issues. The response was met with further sympathy.

Emma quickly looked through the rest of the thread, not for a
moment doubting who in the Prytz family she felt most sorry for. The
only mitigating factor she found about the thread was that it was anony-
mised.

Several other emails from the women's aid website were among the
deleted messages. The next one down was from May, alerting Prytz to a
response to a post about her daughter's broken arm, and how

AnonymousUser thought her husband was to blame. He had been too rough with her during an argument, it said, and restrained her daughter, forcefully.

In another thread, AnonymousUser sought advice on how to break out of an abusive marriage. A marriage that was not only physically painful, but also psychologically, because she never knew when he was going to hit her next. When he got angry, it was like someone flipped a switch. In the responses to her post, she was encouraged to leave him, to seek help – there were centres for people like her, poor thing. In one of the threads, AnonymousUser wrote that she was worried that her husband was going to kill her.

It couldn't be anyone but Oliver she was describing, Emma thought. But had he really been violent?

AnonymousUser wondered if her husband was cheating on her too.

She had been abandoned once before, it said, by her child's biological father. It was unbearable that the same thing might happen again, this time, leaving her for a woman – 'let's call her Maria' – who was much younger. Desperate, she asked for advice on what to do.

The answers ranged from 'you need to hire a private investigator' to 'cut his balls off in his sleep'. One last comment said that 'someone should teach people like Maria a lesson'.

'Shit,' Emma exhaled, taking a quick look around before reading more.

In another, more recent, post, AnonymousUser was worried about a quiet, withdrawn eight-year-old who had been outgoing when she started school and who had scored well on her tests. Now she was doing worse and worse, and she just wanted to stay in her room. She had quit gymnastics. AnonymousUser suspected that something traumatic had happened, but it was impossible to talk to her daughter.

'Oh my god,' Emma said out loud. 'She's insane.'

She leafed through the rest of the threads and found several examples of various forms of disorders her child had, for which she sought advice and support. All with different ages and time markers.

It was as if Victoria Prytz was playing out a fantasy world online, where she took on various victim roles and blamed the system, the government, and everyone else for her problems. Emma was intrigued but appalled by this hidden part of the businesswoman's life.

Emma sank back in her seat, wondering what other dark sides Victoria Prytz had.

50

The reception at Furulia nursing home sprang to life when Blix entered with his father. Two nurses rushed towards them. One – a young woman with long blonde hair – asked if everything was okay. There was genuine concern in her voice.

'Yes,' Blix replied. 'He's still in one piece.'

The carers took over.

Blix stood and watched the interaction between them and his father. It was like he'd never met them before. The building also seemed strange to him, but he finally allowed himself to be led towards the lift. They walked calmly, slowly. The nurses spoke to him in friendly voices, as if nothing had happened. His father turned slightly, as if to see if Blix was following them.

Blix's phone vibrated. He pulled it out to see another message from Tomine. He was about to open it, when someone approached. Blix recognised him. Petter Thaulow. The carer held out his hand. Blix took it.

'I'm glad everything went okay,' Thaulow said. 'Which it usually does, luckily.' He smiled sympathetically.

Blix didn't know what to say. He looked up at the corners of the ceiling. 'You don't have surveillance cameras in here, I see.'

Thaulow shook his head.

'Dad says he was driven home,' Blix continued. 'Either he went out, and was then picked up outside – which I think is unlikely – or someone came in and took him out.'

Thaulow stared at him, as if he were choosing his words carefully. 'You have to remember that your father is cognitively impaired,' he said.

'It's too far for him to walk home,' Blix said. 'And he's unlikely to have taken the bus. He wasn't wearing a jacket.'

Thaulow didn't answer that.

'How long have you been at work today?' Blix asked.

'Since this morning.'

'Do you know if anyone else working today saw anyone with my father?'

The carer shook his head. 'We talked about it upstairs. A number of relatives have visited some of the other patients, but no one saw anyone with your father.'

'And you know these visitors, I assume?'

'Yes and no. We get a lot of people coming and going here. Some of them are here often. So those people, we get to know well, of course.'

'I need the names of everyone you remember visiting today,' Blix said, aware that he wasn't actually a policeman anymore. 'As many as you can,' he added, hoping for goodwill.

'We can try,' Thaulow said. 'Do you want to come upstairs?'

Blix nodded.

They walked towards the lift.

The lift trundled slowly upward. The silence in the narrow space became oppressive.

'Lina Marie Jansen,' Blix said. 'Does that name mean anything to you?'

The doors opened again. Thaulow stepped out. 'The psychologist? Yes, I would imagine we've all heard about what happened to her.'

Blix followed him as they headed onto the ward.

'What do you mean?' he asked.

'Her disappearance,' Thaulow said. 'It was in all the newspapers here for a while.'

Blix came up at his side.

'I didn't know her myself,' Thaulow said, 'but her daughter worked here for a few years. Ann-Kristin.'

Blix frowned. 'Is that so?'

Thaulow pressed a button on the wall, and the doors in front of them opened.

'Ann-Kristin was nice, smart. Was planning on following in her mother's footsteps, I believe, which is why she moved to Oslo. Continue studying and all that.'

'Are you still in touch with her?'

Thaulow shook his head. 'It's been a while since we spoke.'

A new thought gripped him. 'You don't have her number by any chance do you? I need to talk to her.'

Thaulow raised his eyebrows at him. 'I'm sure I do ... somewhere.'

Hesitantly, the carer pulled out his phone and scrolled through his contacts. He typed something in and stopped, so that Blix could see the digits on the display and type them into his own phone.

'Thank you,' Blix said. 'I'll try calling her now.'

'I'll go ahead and talk to the others. Get started on that list.'

The carer disappeared into the staff room. Blix remained standing in the hallway. He brought the phone to his ear. It rang a few times, and someone picked up.

'Ann-Kristin speaking.'

'Er hi,' Blix began. 'I'm sorry to contact you on a day like this. I'm Alexander Blix, former investigator for the homicide unit of the Oslo Police.'

'Okay ... and what is this about?' Her voice was thin and weak.

Blix hesitated, considering how to go about this.

'First of all, I want to offer my condolences,' he continued. 'I didn't know your mother, but ... I know how difficult and harrowing a case like this can be.'

Ann-Kristin Jansen didn't comment.

'I have been somewhat involved in the investigation,' Blix continued, without going into detail. 'I hope you can bear with me, but ... I have a bit of a strange question.'

'Uh, sure?' He could hear her trepidation.

Blix decided to go for it.

'You ... haven't received anything in the mail lately that struck you as a little ... odd?'

'What do you mean?'

'A letter, for example, which...' Blix closed his eyes, hoping he didn't sound crazy. 'Which might have been about your mother in some way?'

It was quiet at the other end. Blix was sure she was going to chew him out and hang up.

Instead, she said: 'I have, actually. It arrived yesterday.'

'May I ask what it said?' Blix said, fired up now.

'It said something about how my mother didn't ... deserve to live. And then there was a quote underneath.'

'A quote in English?' Blix pressed.

'Yes! How...' She stopped herself.

'Was it "All that I am, or hope to be, I owe to my angel mother"?'

'That was it!' she said. 'But ... I don't understand how...'

'It's not that easy to explain,' Blix said. 'I just need you to trust me for now. I promise to call and explain when I know more myself.'

Blix could sense that Ann-Kristin Jansen was now even more confused, but she eventually accepted what he said. He thanked her for the information and hung up.

Things were starting to come together, Blix thought. Or, there were at least elements that made sense, that seemed connected.

You're getting close, he told himself, and felt a kind of warm sensation in his chest. He was excited. It was a feeling he was a little ashamed of. But he couldn't help it.

51

A quick internet search told Emma that dogs could sleep for twelve to eighteen hours a day. With traces of poison still in his body, there was no reason to be concerned that Terry's eyes had spent more time closed than open. Still, she occasionally glanced into the back seat to watch his chest rise and fall.

Emma felt that she needed some sleep herself.

She had thought that with freedom from work, it would be easier to make choices that were in her own best interest. More sleep, more peace and rest, more time for 'personal development'. But the idleness had made her more stressed than anything, precisely because she had so few answers to the questions life threw at her, no clear path ahead.

She had to admit that the last few days of digging into the case had awakened something in her. When they found the traces of blood in the canoe, she had felt more excited than she could remember being in a long time. And she enjoyed being around Blix too, tapping into his police brain. Helping him, but helping herself too. Maybe there was, really, no good reason to deny what and who you were.

But could she bear going back to her life as a journalist?

The doors to the nursing home opened. Blix came out and strode over. Emma started the car. The hum of the engine made Terry's eyes open.

Blix opened the door. 'He's sent a letter to Jansen's daughter as well,' he said before he had time to sit down. 'The same type of letter, with the same quote.'

Terry pulled himself up, trying to say hello. His tail was wagging.

'The Abraham Lincoln one?' Emma asked.

Blix closed the door behind him. 'Yes.'

He twisted around, reached for Terry. *"All that I am, or hope to be, I owe to my angel mother",* he recited as he scratched behind the dog's ear. 'He was critical of Jansen too, said that her mother didn't deserve to live.'

'The same message Tomine Eie was sent,' Emma said. 'Which was more for Elisabeth's daughter, Julie, than for Tomine.'

'Exactly.' Blix turned back in his seat and put his seat belt on.

'It sounds like he's preaching almost,' she said. 'Like he has some need to communicate something, both to you and to the victims' relatives. He wants you to know *why* he's doing this.'

'But he hasn't killed either of *my* parents,' Blix said. 'He could have done that by now too, if he wanted, but ... he spared my father.'

'And there must be a good reason for that,' Emma added.

They both sat there in thought for a few moments.

'He wanted me to find that letter,' Blix said at last. 'That's why Dad was taken out of the nursing home. So I would be called out here. So I would come and find him, and the letter. He *wants* me to find him.'

'And these messages,' Emma said. 'It doesn't sound like he's gloating or taunting you. He's literally just ... telling you. Explaining.'

'And then includes a cryptic note about mothers.'

A few raindrops hit the glass. Emma turned on the windscreen wipers.

'I don't think it's cryptic at all,' she said thoughtfully.

Blix looked at her. 'What do you mean?'

'It sounds more ironic than anything else. All that he is, all that he hopes to be, he can thank his angel mother for?'

Blix waited for the rest of her reasoning.

'It sounds different coming from an American president,' she said. 'That he can thank her for what he has achieved. Coming from a murderer though it's ... not the same. It's like he blames his mother for making him who he is.'

Blix nodded. 'Which might have been why he was sent to Lina Marie Jansen.'

'So maybe Jansen wasn't very nice to him either? Or maybe she abused her own child, and the perpetrator knows the daughter? *That's* why he killed her.'

Emma released the handbrake and pulled out onto the road.

'I looked Jansen up while I was waiting for you,' she said. 'Did you know she was quite controversial?'

'How so?'

'Well, I don't know how controversial it is really, but she was of the opinion that parents need to be kinder to themselves if their kids turn out to be bad human beings. The children themselves have just as much responsibility for that, she believed. She pointed to the fact that there are many examples of siblings who have had the exact same care over the years but go off in completely different directions as adults.'

'As in, some grow up to be kind, while others are abusive?'

'Yes. She said it's too easy to blame the parents. That children are too quick to take on the role of victim.'

They drove in silence for a while.

Blix suddenly sat up.

'Turid Nyjordet,' he said.

'Hm?'

'The one missing in Oslo,' Blix clarified. Emma could see he was on to something, there was an eagerness to his voice. 'We don't know if it *is* the same man who has taken her, but she...'

Emma didn't want to interrupt his train of thought.

'You should have seen her,' he said. 'In the shop. How she was acting towards her son. Maybe...' He scratched his head. 'He's punishing bad mothers,' he continued. 'Maybe that's what this is all about – he's taking his revenge, taking out his anger and hatred for his own mother on other women. Turid Nyjordet – let's just say she is connected to all this – if he has taken her too, then it may have been as some kind of punishment for, or prevention of, damage she has or was going to inflict on her own child, whatever form that might take. He was so beaten down by his own mother that he wants to prevent others from suffering the same fate.'

'That ... might just make sense.'

'He told me that when he called to confess,' Blix continued. 'He said that fathers are important, that some people believe that mothers are the most important people in a person's life, but that he had a "soft spot" for dads. That may be why he didn't do anything to my father. Although, Dad...'

He stopped himself. Emma glanced at him, could see he had disappeared into his memories again. Back to his childhood. He blinked a few times, rapidly, and straightened up.

'I did try to ask why he had killed Elisabeth Eie,' he said.

Emma recalled their conversation about it: 'Because she deserved it,' she repeated.

'Exactly,' Blix nodded. 'Which means that Elisabeth Eie's murder may have been spur of the moment. He may have seen how she was interacting with her daughter. She may have become a victim because of the way she behaved.'

'Quite possibly,' Emma agreed. 'But that doesn't explain why he's doing all this to *you*. After all, you worked on the Elisabeth Eie case. The only personal connection here seems to be the psychologist.'

You killed her. Blix's father's words came back to her. She looked over at Blix, who sat staring ahead, his mind clearly racing.

'He feels some sort of kinship with you,' Emma began. 'Something tells me that maybe you didn't have the best mother either?'

They had been tip-toeing around this minefield for some time now. Emma knew it would be difficult for Blix to talk about.

He put his hands in his lap, squeezed them. His legs shook, restless.

'No,' he said at last, with a deep, heavy sigh. 'That'd be an understatement.'

52

A train passed by to the right of the car. Blix followed it with his eyes until it disappeared into the distance.

'Do you think about your mother?' Emma asked.

Blix didn't answer.

'Your father said you killed her,' she continued. 'I'm assuming he didn't mean that literally?'

She said it like a question. Blix felt his chest tighten. He hadn't talked about his mother with anyone but Merete, and even with her it had only been a surface-level discussion.

Blix grabbed the handle above the door beside him. His knuckles turned white.

'My mother...' His voice trembled. 'She was ... disabled.' He cleared his throat. 'For as long as I could remember, and long before I knew what that word meant. I don't know how we managed on just my father's income. People didn't have much money when we were growing up. Joiners ... there wasn't a real market for people like Dad at that time. And Dad ... well. He didn't exactly work his ass off.'

The car jolted as it hit a bump in the road.

'I say disabled ... I don't know what it was, really. It's something you don't necessarily ask about or understand when you're that young. But Mum was sick. There was always something. If I asked her what was wrong, she would just get angry. As if I had to figure it out for myself.'

They had entered an area of woodland, trees lining the road on either side. The rain was starting to ease. The rubber of the windscreen wipers juddered against the increasingly dry glass. Emma turned them off.

'My mother ... and I didn't realise this until later ... had this compulsion – she needed others to feel sorry for her. Support her, give her sympathy.' Blix lay his hands flat in his lap. 'When I was about nine years old, she started, uh, putting medicine ... in my milk.'

He had to stop for a few seconds and swallow – his throat sounded dry, hoarse.

'Not every day and not every time, but ... regularly enough. Enough to make me sick. Very sick, at times. Vomiting, diarrhoea. I was lethargic, dizzy.'

Blix stared out of the window again. The forest was dark, seemingly impenetrable in some places.

'So I was off school a lot, naturally. I asked her if we shouldn't go to the doctor, but she always said no – she used to be a nurse, she said, so she could fix it, no problem. In the meantime, she revelled in all the sympathy. Everyone felt sorry for her, thought she was doing such a good job as a mother. I overheard her on the phone. How awful and painful and difficult to be the mother of a child in so much pain.' He shook his head.

'Jesus,' Emma said, her own voice croaky. 'So she had...'

'Classic Munchausen syndrome by proxy,' he finished for her. 'You hurt your own child to get sympathy for yourself.'

A silence stretched between them for a while.

'People felt sorry for me too, of course. And Mum was one of them – there was no limit to how nurturing she could suddenly be. But then I would get better every so often – I presume because she was giving me lower doses or none at all – so I could go back to school for a while. I had no idea what was going on. But, as a child, you don't – you just do whatever your parents say. You eat and drink what they tell you to eat and drink. If they say it's good for you, it's good for you.'

Blix could hear the rising anger in his own voice.

'Blix,' Emma said quietly. 'I don't know what to say.'

He didn't answer.

'You said your mother gave you medicine. What kind?'

'A bunch of stuff. Mainly baclofen. My grandmother – my mother's mother – had a disease that affected the nervous system. Baclofen is used to treat tension and twitching in the skeletal muscles.'

'So your mother stole medicine from *her* mother?'

Blix nodded. 'I found some old pill boxes among my mother's things after she died.'

'Bloody hell,' Emma said. 'That must have been awful for you. For all of you. Your grandmother too, my god. It must have made her health worse as well.'

'Yes.'

They drove a little further without either of them saying anything.

'And then it was like some kind of ironic twist of fate that she became sick herself,' Blix continued. 'Actually sick. I was twelve or so. Maybe thirteen. That's when she stopped ... poisoning me. There was no point anymore – she received enough help, support and sympathy as it was.' He shook his head. 'I seriously believe it was the best time of her life. When she could be sick without pretending, without having to try. Whereas for me ... I wasn't doing well. Physically, it took a long time to get back on my feet. And of course I ended up way behind at school. Nothing was going well at that time, really. I didn't have many friends because I had missed out on so much. And on top of that, the fact that Mum was seriously ill, and then it eventually became clear that she was going to die...' He waved away the rest of the sentence with his hand. 'It didn't do anything to help my already-dire mental state. Children are happy with their parents. They want to stay with them as long as they can, even when they're abusive.'

'A lot of people think it's *their* fault too,' Emma added. 'The child, I mean, thinks they're to blame for their parents arguing or being unwell.'

'Yeah, those thoughts crossed my mind back then. For a long time, like my father, I thought that *that* was why she got cancer. Because I had been so sick and caused them so much stress. It took me a long time to realise that that wasn't true.'

Darkness had descended around the car. Blix pointed towards the trees.

'Be extra careful around here,' he said. 'There's a lot of elk in this area.' Emma switched on the high beams. The forest lit up on both sides.

'Was it Lina Marie Jansen who helped you realise that?' she asked.

Blix thought about it. 'She played an important part in it, yes – in that process.'

'You saw her for almost two years, did you say?'

'Something like that.'

'Did your father go with you?'

'Sometimes. He didn't sit in on the sessions, of course. It was always just me and ... Lina Marie.'

It was strange to say her name out loud. He had never done that, in the context of her being his psychologist. In his head, he had always referred to her as 'the psychologist'.

'And then, in the middle of all that, your mother died.'

'Correct.' Blix looked down. 'It was difficult enough as it was. I had started seeing the psychologist before that, and I think she had probably had her suspicions about what was going on at home when I described my symptoms, and how they stopped after my mother fell ill. But no great apparatus was ever going to be set in motion to question someone who was terminally ill. After all, she'd stopped doing it at that point. And I was slowly getting better. Physically, at least.'

'And your father – he knew nothing of what your mother had done to you?'

Blix shook his head. 'I don't think so. Dad was ... a rather apathetic father. Detached. He probably felt that he did enough for the family already, given he was the only one earning an income, and that Mum and I got to do what we wanted. He'd had enough, I think, of the responsibility and the burden as the breadwinner. I don't say that to defend him; I just think that's how it was.'

Emma switched off the high beams as a car approached in the opposite direction.

'He hated that I had to see a psychologist,' Blix went on. 'You should have heard him afterwards. How furious he was at "the system", as he always called it, with contempt. How angry he was at me, because I'd always been so much trouble. Dad was this macho alpha-male type of man. If you had any reason to see a psychologist, then there was something wrong with your head. You were crazy, and that was that.' Blix sighed. 'It got to the point where I realised how little he cared, and when I told him that Mum had been poisoning me and he didn't do a damn thing to stop it, he got so furious that he ... hit me.'

In the back seat, Terry got up and shuffled about, trying to find a new position to lie in.

'He didn't even apologise after,' Blix continued. 'And I ... I was in my mid-teens and depressed, because my mother was dead, and because it felt like my life was doomed long before it was supposed to begin. I ... had to get out of there. Get out of that toxic house. It didn't matter where, just that I left.'

Emma slowed down as they approached a residential area.

'Where did you go?' she asked.

Blix took a breath. 'Luckily, my grandmother was still alive. She also lived in Gjøvik. She had never got on well with my dad, and he wasn't interested in me coming back. So, it worked out. I lived with her up until she died. Then inherited her apartment.'

They drove through the centre of Skreia, turning southeast. Blix cast a long glance at the roads he had walked and cycled on over the years.

'I think Dad was just happy it was over and done with. No responsibilities, not having to deal with anyone else. He could be alone and please only himself. His whole existence shaped only around him. He could drink his beer, watch TV, solve a few crosswords. Some woodwork here and there.'

A sudden realisation hit Blix and he glanced over at Emma.

'My grandmother sort of saved me,' he said. 'Just like *your* grandparents saved you. You and I are much more alike than we might think.'

He smiled weakly, but Emma wasn't looking at him. She seemed deep in thought.

'How common is it for mothers to mistreat their children?' she asked.

'I don't know,' Blix replied. 'Most cases are probably not reported or diagnosed. It didn't happen in my mum's case, anyhow. No one figured it out. Straightforward neglect, a lack of real care, is more noticeable, I suppose. Why do you ask?'

Emma shifted a little in her seat. 'I'm just thinking about Carmen's mother,' she replied.

Blix listened as Emma explained what she had found in Victoria Prytz's deleted emails. How she had sought comfort and support from strangers, and received it. In bucket-loads.

'Did she harm her daughter in any way?' Blix asked. 'Genuinely?'

'Not that I know of,' Emma replied. 'It could just be that she's made everything up, with the exception of her husband's infidelity.'

Blix shook his head. 'Sounds like she has some kind of morbid need for attention,' he said. 'Almost like a narcissist.'

They drove on in the evening darkness.

'Do you think Victoria Prytz could be behind the murder of her husband's mistress?' Blix asked.

'I don't know,' Emma sighed, looking over at him. 'But she definitely had suspicions about her husband, and there were certainly people in the comments section urging her to take matters into her own hands.'

53

The lights in the meeting room were dimmed. Tine Abelvik pulled the door shut behind them, drowning out the sound of the investigators in the open-plan office.

Walenius was standing by the window. He turned towards them and in the darkness behind him, Blix could see the lights from Oslo Prison.

'Do you have the letter with you?' Walenius asked. His tone was cool.

Blix didn't reply, just stood there and studied the young investigator. Measured him from the head down. His shoes were dirty. He had mud stains on his trouser legs.

'Alexander?' Abelvik asked.

Blix pulled the plastic bag from his inner pocket and handed it to Abelvik.

Walenius pulled out a chair and sat down. Abelvik went round to sit beside him. Blix positioned himself across from them.

They had already read the letter. Blix had sent over a picture. He had given them the list of relatives who had visited the Furulia nursing home that day as well.

'We have to do this formally,' Abelvik said, reaching for the recorder.

Blix nodded and waited for her to press record.

'You may already have put two and two together, but the psychologist they are referring to in the letter is Lina Marie Jansen,' he said.

Abelvik seemed confused.

'The one whose body was found at Leirsund,' Blix clarified.

Walenius leaned forward. 'You were a patient of hers when you were young?' he asked.

Blix nodded. 'It took me a while to recall the name,' he said. 'It turns out her daughter used to work at Furulia.'

He told them how he had called her, and that she had received a letter of the same nature and with similar wording as the one to Tomine Eie.

'"All that I am, or hope to be, I owe to my angel mother"', he repeated.

Abelvik held up a hand. 'Can we take this from the start?' she asked, glancing at the recorder. 'From when your father was reported missing?'

Blix collected his thoughts and began recounting the phone call from Petter Thaulow. He neglected to tell them about the blood found in the canoe at Lake Gjersjøen and that he had been with Nicolai Wibe when he got the message. Otherwise, he told them everything in detail, but could see in their eyes that they were both sceptical of his own conclusion that someone had taken his father out of the nursing home to lure him to Skreia themselves.

'Why do you think this letter has cropped up now?' Abelvik asked.

Blix shrugged. 'That seems to be his approach,' he replied. 'It's part of justifying what he's doing, trying to make *me* understand.'

'*Do* you understand what he's doing?'

Blix looked down at the recorder and hesitated. He didn't want to share any thoughts that would require him to talk about his experiences with his mother.

'Not yet,' he replied.

Walenius took over the questioning.

'What did you have to see a psychologist about?' he asked with a wave of his hand to the letter.

Abelvik squirmed a little. Blix searched for an answer.

'Things went downhill, after my mother was diagnosed with cancer,' he replied. 'She died when I was sixteen.'

Walenius didn't pursue his line of questioning.

'Isn't it strange to write a letter but never send it?' he asked instead.

Blix didn't bother offering his thoughts on the matter. It was not a question that required an answer.

'And save it for so many years?' Walenius continued. 'How long will it have been? Thirty-five years?'

'Something like that,' Blix replied.

'You believe the childhood photo of you and Iselin's drawing both came from your father's house,' Walenius went on. 'And that the perpetrator must have broken in and found them.'

'The crime-scene technicians should look into it,' Blix nodded. 'They might find fingerprints there.'

Walenius noted something.

'You were in Gjøvik two days ago,' he stated. 'Did you visit your child-hood home then, too?'

'I haven't been there in years,' Blix replied, letting his gaze linger on the young investigator. There was a kind of insinuation in his question, that there was a possibility that Blix could have planted the letter himself.

'Emma Ramm was with me,' he added. 'She drove.'

Walenius nodded, turned a page and looked at the clock. 'Where were you at this time yesterday?'

Blix thought about Tomine and the messages she had sent throughout the day. How she had been worried about both him and Terry.

'Why?' he asked.

Abelvik leaned forward a little. 'If you could just answer the question,' she said.

It dawned on Blix what the question was really about. The missing woman from the night before – Turid Nyjordet.

'You took over my apartment from five o'clock,' he began. 'I then took Terry to Emma's place. I stopped off at a shop on Sofies gate on my way there. After dropping Terry off, I went to talk to Tomine Eie. Emma was looking after Terry. She then called from the vet at nine o'clock and said Terry was ill.' He stopped to revise the statement, so that Walenius wouldn't have something to cling on to later. 'In fact, I called her,' he said. 'She had sent some messages. I met her at the veterinary hospital.' He looked over at Abelvik. 'While I was there, you called me and told me about the drawing with Iselin's fingerprints.'

Abelvik nodded.

'And after that?' Walenius asked.

'We were at the vet's until close to midnight,' Blix answered. 'We then took Terry back with us to Emma's flat.'

'So you were at Emma Ramm's last night?' Walenius asked.

'I was staying in her spare room,' Blix nodded. 'What is this all about?'

Walenius opened the folder next to him, took out a picture and pushed it toward him.

It was a still from the CCTV in the shop on Sofies gate. He was standing behind Turid Nyjordet and her son in the queue at the till. They must have traced the use of her bank card.

'This is Turid Nyjordet,' Walenius explained, pointing to her. 'She has been reported missing.'

Blix looked over at Abelvik and down at the picture. He had no trouble appearing surprised. The sight of the image had shaken him.

'I told you...' he said, swallowing. 'That he's following me. He must have seen me there, with her. You have to check all of the recordings. Both inside and outside...'

The magazine shelf where the argument with the son had taken place was included in the background of the photo. The interaction between them must be on the recording.

'There's a pattern...' he began, looking for the easiest way to explain. 'Elisabeth Eie was not a good mother. Child welfare was involved and had accused her of neglect. And the perpetrator said so himself when he called me,' he added. 'He had killed Elisabeth Eie because she deserved it.'

He pointed to the picture.

'Turid Nyjordet was not behaving kindly to her son in the shop. She dragged him about by the arm.'

Abelvik nodded slowly, as if she had seen the footage herself, but Blix could tell that she was still sceptical.

'Lina Marie Jansen also deserved to die,' he continued. 'According to the letter he sent to her daughter.' He repeated the Abraham Lincoln quote. 'That's what this is all about. He's punishing bad mothers.'

'So Jansen was also a bad mother?'

Abelvik's question made Blix think twice.

'I don't know anything about that actually, but he must have thought as much.'

Neither Abelvik nor Walenius said anything.

'Have you found anything else at Leirsund?' Blix asked.

'Our work there has not yet been concluded,' Abelvik replied.

'The missing women,' Blix said. 'The crosses on the back of the Polaroid. There must be one more victim. Take a closer look at those who may have a history with child-welfare services. That is the common denominator. Start with the one from Kolbotn.'

Blix pulled out his phone to find one of the newspaper articles about a missing fifty-seven-year-old woman.

'Laila Larsen,' he explained as he showed them the screen. 'Her daughters are featured in several other articles. They won a case against the child-welfare services because they didn't intervene and remove them from their mother's care as children.'

'We know the case,' Abelvik said without seeming interested in what he was showing them.

Tobias Walenius reached for the recorder, stated the time and declared the interrogation over.

It dawned on Blix that Terry had been waiting in the car for over an hour. He dropped his phone back in his pocket and pushed out the chair to get up.

'We're done with your apartment,' Walenius said, fishing the key out of his briefcase.

'Did you find anything?' Blix asked.

Walenius slid the key across the table. 'Mostly dog hair and paw prints,' he replied.

Blix picked up the key and hooked it back onto his key ring. Abelvik got up to follow him out.

'I have something else to talk to you about,' she said once they reached the lift.

'What's that then?'

'You have to leave this to us now.'

Blix looked at her. 'What do you mean?'

'You don't work for the police anymore,' Abelvik replied. 'You can't go around investigating this.'

'Oh come on...' Blix began.

'You called Ann-Kristin Jansen,' Abelvik interjected, her face muscles tightening. 'The daughter of a murder victim. You interviewed her. We had only just notified her of her mother's death. You asked the staff at the Furulia nursing home for the names of the relatives as well.'

Blix ran his hand through his hair and stared at her. 'Sorry,' he said.

'You really do have to leave us to it.'

He didn't want to debate it with her.

'Fine,' he replied. 'But you have to listen to what I'm telling you. He is punishing bad mothers. People he believes do not have the right to live.'

They had reached the ground floor. The entrance hall was empty. Abelvik looked around, glanced up to the floors above.

A guard walked by. The exit doors automatically slid open for him. Blix followed and stopped outside, tilting his head back to get some fresh air.

'Are you okay?' Abelvik asked.

He glanced over at her. 'Yes,' he assured her and straightened up. 'Terry's waiting in the car.' He pointed in the direction of where he had parked.

Abelvik nodded and stood there as Blix walked away. He thought he could feel her gaze on his back, until he rounded the street corner.

He had left the car with a window open a crack, yet a layer of condensation had settled on the inside. Blix opened the car door and glanced over at the back of the seat. Terry sat up drowsily and stared at him.

A police car with blue lights but no siren drove past. Blix slammed the driver's door shut and got in the back with Terry instead. The dog pushed its wet muzzle up in his face to say hello, and lay down with his head on Blix's lap.

For a long time he just sat there, stroking his hand over Terry's fur while he thought about what to do next.

Terry had fallen asleep when Blix finally got back out and climbed in behind the wheel. He took one last look in the mirror and pulled away, watching the police station disappear behind him into the darkness.

54

The cold morning mist lay low over the south of the city. Emma regretted not checking the weather forecast before leaving home. The jacket she was wearing was far too thin. Her fingers felt frozen already, even though she'd shoved them deep inside her trouser pockets.

Nordstrand secondary school was a colossus of a building. A large development project seemed to be under way in the middle of the schoolyard – a building at least two storeys high. The commotion outside the school made Emma think back to her own teenage years and how lost she had felt during that time. How much she had hated sitting at her desk, learning things she knew she would never end up using.

Emma felt for the students who were walking towards the entrance, most of them tired, their hoods pulled tight round their faces. White ear buds shutting out the world around them. Only a few of them were still standing outside in the cool morning air.

Emma wasn't sure if she would recognise Carmen Prytz when she arrived, or if Carmen would come at all. Blix's memories about how often he missed school had made Emma wonder whether Carmen had also spent much of her youth at home. Emma had no idea what Carmen's life really was, and had been, like. But she was itching to find out.

She checked the time. A few minutes past eight.

The text from Nicolai Wibe had arrived while she was having breakfast. Just a short message, which was probably an attempt to circumvent confidentiality regulations:

Match.

The blood in the canoe must have matched Maria Normann's. Emma could interpret it in no other way. She had tried to get hold of Blix to ask if he knew anything more, but hadn't heard from him yet.

Emma had been thinking about him ever since she had returned home the night before. She had just sat in the living room, alone. Listened to the silence, drank a cup of tea. Blix's story had had an effect on her. It had filled her with a sadness, primarily on his behalf, but also because the reality was there were people who subjected their own children to something so harmful.

It was difficult to understand – the fact that no morsel of rationality or compassion for your own children kicked in at any point. Emma was aware that it was an illness, but still. She would do anything to make sure that Martine, her niece, didn't have to go through any sort of painful experience growing up.

Carmen Prytz showed up a few minutes before the bell was meant to go off. She cycled across the yard and struggled for a moment to fit her bike in the rack.

Emma walked towards her and raised a beckoning hand when Carmen looked up.

'Hey,' Emma said.

Carmen stopped and squinted. Didn't say anything, but looked around quickly and straightened the hood on her coat. Emma hoped that Carmen would take her smile as a friendly gesture.

'Sorry to just show up like this,' Emma began.

'What do you want?' Carmen had ear buds in, but she didn't take them out.

'I wanted to talk to you.'

'You could have just texted.'

'True, but it's always so much better to talk to someone face to face.'

Carmen didn't respond to that.

'How are you?' Emma asked.

Carmen shrugged. Emma tried to look for signs of how she was really doing, but without any points of reference it was difficult. Carmen seemed like all the other teenagers around them – sleepy, sluggish. Her face lacked any colour, but that could be because of the cold, or because she had no make-up on.

'I'm ... fine.' She looked around again. 'What are you doing here?'

'I'm here because I think you're right,' Emma said.

'About what?'

'About your stepfather being innocent. I have reason to believe that

Maria Normann will be found soon, and that the police will realise that they no longer have any reason to hold him.'

Carmen stared at her. 'Found? What do you mean?'

'They're looking for her in Lake Gjersjøen,' Emma explained. 'Again – but in a different area. We've found evidence that places Maria very close to the water. In a canoe.'

'A canoe,' Carmen said quietly.

'It was hidden away a bit,' Emma continued. 'Just a few hundred metres from your stepfather's shop. So everything suggests that the person who killed her took her out onto the lake and threw her in.'

Carmen seemed at a loss for words.

'What ... does that mean?'

'It means,' Emma said, taking a step closer. 'That it would take a lot – *a lot* – to prove that your stepfather did it. Just like you said. He wouldn't have had time to.'

'But...' Emma could see that Carmen was thinking.

'They're continuing the search today.'

Carmen glared at her now. 'I told you to leave this alone,' she said.

'Yes, but—'

'You've been working on it anyway.'

Again, Carmen glanced around briskly, as if afraid someone would see them together. Emma wasn't sure what she had expected. Joy, maybe. Curiosity. What Carmen seemed to be presenting she interpreted more as a deep concern for how her mother would react when she found out.

'Have you and your mother spoken any more about what might have happened?' she asked.

Carmen took out her phone and gave the display a few swipes.

'If it wasn't your stepfather who did it, it must have been someone else,' Emma continued. 'Maybe someone who knew Maria? Or someone close to your stepfather?'

'It could have been anyone,' Carmen replied, still busy with her phone.

'I spoke to a friend of Maria's,' Emma said, lowering her voice a little. 'Helle Lindqvist. She runs a tattoo studio. Do you know her?'

Carmen shook her head. 'What about her?'

Emma didn't know how to explain it. She simply had this feeling that there might be something between Maria Normann and Helle Lindqvist. Or at least something desired on Helle's part.

'I don't really know,' she ended up saying. 'She was supposed to meet Maria that day, but nothing came of it.'

Carmen looked up, seeming interested now.

Emma was going to ask how her relationship with her mother was at the moment, but it was as if the young girl was aware of the incoming question. She looked past Emma and up at the school building.

'I have to go,' she said. 'The bell's about to go off.' She took a step to the side and strode past Emma.

She watched Carmen disappear into the crowd of other students. Frosty clouds of air rose around them as the teenagers chatted and laughed.

The school bell rang, and the students headed into the warmth.

Emma turned and walked back towards the car. She had received a message. She stood by the driver's door and opened it.

The message was from Nicolai Wibe. Just as short as the last one: *Body.*

55

The smell of coffee enticed his eyes open. At the foot of the bed: Terry, fast asleep, his stomach rising and falling, steady and calm. Blix had no memory of how the dog had ended up there.

The night before, however, he remembered well.

How Tomine had welcomed him into her apartment after they had said hello to each other and she had greeted Terry. They hadn't exchanged many words until afterwards, in bed.

Blix had told her about his childhood – about his father, his mother, about Lina Marie Jansen and about the letter from the perpetrator, which he had found on the fridge of his father's home. Sharing his trauma with Emma had loosened something in him – it made it easier to talk about it with Tomine as well. He hadn't been scared or anxious.

Afterwards, she had thanked him for opening up to her, for having the courage to do so after so many years, and especially to her – someone he hadn't really known for more than a few days. She had been patient with him, sympathetic. It had been a nice, warm evening.

'I don't quite know how to say this,' Tomine said. She stood in the doorway and looked at him, a mug in either hand, steam rising from both of them.

'What?' Blix said, sitting up.

'You snore quite badly.'

That made him laugh. 'Sorry,' he said. 'I honestly had no idea.'

'Good answer,' Tomine said. 'That means you haven't slept with anyone else.'

'Or that they didn't want to tell me,' Blix said, winking at her.

She laughed and walked towards him. Leaned down and kissed him.

'Mmmh, good morning,' she said.

'Good morning.'

At the end of the bed, Terry hopped up and wanted to join in the game. It was good to see him eager and alert again, happy between them.

'I like that you haven't pushed him off the bed,' Blix said, nodding at the dog.

'Oh, just you wait,' she said. 'I will eventually. This area...' She pointed to the bed. 'We won't be having any dogs up here getting in between us. That is strictly *forbitten*, as Julie used to say.'

The error made Blix laugh. Iselin had also had plenty of strange words in her childhood vocabulary. Chickenpops – didn't that sound so much nicer than chickenpox?

Tomine walked around to the other side of the bed and slid underneath the covers.

'Aren't you going to work?' he asked.

She replied with a smile and shuffled closer, so that their bodies pressed against each other. The hair on her arms stood on end – goosebumps.

'The shop won't open until I get there,' she said, wrapping her arms around him.

Blix tried to reach for his phone on the bedside table to check the time, but Tomine held him back.

'Not yet.' She smiled and lay on top of him.

His phone rang. Blix grimaced.

Tomine rolled off him. 'Saved by the bell,' she laughed and got up.

He let it ring twice before picking it up. The number wasn't saved on his phone, but there was something familiar about it.

'Blix speaking,' he answered.

'Hello, Alexander. It's Krissander Dokken.'

Blix cursed inwardly and quickly glanced at the clock. It was past nine.

'Hi,' he replied and climbed out of bed. 'Sorry, I had completely forgotten that we moved the appointment to today. I won't be able to get to you in time.'

'It occurred to me that you might have forgotten.'

'Sorry.'

'That's okay. How are you doing?' Dokken's voice was, as usual, gentle and subdued.

'Better,' he said, catching a glimpse of Tomine walking into the bathroom. He felt like saying *much* better, but left it at that.

'Have you been to see your father?'

Blix thought about how to answer.

'I have, actually. Involuntarily.'

'What makes you say that?'

'That ... will take a while to answer, but I can explain when I see you next. The short version is that work...' He stopped, held back. 'I've been dragged into something that involves my father. It'll take too long to explain over the phone.'

'But it has resulted in you having contact with him again?'

'A little,' Blix replied. 'But it's not exactly easy talking to him.'

'Well, that's not so surprising, considering how long it's been,' Dokken said. 'It's probably difficult for him too. People who are cognitively impaired have good and bad days, and the swings can be extreme. Some days they can be very communicative and lucid. Other days it can be the opposite.'

'Very true,' Blix replied.

'Shall we book another appointment?' Dokken asked. 'How about Friday? We can talk about it then. How does one pm work for you?'

'Friday at one,' Blix confirmed without checking the calendar.

'Great. Have a good day.'

They hung up. Blix had several unread messages awaiting him when he looked back down at his phone.

He glanced over to the bathroom and heard Tomine step into the shower.

When he opened the messages, they were all from Emma. The body of Maria Normann had been found in Lake Gjersjøen.

56

From the outside, there was little about Dressed in Ink that seemed inviting. The basement premises were located down a side street off Torggata, and the only thing that told Emma that she had come to the right place was the studio's logo painted onto the black door. Emma wasn't even sure if anyone was in, even though the website told her the tattoo studio should have opened fifteen minutes ago.

She made her way down the dirty steps and pushed down on the door handle. It was open.

She took a hesitant step inside. A bell above the door signalled her arrival. The room was pleasantly warm. It smelled like a mixture of incense and ink.

The walls were covered in framed photos. Close-ups of arms, thighs, hands and torsos covered in figures and letters of various colours. Most of the designs were of a dark and gothic nature.

From a sliding door on the other side of the room, a short figure appeared with a military green hat on her head. Although she had a mask over the bottom part of her face, it was easy to recognise Helle Lindqvist – Maria Normann's best friend – from the tattoos snaking up her bare arms. She was wearing black jeans and an equally black T-shirt. Her hands were hidden inside a pair of rubber gloves.

Helle Lindqvist took them off and said hello. 'Can I help?' She removed her mask as she spoke.

'Emma Ramm. We met at a café a few days ago?'

Lindqvist's eyes widened. Then the rest of her face followed, breaking out into a broad smile. Her tongue piercing glinted in the light.

'Sorry,' she said. 'I'm terrible with faces. But I should have remembered *you*. I recognise you now, of course. Thought I'd scared you away.'

Emma remembered the searching, seductive smile on the other side of the table. The question of whether they should grab a drink one day.

'I'm not that easily frightened,' Emma said, although she had to admit that Helle Lindqvist had been surprisingly direct.

'I've got a customer in at the moment,' the tattooist said, nodding towards the back room. 'Is there anything I can help you with?'

Emma immediately became more serious. 'You ... probably haven't been informed yet,' she said. 'And I'm sorry to be the one to come here with bad news. But Maria has been found. I'm afraid to tell you that she's been found dead.'

Emma studied the woman's face. The tattoos covering her neck. How she just stared at Emma, her mouth half open.

'I'm sorry,' Emma repeated. 'I am so sorry for your loss.'

It took a few moments before Helle Lindqvist blinked. As she did so, a tear fell down her cheek.

'It's just ... odd to hear that,' she said at last. 'I knew, really, but ... you always hope for a miracle regardless.'

Emma didn't know what to say.

'How do you know?' Lindqvist asked. 'It's not been on the news?'

'Not yet,' Emma said. 'But I spoke to one of the investigators.'

She left it at that and didn't mention the fact that Maria Normann had been found wearing a backpack full of stones.

Lindqvist nodded slowly, staring at her. 'So ... why are you here?'

'The discovery of the body means that Oliver Krogh will be released.'

'What?'

'I received the message from his lawyer a little while ago. He'll probably be released sometime today.'

Lindqvist swallowed. 'But...'

'He's innocent, Helle. He wasn't the one who killed her. He couldn't have had time to dump her in the water and then drive as far as he did, before turning and arriving back to the fire. It is simply not possible logistically.'

'But who was it, then?'

'That's the question.'

It was only now that Emma picked up on the muffled music coming from the back room.

'Do you know his wife?' she asked.

That made Lindqvist laugh. 'Me? No. Never met her. Why do you ask?'

'How about Carmen, Oliver's stepdaughter. Did you ever meet her?'

The tattooist took a step closer. A suspicious expression had clouded her face. 'No.'

'Maria never spoke of her, or of them?'

'Yeah, a little. But I don't understand why you're asking me all this?'

Emma held her hands up, realising how intrusive she must sound. 'I'm just trying to get a better overview,' she said. 'Can I ask you what kind of impression you got of them based on what Maria told you?'

Helle Lindqvist turned her head towards the open door to the room behind.

'I don't have time to talk about this now,' she said. 'But I didn't get a particularly good impression, exactly. Not of any of them.'

'How?'

'Carmen was a little drama queen – Maria's own words. Off school a lot. She may have seen herself in her. I don't know.'

'So Maria saw Carmen fairly regularly?'

'Yeah, I think so. In the shop, probably. The relationship between Carmen and her mother also seemed to be kind of unhealthy, but Maria never went into much detail about it. Sounded like the girl's mother was a bit of a bitch. Always suspicious of Oliver.'

'She probably had a good reason for that, given what the relationship between Maria and Oliver was like.'

'Yeah, I guess.'

'Did Maria ever meet her – Oliver's wife?'

'Sure, naturally, after she started working for her husband.'

Emma wondered what else she should ask Helle about, without making it too obvious what she was fishing for.

'Will you see Oliver Krogh again, do you think?'

Helle Lindqvist walked over to the reception desk and pulled out a drawer. Found a new set of latex gloves and put them on.

'Oh, I have no plans to see him,' she said.

'Why not?'

Lindqvist snorted. 'He may well be innocent. He might not have killed her. But he's no saint.'

Very few of us are, Emma wanted to say, but left it.

'I've got to get back to my customer,' Helle Lindqvist said, using her T-shirt to wipe the sweat from her face. 'We can talk more about this later.'

'Okay,' Emma said.

She wanted to ask Helle Lindqvist where she was the afternoon that Maria Normann was killed, but couldn't bring herself to do it.

57

The flag outside Furulia was hanging at half-mast, presumably to mark the passing of one of the residents.

Blix drove into the parking space left by a van that had just pulled away, and went inside.

No one paid him any attention as he made his way through the corridors. He had expected to find his father in the TV room, but it was empty. Blix continued on to his father's room. For a moment he stopped outside the door, which stood ajar. From inside, he could hear the sound of the radio, as always tuned to P1.

Blix slowly pushed open the door.

His father was sitting in a high-backed chair, which supported his head and neck. On the table in front of him was an old copy of the local newspaper, laid out next to a bowl of biscuits.

Blix took a hesitant step inside.

'Hi, Dad.'

His father turn to him with a guarded gaze. Blix didn't know where to look. He saw a chair and pulled it over, its legs scraping against the floor.

Blix sat down on the other side of the table. 'How are you today?'

No answer. Blix searched his father's eyes to see whether this could be one of those days that Krissander Dokken had talked about, where his father might be lucid, communicative. He couldn't tell.

'Did you sleep well?' Blix asked.

His father grunted.

'I thought I'd show you something,' Blix said, pulling a small box from his jacket pocket.

His father blinked hard a few times, as if to focus his eyes. Blix opened the lid of the box he had stopped back at the flat to pick up, and took out a dark fishing fly with an orange-and-green trigger point.

Something about the old man's mood shifted. He immediately became more interested and alert.

'An *undertaker*,' he commented, reaching out to hold it himself.

Blix let him take it and began to tell him details about that particular fly – what colours and materials he had used, even though his father could see for himself.

'Could catch some trout with this one,' his father said. 'Where are you going to test it out?'

He handed the fly back. Blix accepted it and returned it to the box.

'Lake Ringsjøen, perhaps.'

His father nodded approvingly. 'Could catch a big 'un there.'

A hesitant silence settled between them.

'Do you remember the one I caught in Innoset?' Blix asked.

'Almost three kilos,' his father nodded.

He was thinking of the one he'd caught in Langvann, but Blix didn't correct him. The trout he had caught in Innoset had weighed over four kilos. It had been big enough to serve for dinner two days in a row.

They went on to talk about other lakes they had fished in, and some other childhood memories. Once, when Blix was about ten years old, a truck with pigs on their way to slaughter had overturned round a bend just beyond where they lived. The pigs had escaped, and both Blix and his father had helped round them up. His father chuckled at the thought of how they had run around the fields.

Another time the wind had felled a large pine tree behind the house. Blix and his father had spent a week sawing at it and splitting it into fire-wood.

'Got us through the winter,' his father recalled.

The conversation created a rare atmosphere of familiarity between them, and for a while, everything else was forgotten.

Blix reached for a biscuit from the bowl. He had his father where he wanted him.

'You took me to see Lina Marie Jansen too. Do you remember that?'

His father seemed immediately uncomfortable.

'The psychologist,' Blix added.

His father snorted. 'What a load of nonsense.'

Blix agreed with him, just to go along with it.

'You were the one who had to drive me,' he said. 'Do you remember? When Mum was ill.'

His father's gaze seemed to wander. He swallowed, seemed distressed.

'Back when we had the brown Cortina,' Blix continued.

'Good car,' his father nodded. His expression relaxed slightly.

'You came in with me a few times. Sat in the waiting room.'

He scoffed.

'Although you would usually wait out in the car park,' Blix continued.

'Had to.'

'Why?'

'Didn't have anything to say to those people in there.'

Blix straightened up a little. 'Which people?'

Outside the window, the wind was buffeting the branches of a pine tree. His father turned and watched them.

'Which people?' Blix repeated.

'The other people waiting,' his father said.

Blix reached for another biscuit. 'Did you know any of them?' he asked, trying to sound nonchalant.

The conversation with his father had taken the form of an interrogation – he had to weigh his words carefully to extract the right answers.

'Some of them,' his father replied.

Blix felt a surge of hope.

'I remember a boy about my age,' Blix said. 'Came before or after me, I think. Do you remember him?'

His father grimaced. Blix couldn't quite read what the expression meant.

'Must have been Odd Henrik's boy,' he replied.

'Odd Henrik?' Blix asked. 'Who was that?'

His father started to chew on his lower lip.

'What was Odd Henrik's last name?' Blix pushed.

No answer.

'Where did they live?'

His father's gaze wandered back over to the window.

'It's going to rain again,' he concluded.

Blix sank back in his chair, realising that the moment was over. He wouldn't get anything more out of his father.

58

Kalle's Choice, Emma's regular haunt, was busier than usual, but luckily, there was no queue at the counter. Karl Oskar Hegerfors, the café's owner and manager, welcomed her with a warm smile.

'My queen,' he said. 'How nice to see you.'

'My king, hello.'

'It's been a while.'

It hadn't, but Emma just smiled instead of correcting him. She knew him well enough by now to know he meant it ironically.

'The usual?' Karl Oskar pressed a lump of coffee grounds into the portafilter as he repeated an order to the assistant next to him.

'Just a coffee today, please.'

He frowned. 'Not sick, are you?' As always, he spoke in his own blend of Swedish and Norwegian.

Emma smiled. 'No, just not hungry.'

Emma took her coffee, made just the way she liked it, as always, and headed upstairs to her regular spot on the second floor.

A little before 1:00pm, she opened a new tab on her phone and pushed in her ear buds to watch the live broadcast from the police station. On the screen were two men: Chief of Police Gard Fosse and Oliver Krogh's lawyer, Leo van Eijk, both sitting at a press table, serious expressions on their faces. *POLICE* was stamped repetitively across the bright blue backdrop behind them.

It was impossible to tell how many people were in the room with them, but Emma was sure that the press conference would be packed out. This was a case that would be talked and written about for weeks, especially now that the murder investigation had been blown wide open again.

Gard Fosse moved to begin. He cleared his throat and slightly adjusted the thin, black microphone in front of him. He started by thanking everyone for coming. Emma could see that he was revelling in having the room's attention on him.

The chief of police briefly summarised that the divers had recovered the body of a woman at a depth of fourteen metres in the eastern part of Lake Gjersjøen at 08:07 that morning. The body was soon after identified as Maria Normann.

'This case has from the outset been investigated as a murder. The circumstances surrounding the discovery of the body confirm that hypothesis. We cannot say anything more about the cause of death until after the autopsy.'

He went on to explain further procedural details, as well as how the police had conducted the case from day one. In conclusion, he admitted that the discovery of the body weakened their suspicions against Oliver Krogh.

'His lawyer, Leo van Eijk, has petitioned for his client's release. The courts have decided to comply with this. The charges remain for the time being, but Oliver Krogh has already been released from Oslo Prison. Before I pass the baton on to Mr van Eijk, I would like to convey a message from Krogh and his family: they ask for their privacy to be respected following his release. I think it unnecessary to point out that this has been, and still is, a great burden on them.'

Gard Fosse seemed pleased with himself as he handed the floor to Leo van Eijk. The lawyer already had a film of sweat on his upper lip. He took a sip from a glass of water and looked down at the papers in front of him.

'The reason for the release is that my client now has a watertight alibi for the murder of Maria Normann. The place in which her body was recovered rules out any possibility that he had the time and opportunity to commit the murder and move her, with intentions to hide her corpse. Oliver Krogh has, from day one, maintained his innocence. He has not been believed. He has been in custody for almost two months, and has been unfairly branded as a murderer across the country because the police did not do their job.'

Gard Fosse shrunk in his seat slightly.

The lawyer went on to emphasise how stressful all this had been for his client, not least because he had lost a close friend and colleague.

'Nonetheless, he is happy to finally be believed and to be free at last. He is now looking forward to assisting the police further in this case, so that the person responsible can be held accountable.'

The rest of the press conference passed without any other major revelations.

Emma was getting ready to leave when her phone rang. The display told her it was Maria Normann's mother.

Emma answered, her voice gentle. 'Hi there, Hildegard.'

'Hello.'

'I'm so sorry for your loss.'

Hildegard Normann sniffed. 'Thank you.'

Her voice trembled. She was unable to continue at first.

'The police told me how they found her,' she finally said. 'That it was because of you. I just wanted to say ... thank you.'

Emma could feel herself welling up.

'Now they just have to find the person who did this,' she said.

After a short pause, Hildegard said, 'I still think it was Oliver Krogh.'

Emma frowned. 'What makes you say that?' She remembered how much hatred Maria's mother felt towards him.

'Someone else could have driven off with his car,' she suggested.

The idea of an accessory seemed to Emma like an unlikely option. 'Who could that have been?' she asked.

'I don't know,' Hildegard answered. 'But he must have done something ... smart. To fool everyone. I'm not the only one who thinks so.'

'Oh?' Emma said. 'Who else thinks that?'

'A lot of people,' Hildegard replied. 'Just look online.'

Emma didn't know how to respond. She had no desire to enter into any sort of discussion about this with Maria's mother.

'You must come to the funeral,' Hildegard went on. 'I don't know when it will be yet, but...'

Emma thanked her for the invitation, although it felt strange going to the funeral of someone she had never met. She hadn't even met any of Maria Normann's friends, with the exception of Helle Lindqvist.

Hildegard thanked her again, before hanging up.

Just look online.

Emma was a little curious about what people were saying, how they justified their suspicions. A quick look on social media proved that Hildegard was right: a lot of people were still convinced that Krogh was a murderer. 'Where there's smoke, there's fire', someone wrote on Maria's Facebook page. 'Pun intended'.

The waves of online attacks people must have to fight when arrested on suspicion of committing a serious crime must leave you feeling powerless, Emma thought. And that bad feeling towards you didn't just disappear when you were vindicated. It didn't even help that there were voices defending Krogh. People had made up their minds. Fake news in practice.

Emma saw that she had received eleven new friend requests since she had last been on Facebook. Helle Lindqvist was one of them.

Emma accepted and clicked onto Helle's profile. She had also posted something about the latest developments, but it was primarily a tribute to Maria, a kind of mini obituary which she ended by saying that her heart was broken and that she would never forget her 'soulmate'. She had also posted two pictures of Maria: one of Maria alone, and one with Helle. In the latter, a small boy stood between them.

Poor kid, Emma thought. Jonas, was that his name? She knew all too well how he felt. How his life would be, going forward, without a mother. He had no father in his life either.

Emma clicked through the photos on Helle's profile. She was a good photographer – there were many pictures of her work, customers proudly showing off their newly tattooed forearms and chests. There were also lots of pictures of Maria.

Emma scrolled down. Every time she saw a picture of her, she clicked on it. There was no doubt that Maria Normann had been a beautiful woman. Narrow face, dimples, gentle eyes.

A series of images further on made Emma squint, pull the screen a little closer. Helle and Maria, out walking somewhere. Surrounded by trees. Wearing hiking clothes. The photo series, posted on the 11th of July that year, was titled 'Rehab'.

Emma stopped on the penultimate picture.

It was taken on a lake.

In a canoe.

The location had been tagged too.

Lake Gjersjøen.

Emma sat staring at the picture, when a text appeared on the screen.

The message was from Leo van Eijk:

Hi Emma. My client would like to meet you. When are you available?

59

The exit was barely visible. The turning was hidden right behind a large fir tree. Blix slowed down and pulled over. A post box nailed to a telephone pole. Most of the dark-green paint had peeled off. The remains of a name written in black marker was still visible.

Odd Hen—

He was on the right track.

Magnar Eikrem, his father's old match-of-the-day friend, had known who Odd Henrik was. When Blix had been told the man's full name, so much seemed to fall into place.

The narrow dirt road snaked its way through the trees. Branches occasionally scraped against the side of the car. In some places, the deep ruts in the road were full of mud. The tyres bumped into potholes he couldn't even see.

The car radio was on low. The sound of the news jingle made him turn up the volume. The first feature didn't surprise him: the police had found another body in the forest near Leirsund. The discovery was being investigated in connection with the disappearance of a woman from Kolbotn a few years ago.

Laila Larsen, Blix said to himself. The third cross. The name that had been at the top of his own list of missing women.

He finished listening to the segment before he took out his mobile phone and called Abelvik, but she didn't answer. He tossed the phone into the passenger seat.

On the right side of the road, a recently harvested wheat field came into view. Blix drove a short distance before slowing down and stopping. The small, abandoned farm lay at the end of the track, about fifty metres in front of him. It was made up of a main house, a barn, two smaller outbuildings with corrugated iron roofs and the remains of some dog kennels. Several of the grey asbestos sheets on the roof of the house had come loose and fallen off. The plaster on the walls was cracked. Parts of the barn roof had collapsed. The red paint was faded and peeling off in large flakes.

He put his arms on the steering wheel and leaned forward. A large, dark bird took off from the roof of the house, flew round in a semicircle and disappeared into the branches of the nearest tree.

He wanted to kick himself for not having made the connection sooner. That was usually his specialty – checking and double-checking. Connecting events, drawing the lines between them.

He remembered the boy in the waiting room, but he still wasn't able to connect everything that had happened with that boy's childhood. What he was certain of was that something significant must have taken place within the four crooked walls of the house in front of him.

His phone pinged. A message from Emma. She had sent him a screenshot of two women in a canoe. *Maria Normann and Helle Lindqvist*, she wrote. The canoe was identical to the one they found by Lake Gjersjøen.

Blix frowned, worried that she would do something stupid. He called her. The call cut off. Soon after, a new message popped up: *Going to meet Oliver Krogh and his lawyer.*

'Huh,' Blix said quietly to himself, wondering how that could have happened. He raised his phone and took a photo through the windscreen.

I'm here, he wrote. *Call me when you can.* And he sent the photo.

She responded with a thumbs-up.

Blix dropped the phone into the centre console, put the car in gear and slowly rolled forward. Tufts of grass grew in clusters across the yard in front of the derelict house. Between them, he could see tracks in the gravel – a vehicle that had been here recently, had clearly turned round.

The sight made him immediately wary. He turned off the engine, pushed open the car door and sat and listened.

A tractor was working somewhere to the east, on the other side of the forest, otherwise, nothing.

He left Terry in the car and approached the house. Steps led up to a front door. A scythe and a spade were propped up against the wall.

Blix rattled the handle. It was locked. He shook it a few times, just to make sure, before continuing around the house.

The windows were grey with dust and fly droppings. Blix found a gap in the curtains of the nearest kitchen window. A light glowed from the extractor fan above the hob. A pile of newspapers lay on the table just inside. On the other side of the room, a cupboard door stood ajar. He rubbed the glass a little, hoping to get a clearer view. On the hob: a pot with the ladle still in it. Some empty tins stood on the counter beside it.

He caught a similar glimpse into the living room. An oblong table stood between the TV and a shabby sofa. Behind it were some carved wooden figures arranged across the empty bookshelves. Presumably ones Odd Henrik had made himself.

The next window didn't have any curtains. Pushed up against the wall was a bunk bed with a writing desk, otherwise the room was empty.

Blix walked on, around the building. The kennels had been built against the west side of the house. The fence around them had collapsed in several places. The posts that had held it up were sticking out at odd angles. Nettles and other weeds covered the roofs of the individual dog houses. In some places, the outer wall of the house was covered in grooves, presumably from the dogs scratching.

The windows of the next room along had been fitted with internal blinds. One of them hung askew. Blix put his hands to the glass and peered inside. It appeared to be a kind of workshop with an old carpentry bench in the middle. A desk lamp was attached to one corner. Some tools were scattered across it, while chisels and saws of various sizes hung on the wall. On a board beside them were three photos. From where Blix stood, he could only just about make out the figures, but he recognised the wide, white frames. Three Polaroid pictures.

His pulse started to increase.

He pulled out his phone, placed it against the glass and took a picture into the room. He then enlarged it on the screen to get a better look. The images appeared to be of carved figures, which suggested that there would be an old-fashioned Polaroid camera somewhere in the house.

Blix went back to the car and studied the tracks in the yard. The grass up to the barn door looked like it had been driven over and was slowly moving back to its original position. He took a picture of that too before walking over to the wide door and trying to push it open, but without success.

Just around the corner of the building was a door with a window. He had expected to find it locked as well, but it swung open easily when he tried the handle.

Inside, the barn was pitch-black.

Blix stood in the doorway and blinked a few times to let his eyes adjust.

Then he took a step inside, and as soon as he did, he felt something hit him at thigh height, followed by a sharp, stinging sensation. He yelled out, more in surprise than in pain.

He quickly began to feel dizzy. He staggered backward and had to reach for the door frame to keep himself upright. The strength in his hands was gone. Then his whole body felt numb. And he collapsed.

60

Leo van Eijk opened the door of the house in Røa before Emma even had a chance to ring the bell. The last time they met, he had treated her with ill-concealed distain. This time, he smiled warmly and held out his hand.

'Hi Emma,' he said as she returned the gesture. 'Thank you for coming, it's good to see you.'

'Thanks for inviting me.'

The lawyer moved aside to show her into the hall, took her jacket and hung it up behind the sliding doors of a wardrobe. Emma pulled off her boots and stepped inside.

Oliver Krogh was waiting for her in the living room.

The first thing that struck her was how thin he looked. Thinner than in the pictures she had seen of him. He was wearing jeans and a T-shirt that clung tight to his torso. Emma noticed a large bruise on one arm, as if someone had held him in a firm grip.

His hair was slicked back. It looked wet. Emma imagined how good it must be to shower properly again, and if not in his own home, at least as a free man.

'Oliver, this is Emma,' Leo van Eijk said from behind her. 'Emma – Oliver.'

Oliver Krogh stood up. Keeping unwavering eye contact, they shook hands.

'Thank you for wanting to see me.'

Emma had imagined Krogh to have a deep masculine voice, a voice of the wilderness – dark and manly. But it was surprisingly light and meek.

'Likewise,' Emma said. 'I've wanted to meet you ever since...' She had to think. 'About a week ago – ever since I first started looking into your case.'

They sat down.

The living room smelled like a mixture of the fireplace and cleaning products. Something told Emma that Leo van Eijk had had help with both choosing the décor and keeping the place clean. The furniture was classic, tasteful. The colours in the room complemented one another well.

'Can I get you a drink?' Leo van Eijk asked Emma.

'I'll have whatever you're having,' she replied.

'We really should have champagne,' the lawyer said. 'What do you think, Oliver?'

He thought about it. 'The only time I drink champers is on New Year's Eve,' he said with a smile. 'But right now ... I mean, if you have any?'

'*If* I have any – what do you take me for?'

Oliver Krogh smiled.

'Just a small glass for me then,' Emma laughed. 'I'm driving.'

The lawyer disappeared into the kitchen. Oliver Krogh smiled. He had dimples on both cheeks. His face was clean shaven. Even from a distance she could sense that he smelled good.

An awkward silence descended.

Emma could tell that he was uncomfortable. She placed her hands on her thighs and ran them quickly over her trousers. It was hard to look at him without thinking of Maria. Of the two of them, together.

She wanted to know what he had thought about the future – before her murder, before the fire – but it felt a little too early in the conversation for such intrusive questions.

'So...' she said instead. 'What's it like being out again?'

He considered her question.

'Weird, more than anything. It's all gone so fast, in the end. Getting out. From one day to the next, sort of. I have you to thank for that. I...' He searched for the words. 'I am eternally grateful.'

A loud noise from the kitchen made Emma flinch. The cork from the champagne bottle hit something that made Leo van Eijk curse. Oliver Krogh laughed briefly. It lightened the mood.

'I'm glad I could help,' Emma said with a smile.

The lawyer returned holding three glasses and a heavy bottle.

'There was a bit of a mess,' he said, shaking his head.

One by one he filled the glasses. The champagne bubbled up and almost spilled over each rim. He distributed the glasses and then lifted his own.

'Cheers,' he said. 'To freedom and justice.'

They each took a sip and nodded at each other appreciatively. Leo van Eijk found a spot on the sofa.

'What will you do now?' Emma asked.

Oliver Krogh looked down. 'I don't quite know,' he replied. 'First, I'll just try to get back on my feet. Leo has arranged a hotel for me tonight, so ... we'll go from there.'

Emma looked over at the lawyer, who nodded and smiled.

'Have you spoken to your wife, since your release?'

He shook his head. 'She's coming here later.' Oliver glanced quickly at the clock on the wall. 'It's easier to do it here than in Nordstrand. There's probably a whole throng of journalists outside the house.'

Krogh took another sip of the champagne.

'Mmm, that's good,' he said, turning the bottle round to look at the label.

'What are the police planning on doing now?' Emma asked.

Leo van Eijk answered this time. 'They'll have to start at the beginning,' he said. 'They've set up a new call-line for tip-offs. A little desperate, I think. They know they've screwed up.'

'Do they have nothing else to go on?'

'That's the impression I got.'

Emma pulled out her phone. She had sent a message to Nicolai Wibe and made him aware of the picture of Maria and Helle Lindqvist in the canoe. No response yet. She considered showing it to Oliver Krogh, but contented herself with first asking if he knew who Lindqvist was.

He nodded. 'Maria's best friend.'

'Did you ever meet her?'

'She came to the shop once. I was dealing with customers at the time so I didn't have a chance to say much more than hello. Maria lived with her for a while, I think.'

'That's right.'

Emma thought about what to say next.

'Helle helped her get back on her feet,' she said. 'Took care of her. They went for hikes together.'

'Yes, that's how I understood it.'

'They explored the area around your shop as well, right?'

Oliver Krogh held on to the stem of his glass and swirled the contents around a few times.

'Maria loved the outdoors,' he said. 'And it was a way for her to test out some of our equipment. She didn't really know anything about any of it.'

'And she spent time on Lake Gjersjøen too?'

'Yes, she explored it a couple of times, I think.'

'Was that in one of the canoes, or...?'

'It was – I had a used one I kept inside the shop that customers could take down to the water to test out, if they wanted.'

There was a moment of silence across the coffee table. Emma was afraid the lawyer would ask where she was going with this line of questioning, but Krogh broke the silence and took the conversation in a different direction.

'So ... it was Carmen who wanted you to...?'

Emma nodded. 'She's a great girl,' she answered quickly.

'She is. We've always had a close relationship. Even if she's not my daughter – biologically.'

'You haven't spoken to her either then, I presume, since you were released?'

'No. I've not used my phone yet.'

'Her father, he ... isn't in the picture at all?'

Oliver Krogh shook his head. 'He didn't give a damn about her. Poor girl.'

Emma thought through what to say next, and what not to say.

'A few days ago Carmen told me to stop digging into your case.'

'Oh?'

'Yes, I made the mistake of telling your wife that it was Carmen who wanted me to help. I thought it was interesting that Carmen, later that day, told me to stop. She also seemed concerned when I saw her this morning.'

'You saw her today?'

'Yes, outside her school.'

The information made him think.

'I know you suspect your wife of being behind this,' Emma said. 'I ... found a couple of disturbing things when I looked through her email.'

'So you did look?' Krogh said. 'I wasn't sure if—' He stopped himself.

Emma put down her glass and told them about Victoria's posts on the forums of the women's aid website. She hesitated to say anything about the accusations Victoria had made of abuse against her and Carmen, but finally decided to be honest.

As Emma spoke, Krogh shook his head and came out with quiet exclamations at what he was hearing. When she finished, he looked over at Leo van Eijk.

'She's more screwed up than I thought.'

He took a few moments to process what he had been told.

'First of all: I never laid a hand on Carmen. Never. I've had to speak to her quite sternly a couple of times, but show me a parent or guardian who hasn't. I have never been violent with Victoria either. Just the thought alone ... fuck.' He shook his head forcefully. 'She ... has always been a drama queen. Always exaggerating things – every problem always became so much bigger than it actually was. She enjoyed making herself the victim. What you're telling me now though, that ... it's completely outrageous.'

Again he paused, as if to think it all over one more time.

'She's probably thrived on this while I was in prison. Had a whole influx of support and sympathy. Jesus Christ.'

They were all silent for a while. Leo van Eijk took another sip of his champagne – he was well over halfway through the glass.

'She wrote something about her suspicions of an unfaithful husband, too,' Emma said.

She felt uncomfortable about bringing this up, but it was hard to avoid.

'She asked for advice on what she should do,' she added. 'People were ... angry. Aggressive on her behalf. There was no doubt about the nature of the advice she received.'

'That doesn't surprise me,' Oliver said, now staring down at the edge of the table.

'The question is whether she acted on any of it,' Emma continued. 'And I understand you've thought about that too?'

There was silence around the table.

Leo van Eijk finished off his glass and poured himself a new one. Topped up Emma and Oliver's glasses too.

'How have things been, really?' Emma asked. 'Over the years?'

'What do you mean?'

'This might be a little invasive, my asking, but ... I was wondering about how things have been for your family? What the family dynamic was like, during the time you were together?' She posed it as a question.

Oliver Krogh sighed and stared at his glass. Bubbles rose to the surface.

'We met at a photography exhibition, of all things. A mutual acquaintance of ours, a very skilled photographer, had a private viewing on Aker Brygge. We got to talking. It was nice. I'd just come out of a failed relationship, so we both had that to talk about. Common ground and all that.' He started picking at the skin on his fingers. 'In the beginning it was ... good. In every way – we had fun, it was nice. We were taking things slowly. So it took a long time before I started seeing the other sides to her.'

He seemed to hold back a bit, before deciding to explain:

'Victoria is extremely self-absorbed. She always wants to be the centre of attention, both at home and at work,' he said. 'She's done well with her company, but she's stepped on a lot of toes to assert herself, exploiting the vulnerability of others to her advantage.'

That matched the impression Emma had of her.

'The way she behaved, it affected our relationship, and she became quite demanding to be around. I think that made Carmen quite a demanding child as well. She was afraid of all sorts of strange things. Like, in the early days she would be completely hysterical if we had gone out onto the veranda without her knowing. She got better, of course, as she got older. But she didn't have many friends and wasn't out of the house that much. And that was absolutely fine for Victoria – she would've liked to have full control of her. Not let her out of her sight ... ever. We argued about that a lot. But she was somehow unable to look at it from the outside in. She always thought she knew best – who was I to know anything about what her daughter needed? Me, who had never raised a child.'

He rolled his eyes and shook his head. The talking had made his throat dry. He took a quick sip from his glass and set it back down.

'Carmen was never difficult to deal with when it was just her and me. With Carmen and Victoria together, however, the two of them ... sometimes it could be quite...' He made his hands into fists and bumped his knuckles together. 'But you know, that's how it was, and it was normal. If Victoria has said otherwise, she's exaggerating – it's always to make people feel sorry for her. Everything she's "been through".' He made air quotes with his fingers. 'It's called being a mother. Not everyone is fit to be one.'

Emma thought of Blix's mother.

'You thought she was a bad mother?'

He considered the question. 'Bad is maybe not the right word. But I thought she created unnecessary drama about all sorts of ridiculous things.'

He took a few more moments to think.

'Victoria got a little jealous, I think, of the relationship I built with Carmen, over time. She often complained about it, that Carmen would rather be with me than with her. Which wasn't true, of course. But like I said, she exaggerates. Often, though, if Victoria was at work on the weekends, Carmen would come along and help out in the shop. And I thought that was nice – fun.' Oliver sighed heavily. 'Victoria only ever wanted sympathy. She wanted me to say that of course the bond between a mother and a daughter is unique or whatever. She needed validation, Victoria. Always. Eventually it became ... tiresome. And you can imagine what it was like when Maria came into our lives.'

Emma picked up her glass but didn't drink.

'Maria...' He paused and shook his head, as if a tender memory had surfaced. 'She was Victoria's exact opposite, really. In almost every way. Social, outgoing, charismatic. She could talk to a wall and make it blush. She was ... utterly unique like that. And for me...' Oliver paused. 'With Victoria, everything was about her. Her, her, her – day in, day out. We only ever spoke about her problems with this or that, whether it was work or Carmen or...' He exhaled hard. 'When Maria came back into my life, it was as if things suddenly became a little brighter again. For one thing, we already knew each other, so we had a lot to talk about, but it was also fun to go to work again, even if the shop wasn't doing well. It was something to look forward to. And then ... there was clearly a physical attraction there as well. I won't deny it. But I never imagined it would—'

Again he had to stop.

'That it would turn into this,' he finished, a note of sadness to his voice.

The three of them sat in silence for a while.

'Oliver, may I ask – what happened that day? That Sunday?'

He lifted his chin to look at her. Moved his gaze to Leo van Eijk, who said nothing, instead choosing to lift the champagne glass to his lips.

'You don't have to answer,' Emma said. 'I'm just curious.'

Oliver Krogh seemed to be thinking through the events of that day himself.

'I'm guessing you've been given a summary,' he began. 'From Leo.'

'I have. But...'

'There's not much more I can add to that really. I ... can't bear to talk about it.'

Emma respected that.

A moment later, they heard a sound from outside. A car pulling onto the driveway. Leo van Eijk got up and went to the window.

'Christ,' he said. 'They're already here.'

He looked down at his wristwatch.

'They?' Emma asked.

'Carmen and Victoria,' the lawyer explained. 'They weren't meant to come until after six.'

61

A wasp bumped against the inside of the windowpane again and again. There was a couple of seconds' pause, before it started again.

'That,' his father said, nodding towards the wasp, 'is the very definition of stupidity. Doing the same thing, over and over, but expecting a different result.'

He smacked his lips and shook his head. Got up from the table and leaned against the window, opening one side and letting the wasp continue to bounce against the glass until it found its way out.

'I had to do that all the time when your mother lived here,' he said, and closed the window. 'Or I'd have to kill it. She'd go into a complete panic, poor thing.' He rolled his eyes and sat down. 'Not surprising perhaps, what with her allergy and all. I would have been afraid myself.'

The boy wondered if that was one of the reasons why his mother couldn't live with them anymore, but he didn't ask.

His father pulled his chair closer to the table. 'It's the year of the wasp this year,' he said. 'Did you know that there are over five thousand types of wasps in the world?' And before the boy could answer: 'Every summer, the wasp queens can produce over twelve thousand workers. That's no small feat.' He laughed. 'We actually have a huge wasps' nest inside the barn. Have you seen it?'

The boy shook his head.

'It's bloody massive.'

There was always something for his father to talk about. Something interesting about the trees, the bushes in the forest, the roots. The mushrooms. The berries. The animals.

His father nodded towards the chessboard. 'Your move.'

He was the one who had carved and polished all the pieces on the board. He had even coated them in oil, so they would last as long as possible.

'You've got to learn to take care of things, boy,' he always said.

For a few moments the boy tried to focus on the game and the pieces in front of him, but he couldn't see his next move. No strategies came to him.

'Planning,' his father said. 'It's all about alpha and omega. You have to think several moves ahead, always – imagine what your opponent is going to do. *You* have to lead.'

It was the same lesson he had heard a hundred times before. Sometimes he did take the lead. As for the outcome of the game though, it never helped. His father always beat him.

But it didn't matter.

'Okay,' his father said, pushing the board a little to the side. 'I can see you're not concentrating. What's troubling you?'

He looked up at his father, who had laid his worker's hands one over the other on the table between them. The boy didn't know what to say. For the last few days, a darkness had settled over him. It had become harder to smile, harder to laugh.

Suddenly the boy's eyes were full of tears. It only took a second, then he hiccupped too.

'Oh, my boy,' his father said in a gentle voice, and getting up, came over to the other side of the table. 'What is it?'

It became impossible to speak. The words stuck in his throat – he just cried and cried and cried. His father sat down next to him. Placed a hand on his back and gently stroked it up and down.

'Has something happened?' his father asked after a while.

The boy couldn't bring himself to answer that either. It took a long time before he could even breathe.

It was the last day of the summer holiday.

That is, the holidays weren't over, but his stay there – with his father – certainly was. Soon she would come and collect him, and then he would have to go back to Skedsmokorset, to the little red house, to the neighbourhood he didn't like, to the friends he didn't have. The kids who went abroad during the holidays – to Denmark, Spain, Italy – and who laughed at him when he said he wasn't going anywhere in particular. For him, he was happiest exactly where he was, right here, where he had lived for the first six years of his life. On the farm, with his father. For the past seven years, he had only been here every other weekend and for three weeks every summer.

What was the rest of his summer going to be like?

She would be happy for the first few days. She would probably suggest that they should play yatzy now and then and do a couple of puzzles, maybe take a trip to Nebbursvollen for a swim – if the weather was good enough. But then she would inevitably grow tired of being a mother and send both him and the dogs to her grandmother in Leirsund. Or maybe not even that – she might just go out and leave him home alone.

He had never been able to say anything about this to his father.

Not until now, when he stammered out the first sentence as he sat hunched over the living-room table. After he had said the first words, the next followed. Then, they became a years-long testimony of what life with his mother was like. She who, in the past, before he had learned to make cheese sandwiches himself, could let him go for days on end without food. Who would lock him in the basement too, often without explaining why.

Once he fell off his bike and scraped himself badly. The pain and bleeding felt endless. But instead of helping him up and cleaning his wounds, she scolded him for ruining his trousers.

His father said nothing as the boy spoke, just continued to stroke his back, up and down. When the boy couldn't say any more, he put his head down on the table and just cried.

Later that day, she came down the road to the farm in her battered old Corsa. The boy was sitting on the stairs and whittling away at what was supposed to be an arrow. His mother zigzagged like a maniac across the gravel to avoid the worst of the puddles. It had been raining heavily for the past few days.

She stopped and turned off the engine. For a few moments she remained seated, as if she needed to steel herself for what she was about to do. When at last she climbed out of the car, she said, obviously offended:

'What kind of reception is this? Are you just going to sit there when your mum comes to pick you up?'

He slowly put down the knife and branch. It was slightly curved, he realised now – it would be useless for shooting at targets.

He stood up.

His mother was standing next to the car waiting for him. She lit a cigarette. His shoes crunched as he made his way across the wet ground. Once close enough, she threw out her arms and pulled him in tight for a hug.

She smelled of sunscreen and smoke. She was also sun-kissed and tanned – she might have been abroad. She would probably regale him with everything in the car on the way home: how nice it had been, how much fun she had had. She had probably met some guy that she really liked. Last summer it was someone called Mogens.

'Did you miss me?' she asked, squeezing him close.

'Yes,' is all he said.

She pushed him away from her and looked around. 'Not much has changed here has it? Where is he, your father?'

'He's in the barn,' he said.

That made her snort. 'Doesn't surprise me. Where are your things?'

'Inside.'

'Go get them then so we can get out of here.'

'Dad wants to talk to you first.'

'Pfft, I'm sure he does.'

'He's waiting for you in the barn.'

The boy said nothing more, just turned and went back into the house. But he didn't collect his things. Instead, he stood in the kitchen and looked out of the window. Watched as she slowly moved towards the barn door that her father had left ajar.

She went inside.

He had no idea what his father was going to do. For the past few hours he had hardly said a word. The boy stood staring at the barn door, half expecting to hear them shouting at each other – he had a vague memory of what that was like, many years ago.

But he heard nothing.

A few minutes passed.

And then he jumped.

A loud scream – his mother's – followed by another.

He rushed out and ran towards the barn. His shoes almost got stuck in the wet grass, but it didn't take long before he reached the doorway.

His mother was lying on the wooden floor just inside the entrance to the barn. The door behind her was open. Insects swirled around her. Wasps. A swarm of them. Only now did the boy notice the wasps' nest on the ground beside her.

Panicked, she raised her head towards him, while trying to wave away the wasps that only grew more and more furious with her movements.

'Quick,' his mother said, frantic. 'Help me. I've been stung. The car. I have an EpiPen in the car.'

He knew what she was referring to. She always had one of those ball-point pen-like needles with her. She kept one in her handbag and one in the glove compartment in the car. She had taught him how to use them as well, but he remained frozen to the spot. Stared at his mother as she slapped at something on her neck. On her head. Flailing and flailing her arms. Her face was turning bright red. 'Hurry up! I'm dying here, can't you see?'

More and more wasps swarmed around her – they just continued to pour out of the nest.

The boy saw nothing of his father.

Some wasps started circling his own head. The boy turned and ran back to the car as fast as he could. It was unlocked – he tore the door open and grabbed the bag from the passenger seat. Rushed back as he fumbled through the contents, looking for the EpiPen.

He found it, wrapped his hand around it and raced towards the barn, through the doorway. He stopped.

There was his father, standing a short way inside.

He was wearing all-white overalls that covered his face. The wasps swirled around him too. His mother was trying to crawl towards the doorway. Her entire face was swollen. On her neck: several large, red boils.

His father just stood there, watching. He didn't move.

The sound of buzzing wasps mingled with his mother's gasps for air, more and more panicked. She tried to say something to him, but the words wouldn't come.

His father took a step towards her, but didn't look at her – he simply stared at his son. His mother's face grew redder and redder, her breathing increasingly laboured. Centimetre by centimetre she crawled closer. But instead of helping her, he just stood there, looking down at her with a quivering lower lip and watery eyes. And when she couldn't take another breath, the boy squeezed the pen so hard that his knuckles turned white.

❋

'She didn't deserve to be your mother.'

That was what his father had said, afterwards. He had repeated it like a mantra. Standing there in the barn doorway, as he was now, was like reliving it all over again.

When the police came, crying came easily. He hadn't been able to say a word – it was his father who took care of the talking, who explained how his mother had probably come earlier than agreed to collect the boy, and that the two of them had been out in the forest, as they often were. When they returned, they had found her on the floor. She had probably gone into the barn to look for them, at which point the wasps' nest must have fallen from the roof. In the chaos that followed, she must have been stung so many times that she couldn't get to the car, where her salvation – the EpiPen – was kept.

It was a story he had had to repeat numerous times over the years. To the psychologist, to his classmates. He had told Elisabeth too.

Should he mention it to Alexander?

Pah, he said to himself and took a step into the barn. There were sounds coming from his father's storeroom. The former policeman was awake.

62

Two car doors slammed shut on the driveway outside Leo van Eijk's house.

Emma felt her face flush immediately. For a few moments she sat petrified in the chair, unsure of what to say or do, but it quickly became clear that she had to go home.

Leo van Eijk crossed the floor in a few strides and picked up the glasses and champagne bottle. He then disappeared into the kitchen, followed by the sound of the glasses clinking. She heard him pouring the remains of the champagne down the sink.

Oliver Krogh remained seated. His hands lay flat on top of his two restless legs. His gaze darted around.

Emma stood up. 'I ... I guess I'll be off,' she said, trying to smile. 'It was nice meeting you.'

Krogh pushed himself up and squeezed Emma's outstretched hand. It was a much tighter grip now than just half an hour ago.

'Good luck with everything,' Emma said. 'I hope we...' She didn't know how to continue the sentence.

'You too,' he said.

Emma turned and started walking towards the hallway, nervous to meet Victoria Prytz again. Their first interaction had not ended on a pleasant note. And the fact that Emma had been snooping around in Victoria's emails made it all the more uncomfortable.

The doorbell rang and the door was immediately opened. Victoria stepped inside without waiting to be invited in, followed by Carmen. Victoria stopped on the threshold upon seeing Emma.

'You...' she began. '*You're* here?' There was a distinct note of contempt in her voice.

'I'm just leaving,' Emma replied. 'Hi, Carmen.'

Carmen didn't answer, just looked down. Emma could see that the acne on her face had flared up since the morning.

Leo van Eijk appeared in the hallway and welcomed them in. Oliver

Krogh had seemingly decided to wait in the living room. Emma moved back towards the doorway to the living room as the two new visitors hung up their coats. Victoria walked in first, sending a disdainful look in Emma's direction as she passed.

Emma felt like saying something else to Carmen, but didn't want to provoke her mother any further. In the living room, Victoria found a seat on the sofa, but sat as far away from Oliver as possible, without saying hello. Carmen, on the other hand, walked right into Oliver's out-stretched arms. He wrapped his arms around her in a long hug and kissed her on the cheek. Said something Emma didn't catch, but even from a distance she could see his eyes sparkle.

'I'll call you,' Leo van Eijk said, placing a gentle hand on Emma's shoulder.

About what? Emma wanted to ask, but didn't. Instead, she put on her shoes and jacket. Ideally, she would love to be a fly on the wall in the lawyer's home for the next few minutes. She wondered what Oliver Krogh would say, if he would tell his soon-to-be ex-wife what Emma had found out.

She walked out and closed the door behind her. Got in the car and started the engine. Decided to check her phone before driving home and noticed she had a missed call from Nicolai Wibe. The policeman had not left a voicemail or sent her a message. Blix, on the other hand, had told her to call when she had the chance.

Emma connected her phone to her car's speakers and called Blix's number. It only took a moment before the call went through to his voice-mail. She looked at the picture he had sent her. It looked like a small farm somewhere in Toten, she thought. He hadn't sent any further information.

Weird, she said to herself.

She put the car into gear and drove off. Emma had made it some way when her phone rang. She answered immediately.

'Wibe,' she said. 'Hi. I noticed you tried to call?'

'Where are you?'

'Uh, just in the car on the way home. I'm coming up to Ullevål.'

'Okay. I thought you'd like to know: Helle Lindqvist, Maria Normann's best friend, has an alibi for the afternoon of the murder.'

'Oh?'

'She was with a customer at her tattoo studio.'

'Right. On a Sunday?'

'Yeah. It's probably not that unusual. We've also spoken to the customer and checked her bank details. It's a watertight alibi.'

There's that hypothesis gone, Emma thought. She pulled over into the exit lane and slowed down on the approach to a roundabout.

'But thanks for the pictures you sent me. It set the department here into a bit of a frenzy.' He laughed.

Emma could picture it.

A car behind her pulled up dangerously close to her rear bumper. She eased into the outer lane of the roundabout and asked:

'How closely have you looked at Victoria Prytz's whereabouts and activity in the time before and after the fire?'

'I can't go into that.'

So not at all then, Emma thought.

'I'm sure Oliver told you of his suspicions about her,' Emma continued. 'That it might have been Victoria who had someone kill Maria?'

'Yes, and we have, of course, investigated that line of inquiry extensively,' he said.

Emma didn't believe him. The car behind her turned left towards the Radium hospital.

'There's another reason why I'm calling,' Wibe continued. 'The technicians found something a short distance from where the canoe was found. It's currently undergoing an analysis in the lab, but I wanted to send you a picture so we can rule out whether or not it's yours.'

'Okay. Let me stop somewhere first.'

A few hundred metres further on, Emma slowed down and came to a halt in a bus stop.

'It could have belonged to Maria Normann, of course,' Wibe continued. 'Or someone else who was at the scene.'

Emma opened the message. It took a few seconds for the image to download. Gradually a round, dirty object came into view.

Emma swallowed.

'Are you there?' Wibe asked.

Her mind raced. There was no doubt in her mind as to what it was. 'Er, yes,' she said. 'But no, it ... That's not mine.'

'Grand, we'll cross you off the list.'

He said something else, but Emma didn't hear him. She just stared at the picture.

With a start, she heard a sudden, blaring sound just behind her: the driver of a huge, red bus honking at her, wanting to pull into the bus stop. Emma released her foot from the brakes, looked over her shoulder, checking that there were no oncoming vehicles, and turned the car 180 degrees, heading back towards Røa.

63

The light was sparse. At first, Blix could only see the faint outline of a lamp at the other end of the room.

His neck felt stiff and hard when he raised his head.

The roof and walls were made of rough planks, the floor of speckled concrete.

Someone nudged the side of his body with a foot. 'Are you awake?'

A woman's voice, full of a mixture of irritation and despair. Blix twisted round, but was held back by something tugging on his neck. A leather strap that was tied around him so tight that he could barely wedge a finger under it.

He pushed himself up along the wall and gained a little more space to move, but the effort made him nauseous and dizzy.

'Who are you?' the woman asked.

Blix met her gaze. She was dirty. Hair tangled. Trapped in the same way as him. Like an animal, with a leather strap fastened round her neck.

Their hands were free. Blix felt along the strap but could barely wriggle a finger underneath. A metal ring was padlocked to a rusty chain, the end mounted to the wall.

The woman tried to edge a little closer, as far as her chain allowed.

As unkempt as she was, Blix still recognised her.

Turid Nyjordet. Missing for almost two days.

'Who are you?' she repeated.

Blix said his name. The woman obviously had no idea who he was.

'I was an investigator,' he explained.

'What do you mean?' Nyjordet asked. 'That you were an investigator?'

Blix nodded, but didn't explain any further.

It was his fault she was trapped here. He had been followed for days and had taken the perpetrator with him to the shop. He had witnessed what she was like as a mother.

'Your son is fine,' Blix said, clearing his throat. 'He's being taken care of.'

'Mattias...'

The chain link rattled as Turid Nyjordet hiccupped. Blix let his gaze slide along it. The bolt attaching it to the wall seemed solid.

'Do you know who he is?' she asked, glancing towards the door.

There was a strong smell of urine when she moved again.

'Someone I met years ago,' Blix replied.

'Why is he doing this?'

Blix tried to gather his thoughts. He still couldn't quite put into words the tangle of motives and driving forces that had made them both innocent victims. A damaged mind with a skewed sense of reality, a desire for revenge against a domineering mother, but also a sick urge to save others from an upbringing he had suffered himself. The desire to spare others a fate like his own.

'I don't know,' he ended up answering.

There was a sound from somewhere outside. Turid Nyjordet pulled her legs back in, pushed herself flat against the wall and looked towards the door.

The lock clicked. The door opened. The ceiling light came on, bright and piercing. A man entered the room.

Blix took a deep breath.

Skage Kleiven.

'Are you surprised?' he asked.

Blix scrutinised him. He was wearing the same green jacket he had worn when following Blix on the street. But he seemed more confident and secure.

'Yes and no,' Blix replied.

That made Kleiven tilt his head. 'What does that mean?'

Blix thought about what to say.

'I'm surprised you chose me for this game of yours – we've never had anything to do with each other. Not directly anyway. But no, I'm not surprised that *you* are the one behind this.'

Kleiven looked at him, waiting for more.

'You killed Elisabeth Eie,' Blix said. 'The mother of your child. Because she took your daughter away from you. Because she was a bad mother and therefore didn't deserve to live, in your eyes.'

Kleiven tightened his jaw, but said nothing. He paced a little back and forth in front of them.

'You know what surprised *me*?' And before Blix could answer: 'That you didn't recognise me the first time you questioned me. Or the second time, for that matter.'

'Why would I have?' Blix asked. 'Because I'd seen you in Lina Marie Jansen's waiting room nearly forty years ago?'

Kleiven didn't respond.

'You never sent the letter you wrote to me,' Blix continued. 'And even though you wrote that you would try, you never made contact with me. Not back then anyway. But you did after you killed Elisabeth.'

'Because I thought you would understand,' Kleiven said.

'Understand what?' Turid Nyjordet asked.

Skage Kleiven ignored her. Blix measured his gaze, tried to imagine how the situation would pan out. Right now, he saw no way out. The only thing that could work in his favour was time.

'You didn't have it easy as a child, like me,' Skage said. 'And when your mother died you weren't exactly sad either. I saw it – I was at the funeral. I even shook your hand. Told you I was sorry for your loss.'

Blix swallowed. Tried to recall memories of his mother's funeral, but apart from the fact that he hadn't shed a single tear, he had no recollection of Skage Kleiven talking to him.

'You were sent to a psychologist, again just like me,' Kleiven continued. 'But we weren't the ones who were wrong – it was those who were supposed to take care of us, who should have been there for us.'

There was something firm and aggressive about the way Skage Kleiven spoke. An emotional instability he had managed to hide in their previous interactions. The bitterness Blix had suspected in him he had put down to resentment that child-welfare services wouldn't give him custody of his own daughter. If Blix had looked more closely, he would have understood that it ran deeper. Much deeper.

'Don't you think your life would be different if you'd had a different upbringing?' Kleiven asked.

Blix looked away. He had thought a lot about how devastating the years with his mother had been.

'It's all connected,' Skage continued. 'You can trace everything back. Maybe your daughter would still be alive if you hadn't had such a bad start in life?'

The extent of Skage's obsession began to dawn on Blix. For years, Skage Kleiven had followed his life, from a distance.

Turid Nyjordet scrambled up onto her knees. 'Please,' she begged. 'Let me go. I promise – I won't say anything about ... about all of this. I have a boy at home who—'

With one sudden movement, Kleiven yanked at the chain attached to her neck. She screamed as she was dragged along the floor to his feet. She flailed her arms and tried to get up. Kleiven pushed her back down with one hand.

'My mother used dog chains like this on me,' he said over the protests from Turid Nyjordet. 'As soon as I learned to walk, she would chain me up and leave me to my own devices. Only when my father wasn't around, of course. Then she knew I'd be exactly where she left me when she came back.'

He made a movement that made the chain rattle.

'As I got bigger, she gave me a longer line. Long enough for me to go to the bathroom or into the kitchen. But never out of the house.'

He stared down at Turid, tightening the chain even more.

'Didn't you think of your son when you were hanging off that bar?' he snarled at her.

'Please...' Turid Nyjordet sobbed.

'Let her go,' Blix pleaded. 'She's not—'

Before Blix could say anything more, Kleiven rammed the anaesthetic pen into her neck. It only took a few moments before her protests died down. Her movements lost power. After ten seconds she collapsed into a bundle on the floor.

'My own patent,' Kleiven said, throwing away the pen.

'Skage,' Blix said, looking for words to help him connect with the man standing over him, but he realised it wouldn't help.

Kleiven put his hand in his pocket and pulled out a transparent plastic bag.

'Don't do anything rash,' Blix tried to warn him.

Kleiven squatted next to the unconscious woman, shoved the bag over her head and pulled her to him. Put her head in his lap. The plastic stuck to her face when she breathed in.

'The world will be a better place without her,' Kleiven said. 'Her son will have the chance to live a much better life.'

'You don't know her,' Blix said, trying to swallow the nausea that had risen in his throat. 'You know nothing about her or her son.'

'I know enough,' Skage Kleiven said, looking down at the woman in his lap. Her tongue had lolled out. The colour of her face was darkening.

'Let her breathe!' Blix begged.

The plastic began to become obscured by condensation.

'It took three minutes with Elisabeth,' Kleiven said. 'Not quite as long with the psychologist.'

Skage Kleiven straightened the plastic bag on her head a bit, made sure there were no gaps.

'Stop!' Blix yelled. The desperation tore away at him.

'I kept her here for a few days too,' Kleiven continued. 'Can you imagine, blaming children for being neglected as a child?'

Blix felt his throat tighten. He swallowed, realising that nothing he said would change the outcome. Turid Nyjordet was going to die before his eyes.

Skage Kleiven talked on, effortlessly, about how Jansen had tried to hold him accountable every hour he spent in her office. Seeing her on TV all those years later had made him realise how harmful she had been too. Probably not just for him either.

Blix had stopped listening.

He felt like he was underwater. Everything but the sight of the dying woman was shut out.

Until, finally, it was over.

Skage Kleiven removed the plastic bag and shoved Turid Nyjordet off his lap. He stood up and set his gaze on Blix.

64

The sky above Røa was pitch-black. Emma quickly glanced up at the thick rain clouds before locking the car and clutching her jacket tighter around her neck.

At the bottom of the steps she stopped and lowered her shoulders. Slowly released them. She could see her own breath in the cold air. Short, sharp exhales.

Her index finger shook as she pressed the bell.

It took a few moments before she heard footsteps across the floor inside, but no one came to open the door. Emma leaned back a little. Leo van Eijk appeared in the kitchen window. She waved at him but didn't smile.

The lawyer disappeared from the window. Within seconds, he had opened the front door.

'Emma,' he said in surprise. 'Did you forget something?'

'No,' she replied, shaking her head. 'But I was wondering if I could come in. There's something I need to talk to you – to everyone – about.'

Leo van Eijk frowned, continued to stare down at her.

'It's important,' she added.

'Oh?' he said, still uncertain.

'I can explain if you'll just let me in. Explain to all of you.'

The lawyer stood there a moment longer before he finally pushed the door fully open for her.

'Thank you,' Emma said and stepped inside.

There was an open view into the hallway from the living room, where Oliver Krogh, Victoria Prytz and Carmen sat. Emma didn't look at them as she took off her shoes. Her jacket, however, she kept on. She was chilled to the core. Her body trembled all over.

'What the hell is this?' Victoria Prytz said as Emma entered. Three pairs of eyes stared at her.

'I'm sorry to interrupt again,' Emma said as she moved closer. 'I know it's a difficult time.'

'Yes, and this has absolutely nothing to do with you,' Victoria snarled. 'Leo – why the hell did you let her in?'

'I think she has something she wants to share with us,' the lawyer said. 'Why else would she have come back?'

Emma looked at him and thanked him, silently, for his support.

She turned her gaze to Oliver Krogh and wondered how much of the truth he had shared with them. About Maria, the pregnancy and the secret rendezvous they had had behind Victoria's back. None of it, she assumed – and Carmen didn't need to know those details now that he was a free man. While he was in custody, however, the situation was different. Then he had been desperate, willing to go through anything to clear his name. Anything other than being sentenced to prison for a murder he did not commit.

Emma had thought a lot about what Hildegard Normann had said about Oliver Krogh, even after he had been released. To the last she had doubted what seemed indisputable to Emma: it simply couldn't have been anyone but Oliver who had taken her daughter's life. It was the only thing that made sense.

You should always listen to a mother, Emma thought. They had strong intuition. But perhaps not always as good judgement.

She looked at Victoria. Into her angry, accusatory eyes.

Although Emma had heard Oliver's description of the relationship, it was impossible to know anything about what their family life had truly been like. As a journalist, she knew that there were always two sides to a story. Probably three in this case – each with their own story; the truth probably lying somewhere in between. The reasons why a relationship breaks down could be numerous and multifaceted. And the fact that Victoria Prytz was a complex woman seemed beyond a doubt. Temperamental, but she obviously did have a softer side – a need to be loved, cared for, to receive sympathy from others. Given that she had sought that out from strangers, it was easy to think that she hadn't received much of it at home. Yet, she also came across as uncompromising. Determined. Cold, even.

Emma guessed that the meeting they were having, here and now, was about the future. About how the Prytz-Krogh family should build a framework that would shape the rest of their lives, work out how to be around each other until the divorce was finalised. Homes, cars, finances, cohabitation. Even though Carmen wasn't Oliver's biological child, everything indicated that she had a close relationship with him ever since he entered her life. That they were happy as father and daughter. Carmen, who hadn't had a proper father figure in her life before Oliver.

Emma gazed at her.

Carmen sat at the far end of one of the sofas, staring at the floor. She picked at her fingers. The hoodie she was wearing looked uncomfortably warm.

'I don't quite know where to start,' Emma said, feeling her vocal chords quiver.

She put one hand in her trouser pocket and took out the lip balm she always used. She unscrewed the lid, but didn't bring it to her lips.

'There are so many options for these,' she said, holding it up. 'I've tried many of them myself, over the years. But once we find a favourite, we stick to it, don't we?' Emma kept her eyes on Carmen. 'Is that the same for you, too?'

Carmen didn't seem to realise that the question was directed at her. When none of the others answered, she looked directly at Emma.

'Me?'

'Which one do you use?' Emma asked.

Carmen shrugged. 'I don't know what it's called.'

'Do you have it with you now?'

'Er, yeah. Think so.'

'Can I have a look?'

'For god's sake.' Victoria Prytz rolled her eyes and threw her arms up.

'I promise,' Emma said, 'that I'll get to the point soon. Carmen – can you show us?'

Oliver Krogh shifted his eyes from Emma to Carmen, who reluctantly reached into the pocket of her hoodie and took out a round, dark-blue box. Hesitantly, she held it up. Victoria leaned forward a little so she could see too.

'Thank you,' Emma said. 'I always have several in rotation. I lose them so frequently or I can't remember where I put them.'

She paused before continuing:

'The police found one just like that at the scene,' she said, pointing to the tub in Carmen's hand. 'The exact same make. Not too far from the canoe used to transport Maria Normann's body out onto Lake Gjersjøen.'

Carmen's face twitched. Her gaze hardened. Her hand tightened around the tub.

'Before I came back here,' Emma continued, 'I called Helle Lindqvist, Maria Normann's best friend. Maria lived with Helle for a while. They knew each other inside out. I asked if Maria ever used this type of lip balm, and showed her the photo that the police had taken at the scene. Helle just laughed – Maria never used anything like that. So it couldn't have been hers.'

'But so what?' Victoria Prytz barked. 'There are thousands of people who use these, right?'

'There certainly are,' Emma replied. 'But there aren't thousands of people who use this lip balm, have knowledge of the local area, and knew the stock at Bull's Eye.' She turned her gaze to Oliver. 'Or who knew that someone would be there that day.'

Neither of them protested.

Emma thought of the first time she had met Carmen. How her phone had slipped out of her hoodie pocket. The scratches on the screen had made Emma think that Carmen was like any other teenager: bad at taking care of her things. Emma had been the exact same when she was that age. Scratching the phone screen was easily done. Especially if you were moving about.

'For the police,' Emma continued, 'a find like that is worth its weight in gold. The fact that these tubs have lids means that the police will definitely be able to extract DNA from it – it's only a matter of time. They are analysing it as we speak.'

Oliver blinked rapidly, as if trying to process what Emma had just told them.

'Carmen,' Emma said tenderly. 'Was it your lip balm they found?'

'Honestly, Leo,' Victoria Prytz started again. 'Are you going to let her go on like this? It can't have been Carmen's.'

The lawyer didn't answer her. Only now did Emma realise that he had sat down on a chair behind her.

'How was Carmen supposed to get out there?' Victoria Prytz continued to object.

Emma didn't bother pointing out that it wouldn't take her more than half an hour to cycle to Bull's Eye from Nordstrand. Nor did she mention that Carmen had probably cycled there several times before.

'You were at a viewing that day, right?' she asked Victoria instead. 'In Smestad?'

Victoria cast an uncertain glance at her daughter.

'So you don't really know where Carmen was or what she was doing that day,' Emma argued.

'She was at home,' Victoria said. 'She's always at home.' Her words were firm, but an anxiety, an unease, had crept into her voice. 'Carmen?'

No answer.

Emma looked at the vain and self-centred woman in front of her and thought about how detrimental her selfishness had been to her relationship with her daughter.

'Were you in touch with Carmen that afternoon?' she asked.

'No, I ... was busy.'

'You were at work.'

'Yes. And then the police called and said the shop was on fire, and then ... I went straight there.'

'When was the first time you spoke to Carmen after you heard about the fire?'

'I ... well ... I tried to call her, but...' A tormented expression had contorted Victoria's face. 'I don't know. Later that night, maybe.' She squeezed her eyes shut, hard.

'Carmen,' Oliver said quietly. 'Is this correct? Was that your lip balm?' His voice was shaky.

Carmen said nothing, just shook her head almost imperceptibly. Kept her eyes fixed on the floor. Spun the tub of lip balm round and round between her fingers.

Emma looked at Oliver. 'Earlier, you didn't want to talk about what had happened that day. But if I can ask you this: Carmen knew you were going to the shop, isn't that right? You talked about it in the house, I presume, before you left?'

Oliver just stared at Emma. His lips parted. He looked quickly at Carmen. 'You ... asked if I needed help at the shop,' he said quietly. 'You ... I...'

But you didn't need help, Emma thought. You didn't want Carmen to go with you, because you were going to meet Maria. And she had something she wanted to talk to you about.

Oliver stood up abruptly and interlocked his fingers on top of his head. Then he quickly stroked his neck as he stood with his back to the sofa.

There was a strange, almost electric atmosphere in the room. As if it could ignite at any moment. All it took was a spark.

'I...' There was barely a sound as Carmen tried to speak. The next moment a tear ran down her inflamed cheek.

Emma thought about Carmen's upbringing. Victoria, who had been attention-seeking and protective; her biological father, who had moved to another country and had never wanted to be a part of Carmen's life. Oliver, who had stepped in and taken on the role of father, but who had later found another woman, whom he had subsequently made pregnant.

'I ... didn't want to,' Carmen said. 'I ... didn't mean to.'

Victoria Prytz gasped, her hand flying up to her mouth. Oliver Krogh said nothing, just stared at Carmen. Leo van Eijk's eyes were wide open.

Everyone waited for Carmen to continue.

She cried. Sobbed. Pulled her hood over her head. She could shut the world out just a bit that way, even though everyone was staring at her.

'I didn't mean to,' Carmen repeated, heaving. 'It just ... happened.'

Victoria Prytz had also started to cry. Carmen lay down on the sofa. She couldn't get a coherent sentence out.

Emma realised that this was not the time to push the young girl. In time, through questioning with the police and presumably conversations with a psychologist, the details of what happened that afternoon would eventually emerge. Right now, they had their answer – the most important one.

Emma took a step back.

Leo van Eijk got up slowly and followed Emma to the door.

'Do you want to call the police?' she asked. 'Or should I?'

'I can do it,' the lawyer answered, glancing towards the sofa, where Victoria Prytz and her daughter were at opposite ends, both crying. Oliver Krogh had taken a seat in one of the chairs. He rested his elbows on his thighs and sat with his head bowed.

'I'll take care of them until then,' the lawyer added. 'As best I can.'

65

Blix tried to keep his breathing calm, controlled, but was unable to hold back the waves of disgust that shot through his body.

Skage Kleiven looked down with contempt at the body of the dead woman that lay between them. He fished a bunch of keys from his pocket and crouched down next to her. With one, swift movement he unlocked the padlock and freed her head from the tight strap.

Blix turned away.

His head was swimming. Everything around him felt blurry and distorted. The sounds were muffled, the colours darker. He had to collect himself, find something else to fix his thoughts on, so he could regain composure.

Tomine.

He thought of Tomine, of Terry, Emma. He had to get out of there. Bide his time and break free.

It must have started to rain outside. It sounded like a steady drumming against the barn roof. He felt his pulse slow down. His breathing became easier.

Skage Kleiven had stood up. Leaned against the wall, watched Blix with a concentrated gaze. Absent-mindedly fingered the bunch of keys. The tinkling sound made Blix say:

'You've been inside my apartment.'

Skage Kleiven looked down at the keys.

'Several times,' Blix added. 'How did you manage that?'

Skage closed his hand around the bundle, so that the sound stopped.

'When I was at the station for questioning,' he said. 'You wanted us to sit at your desk instead of in one of the interrogation rooms. Your keys were on the table.' He smiled. 'I took them while you went to fetch some document for me to sign. Had a copy cut just around the corner.'

Skage seemed pleased with himself. Blix remembered that interrogation, but not that his keys had gone missing the same day.

'I left them at Elisabeth's sister's place,' he continued. 'When I stopped by a couple of days later.'

Of course, Blix thought. That was where he had found them again.

Kleiven picked out one of the other keys on the bundle and held it out between two fingers.

'This one belongs to your father,' he said. 'I took it from his room at the nursing home when I first visited.'

'Were you there more than once?'

He shook his head. 'Didn't need to. I got what I needed.'

Blix nodded slowly, as a kind of acknowledgment, but his thoughts raced.

'You planned all of this,' Blix said, glancing around the room. 'For a long time.'

The acknowledgement seemed to fill Kleiven with pride.

'And you've been following me,' Blix continued. 'You've been inside my apartment. Called me and left traces, both in my home and my father's – all so that I could find you.'

'Yes.'

'You wanted my attention. As you have since the very beginning.'

'Yes.'

'And you've got it,' Blix said. 'So what do you want? What's next?'

Kleiven didn't answer.

'You wanted us to be friends,' Blix continued. 'A long time ago. You said so, in that letter you wrote. That can't be what you want now?'

'I ... thought we were the same,' Skage said. 'That you, of all people, would understand and appreciate what I have done. We are cut from the same cloth, Alexander. We had the same damn upbringing.'

'It wasn't the same, Skage. No two people can have the exact same upbringing. We are not the same just because we both had a bad mother. And it is entirely possible that you can grow up and not let the bad cards you were dealt control the rest of your life.'

Something changed in Skage's eyes. 'So you think it's my fault that my life turned out like this?'

'That's not what I'm saying.'

'You sound just like the psychologist,' he snarled. 'I should have realised that we aren't the same. You sent your father to a nursing home.

When *my* father fell ill, I moved him to Oslo and took care of him myself.'

Blix swallowed. His Adam's apple pressed against the strap around his neck. His father's death had been Skage's alibi around the time Elisabeth Eie disappeared. They had taken it at face value.

Skage snorted. 'You even like dogs.'

Silence filled the small room. The air was raw, damp. Blix's feet were frozen solid. He tried to twist his body round, find a more comfortable position. His back ached.

'You tried to kill Terry,' he said quietly. 'Terry, who never did anything to anybody.'

A grimace crossed Skage's face. 'Mum had dogs,' he said. 'She was more fond of them than she was...' He looked away. 'But she didn't want to look after them either, so she sent them to live with Gran in Leirsund. Like me. I was forced to walk them every day.'

Blix realised that he would have to try a different approach with Skage. Anything to give himself more time.

'My father loved to fish,' Blix said in a quieter, softer voice. 'I enjoyed fishing with him.' Which was actually true, when he thought about it. 'He was the one who taught me how to tie fishing flies.'

The ceiling light flickered, as if there was something wrong with the electrics. Kleiven looked up at it.

'My daughter never met her grandfather. That was ... mostly my fault. I've realised, only now, in the last few days, really, that he missed us, but maybe didn't quite know how to communicate that. You found some of Iselin's drawings in his home. On the fridge.'

Kleiven said nothing, just nodded.

Blix tried to think. But he couldn't come up with what to say or ask next.

Kleiven took a step towards him and stated more than asked: 'You're seeing a psychologist again.'

And before Blix could open his mouth: 'Your former colleagues are wondering if you've got a screw or two loose,' Kleiven continued. 'They asked me how you had behaved when you led the investigation into

Elisabeth's disappearance. I got the impression that they suspected you were acting out of line.'

Skage's gaze was cold. There was something calculating about his voice.

'What do you reckon they'll think when they find you with the missing woman?' With the tip of his shoe he nudged Turid Nyjordet's motionless body.

'What do you mean?'

Skage Kleiven fumbled for a new anaesthetic pen from inside his pocket.

'They won't find you here, of course,' he said. 'But at home in your father's empty house.'

It dawned on Blix that Kleiven intended to blame him for everything. That it had all been part of his plan from the beginning.

Blix pushed himself back a little. The strap tightened around his neck.

'They'll never believe you,' he objected.

'But I'm not going to talk to them,' Kleiven said. 'I'm not involved in this.'

'But...' Blix began.

'And no one'll get to hear your version anyway,' Kleiven added. 'They're going to find you in the ruins of the fire, right under a rafter with the remains of a rope around your neck.'

Blix felt a wave of desperation.

'People know I've been here,' he squeezed out. 'My phone ... they'll trace it to here. I sent photos from your farm.'

Skage Kleiven became somewhat pensive.

'Well, I can explain that, easily. You came here looking confused and disoriented. Searched around for something and moved on.'

Blix tried to push himself up further, his back against the wall. Kleiven's expression shifted immediately. He strode towards him, the pen held out in front of him, like a knife, ready to strike. Blix raised his legs and kicked back. He landed a couple of kicks to Kleiven's ankles, hard enough for Kleiven to wince. He cursed and raised a leg to kick back. Blix twisted away, grabbed his foot and knocked him off balance.

Kleiven tried to bring down the anaesthetic pen, but missed. Blix twisted his foot around and pulled him clean over.

The strap around his neck tightened. Blix gritted his teeth and kicked at the hand holding the pen, but missed. Kleiven lunged at him. Blix shoved his shoulder out, grabbed Kleiven's arm and just stopped him from inserting the needle.

Kleiven pushed with all his weight. Blix had him at arm's length, but would not be able to resist for long. His forearms shook with the strain. The chain tightened around his neck. He had to fight for every breath.

Foam was starting to bubble from between Kleiven's tight lips. Blix stared into his eyes. In an unexpected manoeuvre, he let go of the man and let Kleiven fall towards him. At the same time, he twisted Kleiven's wrist backward with one swift, powerful movement. The sound of something snapping.

Kleiven screamed in pain and lost his grip. The pen fell to the floor. Blix fumbled to get his fingers around it and managed to hit the tip so hard into Kleiven's thigh that the pen stuck there.

Skage Kleiven crawled backward, frantically slapping at his leg, and knocked the pen loose. He tried to get to his knees and onto his feet, but passed out.

Blix forced two fingers between his neck and the strap and let himself breathe freely for a short while.

His pulse calmed down. As did his thoughts.

But he was still shackled.

Kleiven had the keys in his trouser pocket, but he was out of reach. If Blix stretched out one foot, that was as close as he could get to him.

He tried jerking the chain away from the wall a few times. But the wall mount it was bolted to seemed far too solid to give way.

His gaze slid along the chain itself. No weak links.

Outside, the rain had increased in intensity. Blix rested his head against the wall behind him and looked up at the dirty bulb on the ceiling. A heavy realisation sank in. He would still be chained there when Skage Kleiven awoke.

66

You should be happy, Emma told herself. Glad that the case was solved, and that an innocent man had escaped a long prison sentence.

But there was no joy, no elation at what she had contributed. What she felt most was a sense of emptiness. She felt sorry for the Prytz-Krogh family. What had happened tonight was – for them – a before and after, the aftermath being somehow so much worse. They might have thought they had hit rock bottom when Bull's Eye burned down. And again, after, when Oliver Krogh was arrested.

Emma headed back to the city centre. The car was still cold, but the seat warmers provided a growing heat. She reconnected her phone to the speakers, and tried, again, to get hold of Blix, but once again only reached his voicemail.

It wasn't unlike him to disappear every so often, she thought. After he was released from prison, he had occasionally closed himself off from everyone and everything. But things were different now. *He* was different. Besides, he was the one who had asked her to call.

He should've been back from Gjøvik ages ago, Emma thought while she was stuck in traffic from the junction at Smestadkrysset. Maybe he had managed to get something out of his father.

A few raindrops hit the windscreen. Emma turned on the wipers. Her head full of thoughts, she drove through the city and onto Tøyengata. Slowly rolled past number nineteen and looked up at the windows. There was a light on in Blix's apartment.

Emma parked up in a side street and ran back round to the apartment building. The doorbell buzzed a few times but no answer. She tried two more times, before going back to the car.

He could be with Tomine, she thought. She didn't have her number saved, but looked it up online. It took a few rings, but then she picked up.

Emma introduced herself. 'I work with Alexander Blix occasionally,' she continued.

'I know who you are,' Tomine said – there was a smile in her voice. 'Hi.'

Emma glanced in the mirrors and pulled back out onto the street.

'I'm trying to get hold of him,' she said. 'Is he with you?'

'No. I've been trying to call him too.'

'When was the last time you spoke to him?'

'Earlier today. He was going to see his father, in Gjøvik. Is something wrong?'

Emma turned north, towards the E6.

'What's going on?' Tomine asked. 'I'm getting worried.'

Emma weighed up the best thing to say.

'He's probably just busy,' she said in the end. 'Could you text me if you hear from him at all?'

'Absolutely, and likewise please.'

They hung up.

Emma stopped for a red light. She wasn't sure how much Blix had been in contact with Tine Abelvik lately, but she sent the police investigator a message anyway, and asked if she knew where Blix was. The light turned green. No response from Abelvik. She was presumably still busy in Leirsund.

She exited the roundabout at Carl Berner. The roads were pretty clear. She continued with one hand on the steering wheel while she pulled up her messages on her phone with the other.

At 3:12pm Blix had asked her to call him back when she had finished with Oliver Krogh and his lawyer, and sent her a picture from a small farm. *I'm here*, he'd written.

And then it dawned on her why he'd sent the image.

She quickly clicked on the photo and pulled up the information about where it was taken: the coordinates brought up her maps app and placed Blix's location as somewhere called Balke, about three miles south of Gjøvik.

Emma alternated between looking at her phone and checking the traffic in front of her. She clicked on the directions and checked the route. From here, it would take an hour and twenty-six minutes to drive.

Balke, Emma thought. It wasn't a place Blix had mentioned to her before. It was also a good distance from the nursing home.

Using her thumb and forefinger, Emma zoomed in on the map. She glanced quickly at the road again, before seeing that the Balke area was characterised by a huge expanse of forest and not that many roads. The houses and farms seemed to be a great distance from one another. It was impossible to find out exactly what the farms were called on the map, but it would be possible to find the address.

The car had started to veer across into the oncoming lane. Emma quickly yanked the steering wheel back and looked around for a place to stop. She eventually pulled over onto the hard shoulder. A brief search of the address told her that the farm seemed to have been owned by an Odd Henrik Kleiven until two years ago. Rainwater from the passing traffic splashed against the side of the car as she searched for further information. She found a short obituary about Kleiven in the local newspaper, but found no information about who had taken over his farm. Presumably it had passed down to his family.

Bright lights appeared in the rearview mirror.

Emma waited until the SUV had passed, then pulled back onto the road. Again she tried Blix. Same result. From her call log, she pulled up Nicolai Wibe's number. She assumed he would be busy, but the investigator answered her almost immediately.

He began by telling her that Carmen Prytz had confessed to him as well.

'It seemed like it was good for her to get it out of her system.'

'She claimed it was an accident,' Emma said. 'What else did she say?'

'That she cycled to Bull's Eye that day because she had nothing else to do, and then she realised that Oliver and Maria were inside the shop ... together. Carmen said that it felt like her world was collapsing around her when she saw them. She became enraged. And afraid, presumably, that Oliver would leave her too, just like her father.'

Emma decelerated as she came up behind a slow-moving car.

'After Oliver drove off, she entered the shop and ambushed Maria – the person she thought was going to destroy everything. The fact she then fell and hit her head does sound like an accident. But what she did next was quite disturbing. She placed Maria in a canoe and wheeled her out, tied a backpack filled with rocks to her. Then she set the shop on fire and dragged the canoe down to the lake. She must have paddled out as the flames spread and the sirens approached. Dumped Maria and the canoe trolley.'

Emma imagined how Maria's body would have immediately sunk in such deep water, and how Carmen had made it back to shore afterwards. How she must have then cycled back to Nordstrand, to a house where no one was home. With an absent mother with whom she often argued as well, Carmen could get away with spending a lot of time over the next few days in her room.

'She must have been so upset when her stepfather was arrested,' Wibe said, 'she decided to seek help and contact you. Which I think shows she isn't entirely a monster.'

The remains of a small, dead animal lay on the side of the road. Emma swerved without slowing down.

'We'll need a formal statement from you,' Wibe continued. 'Where are you now?'

'I'm on my way to Gjøvik,' Emma replied.

'Gjøvik?' Wibe repeated.

'That's actually why I called,' Emma explained. 'I'm trying to get hold of Blix.'

She felt the knot of concern tighten in her stomach as she said it out loud. It was now hours without any sign of life from him.

'I actually tried to call Abelvik first,' Emma continued. 'As she knows the case and the details.'

'I presume you've heard that another body has been found in Leirsund?' Wibe said.

'Yes, so I realise she's busy, but—'

Wibe interrupted her: 'I'm on it,' he said. 'I'll get her to call you.'

Emma looked at the clock on the dashboard.

'Thank you,' she said, pressing her foot down harder on the accelerator.

67

His throat was dry. His body heavy. He raised his hand to his face and wiped some drool from the corner of his mouth.

When he opened his eyes, he met the gaze of Alexander Blix.

The ceiling light above him flickered.

Skage Kleiven tried to recall what exactly had happened. He didn't know how long he had been unconscious. But nothing seemed to have changed in those missing moments. Blix was still chained up.

'I've been thinking a bit,' the ex-policeman said. 'We must be able to find a reasonable solution to all this.'

Skage moved his wrist. It ached, but it wasn't broken. He pushed himself up, feeling weak and unsteady, and knew he had to sit for a while before he could try to get to his feet.

'Let's talk,' Blix said.

Skage cleared his throat, but didn't answer. There was nothing to talk about. He had an extra anaesthetic pen inside the house. The last one. He would just have to proceed more carefully. Ideally, he would have chained Blix by his arms and legs, but that would have left visible evidence that he'd been held captive. The marks around his neck could be mistaken for injuries from the hanging, if the fire didn't eliminate every trace of him.

He pulled himself together, staggered to his feet and headed for the door.

'Think about it,' Blix said. 'No one is going to believe that I'm behind all this.'

Skage glanced quickly back into the storeroom before pulling the door shut behind him, leaving Blix alone with the dead woman.

✳

The rain fell hard against the tin roof. He walked away from the storeroom towards the barn door and stood a moment on the threshold. The cool air cleared his mind.

Blix's arrival had not been part of the plan, but rather an opportunity he'd seized. The final outcome would be the same as he'd intended. Transporting them was going to be a challenge, and the most difficult part would be getting both bodies into Blix's childhood home unseen.

He would have to do it via the cellar door at the back of the house. In any case, there wasn't much time. The anaesthesia only lasted up to two hours. During that time he had to get both Blix and Turid Nyjordet out into the car, drive off with them and then set them up properly in Gjermund Blix's house.

A dog started barking. The sound came from Alexander's car, which was parked beneath the lamp in the yard.

Skage went out into the rain and over to the car. The terrier was standing alert in the back seat, peering at him through the fogged-up window.

His mother's dogs had been bigger.

Even after she died, he had had to look after them. His grandmother in Leirsund hadn't had the heart to give them away, or have them killed.

Boso was the worst of them.

On one of their walks into the forest, he had found a bag containing leftover barbeque food. He had let Boso eat it before putting the bag over his head and tightening the band around his neck.

The barking from inside the car stopped.

It'd been faster with Boso than the women.

He had gone back out, later that night, with a shovel, to where he had left the mongrel. The place he had found for Boso was hidden away, but he had returned several times after. Had witnessed the mound grow over again.

A gust of wind shook the nearest trees. Skage opened the car door and stood in the opening. The dog whined and tried to squeeze out. Skage undid the collar, pushed him back into the seat and closed the door again.

A kind of warm satisfaction filled him, making him smile. He was able to improvise when needed, add new elements to a plan and make it more solid. The collar was adjustable. It would fit around Turid

Nyjordet's neck. If the police found out where it came from, that was simply one more detail that would point to Alexander Blix.

The rain started to soak through his clothes. He strode over to the main house and unlocked the door.

The anaesthetic pen was in the fridge. He grabbed it and thought through how he could ensure the rest of the plan went smoothly. He would open the barn door all the way, drive his own car out and back Blix's car as close to the storeroom as possible. He'd then place Turid Nyjordet in the boot and cover her in the petrol cans, before taking care of Blix.

It would be a long way to walk back from Gjermund's, but he knew the forest and its paths well.

He headed back out onto the front steps, to the sound of something approaching. A pair of car headlights appeared between the trees.

Blix's dog started barking again. Skage cursed, flew down the steps and stood in the shadows at the side of the house.

68

It was past 10:00pm.

Emma drove slowly. The gravel road was narrow and riddled with potholes. The rain made it hard to see her surroundings, but she could make out the open fields and rolling countryside on both sides of the track. A white fence close by on the right. Scattered houses further away, lights shining from the windows. The people inside probably wondered who was driving about their neighbourhood so late at night.

She followed the directions on her phone. The bad weather had made the trip from Oslo longer than she had hoped it would take, but she was close now.

Forest surrounded the farm she was approaching. The first thing she saw when she emerged at the end of the short drive was a house and barn, as well as a car parked in the middle of the yard: Blix's Volvo.

His car was bathed in the light from a lamppost.

Emma turned off the engine but kept the lights on. She switched on the high beams, which stretched deeper into the woodland beside the barn. All she saw there were branches swaying in the wind.

And then movement in the Volvo's rear window.

Terry.

The dog immediately started barking.

Blix would never have left Terry in the car alone, she thought. Not for seven hours. Emma was about to climb out of the car when the phone rang.

Finally.

Tine Abelvik.

'Hi,' Emma said with a sigh. 'Thank you for calling – I need your help.'

She briefly explained what had happened during the day and evening, where she was and that Blix's car was here. Abelvik apologised by saying that it had been hectic in Leirsund after the last body was found.

'Who lives there?' she asked.

'The registered owner is dead,' Emma explained. 'Odd Henrik Kleiven. Does that name ring a bell?'

'Kleiven,' Abelvik repeated slowly to herself, thinking. 'Does it look like anyone lives there now?'

'Not really,' Emma said. 'There are no other cars here.'

Emma heard the policewoman flipping through some papers. It took a few moments.

Then there was silence, as if she had stopped suddenly.

'What is it?' Emma asked.

'Odd Henrik Kleiven is Skage Kleiven's father,' Tine Abelvik said. 'Skage, the father of Elisabeth Eie's child.'

'Oh shit. I didn't know he lived around here—'

'He doesn't,' Abelvik cut in. 'Regardless, I'm sending a patrol car from the local sheriff's office. Wait for them before you do anything.'

Emma didn't know if there was time to wait, but she agreed to anyway.

'I'll let you know when I find out how far away they are. Text me the address. We'll also send someone out from Oslo.'

Oslo, Emma thought. Even with blue lights on it would take them well over an hour to get there.

They hung up.

Emma sent Abelvik the address, and then studied the windows of the house. No movement, no flashing lights to indicate a TV was on. She opened the car window, but only heard the rain splashing against the roof and the ground outside. Terry continued to bark.

Poor thing, Emma thought. He must be starving.

She pushed down the door handle and stepped out. Immediately felt the raindrops hit the top of her head. She pulled her jacket tighter around her and shivered. The rain was freezing cold. Some of it trailed down her neck.

She walked over to the Volvo. Terry came right up to the side window and scratched at it with his paws. Emma pulled at the handle, relieved to find it unlocked.

Terry jumped up at her, happy for the company. She patted and hugged him a little and made a fuss.

'Where's Blix?' she said to him. 'Where is he?'

Terry jumped from her arms, out of the car and onto the ground. For the first few seconds he just wandered around, seemingly over the moon to be out of the car. He quickly returned to Emma, before setting off again, this time towards the house.

She followed.

Her phone buzzed. A message from Abelvik:

The patrol is out on another case, so they can't be there for three quarters of an hour at the earliest. Keep a low profile until then.

Emma cursed inwardly, but still responded with a thumbs-up.

Although Terry could not have had much food that day, he seemed to be full of energy. The large yard in front of the main house was like his playground. All Emma could think about as she watched him dart around was where Blix could be and what had happened to him. And if Skage Kleiven was here too.

She looked around. Couldn't see anyone.

Terry stopped suddenly and pricked up his ears.

Emma did the same. Was there a sound coming from the barn?

Terry barked.

Emma stepped closer. Yes, definitely something. But it was difficult to tell what was making the noise. The rain pounded against the roofs around her, drowning out everything else.

Skage Kleiven, she thought. The father of Elisabeth Eie's daughter. Who had been refused custody of the child, even though her mother was dead.

Emma turned – there was no one peeking out from behind a curtain in the house. No movement in the woodland next to the barn, or in the outbuildings. All was quiet, except for the rain that whipped against the branches and leaves of the trees.

Forty-five minutes, she thought. She had to assume it would take even longer. Abelvik would have told her the absolute minimum. When it was urgent, you always rounded down instead of up.

They approached the barn. Terry barked even more, as if he had some unfinished business with the door.

'Wait,' Emma pleaded, bending down to get Terry to stop. She tried to listen through the din of the rain. Stood up and clenched her fist. Hammered her knuckles three times against the barn door, as hard as she could. Then: even more sounds from inside. And a voice. A shout.

Blix.

Emma couldn't hear what he was yelling, but she screamed his name. The door had been fastened shut with an old, rusty bolt. She needed some force to push it out so she could pull one of the two doors open, hauling it back to get inside.

It was dark.

A large vehicle was parked at an angle in the middle of the room. Further in was a small storeroom, from which a faint light streamed out. Emma shouted for Blix, and immediately received an answer back.

Terry ran ahead of her, further into the barn. Towards the light. The sounds. Terry disappeared into the storeroom. Emma could hear how eager and happy he was.

'Emma!' she heard Blix shout. 'Be careful – he's still in here somewhere.'

She turned, saw no one, but grabbed a spade propped up against the wall before venturing further inside. She slowly walked towards the room, the light. She stepped into the doorway.

The sight within paralysed her.

All she managed was a gasp, before she registered movement behind her. A kick in her back sent her flying into the room, before she felt something tighten around her neck.

Terry snarled and snapped, but retreated to Blix's side.

Skage Kleiven had looped the collar around Emma's neck. He sat on her back, holding each end of it as he leaned his weight back, like a rider pulling with all his might on the reins of a runaway horse.

Blix roared at him. He threw himself forward and felt the chain around his neck cut into his skin.

Emma's arms shot up to her neck. Her body was stretched back, tense as a bow. Her chin jutted forward, her cheeks reddening. Her eyes flickered, her gaze desperate. She managed to get a few fingers between her neck and the collar and fought desperately to breathe.

The spade she had carried with her had been thrown into the room. Blix tried to reach it with his foot. He could barely reach the tip and managed to nudge it with the edge of his shoe, rolling it a little in his direction.

Emma thrashed around with her free arm, but her screams remained helpless gurgles. Froth had started to gather at the corners of her mouth. Blix made another desperate attempt to reach the spade. The chain tightened around his neck, but he managed to pry his foot under the wooden handle and tip it towards him. With another jolt of his foot, he kicked the spade closer – close enough for him to finally slide it within reach.

He grabbed the handle with both hands. The distance to Kleiven was too far. Instead, he started to use the shovel to smash the mount on the wall where the chain was attached.

The grating, metallic sound silenced Terry. Skage Kleiven looked back at him, but did not release his grip. Emma's eyes had rolled into the back of her head.

Blix turned his back on them and struck again, trying to hit the endmost chain instead of the bolt.

The impact smashed through one of the links.

This could work.

Blix tightened the chain with one hand and struck with the other. This time he missed.

Kleiven released Emma and stood up. She collapsed to the floor.

Blix struck again. The chain shook violently, but he hadn't hit it in the same place as last time. When he turned to check on Kleiven, he had taken out a new anaesthetic pen. Instead of attempting another strike on the chain, Blix swung the spade at him. He missed.

Emma was face down on the floor, gurgling. Skage Kleiven took no notice of her, but stood waiting beyond Blix's reach.

Blix swung the spade at him once more, before lifting the weapon to bring it down on the chain again.

Kleiven raised his arm, poised to stab the pen into his back. Blix threw his body out of the way, swung the spade round and made contact with Kleiven's hand. The needle was knocked out of it and hit the wall before rolling to the floor.

Blix took a step forward to steady himself before launching another swinging strike. This time he hit Kleiven in the upper arm with the side of the shovel. It sliced into his skin like the blade of an axe. Kleiven roared in pain. Blood spurted as Blix pulled back the shovel to hit him again.

Over by the door, Emma moved. Blix barely registered that she had rolled onto her side, holding onto her neck. He held the spade with both hands and struck again before Kleiven could get out of reach. The blow that followed made contact with his head. Kleiven fell to the ground and lay there, motionless.

Emma pushed herself up fully and sat gasping for air. Blix took two more strikes to free himself from the chain, then threw the shovel aside and rushed over to her.

He took her head between his hands and looked at her intently. Her breathing began to return to normal, and she managed to force a smile.

✳

The headlights of two vehicles cut through the darkness. Just behind them: an ambulance, its flashing lights washing the area in blue. All three stopped in the yard outside the house.

Blix ran out into the rain and met the first police officers, gave them a slightly more detailed briefing than he had managed to provide when he had called on Emma's phone.

'Skage Kleiven is in there,' Blix said, pointing behind him, past Emma, who was standing in the doorway to the barn, seeking shelter from the rain beneath the eaves. 'He's breathing, but he's in pretty bad shape.'

The officers sent in the paramedics. Carrying a stretcher between them, they ran into the barn and through to the storeroom.

Blix and Emma stood in the barn doorway while one of the officers unrolled the police tape. The sound coming from the police radios was constant. The officers' earpieces clicked and crackled.

Emma shuddered.

Blix put an arm around her. Hugged her close.

One of the ambulance workers came over and asked if either of them needed medical attention. Blix felt his neck. His Adam's apple was tender. He knew the bruises would develop there over the next few days. The palms of his hands were also particularly sore.

A quick glance at Emma told him that she was battered too, but otherwise fine.

'If you have any water, actually,' he said. 'Otherwise, I think we'll survive.'

Emma nodded in agreement and the ambulance worker returned quickly with two bottles.

One of the officers wanted them to move a little further away.

'We'll go and sit in the car,' Blix said. 'It's warmer in there.'

On his way across the yard, he held Emma by the arm. It was slippery underfoot. Terry trotted along calmly beside them.

All three climbed into the car. Blix started the engine. Turned on the heat, including the seat warmers. Ahead of them, inside the barn, camera lights began to flash.

Another police car drove up.

Tine Abelvik parked right next to them. Walenius got out from the passenger side. He gave Blix a short nod, but said nothing as Blix lowered the window. Blix wanted to make a comment about how the young detective's cockiness seemed like it had been punctured, but he decided to let it be.

Abelvik came over to the window. She scrutinised him, an anxious look on her face, then peered in past Blix to Emma.

'Thank god you're okay,' Abelvik said with a sigh, after Blix had also told her what had happened. 'That was close.'

Blix said nothing.

'You must be tired,' she said. 'But it'd be great if you could stay a little longer. We may need a few more answers.'

Emma and Blix stayed in the car. It was nice and warm. The wipers waved back and forth at regular intervals. The raindrops drummed against the roof of the car.

Terry came up between them and sat on the centre console. Blix gave him a good fuss.

'I keep some emergency biscuits in the glove compartment,' he told Emma. 'Could you...'

She found the pack and opened it. Terry wriggled closer. Emma fed him, bite by bite. Stroked his head and smiled tenderly at him.

For a long time, Terry's chewing and chops smacking were the only sounds filling the compartment. Exhausted, they both stared out of the window, at the investigation going on in front of and around them.

'You knew him, then,' Emma said at last.

Blix straightened up in his seat. 'I don't think anyone actually knew him,' Blix replied.

Several more police cars arrived. And after a while, the first few journalists appeared.

'I'm glad I'm not part of that circus anymore,' Emma said with a sigh.

A couple of camera flashes went off when Abelvik came out of the barn door. She beckoned the two of them over. They got out.

'It's okay,' Abelvik said to the officer manning the cordon. 'They're with me.'

Emma and Blix ducked under the tape.

'You probably want your phone back,' Abelvik said, handing it to Blix. He accepted it, and saw that it had been turned off. He turned it back on.

'We found this in his car,' Abelvik announced, pausing at the large four-wheel drive, now with a white sheet stretched over the hood. On top of the sheet was an old, burgundy suitcase with a broken lock. The contents had been laid out beside it. There were pictures and sheets of paper on which words and dashes had been scrawled, seemingly without any meaning. Times and addresses had been jotted down haphazardly. Blix's name came up again and again.

Next to the ramblings were children's drawings, old photographs and handwritten letters. There were two phones and documents from a foreign telecoms company, as well as piles of newspaper clippings and printouts from the internet, several of them with pictures of Blix, as well as a few articles about Lina Marie Jansen and the various debates she had taken part in.

Abelvik held up a brown envelope. It was closed but not glued shut. She shook out the contents. A collection of Polaroid photos spilled out. Blix recognised Elisabeth Eie, as she had been in the picture he had received in the post, but there were also pictures of the other women.

'I thought he believed he was a victim himself and would probably claim he killed them to make the world a better place,' Blix said. 'But this?' He shook his head. 'This suggests he was even more addled.'

The paramedics left the storeroom with an empty stretcher. The senior medic looked over at them and shook his head.

Blix followed them with his eyes. They would never have all the answers, but at least it was over.

EPILOGUE

Three weeks later

'When you worked as a policeman,' Emma said. 'What did you like most: the search for the answers – the process itself – or the sense of achievement you felt when you eventually found all those answers?'

From the window table, Blix looked out at the water and the sculpture in front of the Opera House. Some loud seagulls had gathered just outside on this sunny November morning. He raised the coffee cup to his lips and smiled as he pondered the question.

'I liked ... Well, there was something very satisfying about being able to put two lines under the answer. You could breathe easier, as it were, afterwards.'

She could tell that he was still thinking it through.

'But then that meant it was over, in a way, and with that came a certain ... restlessness. But that was quickly satisfied by other cases that either appeared or we would return to. So we never got much time to pat ourselves on the back.'

He put the cup back down. The porcelain clinked against the plate.

'Am I allowed to answer "both" to your question?'

'No.' He laughed.

It was nice to see him smile again. It had happened more and more often recently. Emma occasionally saw him withdraw into his old, dark shell again, but he didn't stay there as long as he had before.

'You know,' he said. 'Police officers are actually quite boring. We much prefer it when there's as little drama as possible – as little as there can be, as few questions as possible to find answers to. Most cases start with a known perpetrator. So, fortunately, most police work is spent sorting through papers, putting them in the right order and presenting them to a court, so that the person responsible receives the punishment he or she deserves according to the law.'

'God, you're so boring.'

He laughed. 'Like I said.'

They smiled at each other. Emma took a bite of the cinnamon bun.

'But it was probably the process that I found most captivating, yes,' he finally concluded. 'Which is probably why I ended up divorced too.'

That, and the fact that you shot and killed my father, Emma said to herself, happy not to say it out loud.

'But that wasn't why you wanted to meet me, I assume? To talk police philosophy?'

'No,' Emma replied with a chuckle.

She fell silent for a moment, thinking about how she should word what she wanted to say. She grabbed the tall latte and put her hands around the glass.

'I've been thinking,' she said. 'About the future.'

'Oh?'

'Me and you, we ... work pretty well together, I think.' She paused before finishing: 'I've set up a company for us.'

Blix stared at her. 'You've what?'

'A private-investigation and security-consulting company,' she explained.

He laughed. 'Private investigators,' he said, swallowing the words with a gulp of coffee.

His reaction was as expected.

'I mean it,' she said. 'We've both got pretty good noses. And I'm like you, I like the process best. That's where I thrive – I can't seem to let it go once I've picked up a trace of something.'

He stared at her.

'Neither of us have other jobs stopping us,' Emma continued. 'Why can't we just make our own?'

Blix's smile had hardened.

'I know you'll always think of yourself as a policeman. And you are, even if you don't have a badge and a service weapon. But there's so much you can do still, even if you can't arrest people and haul them into an interrogation room.'

'Like what – find missing cats? Expose people having affairs?'

Emma sighed. 'There's more to the job than that. Look at what happened to Carmen Prytz. She came to me because she was looking for help.'

There was a brief pause across the table. Emma wiped some sugar and cinnamon from the corner of her mouth.

'Why did she do that, anyway?' Blix asked.

'Carmen wasn't like Skage Kleiven,' Emma said. 'She may have been the victim of a bad upbringing, but she didn't kill Maria Normann to take revenge or to save her son from a bad mother. She was just afraid of losing the person who was the closest thing she'd ever had to a father. Afraid that he would love the other child more than her, perhaps.'

'You'll have to explain that to me.'

Emma took a sip of her coffee and told him all she knew about Carmen's early years, and how close and stable the relationship she had developed with Oliver Krogh had been.

'She didn't want him to end up in prison, because then she would definitely lose him, maybe forever. Which is why she came to me. After all, she knew he was innocent.'

'And the fact that she herself could end up in prison, that didn't occur to her?'

'Sure, on some level, but she had also thought that she'd managed to get away with it. She had hidden Maria well, the police had searched Lake Gjersjøen without finding her, and there was no evidence linking Carmen to the murder.'

'Still,' Blix said, 'it's a bold thing to do. Hire someone like you.' He winked at her.

'She didn't *hire* me,' Emma said. 'She didn't pay me a penny. If we had a company though...' She let the sentence trail off.

Emma could tell that she had given him something to think about. He looked out of the window, put a hand to his face and slowly stroked the stubble on his chin.

'When I was chained up in Skage Kleiven's barn,' he said after a while, 'I had time to think about everything. Before all this with Skage ... I wasn't all that afraid if something happened. To me. I could die, and it ... didn't bother me. The opposite, actually.'

Emma gazed at him.

'But when it suddenly became very real, and on someone else's terms, then … I didn't want it at all. I wanted to stay, here, a little longer. Here – living. In that moment it was just about survival, but I've been thinking about it since. What you do with what you've been given. The opportunities life hands you. It's all ultimately … a choice.'

'It sounds like your sessions with Krissander Dokken have helped,' Emma said with a twinkle in her eye. 'Have you tried that GDR stuff?'

Blix laughed. 'EMDR,' he corrected. 'I have, actually. I don't know if it's helped that much, but…'

'Christ, you'll be doing yoga next,' Emma laughed.

He smiled. 'Tomine and I have actually signed up for a class.'

Her eyes widened. 'Have you?'

This time it was Blix's turn to laugh. 'No, of course not,' he replied, before immediately turning serious again. 'But there is something to it,' he continued. 'I'm going to start bouncing off the walls if I don't do something. But it can't just be anything – it has to be something I'm good at, something I enjoy.'

Emma clapped her hands together. 'Right?'

Blix smiled but said nothing. Instead, he picked up the teaspoon lying on the plate next to the coffee cup and twirled it a few times between his fingers. Emma studied him. His phone buzzed on the table between them, but he let it ring. Didn't turn the display to see who it was.

His gaze rested on the teaspoon.

The table stopped vibrating.

He slowly raised his head to look at her.

'So?' she said when he didn't speak. 'What do you say?'

ACKNOWLEDGEMENTS

(Ping – text message popping)

Jørn: *Hey.*

Thomas: *Hey yourself. Nice opening line. I'm all intrigued now.*

(Seconds passing)

(Nothing happening)

Jørn: *You there?*

Thomas: *Yes, Jørn. Biting my fingernails.*

(Seconds passing)

(Nothing happening)

(Phone rings)

Thomas: Hey, what's going on? What's wrong?

Jørn: Nothing's wrong. Why do you ask?

Thomas: Why indeed would I?

(Beat)

(Beat)

Thomas: I'm going to take a wild guess here and say that you probably have something on your mind.

Jørn: Yes.

Thomas: I should be a police investigator or something.

Jørn: Sometimes you are.

Thomas: I suppose I am.

(Beat)

(Sigh)

Thomas: If our books stop selling, we can always do stand-up. The two of us.

Jørn: You think so?

Thomas: No.

Jørn: So why do you—?

Thomas: (getting tired) What is it, Jørn?

Jørn: It's that time again.

(Beat)

(Beat)

Thomas: What – that time of the month?

Jørn: No.

Thomas: Is ... there something you'd like to tell me, Jørn?

Jørn: No, no.

Thomas: You sure?

(Beat)

(Beat)

Jørn: I'm not sure I understand what you're talking about.

Thomas: I'm not sure I understand what *you're* talking about.

Jørn: I'm talking about our latest book being out and that we need to do our acknowledgements.

(Beat)

(Beat)

(Beat)

(Beat)

Jørn: Are you there?

Thomas: Yes. Just ... trying to...

Jørn: ...Are you okay?

Thomas: I hope so.

Jørn: What's—?

Thomas: Never mind, Jørn. Acknowledgements.

Jørn: Yes.

Thomas: Which one is it this time?

(Sigh)

Jørn: *Victim.*

Thomas: Ah yes.

(Beat)

(Beat)

(Sigh)

Jørn: Any thoughts?

(Long sigh)

Thomas: I think ... I'm going to thank my dad this time.

Jørn: Oh.

Thomas: Yes, he passed away last Christmas.

Jørn: I know. I'm sorry.

Thomas: Yes, me too. I have a lot to thank him for.

(Beat)

(Beat)

Jørn: I know it's hard, but would you like to be a bit more specific?

Thomas: Well, for one, he introduced me to Manchester United.

Jørn: Oh.

Thomas: Yes. I was only two years old.

Jørn: Are you sure you want to thank him for that?

(Beat)

(Beat)

Thomas: No comment.

Jørn: You have my condolences.

(Beat)

(Beat)

Jørn: About your dad, I mean.

Thomas: Mhm. Thanks, Jørn.

Jørn: Don't mention it.

Thomas: I won't. Ever again.

(Beat)

(Beat)

Thomas: How about you?

Jørn: I gave thanks to my dad in the second book I wrote.

Thomas: You've written about 734 of them, Jørn ... When was this?

Jørn: It's twenty years ago now.

Thomas: What about your mother – have you ever thanked her?

Jørn: Plenty of times. I dedicated a book to her as well. I've done the same for my wife and kids.

Thomas: Wow.

Jørn: I even did one for Theodor, my dog.

Thomas: Man.

(Beat)

(Beat)

(Long sigh)

Jørn: He passed away this spring.

Thomas. Oh. I'm sorry.

(Beat)

(Beat)

(Beat)

Thomas: Wow, that's...

Jørn: I know.

(Beat)

(Beat)

Thomas: Proper stand-up material, right here.

Jørn: Hm?

Thomas: Never mind. Okay. Take a deep breath now and go for it.

Jørn: Go for what.

Thomas: The acknowledgements.

Jørn: Oh. Right. I'm going to thank Karen and West and Danielle and Cole at Orenda Books. Our publisher.

Thomas: Good. Good!

Jørn: Without them, no book.

Thomas: Indeed.

Jørn: Without us there wouldn't be one, either.

Thomas: I may have said so before, but your powers of deduction know no bounds, Jørn.

Jørn: Thank you.

Thomas: Sounds like you want to thank us.

Jørn: Hm?

Thomas: Since we wrote the book, I mean. No us, no b—

Jørn: That would be a bit silly, wouldn't it?

Thomas: I did that once.

Jørn: Really? You thanked us?

Thomas: I thanked *me*. But then again, I am a bit silly, from time to time.

(Beat)

(Beat)

Thomas: It wasn't for one of ours, Jørn.

Jørn: Oh. Okay, then.

(Beat)

(Sigh)

Thomas: We can thank ourselves if you want, Jørn.

Jørn: No thanks.

Thomas: Okay.

(Beat)

(Beat)

Thomas: Good talk. We should do this more often.

Jørn: Yes. Giving thanks is a good thing.

Thomas: Thank God it's that time of the month only once a year.

(Beat)

(Beat)

(Beat)

Jørn: Hm?

Thomas: Never mind, Jørn.